Look Before You Leap

ALISON NORRINGTON

POOLBEG

Published 2004
by Poolbeg Press Ltd
123 Grange Hill, Baldoyle
Dublin 13, Ireland
E-mail: poolbeg@poolbeg.com

© Alison Norrington 2004

The moral right of the author has been asserted.

Typesetting, layout, design © Poolbeg Group Services Ltd.

1 3 5 7 9 10 8 6 4 2

A catalogue record for this book is available from the British Library.

ISBN 1-84223-133-2

Typeset by Patricia Hope in Palatino 10/14
Printed by
Litografia Rosés S.A., Spain

www.poolbeg.com

About the Author

Alison lives in Cullenstown, County Wexford.

Her bestselling debut novel, *Class Act*, was published by Poolbeg in 2003.

She has written for *The Irish Star*, *Irish Tatler* and *Times Educational Supplement*.

She is currently working on her third novel.

Acknowledgements

I really enjoyed writing *Look Before You Leap* and have to thank a number of people for their help.

Thanks to you, Mum – first and foremost once again. Your support and encouragement are endless! Thanks for the time in Paris – no, thank *you*. Mr Akavani!!

Thanks to my brother Ian. You sat with me in 5 Weald Road and we had fun working out part of this story. For your love and help. Always. Love ya.

Ryan & Conor – for your sense of humour and tenderness. Thanks for putting up with my half-attentions sometimes and for keeping me on the ball. For your love and understanding.

To Poolbeg – for the publicity for *Class Act* and your support and advice. To Paula, Sarah, Brona and Conor – thank you for helping me understand the industry. To Sarah especially, thank you for carrying that bottle of wine around Dublin for me! As if you didn't have enough to do!!

To Gaye – for your patience and calm approach. For being able to laugh with me at the crap bits and for painstakingly editing over the phone.

To Ger – my agent, for your advice and insight. For champagne and a fantastic lunch at Greystones too!!

To all the booksellers who wholeheartedly enjoy their work – thanks for the publicity and your interest.

To Jillian Edelstein – for an insight into a freelance photographer's life. And congratulations on getting your book published too. Thank you.

To the staff at Joyce House, Dublin, for answering my many questions regarding the registry procedure. (01 671 1968)

To Vanessa & Ciara from *Irish Tatler* – thanks for your support and encouragement.

To Moira Hannon from *The Star* – thanks for your kind words and help.

To Kieron Wood, a Dublin barrister who has written extensively on marital law.

Email:barrister_at_law@hotmail.com

Thanks to Lynda and Maggie from Burns bookshop in Wexford.

Thanks to Ned for his support and friendship; to Allie for reading the first draft on a particularly hair-raising flight back to London; and to Belinda for being my sounding-board (amongst many other nice things!).

Finally I'd like to thank the many people of County Wexford for the brilliant reception you gave to *Class Act* – and for making it all such fun too . . .

With love to Ryan & Conor –
look before you leap . . . xx

Frightened to jump?

Or frightened to land?

It's the trip in between that you can't understand.

Excerpt from "materialistic"

by IAN NORRINGTON

Prologue

Aside from putting the starchy white serviettes on their heads and chanting "Here comes the bride, all fat and wide!" far too loudly for Luigi's usual Friday-night crowd, Niamh and Anna reacted much as I'd expected them to.

Of course, the chant swiftly mutated into drunken variations including, "Here comes the bride, Dublin's greatest ride!" and the even more embarrassing: "Here comes the bride, Simon you'd better hide!" OK, and then finally, although I loathe to mention it really, especially on the grounds that it doesn't even rhyme: "Here comes the bride, thirty-three and desper-ide!"

Well, apart from all that, they reacted to my news more or less how I'd initially expected them to.

With contempt and horror.

Niamh leant in onto the table, resting her set jaw-line in

1

her slender hands, ignoring her half-full glass of red wine. An
ominous sign that she meant business.

"Tara McKenna, you mean you go along with that
crusty old bullshit that women have only *one* day every
four years to profess their love for the men in their lives?
Feckit, Tara, just listen to yourself! I mean, how far *have*
we come?"

She had continued to challenge over huge spoonfuls of
dessert.

"You've only been going with him for a few months!
What's the rush?"

Anna was kinder with her words, true to her charitable
personality, although the brief lukewarm soak of her
compassion had been abruptly terminated as Niamh burst
out again, "So you believe the best form of defence is
attach? Christ, Tara, you've been through more men in
this last year than Anna! Why *marry* one of them?"

Resisting the urge to burst out laughing at the sight of
Anna's indignant expression, I finally got the chance to
defend my wild announcement.

"Because I'm thirty-three and I *want* to be married.
Simon's The-One-For-Me. I just know it."

"Oh yeah," hissed Niamh, her finely shaped
eyebrows raised in wings of mock surprise, "Mr-
bloody-Right. A Mr Right for our Little Miss Not-So-
Bright."

"We're not Mr Men characters, Niamh. This isn't a
child's story. It isn't a joke. It's my life!"

"But still, Tara," Anna interrupted, "why do *you*
have to propose?"

Niamh nearly choked on her wine. "Why? I'll tell you why. Because it's so ridiculous, that's why. She knows he'd never dream of asking her to marry him. She's just an athletic bedmate as far as he's concerned!"

I hadn't realised my stamina was so widely appreciated, but then, as she spooned in a disturbingly large mound of zabaione, she added cruelly, "Ha! What a way for him to realise that every shag has its tag!"

Subsequently, over the next forty-eight hours I'd been exposed to many, I feel unnecessary, remarks, including:

"God, Tara, at least rub the rough edges off him first! You've only known him a few months!" *Courtesy of Kate, my next-door neighbour.*

"Why promise to marry one guy today, when you never know who you'll meet tomorrow?" *No surprise to hear that repeatedly from Niamh, once she'd sobered up.*

"You don't have to get *married*. Why not just carry on as you are?" *The sober other half of my best-friend duo, Anna.*

And then, totally unexpected and out of character, "Oh," *with a wry grin, and then with a titter,* "A wedding! So quaint!" *I mean, you'd nearly think she was taking the piss. You'd almost think she found me amusing! My mum of all people.*

Sometimes she could be such a bitch.

The most thought-provoking though, had come from Yannis, my cuddly, hairy splash of Mediterranea who owned the deli on Lower Baggot Street. As he'd leant his chubby forearms on the glass shelf, inadvertently poking his round and extremely hairy ouzo-house into the chiller cabinet, casting a shadow over the taramasalata and tzatziki, he'd croaked, "You kno', ee's a Greek superstition that marrieeeng een lep year ees bad luck," *to which I'd turned on my heel and hissed at his wife (courtesy of months of over-the-counter tuition from Yannis himself),* "Aftos o anthropos einai bellas!" (*"This man is trouble!"*)

*After all, enough was e-bloody-*nuff.

Chapter 1

One year and a bit later . . .

So a year and a bit later, see how my tone has changed. See how my galloping enthusiastic banter has been replaced by this pitiful whisper as I've got my head between my knees, kissing my battered and bruised matrimonial derrière.

They were right.

OK! So I've said it.

I've admitted it.

Of the hundreds of emotions we're designed to experience Regret stands right up there as the most nauseating. Paying scant attention to the uproar of objections that my wedding had ignited was probably the most insular thing I've ever done.

That – and having an affair.

I mean, what kind of person has an affair before they've even celebrated their first anniversary?

Paper. That's what the first wedding anniversary is supposed to signify.

The only paper worth mentioning that I handled on my first anniversary — other than the handful of therapeutic women's magazines I loafed through — was Simon's letter. Tight-lipped and succinct, informing me that he, categorically, would not be returning. On the grounds of adultery.

But I was married for ten months and twenty-two days, three hours and fifty seconds though, without even looking at another man.

And I had only been out with "Him" nine times.

And had wild orgasmic sex with him.

Seventeen glorious times . . .

The doors of the smog-peppered DART bounced vigorously off Niamh's sturdy hold-all as she struggled to get on with the numerous large bags responsible for protecting her equipment so snugly. Owning eight cameras, she seemed always to take at least five on every shoot and now was cursing her new freelance assistant for not packing her bags as economically as she expected. Flexibility not being Niamh's prime strength, she shunted and heaved at the strong handles as her luggage stuck between the sliding doors, unwittingly elbowing a Chinese man in the ribs as she did so. Feeling particularly dynamic after a gratifyingly successful day, she gave an ambitious push to squeeze her pert bum in before the doors slid closed on that also. Ignoring the scowling sea of faces that shuffled backward to accommodate her and her baggage, she silently congratulated herself on previously researching the celebrity that she'd "shot" today. He'd warmed to her instantly as she dashed her suggestions to him, asking if he'd be nominated for an Oscar for his most recent performance, "Face toward the door, but look at me, please!" – *Click! Click! Click!* She didn't often favour the posed style, but, as she was attempting to evoke a sombre and determined mood for this particular project, she'd deliberately used black and white film coupled with yellow and orange filters to diminish the many blemishes on his pock-marked skin. As the train galloped toward Pearse Station the lights flashed off temporarily and then on again, illuminating a mass of unconcerned, almost inhuman expressions. Amongst the throng of tired-looking phizogs arranged at varying heights, she couldn't help but be aware of the garlic-breathed "suit", his hair complete with Ma Nature's badger stripes from temple to crown, who was grinning and winking at her. His being the only face remotely animated she instantly took in his M&S suit, Penney's mac and Next tie and scowled at him, making sure she first deliberately cast her eye over his stripy greying hair, in a bid to shatter any illusion he may have had about himself. Niamh wasn't slow in coming forward when eating men and spitting them out was concerned. A resolute lust-for-the-upper-crust drove her to be an expert at sniffing out the rows of platinum plastic filed neatly in slim wallets and recognising the subtlety of designer clothes. Badger-stripes had neither. She suspected he was already in the latter part of his mid-life crisis, probably with a wife and half a dozen kids waiting in his Wicklow mid-terraced home. She supposed he drove a family car – possibly a reliable Volvo or Cavalier, probably an estate-in-a-state – and fancied himself as some City man with a secret life.

"Moron!" she thought to herself, gathering the handles of her baggage tightly in her clenched fists as she shuffled round to face the arched doorway of the DART in preparation for getting off. She dreaded the walk across Merrion Square to Baggot Street with all her appendages.

"Shit," she cursed under her breath, "why couldn't I have rung Anna to come and help me with these? She must have left work by now."

The train glided to a halt as the sardined prisoners waited silently for their release. The automatic doors slid open and the hubbub began. Forced by the crowd behind her, Niamh was swept onto the platform and out of the station, into the exhaust-fumed evening air.

Niamh had succeeded exceptionally well, swiftly bounding up the proverbial career-ladder two steps at a time as she grew from a photographer's assistant to a well-known and frequently commissioned celebrity-portrait photographer. She'd done her time as a press photographer and had covered incidents across Europe, receiving much acclaim among the contemporary women's magazine editorial teams. All she yearned for now was an eligible bachelor who'd be ready to accept her at face value, uninterested in her humble beginnings, but so mad-keen in love with her that he'd move her into his Dalkey home and marry her –

bestowing on her the unconditional use of all credit cards and unlimited access to a joint account.

"Thank God I don't have to do *that* every day!" she proclaimed to her watch as she pulled up her sleeve to check the time.

In reality, to have commissioned work every day would be the ideal, but in the tumultuous world of photography Niamh just had to roll with the punches, taking what she could, and when. Breathing in the polluted air she bent at the knees, once again gathering her equipment. Straightening with a sigh, she wondered how she'd ever make it home without looking like a pantomime pack-horse.

Only three minutes into her walk home a shrill bleeping sound issued from her jacket-pocket causing her to stop. She shuffled into a shop doorway and grabbed the small mobile that squealed so irritatingly. She pressed the small rubber buttons diligently, smiling at the latest text message, oblivious to the appreciative stares that she commanded. Leaning back against the wooden door frame, she brought her left leg up beneath her, resting her snakeskin-booted foot on the wall. There were striking similarities between herself and George Michael in the 'Faith' publicity shots, although she took immense pride in never having been *caught* performing fellatio in the gents' toilets and had considerably less facial hair. Her black-leather trousers, tight across her crotch, the hip-band exposing her lithe tanned torso crowned with an emerald stud in her navel, caused quite a stir in the dormant corporate boxer shorts of the pin-stripes passing by. For others, the boob-men in particular, it was the mere suggestion of what caused her shocking-pink t-shirt to stretch so promisingly across her ample chest that did the trick. Her nimble brown-varnished fingers deftly squashed down the spongy keys to reply. With a wicked glint in her eye and a renewed spring in her step she shoved the mobile back into her pocket, smiling at the prospect of the evening ahead of her. As she marched home intently, the weight of her luggage now far from her thoughts, her Nokia bustled in her pocket, the green LCD screen still illuminating Karl's message:

"R U UP 4 IT 2NITE?"

Initially so loving and affectionate, Simon soon transmuted into a man seemingly unaware that True Romance was anything more than a mere section in the library. Looking back on those heady, early weeks of marital bliss is painful now, yet it seems almost like a hallucination. He was so refreshingly communicative, funny and keen. The crystal vase of red roses were a permanent fixture on the coffee table and the fresh red and white chrysanthemums that he insisted went on the antique wooden sideboard in our bedroom every Saturday morning meant "I love you" and "Truth". Or so he told me.

Ironic now, really . . .

But yet, shortly after those romantic, luxurious few months it had all taken an abrupt nosedive. Slowly at first, but it soon became par for the course that he'd slam the glossy front door behind him on a Friday evening and I'd tense at the noises that punctuated his return from work, always listening for the familiar sounds of the thud as his briefcase hit the wall and slid onto the hall floor, and the jangling of his keys as they were launched onto the limed oak ottoman.

Despite a headache and a binful of washing at the end of a tiresome day, Tara felt a surge of affection flood her as Simon threw open the lounge door and marched in, on cue with the chiming of the grandmother clock's seven bells. Her eyes danced as they had done on the night of her proposal, which had instigated the transition for her from nearly-wed to newly-wed. But as she stood to hug him, she kissed the draught he created as he strode past her and straight into the kitchen.

"Anything on for dinner?"

Slightly disgruntled at his insensitivity, despite its frequency, she'd dismissed it once again as the result of a hard week at work.

"Yes, there's a bolognese on the go. Your favourite. And I've got some Pavlova for dessert and a bottle of Shiraz in the cupboard."

Simon frowned. "Oh Tara, I'm so sorry, honey. I've just realised that I've left something in the office. I'm going to have to go back for it."

The dance faded from her eyes as she hunched slightly in disappointment. "Can't it wait until the morning, Simon?"

And then he hugged her and consoled her with, "I'm sorry, babe. I promise I'll make it up to you. Look, keep the food warm for me. I won't be too long. I promise."

His voice trailed off as he strode back down the hallway and once again slammed the front door behind him.

And still, I waited for him. You see, I desperately wanted to play out the role of the wife. I didn't want to be like my mother – left a spinster since my father had disappeared at the sight of a podgy wailing Me in nappies.

As the signature tune of *The Late Late Show* trumpeted into the silence of the lounge, she'd heard the rattling of Simon's key in the front door.

As he opened the lounge door for the second time that evening, I realised instantly that the alcohol had done the trick again for him.

"Sorry about that earlier, pet. It was just so important, you know. And you know how much I'm working for promotion."

She stood and hugged him, inhaling the heady aroma of perfume, aftershave, stale beer and cigarette smoke.

"Oh Simon, your jacket stinks of pub!"

He laughed at her grimace, sliding the offending garment from his shirt-sleeved arms. "Sorry, pet."

She was aware that part of his important job as Sales Director was to be travelling around the country in the company of expensively fragrant women and potent-cigar smokers and so made sure that all of his work clothes were dry-cleaned regularly. Especially as he'd often be away on business for a week or two at a time.

By usual standards he was exceptionally well house-trained, insisting on buying his own clothes, socks —

underwear too. To be honest, I felt slightly cheated at my wifely redundancy when it came to outfitting my husband. Although his independence overwhelmed me, I was reassured by his great taste in clothes.

Having removed the malodorous jacket from the room he returned, ruddy-cheeked and smiling. Grabbing her by the hand he led her to the sofa, pushing her gently down onto the plump cushion.

"I'm sorry about that, honey – I know you're mad at me," he chuckled, suddenly seeming childish and unprincipled. "I was just so tense when I came in from work. Don't be too mad at me. You know how much I love you."

"Hey, no. No, don't worry," she tried to laugh it off feebly, to disguise her hurt and humiliation, "don't worry. I don't mind about that. Look, em, I think I'll go up to bed now. You know, I'm a bit tired and all that."

Contented with the righting of his wrongs, Simon kicked off his shiny Gucci shoes, letting them first thud onto the beech floor and then bounce onto the Aztec-print rug as he swung his legs up onto the settee and pressed the buttons on the remote control.

OK, so on reflection our sex life was questionable. He was a terrific Cunning Linguist – great at talking dirty, getting me all worked up asking me if I was wearing knickers, leading me along in the anticipation of bed-breaking, chandelier-swinging sex. I remember only three months before our break-up, before I'd met the life-changing "Him". . .

One night when Simon thought I was already asleep. . .

"Coming up already?" Tara had quizzed, with a

twinkle in her eye and a stirring in her pyjama bottoms at the sight of Simon at the bedroom door. She'd read a lot about the first year of marriage and how many newly-weds fell pregnant in the first year. She had almost looked forward to an impending bout of cystitis brought on by newly-wed shagathons.

"Ugh," Simon had grunted in response, unaware of her gross misinterpretation of the peeling-off of his trousers and annoyed that she had dared still be awake.

The mattress had dipped slightly, taking the weight of his solid frame as he slid his firm, hairy legs under the cool marshmallow duvet. She'd smiled as she slid her arm across him, running her hand over his legs, caressing his firm downy thighs. She still felt an intense sense of security at being married, a wife!

I found myself repeating to myself "Jesus, he is my husband!"

But her thoughts were halted as she felt Simon's body stiffen beneath her touch. Not quite the desired effect – she'd wanted some stiffening, but not of his upper lip. It seemed she was, as usual, having the opposite effect on her husband. Irritated, he moved her hand away.

"Sorry, I'm exhausted," he'd snapped as he leaned over to switch off the bedside lamp and then resettled himself as near to the far edge of the bed as he possibly could without falling out. His apology hung in the air, resonant.

It was, in reality, no surprise to Tara.

In confession, we'd only had sex twice in over two months.

14

Sure, I'd reasoned, aren't all married couples like this eventually anyway? I mean, he's hardly Peter Stringfellow, Hugh Heffner!

In reality, he made me feel like a Passion Assassin.

If anyone had ever attempted to tell Tara that she had been anything more than slightly myopic in her fantasies regarding marriage, they'd have been hailed either a dead-man or a saint. Her perception of Simon had been painfully stuck in her imagination, caught up in the cliché of expected marital bliss.

And then she'd met Graham . . .

So now Tara lay on the bare mattress, a bundle of tangled bedsheets haphazardly entwined between her knees and ankles. She lay with her eyes clamped closed, trying to ignore the gritty irritation of the sleep which had gathered in the corners. Staring at the insides of her eyelids, a thousand images flashed before her eyes, the blank canvas of shut-eye providing a backdrop to the vivid pictures she saw. The mediocre sex they'd shared in the early days, the red roses on Valentine's Day and how Simon was so unaware of her intention of prosposing.

How I wish I could bottle hindsight – everyone's just so smart-arsey wise with it, but totally lost without it. It's only now I'm realising the foolishness of the whole proposal thing. The warnings I'd got were as obvious as the phoney ring on my finger, the vastness of my huge empty bed. But it had been so heady in Renard's that night. The 29th of February, the day of the proposal. The day I now bitterly regretted. Still,

I'd only have to suffer the anniversary of it every four years.

The wedding plans had scooted along famously, culminating in a small "do", giving neither of them time to consider the vastness of what they were "about to receive".

Life had settled, warm and secure at first, although weekends were always an unspoken problem. He had rarely wanted to mix, preferring to "keep you all to myself" he'd claim. His complete adoration of Tara had reassuringly affirmed how lovable she was. He made her feel attractive and good about herself and his knowledge of the traditional meaning of flowers had really surprised her. It had become usual for him to bring home apple-blossom, promising better things to come, or forget-me-nots, declaring true love and remembrance. But soon after, the monotony set in, along with a blatant disregard for his prior pride in their relationship. Niamh had blamed the wedding, insisting that standards dropped worldwide under the weight of a wedding ring.

But I knew the vagaries of relationships! I knew that my mother had always felt guilty at not working at her relationships more. She'd always blamed herself for my dad walking out when I was still blue and screaming. It had been drummed into me for years that the rot would soon set in. But I hadn't realised how soon, I suppose.

Screwing her eyes up tighter in a tormented bid to both blot out the past and yet hurt herself with it further, she recollected how unsympathetic he'd been when she'd taken the plunge and had her tongue pierced, after weeks of contemplation. How he'd just laughed when her tongue swelled up to the size of an old man's slipper for a week and left her to suffer in silence.

The truth is, I was petrified at having that piercing done. You know, I'm not really a cool trendy type. Not like Niamh. She just oozes style and savoir-faire. I'd just felt kind of "homey", what with being married, and I suppose my expectations weren't being lived up to. It's just not the thing to do, is it? Propose and then feel disappointed at your domestic life? The build-up was actually more fun than the reality of wedlock, you see. And the tongue-piercing was just a way of reassuring myself that I was still young enough to get away with it. I felt pigeon-holed already and I'd only been married a few months. Looking back on it all, I'd been so excited when he'd said "yes" to my proposition. I'd felt so liberated and confident. The sultry saxophone humming its moody music had seemed to wind an invisible silken bond between us as we laughed and drank in the dim lighting of Renard's on that dread night . . .

The heady scent of flowers had hung densely in the smoke-filled air as couples celebrated another annual milestone in their relationships. Renard's had been packed to the rafters and yet had seemed strangely intimate for her and Simon. As Tara fiddled with the stem on her wineglass, she'd pondered in anticipation of asking the big question. As the musicians took their reprieve, the bar staff switched on a softly muted tape, providing Tara with her moment. Breathing deeply, she'd composed herself and then, taking Simon by the hand as she'd leant across the small table, she smiled.

"Simon. I've got something to ask you. Something big."

"Oh."

She caught the fleeting look of apprehension dash across his face. It was at this stage Tara's subconscious crossed the line of reason and went into the irrational wish to fulfil her goal. Sense and sensibility had hidden quaking in the corner, wishing to be no part of this madness.

She now painfully recalled her ecstatic squeal as he consented to marry her, and how they'd kissed, almost burning her hair on the single candle stuck into the empty wine bottle as she'd stretched across the table. And then afterwards they'd walked, hand-in-hand along Dublin's Quays and then over the Ha'penny Bridge, resting against a concrete wall to kiss and caress.

I remember the feeling of detachment I felt at that stage – I can still see the blue-decked houseboat that stood out from the line of others. There had been a lean, jeans-clean guy relaxing on his hammock and I remember feeling strangely lusty as I watched him swaying gently while he sipped at his can of beer and watched the lights sparkle from the city onto the Liffey on that cool spring night.

Simon had misinterpreted her surge of passion and had brought her back to earth as he shoved his cold large hand up under her t-shirt.

His technique had gone desperately downhill from there.

You see, Graham had injected some life into my disappointing

18

marriage. Simple Simon simply hadn't participated in the way I'd expected him and I was suffering from the post-marital doldrums. Apart from the fact that he was away on business for days at a time, I also had this overwhelming fear that no-one would ever fancy me again. It's absolutely horrific when you think of it like that. With Graham it'd been the most fulfilling, exciting sex of my life and I was well and truly addicted. He was the perfect accessory to my imperfect life. Twenty-four with a bevy of young and happening "things" around him, I was more than flattered at his interest in me — after I'd tormented myself as to why me, why now and how would my post-thirty body compare. I'd been initially terrified when he indicated his liking for sex in the shower. I mean, did he have slip-mats? My balance surely wasn't what it used to be? But I'd risen to the occasion admirably and it hadn't taken long for him to win me round.

Hell — I'd had no regrets.

At least, not until Simon found out . . .

That fated day Tara had sat at one of the last vacant tables in The Aqua Bar waiting for Niamh. She recalled how the rich aroma of filtered coffee had stung at her nostrils as she'd admired the haphazardly arranged collage of cows in a field, which hung, with that designer minimalism, on the back wall behind the milk-frothing machine.

Niamh had often joked, "You were a bit like a pent-up pony really, Tar, just gagging to go trotting down the 'bridal path'!"

"You don't understand, Niamh. For better for worse. I've got to take the rough with the smooth — it can't always be a bed of roses. Marriage makes you complete."

"Yeah, a complete fool," Niamh muttered, unconvinced by Tara's fruitless search for her narrow definition of happiness.

And so she'd sat that evening, waiting for Niamh to walk past as usual with her rattling equipment cases, in a bid to call her in and pour out the horrendous revelation to her over an espresso.

The waitress had hovered impatiently by Tara's table that afternoon, clattering the empty mugs onto her tray boisterously. Tara's heavy swollen eyelids were crimson from excessive tears but were hidden behind sunglasses as she scanned the passing crowds, anticipating a sighting of the unsuspecting Niamh. Feeling both conspicuous and fragile, she was aware that the establishment would have preferred that she vacate her table, casting aside her half-empty mug to accommodate some of the more lucrative customers who had begun to form a queue at the doorway.

I kept thinking: if only Simon hadn't heard that phone call. I still can't figure whether I felt guilty for having the affair or guilty at being caught out.

Providing a timely rescue Niamh struggled past the window, carried along by a tide of commuters. Tara caught sight of her and jumped to her feet, rushing toward the floor-to-ceiling tinted window. As she accidentally pushed into the back of an occupied chair, she caused its occupant to spill his cappuccino down his front.

"Christ!" the balding Teletubby spat as he wiped the

dripping brown liquid from his chins, his eyes wildly seeking the cause for this spillage.

"Sorry," Tara barked, her tone of voice unconvincing. She knocked heavily on the glass window, unaware that the majority of the early-evening diners were watching her in amusement. She felt aggravated as Niamh failed to notice her and continued walking. One final hearty crack on the window then caused Niamh – and half of pedestrianised Dublin – to look. Relieved, but rubbing a throbbing knuckle, Tara beckoned her in, returning to her table eagerly.

Niamh bustled and barged through the hungry doorway queue, red-faced and irritated at having been humiliated in public. Dropping her hold-alls noisily at her feet, she sat down, noticing the overweight man with gross coffee-stains down his shirt as he ogled her tanned midriff lustily.

"What's *he* looking at? Dirty old sod. And look at his filthy coffee-stained shirt! Egh!"

"Niamh," Tara gushed, unconcerned with the trivialities of small talk, "Simon knows about my affair!"

Not one to be shocked, Niamh was an expert at the relationship challenge. She grabbed the menu, scanning the page for something light enough to sustain her, yet mild enough not to linger on her breath nor bloat her stomach, in the light of her impending date.

"What's the Caesar Salad like here?"

"Dunno. Niamh! Did you not hear what I said?"

"Yeah. Just wait a minute, I must eat before I meet

Karl tonight. He's fantastic. Nearly as good as Marco. You know, he always seems to get me straight into the sack, and I end up ravenous by midnight. Why are you wearing sunglasses? I didn't recognise you at first when you were banging on the window like Roy-bloody-Orbison."

"I said, Simon knows about my affair."

"*Affair!*" Niamh shouted. Momentarily the sounds of stainless steel on china stopped as the surrounding tables seemed to freeze, holding their forkfuls of food aloft, mouths gaping. As swiftly as it had fallen silent, it began to bustle again, much to Tara's relief.

"Why do you think so?"

"He heard me on my mobile."

"How do you know?"

"I *saw* him. I said Graham's name, for chrissakes."

She paused, as the waitress made an appearance, notebook in hand.

Niamh ordered for them both, her tone dismissive and to the point.

Tara continued, "I was telling him my fantasies – hell, I thought Simon was *out!*"

Niamh grinned wickedly, "Go on, what were you saying?"

Tara rambled on, unaware that Niamh was teasing her. "I was saying how sex was better with him. How he was bigger and better than Simon."

"Go on," Niamh smirked.

"I was telling him that I couldn't wait to see him again. How much fun it was being with him."

"Christ, and Simon was listening?"

"Mm."

"Right." Niamh continued with her drink.

"That's it then, is it?" Tara snapped.

"Whaddya mean?"

"Well, end of story? So what am I supposed to do? Sit back and let it happen? What about the betrayal, the lies?" Tara leaned in to the table and hissed, "For God's sake, Niamh, we haven't had sex for nearly two months!"

"Christ!" Niamh tossed the idea around in her head and couldn't imagine the concept of being celibate for sixty days, an idea more gross than the thoughts of Tara wanting to marry Simon in the first place.

She had tucked into her fresh salad, and as an exceptionally mammoth lettuce leaf struggled to escape from the sides of her mouth, she Ermintrude-d,

"You know, Tara, you needed a lover."

"What?"

"No sex for two months! That's criminal. You need someone like Karl. That's Karl, aka Cunnilingus-King."

"Niamh!" Tara hissed. "Not so loud!"

"It's a bit late to be a prude, Tara," Niamh laughed through her gobful of radish and cucumber. "You need to lighten up! Hey, listen to this: men are like lava lamps. Fun to look at but not actually all that bright." Tara lifted the veil of her sunglasses revealing her swollen eyes, making Niamh feel suddenly guilty.

"Oh shit, Tara. You've gotten yourself into a right state, haven't you?"

"Mmm." Her eyes had begun to fill up again, the pain of having been discovered too much to bear.

"Look, let's get out of here and get some air onto your face."

"Right," Tara whispered.

"Right."

This morning, a week after Simon's finding out about the intervention of the lusty, youthful Graham, Tara's hair sat in unsavoury, greasy clumps – a geometric mismatched arrangement crowning her unkempt self. At a glance, she was barely visible, the room seeming mere dismal shades of grey. On closer inspection however, you could just make out the shape of her shoulders, face and scruffed hair as she slumped against the wall. If you were to step closer into the bedroom, assuming your nostrils could survive the cocktail of smells which included stale bedclothes, cheese and onion crisps and Jack Daniels, you'd see that Tara's pillows were etched with dribble tidemarks, tear-stains the size of corn-circles and black cloggy smears of mascara. Her usually, pre-separation, pristine bedding was now knotted and bunched on the bed, strewn with a bright mosaic of crumpled Penguin wrappers and Hob Nob crumbs. Feeling guilty yet wronged, she found solace in food and her cheeks were still wet from her latest bout of tears. She was miserably lonely and was regretting the fact that, unable to even cope with Ruben her cocker spaniel, she had dropped him off at her mother's house.

She couldn't help but keep reading Simon's letter. It was the ultimate in pain to have it in writing how he would never be back. How their marriage was over. Only minutes before she'd been sobbing into her pillow, almost suffocating herself with a yearning for love when she knew that she least deserved it but most needed it, and asphyxiating herself with regret at the nocturnal saucy shenanigans with the nubile and now invisible Graham. The wedding portrait that had stood so proud within its silver frame on the dressing-table for the last year lay face down in shame, their euphoric grins a painful reminder that they were now a statistic amongst the thousands who had once believed they'd married for life.

So now he was gone. I'd invited him into my home, my life. I asked him to marry me! And now I'd driven him away. He was so bloody irritating at times, but I still loved him. At least I thought I did. Of course, Niamh said I was in love with the idea of being in love, but I wasn't sure if that made sense.

I thought of how a life of monogamy, even cooking and cleaning, now seemed such a rosy option. How we'd spend hours exploring each other's crevices in those heady early days. How he'd instantly agreed that getting married was just the best idea ever. How he'd been so delighted that it all seemed so perfect . . .

Still, Tara had yet to find out that he had more faces than a totem pole . . .

Chapter 2

If the proverbial candle had three ends, Niamh would have been burning them all.

Simultaneously.

She lay, reflecting how the anticipation of Karl had proved the most titillating experience of her evening. Not one to mince his words, marginally less politically correct than a disgusting joke, Karl was a man with sex on the menu. Niamh had been excited by his straightforwardness and clarity. That and his gorgeous muscly shoulders and rather well-developed upper arms.

But her sexual evening had kicked off to a bad start when she was stifled as the lusty Karl pinned her tanned frame down onto his bed.

"Hey, hey! Hold it right there," she'd said, giggling as she tried to slide her legs off the bed in an attempt to find the condoms. Karl had other ideas. Forcing himself down on her, almost unable to contain himself, she felt his slipperyness ominously gliding across the inside of her upper thigh.

"No, wait," she'd demanded, playing for the lighthearted approach. "You know my rules – no glove, no love."

This had seemed to cool him down momentarily as he nuzzled into her neck, his hot breath making her feel unbelievably horny.

"Mmm," he'd groaned into her soft skin, "you are absolutely gorgeous! How come some rich bastard hasn't whisked you off yet, eh? How come you're not married?"

"I wouldn't like my parents to die of heart failure due to excessive happiness, OK? Ohhh, Karl please!" She felt her resolve slipping despite the loud voice in her head, which sounded disconcertingly like her mother's, that was screaming at her to stop. "Mmm, stop, mmm, oooh! Get the condoms, Karl!"

He had laughed, deep and rasping. It was at this point that Niamh realised that he *did* know which buttons to press for her and in the disturbing realisation that he hadn't any protection she knew she had to act fast. Disappointed, she called a halt to the whole scenario immediately, fearing it would otherwise end with the morning-after pill.

She was woken the morning after by Anna who rarely slept in after six a.m. and refused to respect the fact that nobody else did.

"Ughh! Hullo." Niamh's voice was thick and beddy. Anna's, however, was bright and sing-song.

"Hi! I know you're still in bed, you lazy cow, but we need to talk."

Niamh's blank tranquil mind was immediately graffiti'd with the recollection of Tara's ongoing situation and the disappointment of the evening with Karl.

"About what?"

"Tara. Meet me in Brady's at six. You will be there, won't you? Are you on a shoot?"

"No. Not today, the big one was yesterday. Oh, my mobile's bleeping, I have to go." Her voice was still slow and throaty.

"Right," Anna had her organising head on today obviously, "see you there at six then. Don't forget now, will you, please? It's important."

"Right, right, I'll be there."

"Bye then."

"Mm."

Receiving yet another text message from the determined Karl, Niamh pushed the pad to switch off her mobile and turned to face the irritating ticking from her alarm-clock, grimacing as she saw the time. Feeling an involuntary stirring between her legs she turned again, to be faced only with the rumpled sheets. The sole indication that she'd spent the night alone, however, was the fact that she had all the pillows. As the disappointing encounter with Karl started to come back to her sleepy mind, she closed her eyes indulgently and mentally applauded the virtues of DIY sex.

As Tara padded through to the bathroom she consciously avoided looking in the mirror. She knew she looked shit.

She didn't care.

Really, I didn't. I was still far too busy punishing myself for being led by my G-spot rather than my brain.

The small fleshy pad of her finger felt raw as she'd punched the buttons to ring him so many times. She'd tried his mobile and his work, but there was no sign of him. Anywhere. His boss was polite but in a cool, officey manner and merely informed her that he was away on business for three weeks.

But I hadn't been put down that easily and I'd asked for his new mobile number. It made little difference though. Simon just insisted on putting the phone down on me. Time after time after time. He just couldn't bear to talk to me.

Tucking into the coronary sandwich she'd just had delivered by the local kebab house she felt the chilli sauce dribble down her chin. She didn't bother to wipe it off. Simon had detested the concept of doner kebabs, erring on the side of caution when faced with an indescribable chunk of dubious-looking meat as it rotated on the spit. The thought was enough to bring the tears brimming to her eyes once again. Blinking them in, she chastised herself mentally, ignoring the blaring lunch-time news on her constantly screaming telly. She gorged on the greasy food.

I thought: I now know that handsome is not *the sole criteria! Why was I such a selfish bitch? No, why* am *I such a selfish bitch? Oh, I hate myself!*

And stretching her dry lips wide, she forced a chunk of kebab into her mouth and chewed.

She felt that chewing eased the pain.

The sounds of commuter wheels whooshing through puddles temporarily boomed louder in the bar as yet another gaggle of "suits" bustled through the open doors. The bleachy tang that had been stinging Niamh's nostrils, as she watched the barmaid prepare for the influx of Friday-night drinkers, was now clouded by a cocktail of manly scents, courtesy of Gaultier and Chanel – and she suspected she could even recognise the seventies twang of Brut in there somewhere. Niamh rested her elbows on the table, wondering what the collective name could be for a bunch of city boyos who had more money than sense – she supposed "a guffaw of pin-stripe" or even "a wall of pervy macs". Her daydream was broken by the arrival of Anna, her high-pitched humming of "Wonderwall" as she weaved through the jutting tables and chairs possibly attracting the entire canine population of Dublin. Oblivious to the tinny sounds she was so publicly exuding, she smiled widely as she dragged at the chair next to Niamh and plonked herself into it, shaking the wet from her hair. The second she opened her mouth Niamh knew she'd been drinking.

"Christ, Anna! You smell like a brewery. Where've

you been? I know it's Friday but, let's face it, it's only six o'clock."

Unperturbed by her feisty friend's concern, Anna, only slightly tipsy, giggled, "We've bin celebrerting at work. A cheque for half-a-million came threh today. Tiffany got out a couple o'bottles she's had in her desk since 1997."

Her position as office administrator for a relatively new charity was one that she held as one of her greatest achievements, justifying her lack of compassion when it came to children and animals. At least in her own mind.

"Jesus, well, you stink! And what about your diet?" Anna lived in a permanent state of waiting for fat to be the new thin, as she painstakingly disguised her homely tum and heavy thighs, and Niamh enjoyed aggravating her with constant reminders.

"No worries there," she sang back, her voice still thick with her home-town Scottish accent. "I've been on the loo all morning anyway, after last night's date. The date was crap, but the sex was great." She groaned as she rubbed her hand over her curvy tummy. "I'm not so sure about the soggy bolognaise and sticky pasta that he made though."

"Jesus, I hope it was worth it!" Niamh grimaced at the thought of it.

"Well, I doubt I'll see him again, but still – story of my life really, eh? But anyway, let's not exaggerate. I've got worse things to tell you about."

"Come on then, let's order up something to drink and get on with it."

"Right, what'll you want? Coffee?"

"Mmmm, s'pose so."

Anna returned to the table, precariously balancing two cups of hot espresso.

"So?" Niamh prompted, keen for Anna to divulge.

"Well," her voice now a hushed slur, "me mam wants me ta go back to Aber-bloody-din next week. Says I haven't been home in a year. They're missing me."

"Will you go?"

"Jesus, no! At least, I don't think so." Anna's red cheeks were sizzling with the beginnings of post-alcohol flush and she suspected that it had gone straight to her knees. "Y'know, *anyone'd* be depressed at the prospect of a week in Aber-bloody-din."

"Yeah, you just can't wait to see your parents and be consumed by *kilt*."

Their walk back to Niamh's car, bravely left on a double yellow and remarkably un-ticketed, gave Anna enough time to sober up a little and to burden Niamh with the banalities of Tara's marital unbliss, their words lingering in breathy clouds in the warm evening air.

"We *must* go and see her. It's been a week now and I've not heard from her. I'm worried about her, Niamh. She's just not pulling herself out of this."

"No, you're right. I thought she'd just snap back out of it, but she's not. You know it was supposed to be our monthly meal last week? I didn't have the heart to mention it – she'd hardly have been up to it. We'll have to go round there."

"Right, I'll ring her in the morning."

Realising that Anna's definition of morning probably meant the middle of the night for other people, Niamh blocked her path.

"No, Anna, we won't ring and tell her. We'll just turn up, unannounced. That way she can't fob us off with an excuse."

"OK, when?"

"Tomorrow, ten o'clock?"

"You're on. Pick me up at half nine."

"Right."

And as Niamh unlocked her car door with a smile and a goodbye, only two miles away Tara continued to punish herself, tormented at ruining her now perfect-seeming marriage, and so began her second bottle of vodka.

Anna's perfect timekeeping continually irritated Niamh and today was no exception. Customarily early she heard the impatient honking of Anna's car hooter outside her Georgian sash window, which she'd framed, inexpertly and rather distastefully, with creased powder-blue muslin. The unpredictable lifestyle of her career as professional photographer led her to be haphazard and disorganised at home. The Mecca of Niamh's house was the desk buried beneath the computer and mountains of magazines, each dog-eared at specific pages which held her interest for a variety of reasons. She'd got to the stage now where she no longer found it necessary to keep a print of *every* one of her published works, instead keeping a portfolio of only the most exemplary of her projects.

Anna's multi-toned hooter blasted into the misty spring air once again, jarring Niamh from her languorous slumber. Pushing her dead-straight hair from her face and deftly securing it into a top-knot, she groped down toward her bobbly bedside rug and grabbed the faded jeans which had remained obediently crumpled on the floor. Tugging them onto her slender legs as she sat on the bed, she scanned the room for her Marlboro Lights. Another night where she'd fallen asleep flicking through her list of contacts, as she sat up in bed eating a Terry's Chocolate Orange, meant that the offending cigarettes were also crumpled under the duvet, their gold-emblazoned packet decidedly worse for wear. Lighting up a sorry-looking smoke she pulled her baggy black sweatshirt over her head, and made for the front door without a backward glance into the mirror – or over her shoulder at the gaping mouth of the bin as it spewed out cardboard packaging of meals-for-one.

The moment she opened the door of Anna's car she was conscious of being in an exaggerated state of dirtiness. The heavy aroma of Anna's perfume immediately highlighted Niamh's own beddy aura and, as she flopped into the passenger seat, slamming the door behind her, she noticed how perfectly Anna was made-up.

"Jesus. Where're *you* going?"

"What?"

"Looking like that! Why're you all spruced up? Is there something I don't know about?"

"As if!" Anna's tone was slightly disgruntled. She enjoyed putting in the effort, but detested being made to feel guilty for it. In her mind there was only one thing worse than being overdressed, and that was being underdressed. "Just because I make the effort doesn't mean there's a hidden agenda."

"Right," Niamh grinned. "So you're feeling 'bonny'?" She enjoyed teasing Anna about her Scotticisms. She fidgeted in her seat as she pulled on the last of her cigarette, then opened the window and threw out the brown-encased filter which was the only evidence left of her smoke.

That and her nicotine breath.

Whilst knocking repeatedly on Tara's black front-door, which was once so glossy it seemed that it had been coated with hot tar, Niamh felt strangely saddened at its new veil of city dust and smoke, its neglected matt appearance.

Niamh and Anna gasped, they weren't sure whether aloud, as a hung-over, dishevelled, almost unrecognisable Tara appeared. Leaving the door wide open behind her, she failed to register her two friends gawping in amazement as she turned her back and retreated back up the stairs of her two-bedroomed Victorian mid-terraced home. Niamh nudged Anna in over the greening brass doorstep and followed her in silence.

With the maternal instinct taking over in Anna she

made straight up the stairs and for the bathroom, holding her nose and grimacing as she did so, for the mouldy, cabbagey smell of Tara's house was like that of a nursing home. She grasped the taps and rotated them fully until the steaming hot water plummeted into the bath, roaring as it made impact with the dry enamelled surface. Pouring in generous amounts of lavender bath oil, Anna tugged at the cord of the extractor fan, leaving the bath to roar as it filled. She jammed the bathroom door open with a rolled-up handtowel and the steam was soon buffeting from the confines of the small bathroom and out onto the landing. Anna stood at the top of the stairs and called for Niamh. Hearing her booted footsteps as she climbed the stairs, Anna went into the half-light of Tara's bedroom.

"Tara. What the hell's going on, babe? What're you doing?"

Tara had buried herself under the grey duvet, the rustling of confectionery wrappers punctuating her wriggles.

"It's no good hiding under there. Look, Tar, Niamh's coming up now. You know what *she's* like."

Remarkably the threat of the lash of Niamh's tongue resulted in Tara at least revealing her head from beneath her turban of covers.

"I don't care." She was a sulky five-year-old who wasn't allowed to stay up late.

Niamh breezed into the room. "Where's Ruben, Tara?" she asked, swishing the long curtains open, letting in large blocks of watery sunshine as the morning mist began to lift.

"At my mum's."

"Look out there, Tara – the promise of a bright spring morning! Sure, summer'll only be around the corner and look at you! Tortoises only hibernate in winter. Or," she added with a giggle, "should I say Tara-toises?"

Tara and Anna scowled at her untimely attempt at humour. Then Anna left to tend to the bath.

Niamh kick-started into action. "Come on then. No good moping around. Won't bring Simon back. You've done the crime *and* done the time, I think. Time to move on."

"You bitch!" Tara whimpered, burying herself under the covers once more.

"You're calling me a bitch? Listen, Tara," Niamh settled her bum on the edge of Tara's bed, her voice softening as she spoke, "the truth of the matter is that you had an affair and got caught. Not the ideal situation, but it happens. Simon's gone. You've got to pick up the pieces and start again."

Tara wailed a muffled retort from beneath the duvet mountain as Anna reappeared. "But I don't *want* to start again!" Tara wailed. "I want Simon. I want what we had together. I want to live my life like before!"

Anna grimaced at Niamh, whose blunt nature was causing Tara more upset than good. "Tara, love. What you had 'before' has gone. Up in smoke, like an apparition. It's not an option to go back. That's not there any more. You have to move forward, Tar. Look, we'll leave you for a bit – there's a hot bath waiting for you and you've *got* to get into it. You're looking dreadful. C'mon, freshen up and we'll sort out downstairs for you."

Tara cursed and mumbled under her breath as Niamh and Anna left the room, Niamh doggedly tugging at the duvet as she left in an attempt to release it from Tara's vice-like clutches.

The living-room was as much a sight for sore eyes as Tara herself. Despite the tasteful decor and well-balanced eclecticism that she and Simon had so painstakingly organised, there was little denying it needed a clean. Spotting a vase full of brown wilted flowers, Anna picked it up and carried it out to the kitchen.

"Hey," she indicated to Niamh, "dead flowers just get more and more picturesque, don't they?"

The pungent stench of the offensive water caused them both to gag when Anna poured it swiftly down the sink, watching the green slime as it cascaded down and around the saucepans and plates which were piled high. She volunteered to tackle the kitchen while Niamh conquered the living-room. As Niamh began by collecting the small forest of free newspapers that had been so religiously posted through the door day after day, she heard the clattering as Anna loaded the dishwasher.

Anna shouted through, "Fancy pizza?"

"OK, shall we cook it or book it?"

"Book it! I can't even see the oven in here! Get on

the phone there and ring Four Star, will you? It'll be nearly lunch-time by the time Tara emerges."

Niamh's efforts at locating the cordless phone proved fruitless so she tugged her mobile from her jeans pocket and recalled Four Star Pizza's number from the memory. As she sat, waiting for a reply, she looked around Tara's house. She'd always had a natural talent for home design, Niamh thought. She'd cleverly defined the boundaries between the two rooms with a subtle change of colour, giving the appearance of being open plan, but ingeniously highlighting the contrast between the two different spaces. Even the fitted kitchen doors had been brought to life with a backdrop of stainless-steel panelling and contemporary "splodge" handles.

As Niamh attacked yet another pile of discarded magazines, coming across a couple of browning apple-cores and a variety of half-eaten choc bars which were ground into the sofa and rug, she discovered an ottoman buried beneath a pile of ironing and mags. She opened it up. The musty smell attacking her nostrils, she pulled out some four-month-old newspapers and was intrigued at coming across a batch of scrunched and rumpled credit-card receipts. Unravelling the shiny, noisy squares she examined them carefully and then called for Anna to come in and see.

Anna appeared, tastefully clad in yellow rubber gloves, snapping at them with a surgeon's glint in her eye.

"Wha'?" she enthused, liberated by her display of good-Samaritanness in cleaning someone else's kitchen.

"Look what I've found in here."

Anna looked at the fan of till receipts clutched in Niamh's hand.

"God! What's that then?" she asked with a giggle in her voice.

"It's not bloody funny, Anna. These are credit card receipts."

"So?"

"So: *The Sun Kee Chinese Restaurant, Belfast – Erriseaske House Hotel, Ballyconneely . . .*"

"Billy Connelly?" Anna teased, "he's great!"

"Ballyconneely, *Galway*. There's a load of them."

Anna moved around to sit next to Niamh, pulling off the rubber gloves and grabbing a cluster of receipts. She whispered names as she read them with as much amazement as Niamh.

"*Gaby's, Killarney – Blarney Castle Hotel, Cork . . .*" Niamh was gobsmacked. She couldn't understand how Tara had led such a dismal, miserable stay-at-home life and yet here were a mountain of receipts with Simon's scrawled signature emblazoned across the bottom of them.

"*The Wine Vault, Waterford – Talbot Hotel, Wexford,*" said Anna. "What was Simon up to?"

"I don't know. But I tell you one thing," Niamh whispered, folding the receipts into a big roll and stuffing them into her jeans pocket, "I intend to find out."

Anna jumped from the sofa when she heard Tara's bare feet padding across the landing as she crossed from the bathroom to her bedroom.

"What were the dates?" asked Anna quietly.

"There's loads. Ranging from only weeks after their wedding right up to a month ago."

"So," she mused, "they weren't part of a honeymoon-type shagging-session thing."

"Don't be ridiculous!" snapped Niamh. "Look, say nothing of this to Tara. Not yet."

"We'll talk about it later. She'll be down in a minute and that pizza won't be long in coming either."

Niamh went to check that she hadn't left any receipts behind and, as she shoved her hand down the side of the ottoman, she came across a long tube with papers rolled inside. Curiosity not being an emotion Niamh felt comfortable with restraining, she pulled the papers from the tube revealing long-forgotten artwork that Tara had completed in her attempts at design. Her Fine Art degree had stood her in good stead in securing the job in the gallery, selling both famous and contemporary pieces to both famous and contemporary people. The days when Tara worked seemed a distant memory now as Niamh turned her thoughts to the lonely existence she now lived. She'd given up her job in the gallery four months after marrying Simon in a bid to set up an interiors consultancy, in the belief that she had his backing. Instead she had merely become his skivvy, spending time desperately trying to amuse herself away from the nine-to-five world, ensconced in a twenty-four-hour stay-at-home one that she knew little about.

With her new-found knowledge of the credit card

receipts, Niamh wondered what effect Simon's frequent absences had on Tara's confidence. From day one, Niamh had pondered on Simon's reasons for agreeing to marry Tara. They'd all been so surprised when she'd revealed her intentions of proposing, but even more so when he had accepted. It seemed increasingly evident as they scratched the surface of Tara's life, that all Simon had wanted was a live-in maid.

"Ha, no wonder Tara had an affair," Niamh whispered to herself as she imagined herself in Tara's situation. "What a boring existence!"

Niamh's daydream was interrupted as Anna entered the small room with a tray laden with three mugs full of steaming tea and a plate of Jammy Dodgers.

"Come on, Tara, cup of tea's ready!" she called up the stairs to a silent Tara. "And we've ordered pizza!"

Tara muttered a barely audible retort from her bedroom and as Anna drove the third Jammy Dodger towards her gaping mouth they heard the sounds of Tara plodding across the small landing to the top of the stairs. Anna leant across the coffee table and deftly rearranged the remaining biscuits so that they covered the plate more evenly.

"What are you doing that for?" smirked Niamh, intent on aggravating Anna.

"No reason, just making them look nice."

"Yeah, right. Just to hide the fact you've already eaten almost half of what was on the plate in the first place!"

Anna's face squeezed into a scowl.

Tara strode into the room. "Nice to see you two still getting on," she said in a monotone. Wrapped in a mulberry-coloured chenille bathrobe which seemed at least two sizes too big, she curled onto the settee, her wet hair still dripping onto her shining face.

"Hey, look what Niamh found!" Anna said, trying to chirp, clutching the roll of papers they'd pulled from the tube.

Tara barely raised her head to see the sketchy interiors she'd planned.

"Huh, what made you drag that crap out?"

"It's not crap. You're quite talented, aren't you, eh?"

"*Were* quite talented, OK? Get it right. *Were*."

"You don't lose talent like that overnight, Tara."

"Maybe not, but being deserted by your husband tends to knock the creativity out of you somewhat!"

Niamh laughed a loud and exaggerated cackle, as she lifted her legs and swung them back onto the cushions of the settee. "Ha! So we're going for the sympathy vote, are we?"

Tara's face reddened as she turned her head to face Niamh in such a hurry that her wet hair slapped her across the face. "Meaning?"

Niamh continued to giggle to herself. "Meaning! Meaning that you're making a right meal out of this, Tara. You had a brilliant job in the gallery. That's just the first fact of the matter. Meaning that you're still young, well, young-*ish*, and you could have a great future ahead of you. You've got to try and put this self-pity crap out of your mind. It will only hold you back."

Tara had adopted the adolescent arms-folded-high-above-your-boobs look which indicated that she didn't like what she was hearing. Anna took her opportunity to smooth over Niamh's lack of tact.

"Niamh *does* have a point in one way, Tar. You do have a great eye for it. That's what Mulligan employed you for in the first place, remember?"

Loosening her grip on herself, Tara relaxed, surprising Niamh by reaching forward, taking one of her cigarettes and lighting up. Coughing as she inhaled, she explained, "I haven't got the confidence to go for that kind of job again. But my time in bed hasn't been wasted. I *have* been thinking of my future. That's one thing chocolate is great for – it gives you something else to do while planning the rest of your life."

Taking her literally, Anna enthused, continuing to munch enthusiastically on the Jammy Dodgers.

As the blanket of dusk began to fall outside, Anna took on the task of pulling the heavy curtains together.

Tara's hair had dried hours ago and sat untouched, topping her ruddy face. Slightly slurring her words she offered, "You know, as guilty as I feel for hurtin' Simon, I don't actually feel overwhelming remorse for what I *did*. Y'know, the pure thrill of illicit sex."

Niamh grabbed the last bottle of Pinot Grigio by the neck, pouring herself an indulgent half-pint, misinterpreting Tara's wide-eyed amazement for vino-retentiveness. Halting, mid-glug, she apologised. "Sorry, I'm just so desperate to get pissed tonight."

"It's OK," whispered Tara. "I've bin thinkin' . . ."

Niamh giggled tipsily. "Yeah?"

Tara snuggled up to Niamh on the sofa, nestling her arm in and under hers and curling her legs up beneath her so as to wiggle in closer. Niamh enjoyed the closeness of her two best friends.

"Well, I reckon you need to start your own business again," said Niamh. "You need to revive that consultancy idea."

Grabbing a biscuit from the tin Tara questioned, "Doing what, exactly?"

"I think you should start a decorating and design consultancy."

Tara rested her tipsy head on Niamh's shoulder. "Tell me more."

Anna spent the next hour pouring pints of sparkling water and coffee in a bid to sober her two slovenly friends, as they managed to sketch, create and invent Tara's one-way ticket out of the depression she'd sunk herself into.

Only slightly aware of the rowdy late-night boozers who passed Tara's bay window, Niamh rested her feet on the previously admired coffee table and proclaimed, holding her half-empty wineglass aloft, "Here's to the Tara McKenna Consultancy!"

Tara and Anna gawped at each other.

It was Tara who broke the silence. "Here's to what?"

"Tara McKenna Consultancy, your new business."

To which Tara and Niamh slurred in unison: "Tara McKenna Conshultanchy!"

Chapter 3

Declan O'Mahoney ran his fingers through his thick chestnut hair in exasperation. As the rebellious waves settled he reclined into his padded leather seat and pushed the directory across the desk and away from him. His eyes settled on the silver photoframes which remained on his desk. Staring into his ex-girlfriend Paula's still eyes he berated himself for insisting on hanging on to the past. The photographs had, as had *speed-dial number one* on his office phone, outstayed their welcome. They were the hangers-on at a party that was long over. Paula had left him, and he had no right to keep reminding himself of the diamante sparkling of her eyes, the rich velvet tones of her deep laugh and how he'd once thought her heart so full of love and compassion that he thought his own would burst in admiration.

Looking through the horizontal slats of the blind on his glass office in the RTÉ building, he saw his robust secretary busily picking at her fingernails. Just to prove a point, he found himself tucking his shirt into his trousers and reaching for his jacket, just itching to watch her spring into life as she'd busy herself typing *quick brown fox* in a bid to appear overstretched. True to form she obliged, almost flicking herself in the eye as she jumped at the sound of his office door opening.

"Morning," he sang, breezing past her, trying not to smile too overtly.

His initial reaction to the mammoth task he'd been assigned had been enthusiasm, there seeming to be a certain amount of voyeurism involved in this new penchant for what he called "homes porn" and the feelings of inadequacy they evoked if you didn't live up to Scandinavian design standards. Months later his ears were still ringing from the sing-song of wannabe interior designers professing their techniques with scumble-glaze and mosaic-ing. His latest dilemma, which was what now led him to the canteen for his mid-morning breakfast and some neutral thinking-ground, was to find the last "designer" for the team. So far they'd seemed either too flamboyant, too minimalistic or too traditional.

Lost in a daydream as he slid the greasy mushrooms around his plate, he felt himself shrink in the presence of Stephanie, the researcher currently working on *Home Is Where The Art Is.* Despite his obvious intent and sudden interest in his plate, she pulled out the chair opposite him and sat down at it.

"Hey, Declan, you know that *that* will do your cholesterol levels – no bloody good at all!"

"Yeah," he deadpanned, "I know.

"Mind you," she flirted outrageously with him, "a man of your physique needn't worry about such things."

"You know," he spoke through a mouthful of bacon and sausages, without embarrassment, "my ex, Paula – she called it a heart attack on a plate."

"She wasn't far wrong."

"Probably not, but if my mother had half a chance she'd serve this up to me three times a day."

"Ah, old school."

"Yep."

He continued to tuck into his greasy meal, obvlious to Stephanie's adoration, his thoughts now gone back to his mam in Carlow and how she still didn't know the full story on Paula leaving him. He felt a strange lack of fulfilment when it came to his mother. She'd spent the last ten years boasting to his home village of his "success" in broadcasting, despite his early beginnings as office junior and runner. Little did she realise that his life seemed more Albert Square than Times Square, and he didn't have the heart to burst her bubble. He was even less willing to divulge his failure to keep Paula, as she had believed that he'd chosen a partner for life. His reminiscence was interrupted as Stephanie leaned in closer toward the table, allowing him an undisturbed view down her tanned valley of full cleavage.

"Are you coming to the party tonight?"

It was something he religiously tried to avoid, believing there was nothing worse than the traditional hell of office parties with the inebriated men leering over at the glassy-eyed women. In the days of Paula he'd had an excuse to go home early. How he'd loved ending the day, however stressed, in the knowledge that she was waiting for him . . .

Once again Stephanie interjected, "Well . . ."

He imagined she was trying to appear coy, and it had to be said that her large blue eyes were hypnotising and her long legs could play havoc with a man's imagination, but he wasn't interested in her, or any other woman. Hell, he was still struggling to "let go" of Paula.

"Well what?" He wiped the grease from his mouth with the paper serviette, then screwed it into a tight ball before leaving it on the smeared empty plate.

"Well," she teased a strand of her blonde hair, "are you coming?"

"No. I don't really go in for that kind of caper."

"Oh," she pouted, "and I had you up for a man who liked to enjoy himself."

"Ah well," he puffed, lifting his jacket from the back of his chair, "you know what they say: gentlemen prefer bland."

He left her giggling at the table.

On the short walk back to his office he pondered over the changes that seemed to befall a woman in love. He'd spent numerous lonely nights asking himself why Paula'd felt she had to change him into a male version of herself. The clothes, the hobbies, the personality – probably the very reasons she fell for him had suddenly seemed problematic. How, over the period of time, she'd begun to criticise his choice of shirts and ties. How, almost overnight, his CD collection "smacked of bachelor".

"Of course it does," he'd retorted, defending his prized music collection. "That's what I was – a bloody bachelor." But suddenly it had seemed just not quite good enough for Paula. She'd wanted instant metamorphosis from "washing-up-piled-in-the-sink, John-Lee-Hooker-CD-on-volume-fifteen, I-survive-alone-and-enjoy-it" Bachelor Man to "I-only-listen-to-Garth-Brooks-and-go-to-the-pub-once-a-week" Family Man.

Ah well, he mused to himself, it only backs up the theory that a woman expects that she can change a man, only to find she can't – and a man meets a woman expecting that she won't change, and she does.

Once back in his office he felt slightly refreshed for the break and sat at his desk once again.

"Mr O'Mahunny!"

He found the temp's raspy voice both entertaining and irritating at the same time, but today mostly irritating in the way she couldn't – or wouldn't – pronounce his name correctly.

He failed to look up, choosing instead to busy himself at his desk.

She repeated herself, this time more forcefully, "Mr O'Mahunny!"

"What's up?"

"There's someone on the phone for you."

"OK. Who?"

"I didn't catch his name, but he knows yours."

Declan inhaled deeply and shook his head. She was truly one of the worst temps he'd ever encountered, but today wasn't the day to enlighten her on her shortfallings. Instead he flopped down into his leather chair and raised his pewter eyes to meet hers. "OK – I'll take it."

"I'll put it through," she said in a monotone, turning to the door.

"Oh, by the way," Declan found himself saying to the back of her shaved head and curiously thick neck, "it's pronounced 'O'Mahney'."

She turned to face him, puzzled. "I beg your pardon?"

"My name. It's not Mr O'Ma*hunny*. Look, you know Armani? As in the fashion-designer guy with the perfumes and products?"

She was nodding, with a confused expression on her face.

"Well, it's like that – Armani – Mani – O'Mahoney," he felt his voice staccato now, almost spitting the words out at her ridiculous expression. "Mr O'Mahoney. Declan O'Mahoney." He could feel his voice rising but had little control over it at this stage, "You're in Ireland now, Miss –Miss – Miss –"

"Day, Miss Day," she proffered.

"Right." He realised how obnoxious he was being and suddenly felt sorry for her. "Miss Day, it's O'Mahoney as in 'O'Mahney' and *not* 'O'Ma-hunny'."

"OK," she smiled, relieved that he'd calmed down, "point taken."

He was both relieved and amazed when she took the outburst of cruel criticism so squarely on the chins and departed his office without forgetting to close his door quietly behind her.

Rubbing his temples, he exhaled. "This is really stressing me out. I must calm down a bit."

Punching the button on his telephone console, he picked up the phone and barked into the mouthpiece, "O'Mahunny here. I mean, O'Mahoney – who's calling?"

A male voice with a lilt of suppressed humour intoned, "Mr O'Mahoney – my name is George, George Galvin. I'd like to speak to you about *Home Is Where The Art Is.*"

Tara felt only marginally better than she had done the previous morning and every morning for the past few weeks, the difference being that this time, despite the sandpaper tongue and banging headache, she had retained glimmers of the positive attitude that Niamh and Anna had conjured up in her the evening before. Breaking new ground this morning, she dressed, properly – knickers *and* jeans, boots *and* socks and even t-shirt *and* bra – with the intention of going out her front door.

As she stepped over her tarnished brass doorstep, she breathed in the fuggy exhaust-fume-filled air. She felt good despite the beginnings of a nagging pain in her pelvis and lower back, a sign that her period loomed. The Tara McKenna Consultancy was established, though in mind only as yet.

"Haaaay, Ta-raaa! I no see you for long time!"

She cringed as she saw Yannis standing in his shop doorway, and gesticulating wildly at her from across the street. Unable for anything mildly resembling conversation Tara managed to rustle up a cheesy grin and wave. Feelings of guilt once again swamped her as she thought back on her previous light-hearted relationship with the swarthy deli owner and resolved to call in and chat with him on her way back from Easons.

Declan pushed the *Golden Pages* over the edge of his desk, letting it fall with a heavy thud onto the nylon-carpeted floor – despite Ireland's obsession with interiors, it seemed design hadn't yet reached RTÉ. Turning to face his computer screen, he rubbed at his tired eyes to try and rid himself of the feeling that they'd been soaked in vinegar, as he viewed the list of interior design colleges and art schools. He still lacked the final piece to his interiors "team" jigsaw. His office door opened with a click and whoosh of wood on nylon. As he looked up and watched the temp enter, he also noticed the empty open-plan office behind her, the fluorescent strip lighting dimmed for the night.

"What time is it?" he asked wearily.

"Quarter to seven. Here," she placed a pile of papers on the edge of his desk, "what'll I do with these?"

Too tired to be even irritated by her, he held his hand up, indicating that he neither cared nor knew.

"You look tired, Mr O'Mahu – O'Mahoney. You know, if you don't mind me saying so, nothing's the same when you're firing on only half your engines."

"Yeah," he agreed, rubbing his tired head, and in so doing ruffled his hair. "You know what I need?" he asked her, feeling slightly guilty about his earlier outburst. After all, the entire department had left for the evening and she was still there, putting in the hours.

"What?" she asked him, annoyed at the fact that he was probably going to ask her to stay for another hour, but determined not to let it show.

"I need a microwave bed."

Not expecting the strange request, her face contorted into a genuine grimace of confusion. "A what?"

"I need a microwave bed. I need ten hours' sleep in eight minutes."

Relieved both at the injection of humour and his intention of calling it a day, she laughed at his remark, and made her way back over to his desk.

"Come on, Mr O'Mahu– Declan. I'm going to call you Declan – I'm sorry if you don't like it, but I just can't get to grips with pronouncing your name correctly. Sorry. Come on now, enough's enough. Call it a day, huh?"

Too tired to argue he agreed with her, and turned the desk-lamp off.

"You're right. Look, you go now, I'll be off in a few minutes. I have a few things to put away first."

"OK, so long as you do."

Feeling a strange, almost disturbing wave of affection for his temp as she departed his office with a succession of heavy thuds, he switched the banker's light back on, and reshuffled the paperwork on his desk. Faced with thirteen episodes' worth of case-study homes to fill sixteen episodes' worth of broadcasting time, he needed another three homes. There was no way he could leave yet. The agenda was set to find Irish homeowners who wanted a home makeover using primarily Irish products and craftsmen. Setting the digital alarm on his desk for eight o'clock, he decided to put in another hour.

The shrill ringing of his phone made him jump. Turning a self-conscious shade of pink, embarrassed at his jumpiness, he grabbed the receiver. It was George Galvin, again.

"Mr O'Mahoney? George Galvin. I said I'd get back to you. Sorry for ringing so late, but you did say that you'd probably be in the office until now."

"No problem," said Declan, eager to get down to business.

"Right, I've spoken to the other half and there's no problem. You can count us in on your *Home Is Where The Art Is* series."

"Excellent!" Declan blasted with a sudden surge of enthusiasm. He now only needed another two homes. Grabbing his pen, he jotted down George's address on his notepad and spent the next fifteen minutes discussing the property with him.

The Old Schoolhouse sounded just perfect for this new series. It seemed, from George's description, that the converted schoolhouse was already painted in a plethora of bold primary colours, but the study and bathroom needed bringing up to date with the contemporary style of the house as a whole. Having exchanged e-mail addresses, George promised to send digital photos of the interiors to Declan the next morning and they both put their phones down feeling as if something had been achieved.

At seven forty-three Declan once again switched off his desk-lamp and, congratulating himself on the last hour's work, decided to go to Byrne's and celebrate with a few jars.

Mere miles away in Sandymount, Ciara O'Rourke sat alone in her 1930's townhouse overlooking the water, checking the final edit of her fifth and recently completed interiors book. Self-designed and, many would consider, horrendously garish, it was a tumultuous cocktail of zebra prints, black gothic gargoyles and red-stained pine floors. She cockily tossed the completed manuscript onto her cream couch which was cleverly punctuated with black velvet cushions. Getting up from the velvet-covered chair and moving toward the centre of the room, she raised her face towards the abstract mirror which hung diagonally above the fireplace. She smoothed her taut pale skin and flicked her short bobbed hair.

"Right," she said aloud in her clipped Dublin tones, "the time has come to be rid of Unfortunate Feargal."

Sitting prim and upright on the edge of the settee, she grasped the cordless phone, her long red talons clipping on the hard plastic. Punching in the sequence of numbers, a wicked smirk spread across her cold face. Unfortunate Feargal answered the telephone.

"Hullo."

"Feargal – Ciara here."

"Ciara, darling!" His voice immediately swamped with thick honeyed smarm, he sounded delighted to hear from her. "How it going, babe?"

"Shuttup, Feargal, you prick! I'm just gracing you with a call to tell you not to bother calling round here again. You're history, *babe*. You know, you're the original boa constrictor of boyfriends. Oh, and while I fleetingly think of it, do you think your dad was under-sexed too? I suppose he was. Anyway, you might want to find out before your dick shrivels up and falls off through lack of use." She felt a rush of warm adrenalin at her outspokenness. Insults she was good at, interiors she was good at, relationships and manners however, were a consummate problem to her.

"You bitch!" Feargal spat. "Just because you've written a few books on what colour walls go with which type of carpet, you think you're a bloody celebrity! Well, face reality, Ciara – you're a dried-up has-been! You're crap in bed and a complete bore. It's impossible to be in your company for more than an hour without you boring everyone around you with the pros and cons of tatmi mats and bloody paint-effects. The bottom line is, Ciara, you're bloody rude and boring to boot!"

Ciara laughed an insidious laugh, his insults running off her like mercury and before Unfortunate Feargal had further opportunity to respond, she punched the "off" button on the phone, disconnecting him.

Feeling absolutely zero conscience regarding

Feargal's bruised ego, she instead reached into her bag, pulling out an innocent-looking white plastic bag. Its contents she carefully spilled onto the stone-effect mantelpiece, the small coloured tablets rattling and rolling across the smooth surface. Gathering a cluster in her hand she threw them into her gaping mouth and swilled them down with a slug of water. As she raised her face a dribble of the water escaped and ran down her chin. Swiping at it with the back of her hand, she opened her eyes wide and smiled.

"Ha," she said, "that's better. Bloody Feargal!" And gathered her briefcase and laptop. "Yuk," she spat, rearranging her blunt-cut prior to opening the front door, "he's one I'd rather forget."

The moment Niamh turned the corner and through the gate of Tara's Ballsbridge house she noticed the smell.

Immediately.

The pungent acidic odour of white spirit permeated the exhaust-fume-filled air. She felt like one of the Bisto Kids in the ad when they tipped their heads to the sky and sniffed at the brown snaking aroma of the gravy. Only she wasn't volunteering to breathe in the smell, but it stung at her nostrils nevertheless.

Stopping at the open bay window she called through, "You've not become one of those DIY junkies, have you?"

She let herself in through the open front door, its black paint now clean again and the brass doorstep once again gleaming. She soon realised that Tara was trying to let as much air in as possible in order to keep a clear head. Niamh strode into the lounge to be confronted with a scene totally different to the one of only days before. Only the smell before was marginally better than now. Dressed in old ripped denim shorts, battered Timberlands and a faded sweatshirt, Tara's skin and clothes were smeared with a rainbow of paint colours. Taking in the industrious scene, Niamh gazed at the kitchen table which groaned beneath a heaving pile of tester-pots, brushes and ominous slices of MDF.

"Jaysus," was all she could muster.

Tara flinched slightly as she relaxed her concentrated expression, dropped the laden paintbrush and faced Niamh. "Well? What do you reckon?"

"Jaysus!"

"Well, it's not often you're lost for words, Connolly."

Niamh noticed the involuntary flinch as Tara spoke again.

"I'm just so shocked," said Niamh. "Talk about Motivation Girl. It's like a bloody shed in here."

"Fancy a cuppa?" Tara couldn't face looking at Niamh's incredulous expression and tensed up as she filled the kettle with gushing water, and began to explain to Niamh what she'd been doing. She made the tea and Niamh noticed that she tensed again momentarily as she carried the two mugs in.

"You all right?"

"Fine. Why?"

"No reason. Just checking. Still no word from Simon then?"

Tara ignored her question and went on to explain to Niamh how she'd spent a quietly creative weekend despite a few minor hiccups. Her most recent experiment was a mosaic in a bid to customise a piece of junk-shop furniture she'd picked up next door to Yannis's only the day before. The old table legs were, once sanded and revarnished, in pristine condition, it being only years of family abuse that had disfigured the top so badly. Her economically astute acumen, discovered since the departure of Simon and the advent of her income-less lifestyle, swayed her hand toward the cheap end of DIY, resulting in her managing to purchase three boxes of broken tiles at a ridiculously low price.

"Yep," she smiled at Niamh through the permeated air as she stood to glue on the final mismatched ceramic shapes, "this is the beginning of a creative journey for me."

The phone began to ring and, wiping her gluey hands on her shorts once more, she hurried to answer it, her long lithe legs striding, with a renewed spring in her step. Yet still, Niamh was sure she noticed Tara tensing and flinching a little at irregular intervals.

"Damn," she muttered to herself once Tara was out of ear-shot, "I hope she hasn't developed one of those nervous twitches. Stress can bring it on."

"Who you talking to?" Tara asked as she re-entered the room.

"Oh, no-one. Who was that? On the phone?"

"Only Mum. She'll probably call again before the day's out. She thinks I'm about to top myself, I think."

"Overreacting mums, eh?"

"Mm."

"She still has Ruben then?"

"Yeah. I'll take him back as soon as I get this job done."

And then she flinched once again, Niamh was sure of it.

While Niamh stared, Tara went on enthusiastically. "I've done some rubbing-down and varnishing and a bit of mosaic-ing and sgraffito."

"What?" Niamh questioned, walking around the table at which Tara was working, casting her eye over the excellent mosaic'd table top.

"Sgraffito."

"Go on."

"It's scratching to reveal the colour of underglaze underneath."

"Oh, right. So you're taking it seriously then."

"'Course I am. The Tara McKenna Consultancy, as of yesterday, has been well and truly born. I've been to Easons and got a rake of magazines: *Elle Decoration*, *Irish Interiors*, *Image Interiors*, *World of Interiors* – you name it I got it. I spent yesterday as my reading day and then today was my 'hands-on experience'."

Tara was now positively gushing and, despite the offensive smell and the strange twitching, Niamh was impressed at her enthusiasm. She continued without further prompting, and it seemed without taking a breath. "People's places are now defined as people's 'spaces'. Lighting is so important, you see. The effect of it should never be underestimated. Low lamps, which don't allow light from the top, make a ceiling seem lower. Halogen bulbs produce a lot of heat and so they're not suitable for a small room whereas uplighting is uplifting. I'm going to experiment with some coloured bulbs, fairy lights draped on curtain tracks and sample some lava lamps."

Totally overwhelmed, Niamh could only watch the animated Tara.

As she flinched, Tara rested for a breath and then began to doubt herself.

"But look at the state of me. Of my place. Who am I to put my mark on other people's homes?"

"Hey, don't even go there! Let me tell you, from what I've seen fashion stylists are much like interior designers: their clothes are the least fashionable and their homes are the least stylish."

"Great," Tara flinched, "make me feel tons better!"

"Go 'way, you'll be into that Feng Shite malarkey next."

"I don't think so. The very concept that putting a rug on the east-facing wall could have made such a difference to my life is nothing but disturbing."

She began to sing her favourite Macy Gray number aloud, unaccompanied by any CD or cassette. Only when she was in full verse did she realise it was the first time in months that she'd actually sung. Simon had hated her singing, claiming that she thought she had a good voice, but she actually didn't at all. Niamh and Anna had disagreed with him, but he'd seemed to get into her head and she had begun to lose confidence – not only in the vocal department but many others also when it came to Simon. The only thing interrupting her today was the incessant calling of Niamh from the kitchen, bringing her back to reality. Tara twitched and tensed as she turned to face Niamh who was scrutinising her strangely.

"What's wrong?" she called.

"Tara, come and sit down a minute, eh?"

Grateful for a short break, she did so. As she lowered herself into the chair, Niamh noticed how she seemed to be sitting strangely, her back kind of arched.

"What's wrong with you, Tar? Are you in pain? Is there something you're not telling me?"

Tara stabbed at joviality. "Yeah, next I'm painting auld Aunt Maggie's antique mahogany table a dazzling dayglo green, and then I'm stencilling some naff designs all over the top."

Niamh wasn't fazed. "Tara. What's wrong?" She leaned forward and placed a hand on Tara's knee as she twitched once again.

"Oh shit, Niamh, you're too bloody observant!"

"Observant! You'd need to be blind to notice that something's drastically wrong with you."

Tara sheepishly caught the bottom of her shirt and slowly lifted it, revealing a rubber-looking green belt with a computerised contraption slotted into the front. Jutting from the waistband of her shorts was the Slendertone logo.

"What the fuck's that?"

Tara's voice dropped an octave at least, and was reduced to almost a whisper: "It's a Slendertone."

"I can *see* that! Why're you wearing it?"

"Simon bought it for me for my birthday. He said I was getting too matronly around the middle and said it'd put me back in shape."

"The bastard!" Niamh shot to her feet, angrily. "A Slendertone isn't something that you buy for someone as a *present* – it's something that you buy for yourself. You look into your mirror at yourself one day and realise you're a mess. Then you buy one, *alone*, and take it into the privacy of your bedroom and plug yourself in for half an hour, during which you twitter and judder. Though I doubt it'd ever make you half the girl you used to be. Anyway, Tar, you don't *need* that."

"I just think that I could do with looking after myself again, so from now on it's this for an hour a day and a diet of fruit and veg only."

Realising she was pissing against the wind, Niamh conceded, "OK, but let's read the instructions. You've surely got it set too high if it's making you virtually epileptic with every power-surge."

Tara took the belt off and they inspected the strange stretchy design, "uurgghing" at the jelly-like adhesive patches that were stuck to it. Then Niamh regaled Tara with the story of Karl and his anti-climactic approach.

Tara's rejuvenation with MDF and spray paint long forgotten and a couple of cafetiéres of Lava Java coffee later, Niamh found herself explaining her own quandaries to Tara. She'd fleetingly given thought to employing a painter and decorator to decorate her flat. The first quandary being that she couldn't seem to find any that didn't sound like cowboys. The second quandary was how she supposed she'd either fancy them like mad or she wouldn't trust them – or herself. By the end of the third cafetiére, Niamh was offering Tara seven hundred euro to renovate her flat.

"You mean only the bathroom, right?" queried Tara.

"No, the whole bloody flat."

Tara had laughed at her budgeting. "Niamh, how much do you think a professional would charge you for the whole flat?"

"Dunno. You see, Tara, that's why I'm destined to meet a man with money – I'm useless at budgeting."

"Look, Niamh, you're fantasising again. I'll try and do the lounge/dining-room and kitchen for seven hundred euro – and that'll mean *no* profits for me at all. I'll use the full seven hundred on materials. Deal?"

Niamh looked at her through squinted, hazy eyes.

"Go on," Tara urged, excited now at the opportunity to put some of her theory and ideas into practice. "Anyway, I need to start some kind of a portfolio. It'd be a great opportunity."

"All right then."

Tara squealed and hugged Niamh excitedly. "When can you start?"

"Yesterday."

"Done."

Tara leapt from the sofa, reaching for the pile of interiors magazines that she'd collected over the weekend. Feeling unable to participate in any ensuing "homes" discussion, Niamh decided it was time to leave.

Chapter 4

Niamh left Tara's at ten only realising as she walked down the streetlamp-lit path that she didn't want to go home yet. Reaching into her bag for her mobile, she punched in to find the number for Adam. It was handy having contacts across Dublin – it meant wherever she was she could fall back on a satisfying lay, but Adam was the best. Especially in the light of the disappointing Karl experience.

"Yeah," she consoled herself, "all this agony-aunt business is too time-consuming lately."

Adam wasn't at home but in a pub in Temple Bar. Pulling her Afghan floor-length coat tightly around her, she skipped down the steps at the DART station. She'd agreed to meet him in an hour. As the draught caught the woolly filaments of her coat she hugged herself contentedly. Her current love for all things shaggy had meant that she even had her eye on some sheepskin cushions, but decided to draw the line at the woolly-haired Rastafarian busker singing "No Woman No Cry" as she skitted past. As she walked onto the bustling late-night platform she made a mental note to dig out her old reggae tapes once again.

Sitting on a bench by Aston Quay, she noticed the time was now quarter to eleven. In the blackness of the night the Ha'penny Bridge, with its elegant arch over the Liffey, was illuminated almost as brightly as if it were day and was almost as busy. Niamh watched the many tourists, and wondered how many would still pay the halfpenny toll for the pleasure of crossing had they not abolished the idea. She'd always enjoyed the voyeuristic slant on life and presumed that it was this which had steered her toward photography. There was a certain element of onlooking and people-watching involved in setting people into frames and clicking your camera at them. Pulling her Afghan closer around herself again, she laughed as she watched a small bustle of workmen in their dayglo yellow jackets hopping and jigging in their muddy workboots around the plastic barriers within which they were still working. It seemed a twenty-four-hour non-stop lifestyle in the heart of the city and she felt an overwhelming adrenalin rush. At quarter past eleven she watched as the traffic ground to a solid halt at the junction of the O'Connell Bridge with Westmoreland Street and D'Olier Street. Suddenly irritated at being alone, she hopped up and made her way to Temple Bar, side-stepping crowds of chain-smoking French teenagers and clusters of exuberantly dressed theatre-goers. She stopped at a pavement café and ordered a glass of chardonnay, taking it outside with her, opting to sit beneath one of the canopy heaters. Although it was early summer, the nights still had a slight chill to them. The metal chair opposite her screeched in the night air as a young man pulled it out for his girlfriend to sit down. Niamh paid little attention to them. Sharing a table was the done thing here. Watching the busy hubbub as she sipped at the chilled wine, she was conscious of an enthusiasm for life. For this life. The rolling sing-song tones of an Italian family came into earshot and she pulled her feet in beneath her chair as the boisterous father staggered behind his chattering clan. Niamh could feel the intensity of the goose-pimples on her forearms and couldn't determine whether they were caused by the night-air or because of the energy coursing through her body. As she watched couples with their arms draped around each other, the air was punctuated with Italian, French and German tourists greeting each other with quirky double-cheek kisses. A regular to this nocturnal scene she still never failed to be amazed at the true grit of life in the city – the perfumey wafts which clouded the air as theatre-goers passed the homeless and filthy young men asking politely for a spare few cent. Checking her watch for the arrival of Adam she looked towards a small illuminated doorway, its grimy stairs visible through the open battered door which was noticeable because of the small red light bulb and handwritten *MODEL* hanging above it. A cluster of five middle-aged men stood lighting up cigarettes outside.

She actually felt a craving for her camera and chastised herself for coming here without it. These were pictures that told a million stories and she had nothing to capture it. Drawn by these shady men she was dying to know whether they were just going in or had just come out of the "model's" room. Her thoughts were once again interrupted by a tall student type pulling a metal chair from the side of her table and sitting astride it, facing her.

His voice was as hideous as his dental work. "I know how to please a woman."

"Fantastic." Niamh could have eaten him up and spat him out. "Then please leave me alone."

Within seconds he had disappeared up the north-facing street. Giggling to herself as she watched his thick neck blend into the crowd, her attention was drawn to the tinny, velvet tones of a saxophone. She finished the last of her drink and walked toward the sound, only to see a crusty homeless man caressing the tarnished instrument as if it were a beautiful lover in his previous life. An old pram stood by his side, housing a battered car stereo illuminated in orange LCD and powered by a car battery, which provided the basic backing for his music. Intrigued by the talents of this otherwise seemingly useless human, she stood watching while a cluster of Mediterranean tourists stood behind him, a pal taking a tacky photo of them smiling over his shoulder. They didn't even think of dropping a few cents into his empty saxophone case. She pulled a ten-euro note out of her pocket and pushed it into his pram, feeling sickened at the exploitative way they had used him, all in fun. She felt an urge to confront them and point out that this was a reality for the homeless guy. However, reasoning with herself that this was city life, she went back to looking out for Adam, checking her watch for his impending arrival.

She soon saw him appearing down the half mile at the end of the street, looking gorgeous. Gorgeous enough to spend the night or two with, but nowhere near long-term-relationship worthy. Her money-sniffing abilities were finely honed and Mr Wad was top of her list of priorities in a partner. Her heart-breaking relationship with Daragh had put paid to any romance in her mind when it came to men without money. Greeting her with a promising hug, purposely grinding his crotch into hers as he did so, he took her hand gently and they began to walk. Watching a heavily pregnant woman in front of them with her partner's arm protectively around her back as they sauntered through the late-night crowds bought it all back to her, horrifically as painful as the very day it happened. She ached as she remembered falling into Daragh's arms, as he'd walked through the door at the end of a long day, and nearly passing out as white images flashed before her eyes. She felt the weakness in her legs and how she was barely able to stand. Her eyes filled with tears at the thoughts of her miscarriage . . . and then the blank gaps that followed for months after, when they went for weeks in silence, unable to communicate with each other. How it carved a ravine in the relationship – "No," she said to herself aloud amid the jovial throng, "tragedies *don't* bring you closer together."

"What's that?"

"Huh," Niamh was momentarily disorientated. Adam's handsome smile was beaming down at her, highlighted with a pink and blue glow from the neon lights. "Oh, nothing." She stopped and kissed him firmly on his soft full lips.

His face remained amused. "What was that about tragedies?"

"Oh, that – oh nothing. Just something I heard someone say earlier."

"So," he pulled her closer to him by tugging at her shaggy coat, "what's on the menu for tonight then, gorgeous?"

"Well," she toyed with the Velcro holding the waist of his combats, "I thought you might have a few ideas."

"Well," his voice turned amazingly husky as he pulled her even closer to him, whispering hotly into her ear, "I have this one idea. It involves you. And me."

Niamh laughed out loud at him, "Really. And you've got a good imagination, have you?"

"Absolutely fantastic."

"Well, you'd better enlighten me then."

"OK," he smiled, "but I'll have to drag you back to my place to do so." And he slid one hand around her shoulder and kissed her tanned neck softly.

She virtually melted on the spot.

The shards of traditional, early summer rain rattled

loudly on the floor-to-ceiling window in Declan's office. He was mature enough to realise that the concept of seasons was beyond the Irish meteorological office. On the basis that there was nothing logical to it. Summer, winter, spring – made little difference. The Irish weather was as rebellious as a teenage student and held scant regard for the time of year. As he watched his staff arrive, with no surprises as to the usual latecomers, Declan O'Mahoney felt his stomach surge with nausea at the sight of the Alka Seltzer fizzing in the glass. He'd overdone it at Byrne's once again and it seemed life was crumbling around him. Declan's hangover always bought with it thoughts of Paula, and now here she was smiling up at him from the silver-edged photoframe that remained on his desk. The sickness churned within him, a disturbing combination of over-tiredness coupled with eyes-bigger-than-your-belly syndrome in Byrne's last night.

His pain was interrupted by The Temp, entering once again without knocking, and dropping a heavy book down onto his desk.

"There's your final piece of the jigsaw."

Her features seemed almost gargoyle-like compared to the beautiful Paula as he tried to refocus onto her animated face.

Obviously perturbed at his lack of response she repeated, "Final piece of the jigsaw?"

"Go on," he encouraged, "explain. No, take a seat and explain." The contrast between the two didn't stop only at appearances. He now realised that, bitter and nasty, the beautiful Paula was streets behind the questionable-looking but kind-hearted friendly Temp in the personality stakes. He watched as the slight roll of fat bulged over the top of her straining trousers when she took a seat.

"Ciara O'Rourke."

"Go on."

"She's the last designer for your team."

"Too ostentatious!"

"Very flamboyant!"

"Too flashy."

"Very popular."

"A bitch."

"A *celebrity*."

"A fashion-victim."

"A trendsetter." The Temp remained unruffled by his weightless retorts and smiled as he went for one below the belt: "A stick-insect!"

"She could wear her buttocks as shoulder pads alright, *and* has shoulder blades you could slice butter with. Looks good in front of the camera though."

Defeated and still hung-over he conceded with a, "OK then, let's give her agent a call."

"I already have." The Temp grinned confidently, crossing her heavy legs.

"And?" Declan's patience was wearing thin as the liquid contents of his stomach began to churn.

"We're to call him back after lunch."

The mere mention of food was enough to send Declan rocketing from his plump leather chair, past The

Temp and into the toilets, all at approximately twelve miles an hour.

Stirring her Earl Grey with a slightly tarnished silver spoon, Ciara grimaced as she spat into the telephone resting between her shoulder and ear.

"Egh, what's to be ecstatic about anyway, making silk purses out of bloody flea-infested sow's ears. Three days a week stuck in a suburban shite-hole and then standing back proud while they cry their eyes out with delight!"

"Ciara, please," the insipid voice of her agent pleaded down the line, "just think of the publicity and at such an important time too, what with the book and everything. And they are desperate. Could mean serious negotiations regarding fees."

"You're on. Sort it quick and let me know."

Chapter 5

Tara had all the tell-tale signs of pre-menstruality – the black circles under her eyes, the not-the-run-of-the-mill-spot-but-mother-of-all-zits, and then there were the low aches and puffed up, swollen stomach – capped with an almost masochistically enjoyable irritability. As she lay exhausted on the settee, relieved that she'd finished reading the mountain of interiors magazines, she reflected on her conversation with Niamh. She watched the muted telly as *EastEnder's* Pauline's mouth moved faster than water disappearing down a plug-hole, her eyes gawking at Phil Mitchell accusingly. Her mind drifted back to the counsellor she'd heard on the radio that morning who had declared how a household is like a box of balloons with each member nudging for space.

I suppose that's what I was guilty of really, I thought, nudging for too much space, keen to accessorise my miserable life with a virile young lover. Dissatisfied with my marriage,

I merely nudged and had an affair, an affair with someone I thought had real feelings for me. OK – it was really just sex, but I'd thought that if I was in some kind of trouble he'd have been there for me. But no. Strange how I hadn't heard from Simon for ages either...

"Jaysus, Jimmy, pigs!"

The thud of boots as they ran caused Niamh to wake. She wasn't sure exactly whose bedroom she was in, but was used to that feeling. The watery sunlight danced on the orange and black-painted wall, a clear indication that she was *in casa* bachelor. She turned her head to the vacant space beside her, her tangled hair gathering by her mouth. She tugged it into a high knot, enjoying the cool feeling of the pillowcase on the back of her neck. In no hurry to move, she closed her eyes and stretched out in the empty rumpled bed listening to the unconducted orchestra of street traders below the barely open window. Her mind drifted comfortably as she realised she was in Adam's place – the only guy she knew who was up and dressed at the crack of dawn every day. Staying at his flat on Moore Street meant that she had to contend with the sounds of one of the most famous and oldest pedestrianised street markets in Dublin. As she allowed her thoughts to swoosh around in her mind she closed her eyes slowly until her peace was broken once again by,

"No, you're not having any feckin' strawb'rrys, they'll give you hoives!" followed by the sounds of a small child wailing and the rattling of buggy wheels over the wet path. Determined to stay put, she pulled the duvet over her head only to hear her mobile trilling. Irritated, she flung back the covers and grabbed at her bag, tugging her phone from among its catastrophic contents.

"Hello," she barked.

"Niamh Connolly?"

"Yeah."

"Declan O'Mahoney, RTÉ."

She immediately felt a lump in her throat which dissipated the confident tone she'd intended to use.

"Oh, right. Hello," she squeaked.

"Hello. Look Miss Connolly, we're producing a new interiors series, *Home Is Where The Art Is*. We'd like to commission you for the publicity photographs."

"Well, that'd be excellent, I'd be delighted."

"I'm still waiting to hear from a designer in Sandymount. We're an interior designer short, you see. Mind you, I can't see her tearing herself away from her projects for this new series."

Niamh paused to light a cigarette as she swung her legs from the side of the bed and sat up, inhaling, "Still, what do you want from the photos?"

"Group shots of the presenters wielding paintbrushes, screwdrivers, that kind of thing."

"Fine. When did you have in mind?"

"Could you do Friday? Morning preferably."

"Listen, Mr O'Mahoney, not being rude or anything, but I can't check my diary right now. Could I possibly call you back in a couple of hours?"

"Certainly, here's my direct line."

Scrawling his number onto the side of her Marlboro box and then sticking the biro in her topknot, she pressed the rubbery button on her phone to disconnect Mr O'Mahoney and flopped back down into Adam's bed, dragging in her nicotine fix. Before she had the chance to finish, she heard the click of the front door and the thudding of Adam's boots as he climbed the stairs. Throwing open the door of his studio flat he stood, dripping onto the oak floor.

"Raining, is it?" Niamh teased. He looked sexy, standing there clutching two white, wet plastic bags, the remains of the shower still dripping from the end of his nose.

"Got us some fruit."

"Forget the fruit, get over here and let me get you outta those wet clothes."

"But I've got bananas."

"Yeah, and I've got melons . . ."

She got up out of bed, naked except for the biro in her hair, and walked over to him. Morning sex always appealed to Niamh more – it had that slow, relaxing air to it, nothing like the heady, rip-your-clothes-off aura of the night. Tracing her finger over his chest she kissed his nipple, "You know, I think I'm a fan of the Calmer Sutra."

"The Karma Sutra? What d'you know about the technique there then?"

She giggled, "I said the *Calmer* Sutra. C-A-L-M-E-R."

He looked slightly worried, wondering what she was angling at this time,

"I'm not with you."

"Slow, relaxing sex. Calm sex. You just can't beat starting the day that way."

Adam dropped the bags to the floor and succumbed to Niamh's suggestion.

The lunch-time sounds of the market below woke her once again, along with the smell of cooking. She slipped from the bed and made her way to the shower, leaving Adam to enjoy his contented post-coital snooze. It was always good with Adam, her orgasms like a hurricane of butterflies, the kind of lusty sexual encounter that, even days after, makes you aware of every goose-pimple on your body, aware of your whole being. She felt that every single pore was engorged with blood, with sensitivity – with life. Massaging the shampoo into her raven hair she reflected on their night out. They'd got a taxi across the city to a late-night club where they laughed, danced and drank along with the best of them. Their last stop was a taxi base, where they'd taken a quiet corner in the lobby amidst the formica'd tables and ashtrays out of the seventies and listened to a raving late-night phone-in show emanating from a small radio on a ten-foot-high shelf in the corner. As they'd snuggled up on the ripped black PVC chairs, she'd watched the sideline entertainment as a posse of hen-night revellers squawked and giggled while they explained how they'd lost their party and couldn't remember the name of their hotel. And so they'd arrived back at Adam's Moore Street flat as dawn began to rise.

With her hair still damp, Niamh cursed the fact that men never own hairdryers and stepped out onto Moore Street market, her small bag slung casually over her shoulder. The rain had stopped and the canopies bowed weightily over the market stalls prompting the workers to push at them with brooms, causing a percussion of splattering sounds as water hit the pavement. Turning into Henry Street and the heaving O'Connell Street, Niamh dodged the masses and the street-traders as they sold copious amounts of illegal smokes. As she past the Anna Livia fountain, intended as a shrine to the goddess of the Liffey, she noted its now unofficial landing site for used burger boxes. In typical Dublin style, the statue had been monikered with a rhyming nickname, like most of Dublin's memorial statues. Anna Livia was landed with "The Floozie in the Jacuzzi" and even "The Whoo-er in the Sewer". Niamh strode confidently along the quays, watching two gardai who leant on the barrier by the side of the road, wondering if they noticed the three schoolboys who were filling their pockets with sweets in the corner shop. Crossing the Ha'penny Bridge she saw the statue of the two shoppers pausing for breath, "The Hags with the Bags". Niamh had enjoyed the monumental rhyming fever that had hit Dublin, and remembered the nicknames without even trying to. Molly Malone on Grafton Street had become "The Tart with the Cart" and the Millennium clock that had stood temporarily in the Liffey "The Time in the Slime". Niamh passed a multitude of galleries, markets and entertainers on her way to Temple Bar, finally reaching East Essex

Street where she decided to stop for a well-earned coffee. Slumping down into the vacant chair she ordered a cappuccino and sat down to watch the buskers out on the wet cobbles. The shower had brought out a multitude of colours in the ordinarily grey cobblestones. Traces of yellow, red, green and many shades of blue danced on the stones as the white clouds began to break up and a hint of blue sky reflected down onto the pavements. She felt, this morning, that every inch of her body was alive. Adam always made her feel that way; it seemed such a shame that he wasn't loaded. She'd travelled from Dundalk to New York looking for Mr Wad and still hadn't found the man of her dreams with money. She finished her coffee, grabbed her bag and made for Meeting House Square, a large public space used for screening free films on summer evenings and the site of an upmarket food fair on Saturday mornings. She made straight for the oyster stall, paying her €6.50 to be seated and served a platter of five oysters, some fresh brown bread and a half bottle of white wine to wash it down with. As she tipped the knurled shell to her lips, letting the slimy mass of salty oyster slide down her throat, she toyed with the prospect of the *Home Is Where The Art Is* commission. Yeah, she had to ring Declan O'Mahoney when she got in: RTÉ publicity could be just what her thriving career needed.

Tara had woken at ten after only four hours' sleep. Her mind had continued to spin as she got up and began to think about at her promise to Niamh.

Eventually, she threw down the colour chart and dragged her hair from her face.

"Seven hundred euro? Virtually impossible. Why did I have to say the lounge-diner *and* kitchen? I must be unhinged. I'll have to ask her for more. Maybe I can get a little extra out of her too – it'd pay for my new shed." The tinkling of her doorbell broke into her dilemma. Striding to the door she was surprised to see Niamh standing there, laden with plastic carrier bags.

"Hey, what you at?"

"Been to Meeting House Square."

"Market?"

"Yep. Fancy some olives?" She was always a sucker for the Olive Emporium.

"Niamh, just one look at the wooden vats stuffed with the reds and greens and you're sold. You're the same every time you go there."

"I can't help it," she laughed, stepping into the hallway and kicking off her ridiculously high boots. "One sight of the olives being scooped up into the plastic bags and weighed and I just have to join in."

Tara took the bags from her as she took off her Afghan coat, hanging it on the hook in the hallway.

"Come on, I'll put the kettle on."

"Get that cheese out too – we'll make a start on some of these green critters. *And* I got sun-dried tomatoes and feta cheese."

As they chatted and laughed in Tara's kitchen, Niamh realised that she hadn't seen Tara so animated for months. As she waffled on about ice-cream shades, calm and sophisticated blends and Mediterranean trends, Niamh knew she'd done the right thing in asking her to redecorate her flat. Now the only thing bugging her was the pile of VISA receipts that she and Anna had found only days before. Something just wasn't right about Simon and she was determined to find out what it was . . .

Declan had expected Niamh Connolly to call him back sooner than she had done. After all, her claim to a "couple of hours" had been stretched ridiculously once six hours had gone by. He decided to ask Miss Day to check who her agent was. He assumed by her lack of response that she wasn't interested in something as paltry as publicity shots and his delight was difficult to contain when she called back early in the evening on his mobile. Another busy day had only depressed him more. It was the kind of day where himself and Paula would have stayed in bed most of the day, making love, reading, watching a bit of telly, bringing up snacks on a tray from the kitchen and making love again. And probably yet again.

In the dream of their lives they'd never really strayed from the mutual infatuation they'd shared as teenagers.

In reality, she'd met someone else.

And Declan O'Mahoney had forgotten how to spend weekends alone.

Niamh Connolly had sounded full of energy when they'd spoken on the phone, both times. Even her request to bring her friend along to the photo shoot he found slightly unprofessional, almost childlike, but spontaneous. He pulled his sleek phone from his jacket pocket and punched in the speed dial for Anto. Anto Mullins was always out. Anto Mullins knew the Dublin scene better than Declan ever could have. Having worked for a recording company since leaving UCD, Anto knew which bands were where and when and who was worth seeing. He was also an avid jazz fan – one of the few things that gregarious Anto and depressed Declan had in common. The telephone conversation lasted mere seconds, in the way that only phone-exchanges between males can do. Despite not seeing each other for the best part of a year, Anto was pleased to hear from his old UCD pal and had no problems with Declan joining him at the Wexford Inn. Feeling slightly more confident, Declan pulled on his black Ted Baker polo-shirt and slid his long hairy legs into stone-coloured jeans, slipping a leather belt through the loops. Feeling the stirrings of excitement at the blank canvas of the night ahead, he was surprised at a sudden surge of confidence. Maybe he'd begun to feel more of the thirty-something he should be than the fifty-something he'd felt for the last few weeks. He tugged at the light-cord in the bathroom, illuminating his face with an orangey tinge as he looked at his reflection in the mirror. He hadn't shaved for three days but, despite it, looked good. Filling the bowl with warm water he reached for his razor and shaving gel, the steam buffeting up under his chin and around his ears as he began to hum while he waited. Massaging the foamy gel onto his cheeks and chin he reassured himself that the blues session in the Wexford Inn was a night not to be missed and congratulated himself on taking the plunge and calling Anto. Since the departure of Paula he'd rediscovered an early love of jazz and found himself playing the CD's in the car, the office and at home. He stretched his face into an "oh" and slid the razor down over one cheek and then the other. Then he paused and looked at his reflection before splashing the sudsy water onto the remains of the foam and re-emerging with a new look. Wiping his face dry he broke into a wide smile, his handsome face suiting the new image.

"Declan boy, you're looking good," he said, suddenly feeling great about himself. And winking at his new, unplanned goatee'd reflection he turned off the light and, picking up his car keys, checked his watch as he headed for a hard-earned night out.

"Come on, Tar, you've always loved a good night out!" Anna's pleading Scottish accent always won Tara round, however much she dug her heels in. She leaned on Tara's kitchen worktop watching her mush the jelly into the foul-smelling dog-food.

"Anna, I'm really not ready to face the world socially. And I've got to organise Niamh's flat makeover." Tara busied herself with Ruben's ceramic bowl and dog biscuits. The golden cocker spaniel skittered excitedly at her knees.

"Bugger that – you've plenty of time. Come, please! Louis Stewart's playing at Renard's. Please?"

"Who the hell's Louis Stewart?" She bent down to place Ruben's water bowl and food in the corner of the kitchen.

"Tara! How could you not know? A jazz guitarist."

"Oh Anna, but Renard's is so expensive! You're forgetting I don't have an income any more. I'm on borrowed time here, you know."

"But it's free to get in."

"Yeah, but drinks are expensive."

"So we'll go early for happy hour."

"Anna, you know that's only Monday to Thursday."

"And Sunday."

"Anna, today is Saturday!"

"Come on, please! It'll do you good."

"I've got nothing to wear."

"Bullshit. You've always got loads of lovely clothes – you just haven't worn them since, since . . . since . . ."

"Since I went out with Graham last. Since my last adulterous date."

"Look, try and put it out of your mind. Tara, I'm picking you up at nine. Be ready or I'll force you into something and drag you out."

"But Anna, I'm so fat. I've got more spare tyres than an artic."

"Yeah, and I suppose the complimentary Simon told you that?"

"It takes a while to get your confidence back. And . . ."

"And what?"

Tara's voice dropped an octave, "And Renard's is where I proposed to Simon."

"Oh, I forgot."

"Oh, I didn't."

In an attempt to rejuvenate her Anna burst out, "Well, what better reason to go there? Lay the ghost to rest."

"You say it as if *he* was the one in the wrong."

"Oh, I dunno," Anna ad-libbed, her mind racing for an idea to get her off the hook, "I'm not feeling too good about myself either. I could have done with a night out too."

Tara noticed the shadow pass fleetingly over Anna's usually sparkling eyes. "Yeah," Tara conceded, "you're right. It's not all about me, is it? Look, pick me up at nine, OK? But how about we go to the Wexford Inn or somewhere else instead?"

Relieved at being so easily let off, Anna agreed and went to find some chocolate to eat to calm her nerves. It wasn't every day that you got the sack. And the humiliation!

The Wexford Inn was packed. Declan made his way around only to find that Anto hadn't yet arrived and so found himself a seat at the bar, trying to remember a time when he'd felt so good. So independent. The jazz was fantastic and he found himself making promises in his head to come here regularly.

"Haven't I seen you here before?" The voice sounded husky yet feminine and his stomach flipped with excitement. Until he turned to face her. Her lipstick-coated teeth caused his drink to catch in his throat. She continued, oblivious, "I'm heading for Renard's later. Fancy it? You *do* know Louis Stewart's there tonight? I love it there and venues like it often suffer from the big-club syndrome."

He did his utmost to remain polite, deciding that a little practice on the flirtation front wouldn't go amiss, "And what's that then?" he smiled.

"All presentation and no soul. A bit like my ex."

"Come here often then, do you?" He could have kicked himself for the cliché, but it seemed lost on her.

"Of course! My counsellor says it's better than therapy, a little bit of jazz. I mean, why talk childhood when you can listen to the likes of Louis Stewart?" As he glanced down to pick up his drink he couldn't help but notice the wrinkled plaster that hung from the edge of her string-tight sandals. He just had to get away from her, but how. The quandary was solved for him when she stood closer to him, pushing her large thighs toward his knee as he sat on the bar stool. The fleshy feel of her legs through both her hideous black dress and his jeans caused him to feel immediately uncomfortable.

"Excuse me," he managed to say, "must go to the loo."

"Righto," she grinned, oblivious, "I'll mind your drink for you."

As he moved towards the bar his interest genuinely went up a notch or two at the sight of two women tentatively ushering each other through the doorway.

One of them in particular caught his eye. Her cropped hair was plastered down smoothly across her fringe, whilst the back sat jagged and spiky. He felt an urge to run his fingers through it. Hearing a loud Dub accent approaching from the left he turned to see Lipsticked Teeth heading in his direction with his drink. He made for the doorway, embracing Anna and Tara, to their surprise.

"You made it!" he shouted, and as he hugged Tara toward him whispered in her ear, "Please! I've got Godzilla after me!"

Tara giggled at such an entrance and the three of them made for the bar together, watching as Godzilla stopped in her tracks, downed the remains of Declan's pint and left swiftly.

"Thanks, ladies, now what're you having?"

Tara was intrigued by the handsome, friendly man, only disappointed at his hideous facial hair.

Still, I thought, I'm in no position to have opinions about any man, after what I've done with Simon and Graham. I'm not entitled to opinions anymore.

"No, you're all right. Thanks, anyway."

"I insist. There's nothing worse than being eaten alive before your mates have even arrived."

"Well, I'll have a Cranberry Breezer then, please."

Declan turned to Anna who was craning her neck around to check out the scene. Tara nudged her.

"What'll I get you?" he grinned at her.

"Oh, gin and tonic, please."

He returned with the drinks in no time, finding

himself rather captivated by Tara's open friendly face, her slightly hooded blue eyes and quirky dress sense. She seemed to be one of those women who could just throw together whatever sat on their bedroom floor and make it look good. Her pale blue slogan t-shirt and jeans were a refreshing mixture amongst some of the more conservative outfits. And he was sure he caught the glint of a tongue piercing there as she'd spoken to him. Wanting to stay but feeling awkward, Declan coughed to clear his throat. "Well, thanks for that. You know, I'm renowned for biting off more than I can chew."

"Hey, join the club." Tara smiled and couldn't help wondering what he'd be like *without* the goatee. Before she could conjure up the image a loud male voice cut across.

"Hey, Deco, man!"

Anto had the typical Dublin urge to abbreviate every name to something ending in "o", hence his own tag. Tara looked with interest at the scruffy guy and then questioningly at the two beauties that followed him. By the way Anto grabbed one of them around the waist it was obvious they were all together. In an absurd way she enjoyed 'Deco's' slight embarrassment as he thanked them once again, and made his way across to his, she imagined, girlfriend.

Shame really, I thought. He'd probably look great without that stupid beard thing. Still, his girlfriend's style left a lot to be desired. The comfortable confines of a little black dress are hardly the fodder of style icons now, are they? Although she had a figure that made you wonder whether she'd spent the winter striking pilates poses.

"Tara!" Anna's voice stacattoed through the heady jazz music that filled the air.

"Sorry. What's wrong with ya?"

"Will we sit down or what?"

"Yeah, go on. I'll follow you."

They sat at a small table, sticking their bags underneath and leaving mobile phones and cigarettes on the top.

"You liked him, didn't you?" Anna grinned mischievously at Tara.

"Who?"

I know I'm blushing. I just know it!

"That guy. The one who just bought the drinks for us."

"Oh, him." She looked over her shoulder nonchalantly. "Yeah, he was all right. Stupid goatee though."

"Don't you know though, Tar, men have to dedicate so much more time to maintain a goatee."

Tara smirked, just in anticipation of the bullshit that was to follow.

"Yeah," Anna continued, "you need a real steady hand to detail the lines. It has to be even and straight or it makes their face look wonky."

"Anna," Tara declared, lifting the remains of her Cranberry Breezer to her lips, "in my opinion goatees are a bit like Tom Jones – always making a comeback."

"But you still like him though, dontya?"

"Who," she slurped the last of the sickly sweet drink "Tom Jones or *Deco*?"

"Deco, you fool!"

"Forget him. I've learnt now, Anna, that I have what is known as Mr Wrong Syndrome. Whatya having?" She held her empty bottle aloft indicating that she was heading for the bar.

"Whatever you're getting."

"Rightso. Leave it to me."

Tara reached the bar pleading with her body to give off the confident signals that her mind wasn't feeling. Catching her reflection in a mirror behind the bar, she smoothed down her fringe and casually looked toward Deco. It was scant surprise to see the little black dress had draped herself over his shoulder and was making ridiculous amounts of eye-contact. Deco didn't look as if he minded. She watched as a crowd of trendy young girls bustled at the bar and paid for their small bottles of Moët which they began to suck down through straws. She found herself ordering the same when the barman nodded toward her.

Her mind working overtime, she put the bottle down in front of Anna and threw in the statement, "You know, I think we should put an ad in the Lonely Hearts section. You know, see who responds?"

"Oh yeah – what, like: *Wanted – Romantic cardiologist who gets to the heart of the matter*!"

They laughed as they drank down their champagne, enjoying every minute of it.

"Look, Tar, if you're keen on Deco don't let your inhibitions stand between you and his Calvin Kleins."

"Stop going on about him, for chrissakes. He only used us as a decoy. Ha, how about that – Deco's Decoy?"

Six small bottles of Moët later and Anna was regaling Tara with the humiliating tale of her sacking.

"Christ, Tar, it was just sooo embarrassing. You see, I was at the water-cooler this morning. I was parched, especially after the wine last night and then he – the MD – came out of his office and over to me. I feel so stupid now for not noticing how he nodded his head toward Jack Reilly as he spoke. I could feckin well kick meself now, really."

"So what *did* he say?"

"He said, 'I'm really sorry Anna, but I've been told to let someone go, and to make it fair I've decided that it has to be the last person in, first person out, you know?' Well, I just smiled vaguely – my brain was still buzzing from last night! So it was then he said it. And, like I say, I could shoot meself for not noticing the head-jerk toward Jack Reilly."

"Jesus, Anna, what did he say?"

"He said, 'Well, Anna, I'm gonna have to either lay you or Jack off.'"

Tara willed her twitching mouth to remain still, fighting the urge to laugh.

"Go, on," was all she could muster.

Anna continued plaintively, "Well, I couldn't believe my ears, but I thought it was all some kind of a joke – I just wasn't with it after last night – so I only went and said, 'Well, I'm sorry, Mr Gahan, but you'll have to jack off today. I've an outrageous headache!'"

Tara, still trying to look sympathetic, thought her insides were going to burst. And the expression on

Anna's face did little to calm her. They eventually laughed together, especially in the light that Mr Gahan had taken pity on her gross misconstruing and had granted her the next week with pay to find another job.

Nearly an hour later Anna was over the worst and, fuelled by the alcohol, was completing her story – how she had eventually ended up in bed with her direct line manager.

"And you should have seen him running around the bedroom naked, his tackle flinging around like an executive desk-toy. And it wasn't even his wife at the door. It was the Avon lady. I nearly pissed meself laughing."

When Tara finally found her voice through the squealing she said, with an air of seriousness about her, "Yeah, but he's a good-looking guy though. We saw him at your Christmas do, all done up in his designer suit and slick hairstyle."

"Don't be too impressed, Tar, he's a bit like a donkey's willie really."

"A wha'? Howdya mean?"

"He's big when he's out!"

Once again they fell about laughing, oblivious to the uncomfortable and bored Declan who was wishing with every centimetre of his body that he could join them and be relaxing with a drink and a laugh rather than standing here with Anto and his two pre-arranged sidekicks. As temptation finally won out he decided to make his way back over to Tara and Anna and join them. He paused, placing his pint on the bar, then turned to find that one of them was gone.

"Shit," he cursed under his breath, "now there's my chance gone."

And then he saw her along the bar.

It was the first time Tara had really been out for an evening since the departure of Simon.

And I was enjoying myself.

Really, I was. I'd almost put Simon out of my mind, and as for Graham . . . Graham who?

I hadn't had such a scream with Anna for ages and it was all going swimmingly.

Grateful for the few minutes away from the "joviality" of our table, I had taken a stool at the bar and settled myself. I was starting to wish that I'd agreed to go and see Louis Stewart. The saxophone thing catches my interest. You see, I've always loved sex. I mean sax.

Feeling more than slightly woozy I turned to check out "Deco" only to feel slightly embarrassed when I saw him equally checking out me. The neck of him! And with his girlfriend around his neck too! Still, wasn't that what I had done? Shat on my own doorstep, I think is the usual terminology for what I'd been up to.

As Tara pondered over the resurrecting guilt feelings she rested her gaze on a couple, quite clearly in love as they held hands across their table, lustily entranced with each other. Her thoughts swiftly rewound to the day she'd proposed to Simon. In the dreaded Renard's.

How my stomach was in knots that evening, my stupid head full of the romantics of a wedding. How I yearned for the choosing of the dress, booking the venue, drawing up the guest list and the other hundreds of details to make it my special day. I repeat, "my". That was all I'd ever thought about. My day, my wedding. I'd have been better to have found a partner whom I loved first. Still, wasn't I always approaching things arseways?

Tara and Simon's wedding had been a relatively low-key do. Well, low-key compared to what Tara had *really* wanted, although in anyone's book a marquee in the garden and dinner by candlelight wasn't bad going. Tara had wanted the works – the castle venue, the brocade dress, the bevy of chiffon-clad bridesmaids. She'd even planned the "something old, something new" part, right down to the blue sugared almonds on the guests' tables. Instead she'd got a shell-shocked and slightly hesitant family-support network, a matter of weeks in which to organise the event, a limited budget and a groom to lead-by-the-nose.

Little wonder it all went downhill after that. Like Simon's technique.

Less than two miles away in one of Dublin's nightclubs Ciara O'Rourke was sitting on a toilet seat, snorting a line of cocaine and popping a couple of pills. Highly strung and immensely paranoid, she was looking for a "man" for the night, surreptitiously stalking the oblivious revellers as they danced, flirted and generally enjoyed themselves. The place was an eclectic mix of European tourists and Ciara comforted herself with the reassurance that she'd go unrecognised. Her fetish for the recent trend of drug-cocktailing, or "recreational poly-drug use", was starting to cause her more problems than she was aware of and, as she pushed the door to the toilets open, her head spun with a false confidence. She made eye contact with a middle-aged Spanish guy at the bottom of the stairs and pushed herself up against him suggestively, "You know," she drawled into his face, "as Warren Beatty once said to Madonna, 'Get your knickers off, I'm half a mile from your house!' I'm yours tonight, Señor. Come, take me!"

Despite his keenness for *coito* with an Irishwoman whilst on his holidays, the traces of white powder around her nostrils repulsed him and he slid away from her swiftly.

"Ahh," she sneered, "you look like something let out of a hospital anyway!"

As she staggered around the club, ignorant of the stares she was commanding, she failed to notice the two tabloid journalists watching her, soberly, from the bar. Being presumptuous enough to order a bottle of champagne, one paid – with every intention of adding it to his expenses – whilst the other strode easily across to Ciara, armed with a charming smile, a handsome face, a taut body and the gift of the gab.

Oh – and a palmcorder tucked neatly into his bomber jacket . . .

Chapter 6

Thursday morning of the next week Tara was up early for the first time in weeks.

It took me days, but I finally persuaded Niamh to let me go to RTÉ with her for the new interiors programme photo-shoot. I'd pretended that I was on the scout for interiors ideas, but hey – it's not every day you get the chance to go into a TV studio. Call me shallow, but I was really looking forward to it. So much so that I changed my clothes five times in three minutes! You see, Niamh always looked so cool and professional. She managed to carry off those huge silver rings that only the arty types can get away with. I tried one on once and it looked like a knuckleduster on me. And her clothes! She seems to just throw together jeans and t-shirts and they look fantastic on her. I suppose the boobs help. Niamh is blessed with long slim legs, a washboard tum and a big chest. I remember trying the pencil test – you know – the one where you put a pencil under your boob and how quickly it falls determines your pertness? Well, Niamh could put a whole

*pencil case under hers and no-one would even know it was
there. She'd be a fantastic smuggler!*

"OK, ready so?"

Tara pulled on her denim jacket, scruffed her hair a
little and applied a swift coat of lipbalm.

"Yep, think so."

"Got everything?" Niamh knew how excited Tara
was and how much store she'd put into this photo-shoot.

"Yeah, notebook, pen, camera."

"Camera? That's my department, isn't it?"

Tara looked over sheepishly, "Yeah, but still, you
never know – I might get some snapshots of celebrities.
I've never been into the RTÉ building before."

Niamh laughed at her naiveté. Sure, it was nice to
see her smiling after the last few weeks.

"And here was me thinking you wanted to pick up
some interiors and decorating contacts when all the
time you're stalking the celebs. Oh, you've not gone all
dotty over Marty Whelan, please!"

"Feck off, Niamh!"

"Only messing. Come on, the infamous Ciara
O'Rourke will be waiting for us."

"Right. Let's go then."

Niamh and Tara's entrance into the disappointingly
unformidable studios was greeted by a foul-mouthed
screeching woman causing a stir amongst a small
crowd. Feeling suddenly nervous, rather like a fish out
of water, Tara dropped her bag in the corner alongside
Niamh's and offered to wait with the equipment whilst

Niamh found out where Declan O'Mahoney was. Disappointed at not be able to recognise anyone from the telly, she looked at the polished studio floor and the backdrop set for *Home Is Where The Art Is*.

The woman's voice rose an octave, "Look, my name's Ciara, not Clara! I'm not an Austrian hausfrau!"

Tara watched as the overly made-up Ciara O'Rourke stormed through the hubbub, her face ferociously set in a scowl. She watched as a young woman in a lavender dress, with matching designer shoes, held her hands to her face and broke down in quiet tears. Two trendily dressed guys shook their heads in disbelief and began talking softly to a cockney cheeky-chappy clad in hideous purple dungarees with the words *Home Is Where The Art Is* emblazoned across the bib. Niamh, ever confident, stood amongst them and Tara could hear her asking for Declan O'Mahoney. Hearing a sniffing sound as Ciara O'Rourke re-emerged and stood beside her lighting up a cigarette Tara watched her from the corner of her eye. Ciara inhaled deeply, blew out a snake of smoke, and then sniffed and rubbed at her open-pored nose. Tara was just about to make a friendly remark – something like, "You'd always feel better after a fag", when a male voice boomed into the studio.

"Right, what's happening? Not more problems, Ciara plea –" he stopped in his tracks as he caught sight of Tara standing next to the problematic Ciara O'Rourke. Niamh, the dungaree'd handyman John and the other two male designers turned to see what had made him stop so abruptly. Even the red-eyed female designer stopped sniffling and crying to see what had caused the silence. Tara felt herself redden like never before.

"You two know each other?" he questioned, raising an amused eyebrow at Tara.

Before she could reply Ciara stubbed out her cigarette and, blowing out the smoke, intoned, "Of course we don't know each other. I've never even *seen* her before. Now, what *are* you going to do about these godforsaken photos?" She strode across to Declan and Tara felt a wave of relief wash over her as things snapped back to normal. All except the incredulous smirk on Niamh's face. Tara tried desperately to ignore her, as she gawked across at Tara quizzically, but seconds later Niamh was at her side.

"So?" she teased.

"So what?"

I tried to be cool with her, really I did. I didn't even look at her, but Niamh's so persuasive. I just knew that she already knew.

"So *he's* the one with the goatee that Anna was telling me about!"

"Oh, was she? Yeah, we met him last week in the Wexford Inn. I didn't know he was *the* Declan O'Mahoney though. His mate called him Deco."

"Jesus," giggled Niamh, "that's some crack – Deco producing the 'deco'-rating programme."

"Don't like the goatee though."

Tara reddened and Niamh shuffled awkwardly as Declan leaned in over Niamh's shoulder and smiled at Tara.

"Hey, nice to meet you again. You're not with Ciara then?"

"No, no. I'm . . . em . . . well . . ."

Niamh rescued the situation, ever the professional. "Declan, let me introduce my good friend Tara. Tara, Declan, although I suspect you've already met."

"We have had the pleasure." Declan took Tara by the hand and shook it firmly but gently. Mini electrical impulses shot up her arm, exploding in her head. "But I didn't know your name was Tara."

"Well, I didn't really get the chance to talk to you properly."

Niamh steered him by the elbow around to the task in hand and Tara listened as she relaxed the photo-subjects, joking, "So, are youse photogenic or phototragic?"

I watched with pride as she put into practice all the things that she'd tried to teach me in the past. Like never face the camera head on, and how she encouraged them to turn one third of their body towards camera to elongate the figure and give a more flattering impression. I couldn't help but notice the scruffy but cute set designer who had his eye on Niamh as she co-ordinated the pose. Even when shackled with oul' purple dungarees and a hotchpotch of paintbrushes and tape measures, Niamh managed to arrange the "design team" in an array of flattering and eyecatching poses – none of this "Charlie's Angels", pretend-your-fingers-are-your-pistol lark.

The recurring problem was in the form of Ciara O'Rourke. She was doggedly pushing herself to the forefront of the shots, insisting that she was more well known than the other two male and the one female designer and therefore should have maximum exposure. Tara watched as Declan continually pacified Ciara whilst refusing to suck up to her ego, assuring her that the publicity shots were looking just great and she'd get *her* chance at publicity at a more convenient juncture. It was at these stops that Niamh began to make her flirty eye contact with the set designer whose eyes twinkled attractively. It wasn't until the handsome Declan asked the bullied female designer to stand in front of Ciara for a tape-measure shot that the paint-scrapers hit the fan.

"That's it!" Ciara screeched. "Declan, either she feckin' goes or I do!"

"Don't worry, you old has-been!" the young female designer blazed. "If you think I can work with you for the next six months, honey, you're very badly mistaken. Jesus, with the size of your ego coupled with the size of your mouth it's amazing there's room for anyone else in here." She turned to Declan with an apologetic expression on her face. "I'm sorry to do this to you, Declan, but I quit – I'm outta here. There's no way I could bear to be in the same room as that wagon. Sorry, pal – I'm gone."

And with that she grabbed her coat and bag and breezed out of the studio, leaving a smirking Ciara and an amazed Declan.

And a totally exasperated Niamh.

And, as Declan O'Mahoney winked at Tara across the room, a surprisingly blushing Tara.

"Miss Day!" Declan's intended boom came out rather

squeaky. He cleared his throat and gave it his best shot, "Miss Day?"

She appeared, efficient as ever, within micro-seconds. "You look tired, Declan. What can I get you?" She held her notepad and pen aloft, rather in the way a waitress would.

"You can get me a new designer," he said softly, resting his head in his hands, looking down at his new shoes beneath his desk.

"For what? Hadn't you contracted Ciara O'Rourke as the final designer?"

"I have – for my sins. She's so bloody obnoxious that Jessica has quit!"

"Jessica Fallon? The other designer! Oh . . ." She took the liberty of sitting in the spare seat and rested her notepad and pen on his desk. "So is that the only problem?"

"The problem is," he raised his head to look at her, his expression open as he looked her squarely in the eye, "that, not alone do I *still* need another designer, but I have sixteen episodes' worth of broadcasting time and only fourteen volunteer homes. I just cannot believe that I still need another two houses *and* still need a new designer."

"All in a week."

"All in a feckin' week . . ."

With the convenience of a Hollywood movie, much in the same vein as the cop always finding a parking space right outside the "joint" he's about to "bust",

Declan's phone rang. Miss Day took her cue and, not forgetting the pad and pen, made her way quickly from his office.

The male voice crackled slightly down the line. Declan was instantly aware that the caller was using a mobile.

The crackling call proved lucrative – slot fifteen was immediately filled with Sorcha's Waterford townhouse courtesy of some extra persuasion from Stephanie the flirtatious researcher.

With renewed enthusiasm Declan immediately picked up the phone and rang Niamh Connolly's mobile number. He was surprised when he was instantly connected to her answerphone, which tormented his anxious brain with a full rendition of 'Greensleeves'. When the *beep* finally sounded he was temporarily lost for words.

"Christ. Niamh. You . . . have to . . . listen to . . . the *whole* . . . of 'Greensleeves' . . . God, well. Em, right, Niamh, could you please call me? I'd like to discuss a commission with you. We'd like you to accompany us on the production of *Home Is Where The Art Is*. We'd like you to photograph each makeover as they're completed. We're hoping to publish a book on the series, penned jointly by our design team. Anyway, if you're interested please contact me."

Feeling rather like an adolescent boy, he desperately wanted to ask after her friend Tara, but couldn't see how he could slot it into his messsage without being painfully obvious. Anyway, given his track record with women, it was probably best if he didn't go sticking his head in the lion's mouth so soon.

"How come we always say we're coming for coffee and end up stuffing our faces?" Tara questioned, failing to make eye contact with Niamh across the table in the mock-American Café.

Niamh replied, equally distracted by her massive bowl of chilli, "Because the food here is simply adorable. I've even switched off my mobile so we can enjoy it."

"God, you must be hungry!" teased Tara.

"So," Niamh steered the conversation back around to its origins, "what am I gonna get for my seven hundred euro?"

Tara sucked in an extraordinarily long strand of spaghetti; it thrashed against her left cheek as it sped into her mouth.

"I've got some samples and colours here for you to check."

"Oh, really tackling the task like a pro, huh?"

"Sure – I *am* a pro."

"'Course. Come on," she managed to tear the fork from Tara's hand and rest it on the table, "show me what you've got."

Niamh found it hard to contain her praise for Tara as she revealed her plans regarding colours, textures, lighting and furniture arrangement.

"Well, girl, I've gotta give it to you, you've certainly thought it through. At this rate I'll be calling for you next week when we're on location in Wexford. Some of these ideas are simply brilliant."

"Well, I'm relying on you to pick up all the tips for me. I'm expecting daily progress reports on the series."

"Leave it to me."

"I will miss you though. It'll be months!"

"I know, but we're coming back to Dublin every few weeks. I'll still be in touch. And we've got our texting and our e-mails."

"Yeah, and I suppose I've got plenty to keep me busy what with smarting up your place for you."

"Hey," Niamh slapped her on the arm, "it's not that bloody bad!"

Niamh had left for the first assignment in Wexford, her absence bringing with it a period of reflection for Tara. She was proud that she didn't think of Simon as much as she used to do. She was even beginning to realise what a bore he really was. The solitude of decorating brought with it many reflections on her feelings for Graham and Simon. The stretching and stapling of fabric as she re-upholstered allowed her mind to wander in a way that instigated a strange positivity, unlike the feelings she had experienced in her bedridden week. Still, an overwhelming feeling of guilt refused to pass. Guilt enjoyed being acknowledged and once exposed didn't take kindly to being tucked back into his box. Who knows when he'd get the chance to reappear – rather like the genie in the lamp? Guilt, with his smiling, smug face stood between Tara and true happiness. As long as Guilt held centre stage, Tara McKenna felt unworthy of happiness.

I was just sooo in love with the idea of matrimony I failed to concentrate on the most important factor.

The husband.

I had instructed Simon how I'd wanted the guests to affix their photo to the RSVP's so that we could compile them into an album and circulate it on the day. In my mind I'd plans to give each guest a hangover kit post-party containing orange, alka seltzer, ginseng and water. I'd virtually insisted on a meal of Connemara salmon with cream cheese and dill, Kinnity lamb with roasted vegetables and a trio of desserts. And how many times had I driven my parents insane with the talk of the honeymoon dream cruise on the Mexican Riviera?

The fact remained still painfully in Tara's mind that she'd had to make do with three days in Paris. Simon couldn't get time off work. At that stage she'd yet to learn how pedantic he really was.

Organised.

Scheduled.

Anal.

Very.

I suppose it was surprising really that he'd agreed to marry me at all! And so quickly! But I felt such an admiration for him in his enthusiasm for certain aspects of our preparations. He'd begun a wedding list on his laptop. Mainly gifts for him – Davidoff cigars, a DVD player, his 'n' her mountain bikes. I admired the way he'd shied away from the hotchpotch of traditional gifts – the toaster, the kettle, the John Rocha wineglasses and linen. He'd suggested the

Habitat "Blue Daze" chinaware. He had an experienced, exciting air to him.

I remembered how I'd rehearsed in my mind for years the "we are gathered here today" speech and whilst I couldn't concede to "obey", I had stood proud and meant every word when I'd promised to "love and honour till death us do part"...

How cheap she felt her words were now.

But Graham had been so damn sexy.

And she didn't see Simon every week – "between the jigs and the reels", as he used to joke. The truth was, he was always working . . .

Always.

Working.

It was an increasing source of curiosity for Niamh how the brittle Ciara O'Rourke had reached the over-inflated iconic status she had. Niamh knelt on the foam window-seat of the Wexford maisonette, watching through the woodworm-ridden sash window the "public's Ciara" as she signed autographs, stretching her coarse skin into a wide smile and making small talk with the local neighbourhood. An "interiors celebrity" was how she was being referred to on this street, only minutes from Wexford town. Niamh anticipated the metamorphosis from the grinning, approachable TV icon as Ciara stepped over the front door, away from the cameras and local press whose shutters were clicking fervently. Tired of the ego of Ciara, Niamh crossed the room to check her equipment and read the brief for the work to be done on this first assignment. Scanning the style sheets, she began to mentally prepare the lighting and angles for the rooms. Farrow and Ball India Yellow paint for the dining-room to blend with a Louise Mulcahy oil painting of small children playing on a Killarney beach which would stand as the main feature of the room. She'd need floods of natural light. She made a mental note to ensure the French doors which led to the small balcony remained open, introducing a hint of the greenery from the back garden.

As she studied the designs she had to agree with the publicity blurb that surrounded Ciara's work. She had been praised with words such as innovative and eclectic and Niamh could see why. Despite her questionable personal skills she really did have a good eye for interiors. As she turned to view the living-room she felt a yearning for the Kinsella Interiors dresser that caught her eye as it stood in the hallway, envying the guy who owned the maisonette. It surely would take centre stage in his currently dowdy living-room. Ciara really was targetting Irish designers and craftspeople as the brief for *Home Is Where The Art Is* instructed.

Striding back toward the front window, Niamh straightened her sandblasted jeans, pulling gently at the ribbed black jumper that she wore with them. In anticipation of bagging a squillionaire, however unlikely in Wexford, she had fine-tuned her meat-seeking missile and was constantly on the lookout. She'd been told how the Wexford Opera Festival often brought opera lovers from around the world and so wasn't taking any chances with her once-in-a-lifetime opportunity of finding a man with moolah. The fact that the festival was in October – a few months away – had escaped her.

The silence was broken as Declan entered the quiet room, rubbing at his brow and sighing.

"Problems?" Niamh smiled at the stressed Declan.

He sat, his legs wide, on the window seat.

"Yeah!" The sound of him exhaling seemed to echo through the room. "Where can I get a decent designer at the last minute? I just can't promise to see the series through in the allotted time with only three. The brief was for four designers."

"You've surely got someone in mind?" Already her mind was working overtime and she was slightly fearful that the sounds of the cogs and wheels spinning in her head were audible.

"The trouble is, Niamh, I've seen so many that I'm brain-dead."

Deciding to seize the moment, figuring she had nothing to lose, Niamh took her opportunity:

"How about Tara McKenna?"

"Who?" He looked up at her, frowning and puzzled.

She tried not to smile as she spoke, desperate to give off an air of vagueness and detachment.

"Tara McKenna from the Tara McKenna Consultancy."

Declan looked back toward the carpeted floor, despondently shaking his head. "I've never heard of her."

"Oh, but you have." Niamh, an expert at reeling men in once she had a hook into them, rested her pert backside and taut denim-clad thighs on the seat next to Declan, sidling up to him, engulfing him in her aura. "Tara – my friend Tara. Did you not know that she has her own interiors consultancy? Declan, I'm sure I told you."

Declan's mind clicked back to the image of Tara, something that it had been well-practised at for the past fortnight. Strangely, despite only meeting her twice, he simply couldn't get her out of his mind. His only reservations were that she seemed ever so slightly aloof.

Declan looked squarely at Niamh, then squeezed her face in his hands so tightly that she was aware of a small callus on his left palm.

"Well, why the hell haven't you mentioned her before?" he virtually boomed.

Niamh felt the stirrings of doubt. "Well, she's not been going *that* long. And she's not really established, you know, compared to the likes to Ciara O'Rourke."

"No!" Declan jumped to his feet. "This is just what we need. Some new fresh talent. An unknown to work alongside the well-known. What a fantastic mix! The public will just love her, I know they will. How can I get in touch with her?" Oh, how he'd waited for the chance to get at her phone number!

He would have to wait a little longer for that.

"How about I ring her?" Niamh felt suddenly sick at landing Tara in the thick of it so quickly. She'd barely started on Niamh's place, let alone been stuck on the telly for millions of people to watch. Shit, Tara'd kill her!

Chapter 7

The sounds of Tara screaming down the phone were deafening. Niamh was forced to hold the handset a good twelve inches from her ear. Using her most passive and calm voice she spent just over an hour on the phone, convincing and cajoling her, shoe-horning her into the vacant space left by the now-absent Jessica Fallon.

"But what about that Ciara O'Rourke?" Tara squealed.

"What about her? It's nothing to do with her. This is Declan's decision."

"Yeah, and she won't *really* hate my guts. I'm a total unknown! Look what she reduced the other designer to – and she'd be *used* to the business!"

"Look, Tar, don't worry about that biddy. Just don't be intimidated by her. She'd take off her socks and fight with her toenails if she thought it'd get her somewhere!"

"Well, I'd rather she do that than pick on me!"

"She won't pick on you, Tar. We're in this together. Just think about it, us travelling around Ireland together! We'll have a right time!"

And when Tara's tone of voice softened, Niamh recognised that she'd gotten her hook into her and began to reel her in also. "Honey," she whispered downline to the panic-striken Tara, "when Cinderella left her glass slipper at the ball it was no accident."

"What the hell's that supposed to mean?"

"Think about it – it's fate. Me, here. You, the Tara McKenna Consultancy. This was supposed to happen! How's the portfolio going?"

"Great actually. I've got some big, arty photos in there. The pictures of what I've done to your place – all very stylised."

"You've finished? How's it look? I can't wait to see it!"

Tara took a deep breath. "I just hope you'll like it, Niamh."

"Are you happy with it?"

"Very."

"Fantastic!"

"And I've got photos of those makeovers I did at home. Those old bits of furniture I breathed new life into. It actually looks like the kind of things you'd see in *Elle Decor* or *Image Interiors*." She giggled, "It's a con really – it gives the impression that I've done loads of jobs."

"Great! So you're up for it then?"

Tara groaned. "I can't do this. It's all too dishonest.

And what about Ruben? I can't leave him here for days on end while I'm away!"

"C'mon, Tar, where's that old fighting spirit? You know your mum'll take Ruben for you for a few days here and there. And you probably won't even need the portfolio, but when you're working with the likes of Ciara O'Rourke you'd want to be prepared."

"OK," she whispered.

Niamh laughed. "Didn't quite hear that, Tar. Once again, with a little more conviction?"

"OK!" she boomed, and put down the phone and slumped into her armchair. A million insecurities raced through her mind. It seemed as if they all reached the finishing line at the same time, causing only more confusion. As they took off once again My-Poor-Self-Image raced neck and neck with No-Confidence as Lack-Of-Talent and I'm-Only-A-Smalltown-Girl battled for second place.

"*Aaagh!*" she hollered, placing her hands over her ears so as to muffle the thudding sounds of despair as the race continued in her head. Tara suffered a continuous fear of inadequacy. And now she faced not only her personal daily battle of not being good enough, but one which would be broadcast across the country with an audience reaching millions. These insecurities, however, did little to blight her delight at this high-profile opportunity. Despite her paint-stained jeans and sweatshirt she grabbed her denim jacket, tugging it onto her arms as she struggled to close the front door behind her.

She had to tell Anna the great news.

"Tara, that's fan-fucking-tastic! You must be delighted!"

"Well," Tara beamed as they threw bread to the ducks together in the late afternoon air, "of course I am, but what about the look of me?"

Anna turned to face her, a Picasso of disgust on her face as she grimaced, one eyebrow high and the other low.

Tara ignored the dramatic. "Oh Anna, c'mon, you know what I mean! What'll I wear for a start? And then there's the ten pounds that the cameras are supposed to add. The make-up, the spotlights, the way I sometimes talk too fast. It's all going to be there for people to video and watch and scrutinise time and time again."

"I think you're overreacting a little, Tar." Anna threw a huge lump of bread which caused most of the ducks to swim in the opposite direction. "You're there as part of the team, you're not a one-woman show. There'll be make-up artists to sort out your face. And your clothes? It's a DIY kind of thing, isn't it? You'll probably be wearing your combats or your jeans most of the time. You'll have to watch some of the programmes on Sky to check out what the other presenters wear. Tara, you'll be great, stop worrying."

Tara nodded, her mind still racing.

The trouble was, I sounded so vain keeping on about it. But I was at the camera's mercy, wasn't I? I'd be stretching and crouching and lifting, and – well – moving! It wasn't even as if I could just sit perched on a sumptuous sofa and blah-blah-blah my opinions. I was actively involved in the design and revamping of the rooms.

My head was really excited.

It was just taking a little longer for my stomach to catch up . . .

Chapter 8

Tara stood beneath the icy water and felt her skin tighten as it rained down on her back within the mosaic'd shower cubicle.

Simon had hated them.

The mosaics.

Glancing at a bottle of extortionately priced shampoo which she held in her hand, the jet of water washing over its sleek design, she pondered on its claim to be "volumising". Her hair was clean and was passable this morning, but the anxiety knot in her chest suggested that a head of full thick hair would conceal her inner turmoil at meeting the *Home Is Where The Art Is* team. Squeezing an over-generous potato-sized blob into her wet palm, she whispered, "Here goes. It'll probably add half an hour to my get-ready time – what with blow-drying."

As she massaged and lathered her scalp, praying for a result, she continued to question the marketing promises of these new shampoos offering "volume", "sleek and shiny" and even "enriched colour".

I mean, don't we want all of these things? Couldn't I use them all together? How could it really change your hair so drastically in such a short time?

She fingered the base of her skull with soapy fingers through silky bubbled hair.

Shortly after rinsing off the plethora of bubbles she stepped out onto the bath mat and wrapped a gigantic fluffy towel around her. She smiled at the recollection of Simon's teasing that women wrapped, whilst men got on with the job of drying themselves immediately. Lightly frisking her fingers through her damp hair, she applied her stylish serum as her mind raced.

You see, I'd only been halfway through Niamh's makeover when the doubts began to smack me in the face. I absolutely detested what I was doing to her rooms – even as I was doing them I'd got myself into a terrible state. It was only the fact that I didn't have the money to change my plans that had made me see it through. It was simply pure luck that it had turned out so well.

It'd be even luckier if Niamh loved it too.

She sat on the edge of her bed, in a trance.

I was thinking: what if I reek of "amateur"? What if the people don't like what I've done to their rooms?

I'd probably burst into floods of tears and run off down the road. Not exactly professional, eh?

And I was going to be on the bloody telly! I just wasn't sure if I was ready for all this! I mean, me on the telly! It was completely ridiculous. I'd be like a bungling Big Brother *contestant, rocketed into the spotlight in their new role as telly presenter! And then what about those days when I was suffering from pre-menstrual bloating? And then there was the regulatory spot. And what about when my hair wouldn't go right?*

It was just too scary to imagine.

"I'm *not* a chain smoker!" Niamh snorted, blowing out a bluey grey whirl of smoke.

Declan pushed the small plastic button which opened the car window – *her* side.

"Jesus – it's bloody freezing. Do you have to do that?"

"You're stinking. Them fags are rotten. And you just don't stop, do you? It's a constant cycle."

"God, I'm not *that* bloody bad! You make me sound like a real addict or something."

"Well, Niamh, make the most of it. Billy McGee has banned smoking in his apartment in Temple Bar."

"Who the hell's Billy McGee?"

"The guy who owns our second makeover."

"Right, the apartment with roof garden? Sure, can't I step outside and have a puff? It'll be alright."

Niamh just had that way with her. People felt instantly at ease in her company and Declan O'Mahoney was no exception. He'd offered her a lift to Inistioge, in an attempt to find out more about her and also anything he could pick up about her pal, Tara. The winding country roads as they drove from Wexford up through Thomastown looked exceptionally beautiful as the sun shone through the trees, casting mottled shadows on the rough road. Ever the professional, Niamh had to take her opportunity.

"Oh, Dec, just pull up over there for a bit, could you? I must take some shots of this. I just love landscapes."

Declan obliged, grateful for a reprieve from the fumes. Niamh grappled with her camera, leaning her elbows on the car roof as she focused and twiddled.

"The dramatic light is fantastic."

He suspected she was expecting an answer from him, but he was also well aware that she was talking and concentrating at the same time. He raised his eyebrows.

She continued, "Even mundane scenes are amazing if the light is brilliant. It's always the light I'm after. A shot just lacks substance without it."

She'd already enlightened Declan on her "landscapes of Ireland" project that she hoped to complete whilst on the *Home Is Where The Art Is* production. She'd planned a personal exhibition of the landscapes in a variety of galleries in both Ireland and the US.

As Declan enjoyed drinking his slightly lukewarm 7Up from its green plastic bottle he listened to Niamh chattering to herself as she made time stand still on film.

"God, it's great to move away from family portraits anyway. Just wait until I have my studio. Acres of floor space, white walls and high ceilings . . ."

As Tara drove down to meet them in Kilkenny she couldn't help but sneak an odd-angled look at herself in the rear-view mirror. She was delighted with her hair – the visit to the hairdressers had paid off. As short as it was she was sure that her slicked-down fringe seemed fuller and the spiky scruffed back sat in better shape than for ages. She was to meet the team near Kilkenny, in a small village called Inistioge that they had apparently fallen in love with on their search for Irish craftsmen, and where they were now celebrating the success of their first assignment. Tara would then be, officially, a team member.

It seemed mad to make the journey from Dublin only to return in a few hours, but as "the new girl" she understood it would have been foolish to refuse.

And I was hardly in a position to be calling the shots, was I?

"Here's to a successful start!" Declan held his golden pint of Heineken aloft, the first traces of warm summer sun shining straight through it, giving it an enhanced glow. They stood up from the ricketty wooden beer-garden bench that they crowded, and held their drinks up, repeating Declan's words, Tara feeling rather stupid especially as she hadn't participated in "the start".

The Wexford job had proved interesting and Ciara was regaling them with her delight at picking up some fantastic pieces from the Kilkenny Studio Workshops in Bennettsbridge. The Jerpoint Glass Studio had proved the perfect place for the light-reflecting lampshade that she'd intended for the first makeover and they laughed in an exaggerated team-building way about the fiery furnace that they'd looked into at the glass-blowing demonstration. White hot and sensual as the red-hot glass flowed into shape. Niamh had got some fantastic photographs there too. And then how the Nicholas Mosse Pottery shop, which was more than a shop in its fantastic old stone building right on the river, had housed the most amazing fruit bowl which now sat atop the dresser in Wexford like a crown.

Tara looked across the small village, down the valley to the River Barrow, across to the forestry with its clichéd "forty shades of green". Feeling very much the new girl she sat opposite Niamh listening to Ciara ranting about her latest design scoop, her patronising opinion of her "client" obvious by her tone.

"He had this attic room with his hideous record decks set up there. Fancied himself as some kind of DJ or something horrendous. Anyway, I had eighteen tons of deck equipment to incorporate into the design and so decided to keep it open and low. He absolutely loved my Moroccan theme and so I opted for the strong spicy colours – you know, Moroccan blue, azure, terracotta. I fashioned a draped tent effect at one end with Bedouin silky fabric draped in folds, stapled to the ceiling. It was without doubt the ugliest end of the room and so I accessorised with mirrors and candles. The huge spiders were absolutely unbearable and the rotten carpet and rising damp was stinking. Still we managed to sort it – I had to add a grand onto the budget though. Absolutely impossible to work within his budget given the conditions."

Tara was captivated by the speed of her mouth and only realised she was staring when Niamh kicked her under the table, bringing her back to life. Her jerking causing a rippled effect as Declan, who was equally mesmerised by Tara, also flicked his attention back to his pint.

"Hey, Tar, c'mon, I'll show you the small art gallery I was telling you about," Niamh said, breaking the spell and Tara, grateful for the intrusion, straddled her legs back over the wooden bench and followed Niamh toward the river.

They chatted as they meandered in the sunshine.

"How're you getting back to Dub?"

"With Declan. He gave me a lift down, remember?"

"What do you think of him?"

"Nice. Cool." Niamh wasn't about to give anything away. If Tara wanted the latest on Declan O'Mahoney, she was going to have to ask for it. Specifically. She continued, "Shame about that damned goatee though, don't you think?"

"Yeah, isn't it? Where's he taking you?"

"When?"

"When you get back to Dublin?"

"Oh, he's just dropping me off at RTÉ. I need to take some of my stuff into the office."

"Shall I meet you there then, or do you want to drive up with me for the rest of the way?"

"No," Niamh smiled, "thanks anyway, but there's something I need to talk to Declan about."

"Oh, OK."

Niamh knew Tara was disgruntled. They sat on a small stone wall at the riverside.

"What are you doing tonight?" Niamh asked.

"Well, I was hoping that my new shed would be delivered, but it seems they can't do it till tomorrow, so nothin' really. Why?"

"I'm going for a tattoo. Fancy coming along? I could do with a bit of back-up just in case I'm sick or something."

"What, tonight? A tattoo! Why?" Tara wanted to know.

"Dunno, just fancy it, that's all. Do you think it'll hurt?"

"Probably."

"More than a BCG?"

"'Course. But why? You'll look like an arse-scratching roadie! What do you want a tattoo for?"

Niamh smiled and shrugged. "What did you want your tongue pierced for?"

"That's completely different! Anyway, what are you having done?"

"This." Niamh pulled a Celtic design from her denim-jacket pocket and unfolded it. It was a mixture between a Maori-type style and a Robbie Williams job with a bit of Book of Kells added in there too.

"God, it's gorgeous. Where you having it?"

"On me arse."

"What?"

"Not really, across the back of my hips. Whaddya think?"

"Gorgeous. OK then, I'll wait for you in Declan's office."

Niamh changed the subject. "So, show us the photos of my flat!"

Tara beamed. "All finished. *And* eighty euro under budget."

"Go 'way. God, you're honest too. Thought you and Anna would've gone out and spent anything left over."

"Shut up! As if I would." Tara was used to Niamh's sense of humour.

"Keep the eighty anyway," said Niamh. "See it as your commission."

"Very generous," she teased. "You'll have to come over to the car to see the photos – they're in the portfolio now."

"Oooh," Niamh Victor Meldrew'd, "very professional, aren't we?"

They slowly walked beside the river, back towards Tara's car. She pulled the portfolio from the back seat and they sat on a large boulder at the side of the river.

"Here. Don't laugh."

"Don't be so bossy," Niamh tittered, pulling the large file from Tara.

Niamh felt her insides tighten as she rested the file down onto her lap, desperately hoping that the photos would come up to the standard that both Declan and Ciara were expecting from her. She'd taken a huge gamble on pushing Tara forward as the prime candidate and now only prayed that she'd done the right thing. The knot dissipated as the sweet warm feeling of relief swam through her with the turning of each page. Tara had done a really fantastic job. This was just what her disorganised life needed. A touch of class – Tara had truly excelled herself.

By the time the team returned to Dublin everyone had begun to form opinions on each other.

Declan knew for sure that there was no denying it. He fancied Tara McKenna. He could kick himself for continually being caught out staring at her. And that spiky thing she'd done with the back of her hair – how he yearned to ruffle his fingers through it! He'd been surprised when Niamh had brazenly instructed him to lose the goatee but, as she'd explained that from a woman's point of view goatees weren't the most attractive of features, he'd been grateful for the advice.

Ciara felt a mixture of irritation yet admiration for Declan's latest protégé Tara. She seemed terribly "green" in terms of professionalism yet had a raw talent, an eye for balance and co-ordination that even Ciara couldn't belittle. And how she'd tried. Already. She was irritating in that she reminded Ciara of herself, years ago when she'd just started her own consultancy, although she'd been much younger than Tara was now. Her enthusiasm and easy, confident manner were so familiar and yet, while she reminded Ciara of herself, she also reminded her of someone else she kinda knew too.

Tara felt confused. She wanted to hate Ciara O'Ro[...] and really should have after the emba[...] derogatory abuse she'd already hurled[...] Tara prided herself on being an[...]

Declan felt a swell of pride at Tara's handling of the obnoxious Ciara only earlier that day. As he sat in the driver's seat of his car in the RTÉ carpark, the door open and one denimed leg outstretched onto the warm tarmac, tapping rhythmically to his jazz CD, he went over the day's events. How Ciara had run her eye over Tara's ultra-feminine summer dress, pausing unnecessarily and resting her eyes on her bikini line, then blasting her with a nonchalant, "Jesus, honey. A see-through dress. You could at least have shaved."

Declan smiled in his jazz-induced trance, recalling how Tara hadn't even blushed. He felt proud that she wouldn't lower herself to Ciara's bitchy level and yet seemed somehow able to cope with her ignorance. As the saxophone seemed to compete with the bass and drums, Declan lost himself in a foot-tapping mantra.

He didn't realise he was being watched . . .

*"He's just so cool. If only he'd lose the bloody goatee. Doesn't he realise designer stubble went out with George Michael? I'm not sure about his choice of jazz either — it sounds mo*_____ *a musical battle than a harmony. I much prefer* ___ *stuff. He seems to know his music th*____ ___ _____ *ling Niamh earlier how he knows the* ___ __ *s on St Stephen's Green — the one* ___ *ooombowombowooombo" song.* ___ *it now than when he started* ___

hrough my head. ___ *ly beginning to feel* ___ *rude and unkind.*

You know, I felt bullied and intimidated by her, but I'd be fecked if I'd show it. It was strange really, she was more obnoxious in front of Declan, but it seemed to have no effect on him.

I kept catching him looking at me. It was flattering, but I wasn't sure I was ready for this after the way Simon treated me. I mean, you can't polish a turd, can you?

If Tara could have seen Declan at home later that evening she'd be viewing a slightly different picture from the ultra-slick superman she was painting him as. She'd see a man relaxing as he pottered with his house plants, pondering the benefits of having Paula back so they could be lonely together rather than lonely alone. He then remembered her dislike for his fish-tank coffee table, its lid mounted on rubber shock-absorbers so his unsuspecting fish weren't stunned by the clatter of a pint glass or coffee cup. But how she'd adored the kitchen with its cool yet warm stone floor reflected in a blur in the stainless-steel Smeg accessories and chrome appliances. As he loaded his dishwasher his thoughts turned once again to Tara, wondering what she'd think of his bachelor palace. The mere thought of her caused him to smile.

Niamh had hopped out of Declan's car, and come over to Tara's. She asked her to wait a few minutes while she dropped off her paperwork at the office. Tara hadn't minded waiting, she'd simply relaxed in her car watching Declan in his, as he went through his own files. Shortly after, Niamh reappeared and hopped into the passenger seat next to Tara.

"Right, ready now."

"So where are we going?"

"To the end of the road and turn left."

As they'd edged through the rush hour traffic, listening to other people's music through their open windows as they waited at a red light, Niamh casually stated, "I told him to shave off the goatee."

"No!" Tara laughed, "Do you reckon he will?"

"You'll have to wait and see."

Half an hour later, breathing in the thick antiseptic'd air, Tara watched as the tattooist painstakingly copied the design with his purple pen and listened as he calmly explained that although the first few needle strokes would hurt, the pain-reducing endorphins would soon kick in.

I'm sure Niamh thought he said dolphins – I did – 'cos she let out a wild nervous cackle which made him look at her oddly.

Once he'd begun, Niamh began to flirt outrageously with the rugged and bare-torso'd tattooist, delighting in his smooth hands resting on her bare hips.

And by the look on his face, he wasn't too upset by it either.

Once Niamh had *insisted* it felt more like being scratched than cut, Tara went out to the waiting-room and cast her eye eagerly over the brief for the second makeover. She'd heard Ciara pontificating once again about finely woven Japanese grass, but she already had her eye on a fabulous painting by Cliona Doyle up for grabs at the De Veres art auction, hoping it would be her one-way ticket to acceptance as a professional interior designer. Lost in her thoughts of drawing from natural elements, using daylight to its best advantage and using raw materials such as wood, linen and stainless steel, she didn't hear Niamh come into the waiting-room.

"Ready?" Niamh said, her hip jutting awkwardly as she stood over Tara.

"You done?"

"Not quite. He's done the outlines only. I'll have to come back for him to fill in the colour."

"God, you have to go through it all again?"

"Yeah, but it looks deadly." She nudged Tara cheekily. "He asked for my number too. Might get a discount next time! Fancy a gargle?"

"Sure. But I'm starving too. Can we get a McDonald's first?"

"C'mon then. Let's head off."

Tara sat at the only vacant table, watching as Niamh bustled expertly at the counter, sneakily nudging the scourge of tourists and students out of the way. Seated on the plastic seats as she waited for her McChicken Sandwich, a young woman caught her eye, her bandana clumsily folded and tied around her neck. As she chawed on her fries Tara noticed the slight swell of her breasts beneath her "Loopy Lass" t-shirt and then she caught sight of her burgundy fingernails. Expertly painted. With the body of a teenager yet the elegant hands of a seductress they revealed her intentions of adulthood, her inkling of desire to be a woman. Tara knew she was staring as the girl fumbled with a plastic rectangle of ketchup and was transfixed as she squirted it onto the few chips remaining on her serviette. It was then she noticed the toddler in the buggy, as the young woman leant across and fed him a ketchup-coated fry. A crowd of Japanese tourists, complete with camera necklaces, bustled between the young girl and Tara. Yet amidst the throng she saw the girl stand and embrace someone. A friend. No, a man.

Must be her father, I thought.

But yet, something strangely familiar struck Tara and she felt compelled to stand and rise above the five-foot-high wall of Japanese.

It's Simon!

It can't be!

He had the same hair, the same wonky grin and even the same jacket.

Yeah, the one that smelt of expensive perfume.

On her right Tara could see Niamh, all grins and grimaces as she wove through the crowd with a laden tray. She always had two Big Macs to Tara's McChicken and it didn't even seem to touch her. Tara had always said she had the metabolism of a whippet. On her left she could see Simon hugging and petting this girl. Before she could get out from behind her pokey table Niamh clattered the tray down.

"This must be one of the roughest McDonald's in town."

"Why?" Tara stood confused, not sure whether to go over to Simon.

Niamh continued, oblivious. "Every single young one behind that counter has at least one of those blue plasters on them. On their noses, cheeks and chins, I'd say they've gone through a whole roll." She tittered. "D'yeh reckon it's part of the uniform?"

Tara stared at the empty space that Simon and the girl had vacated.

They'd gone.

"Tara? You listening to me at all, are yeh?"

Tara sat, stunned. "I've just seen Simon."

"What? In here? Girl, you're losing it. Simon in a McDonald's? I don't think so, you're hallucinating."

"I'm telling you, Niamh, it was Simon. He was with a young girl."

Niamh felt the huge bite of Big Mac catch in her throat. She'd spoken with Anna only earlier that day about the pile of VISA receipts and it wasn't looking good.

"Oh," she forced the light-hearted tone, "must be a niece or something."

Tara wasn't to be put off that easily. "She wasn't at the wedding."

"Maybe a cousin then. Don't torment yourself with it. Look, there's your chicken thing. Finish it up and we'll get a few vodkas into us."

Tara obediently chomped at her food, but her mind was elsewhere.

Niamh's attempts to brighten her up were completely in vain.

"But you don't understand! I haven't seen him in months! And who *was* that girl with him?"

As they left the McDonald's, Niamh looped her arm through Tara's and tugged her closer in a friendly manner. "C'mon, Tar, don't torment yourself. He's a loser. Forget it. Just for tonight, eh?"

"That's easy for you to say. Jesus, Niamh, he's my *husband!*"

"I know, love. Look, let's stop off in here for a quick livener, eh?"

Before she could protest, Niamh dragged her through the doors of one of the city's newest "superpubs". Tara didn't really like these so much; they were all virtually indistinguishable from one another and she felt they lacked in atmosphere – severely. They waited at the spotlit bar, Tara immediately switching into interior designer mode and taking in the beechwood floors, textured upholstery of the high bar stools and the low, beige leather chairs. Still, it was kooky and she hoped she'd be able to relax there for a while.

And get the misery of seeing my husband with another woman out of my mind.

For a while.

Chapter 9

Despite my squeezing headache, I could remember everything from the previous night.

Well, that's a lie. I couldn't really. It was mostly a vague, disgusting haze.

But I knew that I had seen him.

I hadn't seen him since he left me.

Simon.

I knew it was not all that long in weekly terms, but my mind had stretched it to a painful eternity since he walked out.

And who was the young girl with the baby?

Although the sight of Simon had tormented Tara, the memory was blurred as she'd diluted it with vodka. Herself and Niamh had dashed in and out of the light showers, stopping in an abundance of pubs for "just the one", taking shelter, wetting their palates as the pavements dried. It had been proving to be a rather nondescript night, despite Niamh's enthusiasm as they trawled from the nondescript bar with blue walls and Chinese lanterns, to the nondescript nightclub with the neon lights of purple and blue that x-rayed their white underwear through their clothing. They'd laughed at the divvy tourists who posed for photographs on the gleaming bronze statues, hopping up and screaming as they got wet arses, jumping in shock and squealing. Things took a definite turn for the better when they headed northside to one of the up-and-coming comedy venues. They both loved the storytelling kind of gags and Tara had heard that the open-mike session was particularly hilarious, where the winner – chosen by the audience – got a plastic duck as a prize.

"Do you fancy a turn?" she asked Niamh, her own humour exaggerated by the few vodkas they'd had.

"You're not serious! I begin and end with a camera. I'll leave the funny stuff to them. But I'm up for it. Should make a good change anyway."

It had been just the right thing to put Simon out of her mind. She'd got right in and joined in with the drinking and crazy heckling that went on from the audience. And had taken Niamh by surprise when she'd shouted out a few times at the "have-a-goers" as they improvised and "funnied" at whatever was thrown at them by the crowd.

But my euphoria was shortlived. I could feel my smile sliding with every extra mile that the taxi drove nearer to home. And then when I stepped in over the doorstep into my cosy yet cold home, the absence of Simon hit me even harder than earlier in the day.

I cried myself sober and to sleep.

The second assignment was upon them as were two horrendous hangovers.

And I had to wash the freshly hairdressered hair! It reeked of cigarette smoke. To be honest I thought I'd woken up wearing a wig of fag-butts and I knew as the shower sprayed down on me that my bubble of glamour was shattered. I was back to square one. No, I was nowhere near square one. As if the horror of my first TV appearance wasn't bad enough, it was now tinged with a mosaic of emotional shards at seeing Him.

With Her!

I opted for my hipster jeans with the wide belt and my long-sleeved pink t-shirt. I reckoned it was trendy enough to get me accepted and yet practical enough to paint and decorate. If only my head was more geared up for it. My brain was being ambushed with traumas. Nothing major, you understand, just the fear and dread that my paint wouldn't dry in time, or my shelves would fall. And then there was the dreaded "reveal". What if my homeowners lost their temper at the sight of their new decor?

Or even cried?

Perhaps I'd beat them to it . . .

Armed with her photographic equipment Niamh's stomach lurched with every step up to the already stylish pad with a roof garden in Essex Street, belonging to a young silversmith whose studio was around the corner. The odd-shaped one-bedroomed flat would be a delight to transform, although Tara prayed that Ciara wouldn't go for the deep red she'd initially suggested. Her stomach just couldn't take it this morning. Billy McGee, the silversmith, had quite a clear idea of what he wanted from *Home Is Where The Art Is*.

"I'd like some nice pieces – a combination of sleek modern broken up with eighteenth century Rococo."

"Not much of a bloody challenge," snorted Ciara.

"Piss off!" whispered Niamh as she set up her lighting in competition with the television company's camera crew.

"I heard that," Tara teased, pulling back in alarm as she realised Niamh's state of dehydration. "Christ, you look rough. You OK?"

"Oohhh, no. I feel deadly. I've already spent half the morning yodelling into the toilet bowl."

"Here," the smiling camera-woman bought them over two plastic cups of coffee. "Might just do the trick."

"Oh, thanks a million." Tara took both of the cups from her, handing one to a still groaning Niamh.

"Well," teased Tara taking a sip of the hot bitter drink, "you know what they say, men are like coffee – the best ones are rich, warm and can keep you up all night long."

"Yeah," struggled Niamh, her tongue feeling like snakeskin after the boozy night, "and they're like mascara – they usually run at the first sign of emotion *and* they're like laxatives – they irritate the shite outta ya."

"Hey," Declan boomed, "you ready, Tara?"

She looked across the roof terrace at Declan.

I'm sure I'm blushing, I thought. It's the eye-contact thing. He just holds for so long. And he looks fantastic without the facial hair.

"Yeah, coming."

"Go on, girl," nudged Niamh slightly overexuberantly, causing Tara to spill some of the coffee onto her shoes.

"Niamh!" she hissed, irritably. She grabbed the small print of the Cliona Doyle painting and confidently strode across to Declan and Ciara, ready to reveal her intentions for Billy McGee's pad.

Niamh called her back, "Hey, wind him around your little finger, let him bounce like a spring and then tell us all about it tomorrow night."

Let me enlighten you.

Every month we met for our "monthly meal" – Niamh, Anna and me. It all started just after we'd started work – although we used to meet in Pizza Xpresso in those early days.

And later?

Later we matured to Luigi's, Meeting House Square, Temple Bar. My most favourite Italian restaurant in the world. Well, in Dublin anyway. I'd never actually been to Italy to sample a true Italian restaurant so my palate was somewhat ignorant, but hey! Who cared?

Luigi's. A small cavern of a room in a corner of Meeting House Square. The initial suggestion at taking the four or five steps down in through the wooden doors creates an air of excitement. You know, as if you're going down into something exclusive and mysterious. Then, once you're in, the stone floors and authentic Italian decor, small ricketty wooden tables, roughly plastered whitewashed walls and that gorgeous heady garlicky smell . . . well, I'm hooked. Saturday night really is the best as everyone gets squiffy and takes it in turns to strum guitars.

Coupled with my failure at discretion regarding marital politics, and then the Tara McKenna Consultancy thing, I hadn't joined the others there for the last two months. But, guess what? Yep, we're all meeting there tomorrow night.

The crew sat out on the roof garden overlooking Temple Bar. The glorious midday sun shone down on them. It was only Ciara who couldn't relax as she was afraid the heat would blister her paintwork.

"You *must* remember the 1972 Pirelli calendar. The Parisian one," Niamh insisted.

"'Course I don't. I was only a toddler, how would I? We weren't really the kinda household that displayed Pirelli calendars. I don't think we even had calendars unless Mam pulled out the centre pages of the Christmas issue of the RTÉ guide and blue-tacked it onto the kitchen wall."

Declan smiled, an intense feeling of admiration for Tara and her acceptance, verging on pride, of her inner-city upbringing.

Ciara O'Rourke grimaced, "RTÉ guide! You really mean you didn't have calendars?"

"'Course not. Christ, Niamh, what's your point?"

"The 1972, or was it the 1974? Anyway, one of those Pirelli calendars was shot by Sarah Moon in Paris. She was given no story for her calendar, only the subject: woman. She tested the limits of the calendar. She diffused the shots with Peter Stuyvesant paper from the cigarette packets. She challenged the open-mouthed, semi-naked pictures that were the Pirelli trademark. The 1972 calendar was more about dark eye-shadowed women, failing to make eye contact with the camera as they sat sexily in the Parisian house."

"Yeah," Ciara felt irritated at Niamh's dominance of the conversation. "So?"

"So, I'd like to take some unconventional shots of the makeovers, but I'll need a little co-operation."

"Sure." Declan liked anything suggesting the innovative. "Whatever you need, let us know. But nothing too arty, eh?"

Ciara harrumphed, raising her eyes heavenward, causing the team to disperse, each heading toward their own personal task.

Declan caught Tara by the arm. "How you getting on then?"

"Fine."

I'm blushing again!

"Look, I know she's difficult and you seem well able for her, but are you really OK?"

"Yeah. She is hard to get on with at times, but I think I can manage her. Are you happy with my contribution? Is my work OK? I feel terrible about damaging the mirror earlier."

"Your work is fantastic. And don't worry about the mirror, it's already sorted. I suppose you must be feeling nervous, what with this being your first time in front of the cameras."

Tara blushed even more and did that fluttery glance-away thing with her eyelashes.

How pathetic – I know! I didn't even mean to do it. I mean, what a bloody cliché!

"You know, Tara, I've already had remarks complimenting your ability to make use of dead space and your eye for colour co-ordination. And the Cliona Doyle painting is just the icing on the cake."

"Thanks. I'd hate to be pulling the team's reputation down."

"Not at all. Look, Tara, that night in the Wexford Inn –"

"Oh, look – don't worry about it."

"No, I have to explain. I didn't know those two women. My friend Anto, you know, brought them along."

"Yeah, OK, whatever."

"Well. Would you like to –"

"Taraaa! Are you part of this team or what?" Ciara's screech zig-zagged through the air, knocking the satin edge off Declan's tone and causing Tara to feel suddenly awkward.

"Would I like to what?" she prompted.

"Oh –"

He was sheepish!

"Nothing. I'll catch up with you later on. Better see what madam's after."

I could have sworn he was going to ask me out! Or was that just wishful thinking?

Luigi's was everything Tara, Niamh and Anna had grown to expect and the relief at completing the second makeover was making Tara's chest swell.

Yeah, great, isn't it? And not a chicken fillet in sight! You'd nearly think I was on the road to recovery.

All I was waiting for now was for this little cloud of adulterous guilt to blow over . . .

As long as it didn't break into a rainstorm, and soak me . . .

The swift succession of tapas-style cuisine was the perfect accessory to their intimate conversations. Niamh led the subject, as usual.

"Yep, and we've got a budding romance here between Declan and Tara."

"Ha ha ha! Why d'yeh say that?"

"Oh come on, who are you trying to kid? He's gorgeous! Haven't you noticed the way women flirt with him? Especially that researcher?"

"Which one?" Tara asked quickly,

Niamh smiled at Anna, "That blonde Stephanie one. But don't say you haven't noticed the way he looks at yeh?"

"Don't be stupid, Niamh. Anyway, given my relationship history I hardly think I'm the perfect catch. Have you forgotten? I couldn't even manage my first wedding anniversary?" Tara's tone rose with every syllable she formed her berry-red lips around, and by the end of her speech her cheeks matched her lipstick nicely. Making the wooden chair screech she stood, "I'm going to the loo."

Niamh gulped a mouthful of Chianti, gazing unblinking as Tara marched across the stone floor toward the toilets.

Anna looked on, concerned. "Actually, Niamh, I'm grateful for the opportunity to talk to you alone. It's about Simon."

"Oh, not you as well. Look, forget him. The man was a bore anyway. She needs a bit of excitement in her life."

"Niamh! I've seen him."

"Yeah?"

"I've seen him twice. Once in Dublin and once in Wicklow. Well, now I'm out of work I've got time on me hands, you know."

"Go 'way!" said Niamh. "Tara saw him in McDonald's with a young woman and a pushchair!"

Anna's voice lowered to little more than a whisper, "Well, both times I've seen him he's been with different women and, put it this way, they *weren't* family. They were both dark and petite and were *both* wearing wedding rings."

"Go on . . ."

"Well, d'you think we should tell her? It might help her to get over things a little. He's obviously not pining for her!"

"What did you find out about the pile of receipts?" asked Niamh.

"It's really odd. In one hotel he checked in as Mr

and Mrs Donnelly, the one in Galway he was Mr and Mrs Sullivan and the Wexford one knew him as Mr and Mrs Kelly. Something sniffs, anyway."

"The conniving bastard! Playing away from home! And there's Tara feeling like shite."

"Well, should we tell her?" said Anna. "If guilt's the only thing holding her back from a relationship with Declan O'Mahoney, then surely we should."

"No. Not yet. Let's just give it another couple of weeks. This thing with Simon needs looking into. Let's just bide our time and get to the bottom of his game a little more. Agreed?"

"Yeah, OK. We might even find out – "

Anna noticed Tara on her way back to the table and fell silent.

"What were you talking about so seriously?" Tara wanted to know, as she sat down and pulled her seat in.

"Christmas," said Niamh.

"Youse talking about Christmas already?"

"Yeah," Niamh's mind was racing for an explanation of their conversation. "We were debating the dread of a family Christmas – you know, flatulent grannies and braying children."

Declan lay still amidst the strangely unfamiliar sheets, detesting himself. Giving out to himself for being so stupid. As he lay on his side, feigning sleep, he looked down at the swirly pearly latex on the floor. His stomach churned with disgust at what he'd done. As the woman beside him fidgeted he felt himself stiffen slightly, clamping his eyes closed. She yawned noisily and stretched. He felt the bed rise slightly as she got up and through slitted half-closed eyes he watched her naked butt as she walked out of her bedroom and into her shower. On hearing the blast of water hit the shower tray he opened his eyes and looked at his watch. Six fourteen.

"God, she's an early riser. What the hell possessed me?" He rubbed his forehead, battling with the cotton wool that seemed to have taken residence. Taking his opportunity he leapt out of her bed and grabbed his creased clothes from the wooden floor. Her bedroom was a shrine to the catwalk, her label-conscious clothing hanging elegantly on padded clothes-hangers. Slipping on his leather jacket he quickly checked himself in the mirror, ruffling his wavy hair into shape. As he passed the bathroom he heard her humming to herself contentedly. Begging for the stairs not to creak as he tip-toed down them and reached the front door, closing it behind him with the quietest of clicks.

Starting up his car down the street from her house, he turned down the immediately blaring breakfast radio show and once again questioned his behaviour.

"Hell," his breath formed warm clouds in the early-morning freshness as he virtually wailed, "what the hell have I done?" On the drive back home he tried to piece together the mismatched jigsaw of the night before – only there were many vital pieces missing. The bits that the soak of the brandy had blotted out. He recalled how she'd seemed so easy to talk to at first.

How she'd boasted at knowing the real names of the Hollywood celebs. How Demi Moore was really Demetria Guynes, Lauren Bacall was something horrendously matronly like Betty Joan something. He'd already known about Freddie Mercury being Farookh Pluto Bulsara and Cher being Cherilyn Sarkisian La Pier. He supposed that her admission that she missed her ex, claiming that she missed the way he gently sucked on her nipples, and how she just couldn't do *that* herself, was the final clinch for the night. And so this morning, as the sunshine began to heat the road and the dew lifted, transforming the view as if through a wobbly heat-induced lens, Declan felt rotten, resolving that if he really liked Tara he'd better get his act together. He wasn't prepared to start a lifetime of a succession of disappointing drunken one-night stands.

Tara was delighted. "The Shed" was everything she'd been expecting – and a whole lot more. What had arrived as a twelve-foot square wooden box was now her idea of heaven. Her choice of soft furnishings and the right accessories had turned her humble shed into an extension of her home. It was her turn for a week off, while the two male designers tackled the next makeover and she was grateful for the reprieve. She'd spent a lot of time engrossed in the *Home Is* world lately and was keen to establish the Tara McKenna Consultancy a little more. In only a few days she had completely transformed her new shed. She had stained the wood with a blue wood-stain –

It did exactly what it said on the tin –

And panelled the inside walls, lining them with cream fake fur. A cheap rug was thrown down on the floor for comfort. She had fitted in a workbench and then had divided The Shed into two sections – her beads and fabrics and stencils on one side, and her paints, glazes and colours on the other. Although it wasn't tidy, it was organised and her newly MDF'd drawers and cupboards were a credit to her. Resting up against The Shed, in the sunlight, was the bright yellow chair she was repairing and the wicker basket full of her tools. She paused at her pottering, uncertain whether she'd heard a knocking at the door. She quietly crossed her small back garden and went in through the kitchen. She opened the door. It was Declan.

And here's me in my shorts, I thought. Look at the state of me!

"Hey! Not disturbing anything, am I?"

"Not at all, come on in."

He followed her through the house, pausing as she opened the fridge and pulled out two cans, then taking the one she handed to him. As they stood in her garden she cracked open the beer, gulping at it thirstily.

"I like The Shed."

"Yeah," she nodded, trance-like as she viewed her pride and joy, "me too."

"Have you had it long?"

"A few days."

"You *have* been busy. Mind if I look inside?"

She lifted the can to her lips, swinging her other arm

open to indicate the way. She heard him laugh out loud from inside and went over to the closed door. Opening it she watched as he ran his hands over the cream furry walls and twiddled with the volume knob of her micro hi-fi. The music blasted out and made him jump.

"I love it!"

"Yeah," she smiled, "so do I."

"Do you know, I've got just the thing at home that'd look great fixed onto your outside wall."

"What is it?"

"No. I can't tell you. You'll have to wait and see."

"Right. Thanks."

A silence fell between them and they suddenly felt awkward. He shuffled, gulping down the last of his beer.

"I just wondered how you were. Kind of seems strange around without you now. We'd all got used to having you around the last few weeks."

He was missing me!

"I've only been away for a few days! I'm back next week, or am I? Have things changed?" She felt her voice drop slightly, her feelings of inadequacy flooding back.

"No. Nothing's changed. Yeah, you're back next week."

As they shuffled from foot to foot a dark cloud moved over them, casting grey shadows across her sunny lawn. They looked at each other and giggled.

"Quick, we'd better lock up – looks like it's gonna piss down."

They rushed to carry in the yellow chair and wicker

basket, Tara swiftly locking her shed door, and made a run for the house. The shower just hit the back of her legs as she made it in through the back door.

"Right, so let me get my calendar. Where are we next?"

The quick intake of beer coupled with the shower had made Declan fidgety.

"Mind if I just use your loo?" he asked.

"No problem, upstairs."

She sat at her kitchen table with her wall calendar listening to Declan's footsteps as he climbed the stairs. Flicking back six months to January she was amazed at the markings for the month.

There was a huge section of two weeks that I'd marked for Simon working away. And then a week at the beginning of Feb and five days at the end. He was away for nearly two weeks in March and then a week at the beginning of April. No wonder I had the affair! I didn't realise it at the time, but he was hardly ever here! No wonder I was lonely.

Although, that's a rather lame excuse too, isn't it?

Declan skipped back down the stairs, noticing the darkness which had crept into Tara's eyes and so he decided to make a quick exit – he was obviously disturbing her work. He sat with her at the table, checking through his diary and giving her the dates for the next few makeovers. He watched her intent expression as she noted them down onto her calendar.

He really loved the way that long piece of fringe was too short to tuck behind her ear with the rest of it. It flopped forward, dangling down toward the paper as she wrote – a few single strands of her soft hair. For some reason, it made him want to tuck it behind her ear, smooth her face, and kiss her.

Chapter 10

The Old Schoolhouse in Carlow was a fabulous
converted school. As they gathered in Declan's office
with Stephanie showing the brief, it was the first time
Tara saw Ciara get remotely excited. It seemed both
Niamh and Ciara were anticipating money and class,
especially when Declan explained how this was owned
by two professional, rich men. Tara herself had to admit
a slight surge of butterflies.

It had nearly killed Niamh, the ninety-minute drive
to Carlow with Tara in the front, pondering and
despairing at her indulgence with the lusty Graham.

Niamh had tried to distract Tara from the subject of
Simon.

"You know, Tar, they say a successful man is one
who makes more money than his wife can spend. And
a successful woman is one who can find such a man. I
intend to be a highly successful woman."

"Good luck to you, but I admit to be looking a little deeper than his pockets, Niamh."

"Oh, you're forever too meaningful. Whoever said money can't buy happiness must have been wired to the moon."

Relieved to pull up on the gravel drive of the Schoolhouse, Niamh didn't think she could bear another minute of self-deprecating and sombre reminiscence.

But the wedding had been my fantasy. I'd both given birth to it and then killed it. How do you ever get over something like that? What kind of person does it make me? I'd wanted the full choir – the works, but had settled for the reception at home and drinks on the lawn. The lively salsa band had pulled the whole thing together right up to the speeches and dinner by candlelight. I knew my decision to propose had stunned everybody – probably even Simon. Niamh had told me many times that I needn't wait for the Leap Year tradition – that it had started in the fifth century when St Bridget complained to St Patrick about women having to wait so long for a man to propose. So what? I was enforcing a tradition that was over fifteen hundred years old. To me? To me, it just made the whole thing more romantic, more Rapunzel, more Sleeping Beauty . . .

The gravel crunched beneath their shoes as they filed in through the quirky stable-door of the Old Schoolhouse. Ciara winced at the plethora of colours. They really hadn't seemed so vivid on the polaroids. The magenta-painted walls of the living-room clashed strangely but stylishly with the Tipperary green of the kitchen.

"So?" Ciara questioned loftily. "Where's George and Den?"

Declan responded, "George left a message on my mobile. They've had to go into town for something. We're to set up our equipment and start getting organised before we start shooting tomorrow. Bring your portfolios over into the kitchen and we'll have a brainstorming session."

"Brainstorm or blame-storm?" Ciara sneered.

"Excuse me?" Declan turned to quiz the irritant Ciara.

"Declan, I wonder sometimes whether you are looking for *our* ideas or for someone to blame? Like me? We all know you'd prefer Tara to have the say in most cases anyway."

"Oh Ciara, please. You're totally paranoid. C'mon. Let's get the kettle on."

"No, Declan. I have to drive into town. I've got a designer to meet. He's sourced some fantastic bronze sculptures for me. I have to go and decide on one for this place. Anyway, if George or Den haven't the manners to be here to greet us, then I don't suppose I'm missing out on much when they *do* arrive."

And in a cloud of perfume she slung her zebra-print bag onto her pristine leather-clad arm to match her leather-clad legs, and left them to it.

Minutes later, before Tara was even halfway through her herbal tea – the only choice George and Den had left – she heard the deep, unfamiliar voices which proved to be the owners of the Old Schoolhouse. Niamh, Tara and Stephanie jumped from their seats in the kitchen and peered around the doorway for a sneaky preview. They weren't disappointed. Both men topped six foot, wrapped in a muscled, tanned skin – they were total gods.

Feeling like nervous schoolgirls, or giggly womenfolk from a 1950's film, their aspirations were shattered as they watched the hunky men talk with Declan about lighting, set-up and production plans. Then Den dropped his hand and caught hold of George's huge downy one, and the girls watched as if in slow motion as the two fine examples of maleness squeezed each other's hands excitedly. It was obvious that Declan was trying desperately not to glance down at the obvious hand-clenching, and to ignore the tittering from the kitchen. Tara admired his professionalism.

"Stop it, Niamh!" Tara nudged the guffawing Niamh in the ribs.

"I mean, what a bloody waste!" spluttered Niamh.

"*Sssh!*" Stephanie blasted. "Declan's bringing them this way."

They dashed back to the kitchen table, making an unceremonious clatter as they grappled with the chairs, sploshing the contents of their mugs across the table top.

"Den, George – let me introduce you to Tara our newest designer, Niamh our photographer and Stephanie our senior researcher. The two fellas are outside with our DIY master, sawing up squares of MDF. Ciara O'Rourke, our other designer, has had to go into Carlow for a bronze sculpture or something."

"Not for here, I hope?" Den questioned.

"I don't know. Why?"

"I can't stand the stuff. Don't bring any metallics into our home. We prefer more of a matt two-dimensional effect. I'm *sure* we put that on our e-mail."

"You did," confirmed Stephanie. "I'll make sure she knows."

Niamh, Tara and Stephanie just had to laugh as the three men went out of the back door to meet the rest of the team, realising Declan's diplomacy and Ciara's failure to read the brief.

"No metallics, huh? So who's gonna tell Ciara?" teased Niamh.

The three of them shrugged, grinning widely.

The early morning sunrise washed the gravelled forecourt in a ruddy hue. Ciara, Niamh and Tara rested their bums on the step at the back of the open Land Rover. The lighting technicians and camera operators bustled with jangling equipment as they ferried it back and forth through the church-style front door. The place was a hive of activity – and all before seven a.m.

Clutching the design brief in her perfectly manicured hand, her knuckles white with the grip, Ciara asked, "So – what were they like?"

Ciara's attempt to appear nonchalant was really quite pathetic. It was obvious she was bursting to know about George and Den. OK, so I know it's mean, but sometimes you just can't let an opportunity pass you by.

"Oh Ciara, they're just sex-on-legs!" Niamh gushed.

In reality, it wasn't a lie. They were. But they only had eyes for each other. Nobody dared to enlighten Ciara.

We forgot.

"Ohh, I just can't wait to meet them," she declared, pushing her manicured fingers through her stylish bob.

"You won't have to wait for too long," Declan offered, earwigging on their conversation as he passed with a gigantic board of MDF, catching sight of the two huge-framed men as they jogged over the small wooden bridge which linked their garden to the small country road. Ciara's head swung around in panic and her sharp intake of breath echoed through the vacuum of the Land Rover on which they perched.

"My God – just look at them! And two of them at that! My God!"

"Didn't we tell you they were gods?" said Niamh.

Tara nudged Niamh in the ribs.

Sure, she always just takes it too far.

"My God."

"Yeah," whispered Niamh, "my God . . ."

By mid-afternoon it was Tara's turn to make the coffees. As Ciara battled beside her with the enormous swathings of fabric intended as drapes and the sound of the jig-saw buzzed through the house, she was grateful for the break. She was suffering from primary-colour overload, what with the pillar-box-red painted walls and the bright yellow and deep blue soft furnishings, and so a mug of camomile tea was just what she needed to regain her balance. She heard the sounds of bare feet padding on the wooden floor behind her, and turned to see George. Her stomach flipped at the sight of him in black Nike shorts and nothing else, his toned, tanned thighs and torso covered with a glorious smattering of blonde hair. She stared into the mugs before her, aware that she was stirring the one coffee for far too long. She regained her composure before turning again with an easy smile.

"So, what happened to the *Home Is Where The Art Is* shirts that Declan asked you and Den to wear?"

He laughed.

"Hey, not my style really. I've no aspirations to be on the telly. Den's wearing his – let him be the one they film. That camomile tea smells good – got one on for me?"

"Well, no. But it's not a problem. Here, I'll pour you one."

Tara handed George the mug of aromatic tea and was surprised as he handed it back.

"They the coffees for the workers?"

Tara nodded, confused.

"Here – you take our teas out to the back garden and I'll take these coffees up to them. Meet you out by the fish-pond."

Tara carried the two heavy mugs out to the crisp air, watching the small remnants of dew lift from the grass and flowers beneath the indigo sky. Taking a deep breath and closing her eyes, she sat on a large boulder by the waterside and rested the teas onto her knees.

"Grand," George's deep voice caused her to jerk her eyes open, "now for that drink."

Tara was surprised at how easy she felt in George's company and was amazed at his calm amidst the take-over of his home. There were workmen everywhere and yet George and Den hardly seemed to notice.

George cupped his mug of tea and slurped from it noisily.

Tara giggled, "The sound of you!"

"Tea always tastes better if you make a noise drinking it, I find," he smiled.

Tara tried it, sucking in the camomile concoction loudly.

"Hey, you're right," she laughed.

"See? Thank my middle-class education for that. And my misspent years at UCD."

"You went to UCD? So did my husba – my ex-husband."

George ignored the trip-up. "Yeah, what year?"

"Oh God, left 1988 or '89. Not sure now." She laughed nervously. "Don't think I'll be ringing him up to check though."

George slurped again. "Like that then, is it?"

"Yeah, and some. So, what did you study at UCD?"

You know, what with the artistic style, the liberating, colourful house and the whole aura of George I was surprised to hear what he did . . .

"Sales and Marketing – I hated it."

"That's what my husba – ex-husband studied. You probably know him."

"What's his name?"

"Simon. Simon Cullen."

"Jeeesus, Slimey Simey. 'Course I know him. Still speak to him on the odd occasion. He's your 'husba – ex-husband'?"

"Yeah," Tara blushed.

Feckit, I thought – I never thought they'd know each other. God, how embarrassing!

And he probably knew all about my infidelity and the rest. Here's to the first unravelling of my professional image.

"So," George continued, blissfully unaware of Tara's inner turmoil, "when did you marry oul' Slimey?"

I'll ignore the nickname . . .

"Only last year."

"Right." Now he understood the sensitivity of the issue. Tara's face alone was a dead giveaway. "But," he puzzled, "you look so different from when I saw you at Kevin's wedding last August."

"Kevin who?" Tara's guilty eyes met George's confused expression at close proximity.

"Kevin DeBurra who got married last autumn to that awful Joanna O'Carroll. You must remember – the wedding was in Galway. Didn't you have darker hair then?"

Tara's mind whizzed.

I certainly didn't have darker hair. My hair had been the same for the last three or four years. And Kevin DeBurra? I'd not been to any weddings with Simon.

A brick formed in Tara's throat. She recalled Simon receiving the invite to a "Kevin's" wedding.

Yeah, and how he'd said he couldn't stand him at UCD and they wouldn't be bothered going. Of course – it was the Bank Holiday weekend. And he'd gone to London on business instead . . .

The bitter penny began to slowly drop, but she wasn't about to let George see.

"Oh, of course. No – we had split up for a while in the autumn. You're right – it certainly *wasn't* me at that wedding with him. So you and Den went, did you? Simon said after what a great 'do' it was."

George released a burst of air as he let out the breath he'd been holding, his face relaxing into a relieved smile.

"Yeah, a great time we had. Mind you, Den didn't think much of Joanna. I suppose really none of us did."

"Simon said that too."

I was lying through my bloody teeth, but I just had to find out more. Wasn't it a sickly strange situation? You know that you don't really want to know, but at the same time you just have to . . .

"Well, I thought I was cracking up. I just knew that it wasn't you at the wedding."

"No," Tara feigned humour. "You know, I can't remember who he went to that with. You see, we weren't really getting on at the time."

I tried to casually giggle – you know, as if it didn't really matter . . .

George laughed as he downed the last of his tea. "That was bloody obvious from the way he was all over *her*. It got to the stage where it was embarrassing. I mean, they were like teenagers."

161

Tara felt sick, grateful for George plucking the empty mug from her hand and leaving her knock-kneed on the boulder, alone. A waft of synthetic perfume permeated the fresh aroma of the flowers as Ciara stepped into the garden, blocking George's path.

"Geooorrrge, honey!"

Tara looked up through hooded eyes to see Ciara smothering George's large frame with her invisible force-field, encroaching on his personal space.

"Ciara," his tone was clipped yet pleasant.

"I see you have your hands full." She lifted her leg slightly to rub her thigh against the silky crotch of his shorts. George remained composed,

"I sure do, but here's someone to help me."

Den skipped down the few steps into the sun-drenched garden. The eye-contact between the two men was electric.

"Here," offered Den, "let me take those in." His handsome open face smiled at George's as he took the two mugs. George handed over the mugs and, as he did, met Den's lips as he reached towards him, planting a firm but resounding kiss first onto his firm stubbly jaw, and finally onto his thin pink lips.

I nearly fell off me boulder. Ciara's face was disgusted, but she was rooted to the spot. She first went red, then a kind of yellow, and finished up with a rather flattering shade of green. That was before she grabbed the mug from Den and threw the tinted remains of cool camomile tea onto George's bare chest.

To which he laughed and said to Den, "I think that

was intended for my face," and he wiped off his chest with his hand.

Thankfully the afternoon sped by. Tara suffered as she felt like a holiday rep, forcing an air of joviality upon herself, smiling at her colleagues for the camera and commenting on the beauty of the hideous bog-oak sculpture Ciara had exchanged for the bronze work she'd intended for the Old Schoolhouse.

Two people saw beyond the polished veneer: Niamh and Declan. Between shoots Niamh grabbed her by the arm, tugging her towards her, tripping over the tripod as she did. "What's happened? You're not yourself."

Tara smiled through gritted teeth. "I'll talk to you later."

"No, now."

"Look, put it this way. It seems Slimey Simey wasn't all he was cracked up to be."

"Slimey Simey?"

"Simon!"

"How?" Niamh challenged, slightly fearful that Tara had happened upon the batch of receipts.

"I'll talk to you later. Please, let me finish this first."

Niamh let her go, wondering when the revered Simon had mutated into Slimey Simey.

Chapter 11

George and Den were delighted with the results. The makeover was, in the opinion of everyone but Ciara O'Rourke, a resounding success. She'd muttered and whinged about the lack of depth, criticising the primary colours and blocks of bold shades, but the majority of the team had found it refreshing to be involved in such an extravagant theme, and in such a quaint location too. As was proving to be the routine, the *Home Is* team dispersed, heading for a local pub. Tara deliberately went in the opposite direction, focusing on a grimey-looking pub with filthy windows and tobacco-tinged nets. Niamh had followed her, much to her irritation. As Niamh stood at the bar Tara waited, seated in the church-type pew. Her eyes filled with heavy tears. She stared down at her paint-splodged jeans and, as a heavy tear fell and splashed onto her indigo thigh, she realised that she'd fantasised about this moment. Or at least, a moment like it. OK, so she wasn't quite Anna

Ryder-Richardson – even considering the difference of a stone and a half and years of experience – but she had looked forward to what she'd imagined this feeling to be like. Her moment of fantasy was dampened now with the grey shadow of Simon and the quandary of Kevin DeBurra's wedding versus Simon's business meetings in London.

Niamh bustled from the bar with two gleaming pints of Guinness.

Not my usual drink but hey – I wasn't feeling my usual self. I'd coped with Guilty-spouse Syndrome, Traumatised-ex-wife Tales and even Newly-single, Newly-minted, but I can't do, haven't had to do, the Lied-to-In-The-Dark Divvy.

Niamh got the blurted low-down on Simon's mystery wedding guest and Tara's humiliation at the lies. Then her rage that he'd never even admitted he'd been to the wedding. She'd blasted at his deceit in its most disgusting marital guise, and so Niamh was now trying, once again, to make Tara realise how much better she was without him.

Tara stared into the blackness of her pint.

Niamh continued, "Remember how anal his sense of humour was?"

"No. Remind me. Right now he seems like a mixture between Michael Barrymore and George Clooney."

"Christ! OK, how about how I used to torment him with my cow-fascination. Remember the time I wound him up with my knowledge of Belgian Blues and Herefords? He was bloody furious with us for laughing at him. Remember?"

Niamh clocked Tara's slight intake of breath, recognising it as indication that she was beginning to relax. She continued, hurriedly now,

"And then at the Christmas do, when we dressed up as a pantomime cow and how horrified he was at the pair of us. And there he was, dressed up in his hired costume as Mark Anthony."

Tara wailed into the Guinness, unexpectedly.

"What?" said Niamh.

"Niamh, you're making it worse! He looked bloody gorgeous in that costume, don't remind me! It's my fault – that's it. If I'd been more of a woman and less of a matron then he'd never have gone off with his sexy secretary. It's all my fault!"

A tirade of expletives followed as Tara expressed her pent-up frustration, causing Niamh to gulp copious amounts of Guinness to mask her embarrassment. At this stage the line-up of builders at the bar turned to face them, watching her – unimpressed yet slightly amused.

Niamh forced a smile onto her frothy moustached mouth and tittered, lamely, "Hey, have you got Tourette's?"

"Shit, shit, shit!" Tara replied, banging down the Guinness and storming toward the toilets.

Niamh plastered a grin onto her face, scraped back her dark hair from her face and flirted with the chunky, dusty builders.

"Well, you know what they say, ten per cent of men kiss the wife goodbye when they leave home, and the other ninety per cent of men kiss the home goodbye when they leave the wife."

To her embarassment, not one of them laughed. The Guinness moustache probably did little to help.

Declan made a slightly late appearance in the grimy pub, due to his scouring of the locals in search of Tara. Despite the mottled appearance of her eyelids, he suspected nothing of her outburst and so cheerfully ordered himself a pint and took the liberty of refilling the two empty pint glasses, the traces of frothy Guinness foam clinging to their sides. He brought over the fresh drinks to Tara and Niamh.

"He hasn't the hands to wipe his arse!" Niamh spat.

Declan beamed, feigning offence, "Thanks. And me after buying you drinks too."

"Oh, thanks, Dec. No, not you. Private convo, you know . . ."

The nod was more than sufficient – Declan was a man who knew when to change the subject.

Staring at Tara over the lip of his pint glass as he sucked down the thick creamy liquid, he queried mentally her shaken appearance and red eyelids, yet decided to steam ahead regardless.

"Tara. How d'ya fancy a few days away? Business, of course."

Tara looked up from the woodworm-riddled table that she was so intently staring at.

Sometimes the little holes make up patterns, you know . . .
"Why?"

"One of our families want a makeover with a French

feel, but still keeping the Irish-crafted arts theme. Fancy a few days in the good name of research?"

"Why me?"

Declan inwardly cursed her questioning. He could have asked any of the other three designers to make the trip to Paris, although the idea of a few days away with one of the male designers or Ciara didn't have the same appeal. Of course, one of the researchers could have taken the time, but on reflection, Stephanie might have been a bit of a handful. He took a deep breath and lifted his glass, tipping it toward her in a cheers-type *slainté* move.

"You're the newest designer on the team and we're getting an extremely positive response about your style. I'd like to give you the opportunity to widen your expertise. This will be one of the more challenging of the *Home Is Where The Art Is* makeovers, and I suppose I just wanted to give you the opportunity. But if you're not interested . . ."

"No," Tara sprang to life, nudging Niamh as she did so and causing her to spill the froth of her drink, "I'd love to. When will I be going? And with who?"

"Next week, and, unfortunately for you, with me."

I was blushing! I couldn't even manage to keep my skin under control! With Declan! God, what would I wear? How many clothes would I need for a few days? I think I'd already shopped until my credit card had cracked. Compose yourself, woman, for God's sake. . .

"So, that's grand. Where will we be going to?"

"Paris."

"Wha'?"

OK, so the colour left my cheeks and I suppose I'm now an even more unflattering shade of grey, but Paris! And you know how they say your ghosts come back to haunt you – my ridiculous fear of flying has yet to be revealed . . .

Declan repeated himself, slowly, a hint of amusement dancing across his eyes, "Paris."

Tara tried to smile at Niamh, but then wailed, grabbed her bag and headed for the toilets once again.

Declan stared at Niamh with a look of total confusion.

Niamh merely shook her head and explained, "Where she went for her honeymoon . . ."

Yes, Simon had been surprisingly well-informed about weddings. He'd known that bridal flowers had traditional meanings – that daisies signify "Innocence" and ivy stands for "Eternal Fidelity". He'd so confidently taken the lead as first on the dance floor and had even chosen the music. He'd really lapped up the day. I'll always remember his beaming smile, his quiet confidence and ease. While I'd been a total bag of nerves, he had calmed and soothed me . . . Despite his slightly dubious lack of personality, when it came to our wedding I have to say, he really knew his onions.

Shame they only brought tears to my eyes . . .

On their arrival back in Dublin the next day, Niamh and Anna took their opportunity whilst Tara went out with Declan – *purely on business of course, to discuss our trip to Paris* – to try and get to the bottom of the clutch of VISA receipts they'd located at Tara's. Her chirping, vibrating

Nokia in hand, Anna sat in Niamh's newly decorated seventies retro lounge, the carefully selected funky post-millennia stamp quite clearly Tara's.

"Go on then." Niamh rested her elbows on her knees, cupping her chin with her right hand.

"Right," Anna shuffled the slippery receipts. "I've been making good use of all this extra time on my hands. Shame I'm not getting paid for it really," she deadpanned. Niamh ignored the heavy hint. "I rang the Erriseaske House Hotel in Galway and he'd checked in as Mr and Mrs Barry. The Blarney Castle Hotel in Cork had them down as Mr and Mrs Harpur. It seems that every single booking was in an alternative name."

"Bastard!" Niamh launched herself from her re-upholstered orange sofa, complete with circular logo'd furry cushions. "That fecker was having affairs long before Tara even met Graham. And," she span to face Anna, "you haven't heard the latest about the wedding and the business trip to London, have you?"

"The what?"

Niamh explained the indiscretions of Slimey Simey and the nuptials of Kevin DeBurra.

"Y'know, I never really took to that pompous prick!" said Anna. "I mean, seriously, any man who overused that patronising expression 'pet' as frequently as he did was in serious breech of social 'petiquette'."

"Bastard! He's nothing but a knuckle-dragging bumpkin."

"So what do we do now?"

Niamh smoothed her hair into a low bun and speared it with a biro to hold it in place. Anna wished she could be as adept with her own tangled arrangement.

"Well, the only link we have is George, really," said Niamh. "If we could just find out who that woman at the wedding with him was. It'd be a start, wouldn't it? I think that's where we begin – with George."

Declan had taken a good quarter of an hour extra to prepare for his afternoon with Tara. He'd decided to book a table at L'Hirondelle to invoke the Parisian atmosphere, he hoped in a positive way given the honeymoon revelation. As he buttoned his shirt, tucking it into his stone-washed jeans, he wished he had the confidence to throw himself a cheeky wink in the mirror like they did in the aftershave adverts. Instead he switched off his bedroom light and made for the DART.

Tara had been equally nervous. A "date" in the afternoon always posed such a relentless problem.

Do you go vamp or is that just too evening? Does the navy linen trouser-suit scream "office"? I didn't want to give the impression of vulnerable female and opt for my floral summer dress, but hey, what if I topped it with my slightly knackered-looking denim jacket? No, still too summery looking. Perhaps I'd play it safe with my old faithful – the suede trousers and cream t-shirt always get me through the most difficult of situations.

Tara arrived fashionably *en retard* to see an anxious-looking Declan already seated as he watched couples happily slurping down rock oysters from their shells. As she made her way through to the bustling restaurant she caught the aroma of onion soup and the delectable hint of pan-fried foie gras and her stomach flipped in excitement and anticipation.

Yeah, that and *the fact that Declan O'-feckin-Mahoney looks gorgeous.*

The French staff welcomed them with fresh walnut and raisin bread, after which Tara ordered seared salmon on fresh tagliatelle with basil and olive oil and finished with a raspberry and vanilla mouse which was dabbling its rear end in a raspberry coulis.

"So, you're a fan of the Dublin jazz and blues scene then, Tara?"

"Pardon?"

"The night I met you for the first time. The night you rescued me from that hideous woman."

"Oh yeah," the realisation sank in, "the night you met your girlfriend and the other couple."

"My girlfriend?"

"Yeah, the tall blonde lady who couldn't leave you alone."

Declan felt his throat constrict, threatening to choke him on his wine.

"I told you she wasn't my girlfriend!"

"Yeah," she teased, the afternoon sunlight dancing in her eyes, "sure she wasn't. Have you told her that yet?"

"You can blame my friend Anto for that. He's

always pairing me off with someone, especially after Paula . . ."

Tara noticed how the illumination of his face faded and, whilst clocking the change, chose not to further the conversation.

"You know, I'm really dreading going to Paris – in a way."

"Why? 'Cos of the honeymoon?"

Tara laughed, throwing back her head, and bringing her blonde hair to life. "Not really. But you know, Paris is a rather sick anagram of 'pairs'. The place seems to be full of 'em."

Declan laughed, "Yeah, romantic capital of the world."

"Still, we'll have more than enough to do."

Declan wasn't about to be thrown from the subject so easily. "You know, we could try some of the jazz clubs in Paris. After our day's researching, of course."

"OK, but I'm more of a Billie Holiday, Ella Fitzgerald fan rather than the contemporary stuff."

"Yeah, let me guess – Louis Armstrong, Charlie Parker? You haven't even tried anything else . . ."

"Such as?"

"Put it this way, a lot has happened since Louis Armstrong was born a hundred years ago. Jazz means different things to different people. There's plenty of debate as to what the legacy actually *is*."

"I'm confused."

"Well," he placed his warm hand over her slender one, "let me enlighten you. Paris is a jazz-crazy capital. Give me one evening to take you around!"

Tara's eyes lit up at the promise, "Sure. Where did you have in mind?"

You know, I didn't really expect him to know where to go for jazz. Least of all in Paris, but he did. He really surprised me.

I said surprised – not impressed . . .

"Le New Morning on Rue des Petites-Écuries would be a good place to start. All the big names have played there from Art Blakey to Dizzy Gillespie. Honestly, whatever your style, there is no lack of jazz action in Paris – for instance, Le Duc des Lombards is a New York style corner bar but Le Petit Opportun is a snug kinda medieval cellar bar."

"Well, you're clearly the expert. I'm in your hands."

"And there you'll be safe enough."

Christ, my stomach was doing somersaults. It wasn't going to be easy keeping a professional distance between us. I'd have to make sure to focus on our research.

"I've been looking into some French interiors," Tara said.

I'm gushing and blushing.

"Go on."

He's laughing at me, I know he is!

"Autour du Monde is a small shop concentrating on the natural look. I thought it might be a nice twist between traditional Parisian and the Scandinavian feel. It has lots of recycled furniture and traditional antiques. But, of course, I haven't seen the Dingle residence yet."

"I have photographs to show you."

"OK, but I wondered how you felt about a touch of

Parisian chic coupled with country-house in Provence? We'll have to remain focused on the Irish nature of the programme though. You might have to stop me from buying the products there and then – we'll have to only take ideas back to Ireland and source our craftsmen here."

Declan was encouraged by her enthusiasm. He hadn't made a wrong choice. Both professionally and personally.

"Mis en Demeure on Rue du Cherche-Midi is uber-chic, where we can find ideas for kitchens and bedrooms." She looked at Declan's expression and read it for blank. "I'm boring you."

"Not at all." Declan snapped out of his admiration of Tara, annoyed at himself for slipping. "OK so, we fly out on Tuesday at eight thirty from Dublin. Will you need a lift to the airport?"

Despite her yearning to say yes, she maintained her distance and refused. So as Declan charged the bill to that trusted corporate friend – Expenses – and helped Tara with her suede jacket, both of them were equally looking forward to the following week.

You know, I really liked him. He's so different from Simon – makes me wonder what I ever saw in him. . .

"You know," Niamh laughed with Anna, "men are like snowstorms. You never know when they're coming, how many inches you'll get or how long they'll last." She loved playing this new "game" that Tara and Niamh had invented on the set of *Home Is*.

Anna laughed, falling back into the comfort of the ricketty armchair that Tara had added to the furnishings of The Shed. Whenever the weather was fine, The Shed had become "the place" to congregate, her lounge now playing second fiddle to the wooden structure in her garden. Tara only wished that she'd thought of getting it at the beginning of the summer. Niamh and Anna had squealed when they'd first seen it, especially the inside. It seemed that a ritual had started that whoever saw "The Shed" had to bring a token to add to its character. Declan had given her an old metal tobacco sign which used to adorn the outside of a corner shop about a hundred years ago. It looked fantastic on the side of The Shed, with its scratched white background and old-fashioned red letters. Niamh had brought along an old lamp that Tara had since re-shaded and Anna brought along a holey galvanized bucket – which had probably been used for milking cows two hundred years ago. Tara had planted flowers into it anyway.

"Hey, I've got one!" Anna blasted. "Men are like horoscopes. They try to tell you what to do and are usually wrong!"

The two friends overreacted as they curled up laughing, completely forgetting their plan to try and bring up the subject of the receipts found at Tara's house. They didn't notice her as she walked across the garden, heading towards them.

"Jesus, I thought she'd be ages in the kitchen. Quick, Niamh, put away those damn receipts. We haven't talked it through yet!"

A quizzical Tara viewed their strained grins. Then she saw the remains of the pile of small crumpled papers on the floor. Niamh caught sight of Tara's gaze and grabbed at the receipts nervously, cramming them into her jeans pocket.

"What are you doing?"

"Oh, nothing!" Anna jumped in, attempting to be breezy but failing dismally.

"So what has Niamh just stuffed into her pockets then?"

"Oh," Niamh looked down at the posy of screwed paper spilling over her pocket, "these? Nothing – just rubbish."

Tara stepped toward Niamh accusingly. "So what kind of rubbish can't I look at then?" She thrust her hand forward to grab the papers, but Niamh was too swift for her and darted to the side, stuffing the loose receipts deep into the confines of her jeans.

"I've got a new fella," stated Anna, by means of changing the subject. Her proud tone caused both Tara and Niamh to stop in their tracks and look at her.

"Excuse me? Since when did you have a relationship?" Niamh questioned. "I thought you were Queen of the One-Night Stands?"

"Since I met Hugh."

"Hugh? Hugh who?"

Tara and Niamh laughed at the sound, which caused them to mock and cat-call as they trilled, "Hugh who? Yoo-hoo?"

"Don't take the piss," chided Anna. "He's a very

up-and-coming accountant who very soon will have his own firm. Actually, he's loaded."

"Oooh," teased Niamh, "'Hugh' wants to be a millionaire!"

Tara laughed, once again relaxing with her friends, all thoughts of relationships, Paris, jazz and Declan O'Mahoney temporarily forgotten.

"You've met him, Niamh."

"I have? When?"

"At that charity do last year. You know, the one for the homeless."

"Not him! Jesus, Anna, he was rotten!"

"Don't be so bloody rude. And how would you remember?"

"I remember he was wearing shiny trousers for a start."

"Yeah? And they're trendy!"

"They didn't *start* shiny – they were bloody shiny through wear and tear!"

"Don't be ridiculous," Anna retorted. OK, so she had horrendous taste in men, but rather resented her choices being commented on by the high-standarded Niamh.

"Well, I've just joined an 'elite' dating agency," said Niamh.

"What's *that?*" Anna scowled.

"It's all part of my plan for a man with money. I've tried Dublin's financial district only to find that it's a ghost town at night. And then I realised that they all start early for international trading. So, I've taken the plunge and joined up with Millionaire Match Club."

"God, it sounds like a cheap game show."

Niamh laughed, "Hardly. Not with an eight hundred euro joining fee."

"You're not serious!" Tara nearly choked.

"I am. At least it keeps out the riff-raff."

"Yeah, *you*!" Anna giggled.

"Only it didn't keep me out, did it? They claim they help romance and success meet. You don't *have* to be rich or famous to join, but Carolyn, the agency manager, did mention that if you own a chain of hotels or are a well-known brand name it does help."

Tara and Anna were aghast at her incessant search for money, especially when she was relatively successful herself.

Niamh was on a roll. "I picked up loads of hints from Carolyn. She said that spotting a millionaire is as simple as looking at their watch."

"So my Timex is out of the running then?" Anna quipped.

Niamh ignored her, "Apparently it's not the gold Rolex that you should be checking out but the not-so-well-known brands that are discreetly expensive without screaming."

Tara shook her head vaguely. "Such as?"

"Panerai, IWC or a Franck Mueller for example."

Anna folded her arms and sighed, "Well, I'm lost for a start."

Just as Niamh was about to launch into her next millionaire-seeking hint, to offset against another derogatory opinion of the cheesy Hugh, her mobile rang. She answered with a grin, ready to cut short the caller and continue aggravating Anna. Looking at the display on her mobile the name "George" flashed in accompaniment with the ring tone. Realising that this could be a call that she'd rather take out of the proximity of Tara, she paced casually through to the kitchen before pushing the rubbery button.

"Hey!" she tried to sound casual.

"Niamh. I have the lady's name for you. Apparently she's been seen with Simon a lot recently. Mind you, it's little surprise really."

Niamh held the phone close to her mouth and whispered, "Tara's here with me."

"Oh, right. Look Niamh, it's not looking good. I feel bad really. You've put me in a very difficult position. I still see Simon now and again at reunions and mutual friends' weddings and that – you know. But look, don't involve me any more and you *haven't* heard this from me, but –"

"But wha'?" Niamh hissed, aware of the sounds of Tara's footsteps approaching the small kitchen.

"But the lady with Simon at Kevin's wedding was Una Cullen."

"Yeah?"

Tara was now standing right in front of Niamh, looking up into her face. Niamh forced a grin as George repeated: "Una *Cullen*. *Mrs* Cullen. Simon's *wife*."

Chapter 12

Isn't it strange how excitement and anticipation are diluted with a burst of reality? I suppose I should have known better. Despite a lifetime of trying to escape reality, it always seemed to catch up with me. I was brought up on an estate where the daddies would scramble of an evening to park their cars at the top of the hill so they could get the maximum speed up as they rolled them down in the damp Dublin mornings, just to get them started. Back then the baked beans were straight from the tin — no microwaves in those days.

And so here I was now, six thirty a.m., another damp morning, staring down at a plate of barely warmed beans and soggy lukewarm toast at Dublin airport, trying to look as if my eyes weren't really out on stalks with tiredness. My stomach was doing somersaults with anxiety and there were already queues at the Aer Lingus desks.

I was having serious doubts about ever agreeing to these few days of madness.

With the newly smoothchined, gorgeous Declan or not.

Tara's surge of insecurity was interrupted as she earwigged on the conversation going on between the couple behind her. As she listened to the muted tones, she thought she recognised the slight twang of an American accent.

"And you know, I just love the taste of hot garbage."

"You had *that?*"

"Yeah. And just wait till I tell Sven."

"So, with what?"

"Garbage with carrots and parsnips."

Jesus, they're bloody Scandinavian, not American! And the "garbage" is "cabbage"! I'm such a sad eejit, I couldn't even get that right. I just knew those few days were set to be a disaster. Those couple of days in Paris would reveal the real me to Declan – the working class, struggling Tara rather than the professional interior designer.

Count on it – my days on "Home Is" were numbered, I was sure.

An hour later she was sitting beside Declan on the plane, crammed into the narrow seats, over-heating as she fumbled and struggled with the seat belt. A bustle of businessmen cockily breezed past in a wave of leather attaché cases, confidently throwing their macs and bags into the overhead lockers and slamming them closed. As her stomach churned she pondered at their confidence. Only fifteen minutes into the flight and she began to relax. Despite the initial battering as the turbulence hit them through the grey clouds, she actually found herself unwinding.

In the taxi from the airport to their hotel she viewed

the painfully familiar reminders of her honeymoon with Simon. As the rain cascaded down the windows and rattled off the roof she watched *les gendarmes* as they blew their whistles on the street. As the taxi sped into the city centre, she saw with a gut-wrenching yearning feeling the wrought-iron-clad balconies, almost in sepia but for the bright spruce of green conifers and topiaries punctuating the muted tones of the architecture.

Tara was just so glad that she'd done her homework. Once they'd checked in she led Declan straight to Galeries Lafayette and Printemps, reckoning that the two famous department stores would be a good place to start. She desperately wanted to visit the store of her favourite designer, Agnès b on Rue du Jour, especially in the style guru's home town, but knew this would have to wait until later.

In reality, I can't get away from Declan.

And I don't really want to . . .

The early afternoon was time well spent as they'd handled fabrics, and seen colours and designs that were typically Paris. They headed north of the City for Saint-Ouen. The Marché aux Puces at Porte de Clignancourt was a flea-market with over two thousand stalls that had been recommended to her. Tara and Declan made their way through the crowds, taking great pleasure at the many specialist markets full of antiques and junk. She fell in love with an antique chair, upholstered with buttercup velvet, the solid arms and seat slightly worn and threadbare. Urging Declan to translate for her, she managed to haggle a good 20 per cent off the price and was thrilled to find that the stallholder worked with an international carrier who could arrange delivery for her. By late afternoon they were both hungry and so agreed to lunch at Sacré Coeur, elbowing their way through the gaggle of bus-delivered tourists. They lunched at L'Été en Pente Douce, a pleasant little café with a terrace at the foot of Sacré Coeur.

"What does the name of this café mean?" she asked Declan, tucking into her traditional salad, the sunshine now warming her skin as they sat at the chrome table and chairs with a view up toward the impressive Sacré Coeur.

"Summer on a gentle slope."

"God, that's lovely. No wonder this place is known as romantic capital of the world. So what does Sacré Coeur actually mean then?"

"Sacred Heart."

"Ooh," she giggled, trying to lighten her mood, "named after me then."

"How do you figure that?" Declan wiped the remains of his salad dressing from his lips, scrunching the serviette onto his empty plate.

"That's me all over. A sacred tart."

"I hardly think so." He laughed, nodding to the waiter for the bill at the same time.

The ache in Tara's arm from scribing hurried notes in her book had subsided and when Declan suggested time out in the Louvre she had jumped at the chance.

"Well, will we skip to the Louvre, then?"

Tara put her pen down and turned to face him,

unaware at how relaxed she looked with her hair pulled from her forehead, secured by the Chloe sunglasses she'd recently bought.

"Will we what?"

Declan smirked. "Skip to the Louvre – as in the song –"

"Oh, I get it." Taking the pen from the table she plunged it deep into her handbag and smiled. "Sure, you lead, I'll follow."

I'd really wanted to go into the Louvre on my honeymoon, but Simon had refused, completely ruining the afternoon with his moaning. He simply failed to understand its attraction, deeming it a total waste of an afternoon. Still, they say one man's heaven is another man's hell.

She felt heady with excitement as Declan hailed a taxi which sped down the Champs Elysées, past the Arc de Triomphe. They'd turned just prior to Jardin des Tuilleries and had stopped at the Louvre.

They got out and, excited beyond belief, Tara grabbed Declan's hand. It was only when he pulled on her arm as he reached to pay the taxi-driver that she realised she was holding his hand. She let go as if an electric spark had gone off between them. She thought Declan noticed, but he said nothing.

Tara picked up one of the free orientation leaflets at the entrance, knowing from her research into the Louvre in preparation for her honeymoon that the secret is to be selective. They sat on a wooden bench and scrutinised the leaflet together, Tara's blonde hair slightly tickling Declan's cheek as they did so.

"Right then," she was clearly taking control, "if we

begin in the Richelieu and Sully wings we can see the French paintings including Poussin's *The Four Seasons* and the landscapes by Claude Lorrain. Then we'll have to head for the Denon wing overlooking the Seine."

"Why?" Declan was trying to lean in closer to her. The smell of her perfume and her clothes were starting to cause a stir in his jeans. Tara continued, oblivious. "Denon wing – first floor – Italian painting. Leonardo's *Virgin on the Rocks* and *The Virgin*. And the *Mona Lisa* is in the Salle Rosa. We *have* to see that!"

"Why?"

"It'd be a sin not to!"

The General Register Office, Joyce House on Lombard Street, is the central repository for records relating to Births, Deaths and Marriages in the Republic of Ireland. The queues in the General Register Office were like nothing that Niamh and Anna had ever come across before.

"You know the records here date back to eighteen-sixty-something?" Anna reminded Niamh.

"Well, how about we concentrate on the last four years, for starters."

She'd checked out the procedure to make a search in the public office, and had convinced Niamh that they *weren't* being disloyal to Tara by making an enquiry. Her mobile bleeped to signal that a photo message had been sent to her. Grabbing the phone, she felt a warm tingle to see that it was from Adam and the photo was of The Yacht with a blackboard outside advertising that

The Long Johns were playing there tonight. She knew it was an invitation and she was pleased as they had such similar tastes. It was such a terrible shame that he was low on her list of monied men. Still, she sent back a photo message of two ice-cubes. She knew he'd understand that it meant "cool".

"Right, Anna, let's get at it. I just hope we find something concrete here."

They paid their two euro for the five-year set of books and set out to check anything that could track back to Simon Cullen. The huge books were like telephone directories and listed entries by name, then giving area of marriage and age. After each entry was a code which the clerk would input into the computer for a full listing.

"If the marriage is recent then it mightn't be in the book," informed the clerk. "The computers are updated much quicker than the books."

"How recent is 'recent'?" queried Niamh.

"About the last couple of years. Anything in the last two years mightn't be in the book. But if you know what you're searching for, then I can do a check on our computers files for you."

"Thanks."

Three and a half hours later Niamh hit upon something.

"1998!"

Anna leant across to her, anxious to see what she'd found.

"1998, Simon Anthony Cullen, Foxrock, aged 32."

She jotted down the code beside the entry and raced to the desk. The clerk obliged and punched in the code to her system. Within seconds it was all there in front of them.

Niamh read it out: *"Simon Anthony Cullen and Una Mairead Slattery. Married in Foxrock, 4th June 1998. She was 31."*

"Oh no." A wave of sadness swept over Anna.

But Niamh, ever the perfectionist, was still looking for more. "Now we need to look for a divorce entry. If Una Slattery or Cullen, or whatever the hell she's known as, was at that wedding with Simon last year it means one of two things."

The clerk interrupted. "I don't think there are records for divorce. Not centrally anyway. Prior to every marriage you have to sign a form to declare that you know of no impediment. I suppose a lot of it is taken on trust."

Niamh's eyes narrowed as she asked the clerk, "So if you didn't admit to already being married, then there'd be no way anyone would know?"

"Exactly. Unless you were married by the same registrar, and he had a quick eye and recognised you. No, there's no way of tracing divorce."

Anna looked on, wide-eyed.

Then Niamh hissed at Anna, "Either Slimey Simey is still seeing her after their divorce or *they're still married!"*

Five thirty was closing-time at the General Register Office and Niamh was seriously disgruntled at being

188

asked to leave at quarter to six. She'd been talking with the clerk for hours, trying to find out how to track a divorce record.

"Fancy a beer?" Anna asked, fully aware that Niamh was volatile when in a lousy mood.

"Yeah, anywhere will do."

"How about Dockers'?"

"Anna, Bono won't be there – you *do* know that, don't you?"

Anna blushed slightly and shrugged as she replied, "'Course I do!", irritated at being so apparently transparent.

They walked along the Quay and Anna desperately tried to be discreet as she walked into the small pub. Niamh, however, noticed her surreptitious glancing.

"They're not recording in Dublin at the moment, Anna. Haven't you seen their live concerts in Japan on MTV?"

As Niamh made straight for the loos Anna poked out her tongue at the back of her retreating head.

The barman laughed at her. "Annoying ya, is she?"

"Yeah," Anna smiled. "Two pints of Guinness, please."

The barman swiftly obliged, omitting the obligatory shamrock shape on the top of the pints that they save for the tourists' benefit.

As they sat on the wooden chairs in a quiet corner Niamh pronounced on the afternoon's findings. "So that bastard was married before Tara."

"But how can we find out about their divorce?"

"Don't worry, Niamh – maybe we'll ring that solicitor in the morning."

"Do you fancy a casino?"

"Oh, Niamh, do you never give it a rest? Looking for a high-roller, eh?"

"Oh, just get me in my slinky Gucci! I can even handle the thoughts of slimy foreigners sidling up to me and asking me for numbers for them to bet on."

"Sorry, Niamh, I just don't fancy it."

"Oh, Anna, don't be so dry. I thought in your current state of unemployment you'd be looking out for old money. You just have to look at the quality and shine of their shoes. Forget the Gucci or Prada, the old money will be wearing unbranded shoes. And they'll *always* pick up the bill."

"Niamh," Anna was exhausted and tormented by the findings of the day and the last thing she wanted was a night out with Niamh – especially as she was in one of her shallow moods.

She downed her pint and, ignoring Niamh's mad texting fit, strode toward the bar for a reorder.

They spent the afternoon mostly in the Denon wing, lingering over the European sculpture on the ground floor – Michelangelo's *Dying Slave* and *Rebel Slave*, and the *Venus de Milo* amongst the Greek antiquities. Later, things only went from better to – well – even better still as they wandered along Boulevard Saint-Germain, and Declan steered her into a small doorway. Hesitantly Tara entered and allowed Declan to take her hand, leading her up the aromatic stairway and into a traditional Lyonnaise cuisine restaurant. She was amazed to find that he'd made a reservation. As Madame LeGrand, the owner/hostess/waitress *and* bartender showed them to their table in the already humming but small restaurant, Tara grinned at Declan.

"How do you *know* about this place? Seriously, I'd have walked past hundreds of times without noticing it."

"And no background music." Declan cocked his ear upwards, making her aware of the low relaxed hum of conversation.

Tara watched as sumptuous appetisers and pâtés served in terrines were delivered to tables around her, and felt a tingle as she soaked up the atmosphere of this exquisite yet humble place.

"But do tell me, how did you find this place then?" she asked a relaxed Declan

"Can't really remember to be honest. I've been coming to Paris for the last fifteen years. I think a friend of Madame LeGrand told me she was opening this place. That must be a good ten, eleven years ago now."

"The food looks fantastic."

"It surely is. My favourites include *quenelle de brochet;* it comes up to the thickness of my arm! And she prepares a heavenly *soufflé aux tourteau*. But you see, some of these dishes take time to prepare and Madame will serve you a slice of one of her pâtés while you wait."

Tara watched as nearly all conversation stopped when a soufflé was served to a couple at the next table. A golden cloud of whipped eggs with a rich crab lining and a light *salade au noix* was served in a giant glass bowl – enough for a whole table.

"So what will you have, Declan?" She began to feel a little nervous at her distinct lack of knowledge regarding Lyonnaise cuisine.

"The main dishes are just huge," Declan confided.

"So what will *I* have?" Tara mused, confused.

"Do you like beef?" Declan offered.

"Only well done. Can't stand that blood running out onto my plate, you know."

"Leave it to me then."

God, I love it when a man takes control!

Tara listened intently as Declan ordered their meal in fluent French and Madame LeGrand nodded rather than jotted down their requests.

Two glasses of wine later Madame LeGrand placed a *boeuf ficelle* in front of Tara. It looked like a Dutch master painting. Rolled loin of beef tied with string and poached, served with a huge marrowbone, a wine reduction sauce and cracked pepper and sea salt. Tara's tastebuds exploded as if feeling the sensations of textures and flavours for the first time.

To complete their meal, the small table almost buckled as a whole *crème caramel*, a bowl of *mousse au chocolat*, a bowl of *riz au lait*, a bowl of *bugnes* dusted in icing sugar, and a plate of *oeufs* à *la neige* with a vat of *crème anglaise* were placed before them.

"What's the story here, Declan? These are family-sized servings! Is it all for us?"

"Just take a spoonful here, and a scoop there."

As Tara slid her fork down through the *choux à la crème* Madame LeGrand approached with a whole *tarte au citron.* She cut a small slice and nudged aside the *choux à la crème* to make room on Tara's plate. The *choux* were pastry hot-air balloons with a silky almond cream filling to push them aloft and as Tara ate them she felt as if she was lifting off her seat. Declan tucked into a *bugne*, a crisp fritter which dissolved in his mouth into pure sweetness.

"But Declan," Tara whispered across the small round table, "the lemon tart – why did she serve only a small slice – should we leave it till last? Does it mean something?"

Declan just smiled, familiar with the intricacies of Madame LeGrand's repertoire. "Yes, leave it till last."

Anxious to try the *tarte au citron* Tara lowered her fork and broke off the tip of the slice. The lemon aroma wafted and as she bit into the soft yet firm tarte she experienced the perfect balance of tangy and sweet.

Feeling satisfied and full, Tara finished the last of the red wine and watched, slightly tipsy, as Declan paid the bill.

"Did you ever realise that Evian backwards is *naive*? Do you think it's all a cruel con?"

Tara knew she was slightly slurring her words, but was enjoying it. They were in New Morning on Rue des Petites-Ecuries, one of the most popular jazz venues in Paris.

"Do you know most of the top names have played here?" Declan was totally absorbed in his surroundings and the fantastic sounds of James Brown's tenor saxophonist getting it on with trombonist and old friend Fred Wesley.

As she cupped the red wineglass in her palm, Tara swigged down the remains. Before Declan could continue she came up with another interesting perspective. "*And* do you realise that, generally, Frenchmen aren't really worthy of Frenchwomen."

She was amusing him. He bit back the overwhelming urge to kiss her, wary of crossing the line between professionalism and friendship. He also didn't wish to be seen as taking advantage of her insobriety. He lightly took her hand as he responded, "And how do you figure that then?"

"Well," she wobbled on her stool, "take Frenchwomen – they're groomed and coiffed and styled! And then Frenchmen? They're either poncy-looking or dirty leering cardigan wearers!"

"Now you're exaggerating! Sure, look at her over there. Groomed, coiffed and styled! Yeah, right!"

Tara looked across at the doorway to see a woman whose g-string sat higher on her hips than her jeans, pushing ugly bulges of lardy white flesh out between the restrictions. She giggled as she reached across the table and lifted the empty wine bottle. She looked into the bottle with one eye clamped shut in a bid to see whether there was any at all left. There was none. She continued, nonetheless. "All I know is that I haven't seen *one man* that'd be fit to be in a martini ad. I feel cheated."

Declan laughed at her reasoning, feeling strangely protective of her in her semi-pissed state.

"So you're saying you judge a man by his appearance?"

"No. I'm saying that they don't look like the cliché, that's all."

"So, Tara, what is it you want from a man?"

"Declan," she leant in across the table, trying to focus blurry eyes on his handsome face, "I'm in desperate need of *intellectual* intercourse."

"Ha," he laughed, "so you *want* him to fuck your head?"

"No! I mean I want a man to give me mental orgasms . . ."

As they staggered back to the Métro at Château d'Eau, Tara clenching a plastic bottle of Evian, her inhibitions at linking Declan's arm were forgotten.

"Me feeet a kill'n me," she moaned, unable to walk straight after the day's researching and the night's dancing. The sultry sounds of the jazz club still ringing in her ears, she knew she'd had too much to drink and was necking the mineral water at a rapid speed.

It's lovely here.

Chapter 13

The walk back through the Latin Quarter, into the
dixième arrondisement to the Hôtel des Grandes Ecoles
went a good way towards sobering Tara up. That and
the mineral water she'd been drinking. She had begun
to feel slightly embarassed at dropping her professional
guard in front of Declan so soon and chided herself
about that. Their two single rooms were adjacent to
each other and Declan saw her into her room with a kiss
on the cheek and a smile. Tara kicked off her shoes,
liberating feet that had been feeling like two kilos of
corned beef squeezed into one-kilo tins. They throbbed
with relief as she padded across the room toward the
French windows which overlooked a leafy garden. The
wrought-iron filigree balcony was cool in the night air
and reflected a blue tinge beneath the moonlit sky. She
sat on the antique wooden chair on the balcony and
rested her hands upon the lace tablecloth which

covered the small round table in front of her. She closed her eyes and breathed in the slightly chilly night air.

I now realise what is meant by dealing with problems on neutral ground. There's a peace and serenity to be found by distancing yourself from your life. As my mind unravelled back to my disastrous marriage, it was less absorbing to reflect on it now.

Away from Dublin.

Her wedding day had been idyllic. Simon's job as a sales director had meant that he'd met many people and, Tara reasoned, had experienced a lot of the finer things in life.

He knew what would be just perfect for our wedding day. And he'd been right.

Except in his choice of bride, I thought wryly . . .

Tara poured the remains of the bottled water into a wineglass which rested on the small table. As she took a large sip of the by now lukewarm water she thought back further to Simon's parents. He'd been so upset that night when he'd told her the sad story of the massive family argument. They now lived in Chicago and he hadn't heard from them for over ten years. It was one of the very few things she'd been disappointed at on her wedding day – that she still hadn't met her mother and father-in-law. She'd always wanted a mother-in-law – someone who knew your husband as well as you did, someone to go shopping with.

No, perhaps not.

But at least someone to moan about.

I'd felt so sorry for him. He had so much love to give and was so distressed at his inability to patch up the terrible argument with his parents. He was never able to tell me what it was all about though. Poor old devil, it was just too painful for him . . .

Feeling saddened at the memories, she stood and glanced down into the quiet garden, amazed that she was actually in the midst of Paris, yet it seemed to be in the country. She looked at the old metal staircase that ran up alongside her window, and stretched her head out to see what was on the small landing above. She noticed an ugly external door, entitled *blanchisserie*. Grappling into her loose handbag for her French/ English dictionary she looked it up to find it meant *laundry*. She leaned toward the other side of the window, cheekily trying to see what she could of Declan in his room. As she overstretched, her grip on the iron balcony slipped and she knocked the table with her leg causing it to scrape on the floor. Embarassed that Declan would go to his window to check out the disturbance she swiftly closed the French windows, securing them with the quaint latch. She wished it had been warmer so that she could have left them open and maybe only closed the louvre doors either side of the window. At the foot of her bed was a small step leading up into her bathroom, the regulatory French plug-hole in the floor and a shower above it. Looking at her reflection in the small mirror by the bathroom window she decided against removing any slight traces of make-up that remained.

She was just too tired.

Sleep found her almost immediately. Peering through

the darkness at her watch she saw it was just past one in the morning. As her mind swam with muddled thoughts of Declan and Simon, jazz and bronze sculptures, she relaxed into a deep, peaceful sleep.

It seemed she'd slept for hours when she was woken by muted banging sounds. The few glasses of wine had delayed her waking, but once she'd tuned in, she could pick out a distinct sound of insistent although muted, banging on metal. Sitting up in the bed with a start she flicked on the bedside light, looking for the time. Quarter to three in the morning. She'd barely been asleep a couple of hours.

There it was again. The banging sound. Tara realised with a wave of intense panic that the banging was on her bathroom window. *Her* bathroom window! And this time could make out a man's voice insisting to the window, "*S'ouvrir! S'ouvrir! S'ouvrir!*" and with each declaration hitting on the rattling old metal window-frame. Sitting up in bed, her head spinning with fear, she listened, frozen at the sounds of this strange man who was trying to break into her bathroom. The sound of the ricketty window-frame bursting open jolted her into action and she screamed and attempted to get up, only to find that her feet were tangled in her bedsheets. Pulling at the sheets in her panic, she only tightened them. At last freeing herself, she grabbed her mobile and ran for the door, managing to open it, but then feeling her knees soften and a swarm of bees buzzing in her ears, filling her head with cotton wool . . .

She awoke to find herself slumped in the corridor

with Declan gently tapping her face. He'd heard her screams and run straight to her door, just in time to see it open and Tara fold into a heap, her legs and feet still in her room as she fell into the hallway. He'd already called the hotel staff and, as he helped her up and into his room, her room was already being inspected.

"Well, whoever it was, there's no sign of him now," he told her reassuringly.

Tara's terror returned and any remains of colour drained from her face.

"He was in my room," she whispered and then sobbed, "He was in my room. I couldn't get out of bed. My feet were tangled. I just couldn't get out."

Declan wrapped his two arms around her and hugged her as she sobbed against him.

The hotel manager appeared at the doorway, his face awash with apology, and his English perfect. "He has gone. There is no sign of him. I have called the gendarmes, but it seems clear that he climbed the external fire-stairs to try to break in through the laundry. He was breaking into the wrong room."

"*Any* room was the wrong room!" Declan suddenly felt angry at the situation. "We expected to feel safe and comfortable here and we clearly weren't. Look at the state of her. She's terrified!"

A gendarme appeared at the door, the holster on his belt housing a small black handgun, alarming Tara further. He smiled at her and spoke loudly to the hotel manager.

As he finished the manager said to Tara, "The

gendarme will watch the hotel for the rest of the night in case he returns. We have had this problem here before but have been unable to catch him. But it is safe for you to go back to your room, Madame."

"Safe!" she squealed. "How the hell can it be safe? What if he's angry at me for disturbing him now? He could be some drugged-up lunatic!" She turned to Declan and her expression switched from anger to fright, "What if he's coming back for me? I can't bear to be in there again."

Declan led the hotel manager into the hallway, explaining quietly that they'd deal with this matter in the morning. He came back and closed the door behind him.

Tara was sitting on the edge of the antique bed.

"Come on, Tara. You can stay in this room with me if you like. No funny business, I promise."

"I just can't go back in there. I'm fucking terrified now."

He sat and put his arms around her again, rocking her gently as she cried. Once again he resisted an overwhelming urge to kiss her on the top of the head. Her blonde hair was so soft and slightly ruffled from her sleep. He looked down at her and felt a disturbing movement in his jeans as he realised she was wearing only silk pyjamas. He broke free of the hug immediately. He'd thrown on his jeans and nothing else. The last thing he wanted was for Tara to be face to face with his swelling crotch! Well, he *did* want that, but this was severely bad timing.

He managed to calm her and reassure her by checking both his windows, looking down into the courtyard and the gardens and checking that the windows were locked. He switched on the small telly in the room and channel-hopped for something soothing. *France 2* was broadcasting an old cop series, *M6* brought an old, imported *Ally McBeal* into the room. He felt intrigued by French television and was slightly distracted to realise that the hotel also had cable and satellite channels. *Paris Première* featured a fashion show, *Planète* hosted a documentary, while *BBC Prime* showed an up-to-date *EastEnders*. He finally settled for *CNN* and it's 24-hour global news, the softened sounds providing a strangely relaxing backdrop. Tara had relaxed enough to move from the chair by the door onto the bed.

Declan's bed!

Her eyes were pink from the tears, but the colour was slowly returning to her cheeks.

"You know," she whispered to Declan, who sat on the edge of the bed, remote control in his hand, "I'd always kinda imagined a situation like this. You know, you'd try and plan what you'd do – how you'd be."

He turned to smile at her, "Yeah, and?"

"And I'd always thought I'd be a right *Charlie's Angel*. I'd leap up and karate-kick him in the balls. You know, a kind of 'How dare you disturb my sleep?' kind of thing?"

"And you didn't do that."

"No. I thought I'd be a *Charlie's Angel* and I was just a right 'Charlie'!"

She began to cry again. Declan moved up toward her on the bed and lay beside her, hugging her again, silently willing his willie to behave this time. She rested her head on his bare chest and he smoothed her hair gently.

"Look," he whispered, "Parisian sunrise."

Through the shutters the dawn sunrise shone onto their wall in orange stripes.

"Will I open the shutter and we can watch the sun rise?"

"Yeah, I'll be much happier when the darkness has gone."

Declan obliged and returned to the bed, lying on his side as Tara began to talk.

"Do you remember your childhood?"

"Yeah, seems ages ago now though. Why?"

"I don't think I've ever felt as safe as I did then. Apart from now. Here with you. I suppose that feeling was what I was trying to recreate by getting married."

"How?"

"I love that feeling of being safe. Of being cared for. Looked after."

"But it didn't work that way?"

"No. I messed it all up."

"So what do you remember of your childhood then? What were the good bits? Apart from the safe feeling?"

"Hopscotch."

"Hop-bloody-scotch!"

Tara giggled at his expression. "Yeah, skipping, handstands."

"Bet you couldn't do one now."

As they laughed Tara felt suddenly overwhelmed with tiredness and yawned. Declan lay with her and hugged her.

"Lie here with me and sleep. Probably the shock's hitting you now. I'll keep you safe, promise."

And Tara snuggled down in the warm sun-washed room, nestled into Declan's side.

I think I'm in love, I marvelled . . . he's so nice to be with . . . so nice and he hasn't even tried to lay a hand on me . . . it's obvious he's been hurt too . . .

The sounds of muffled footsteps from outside woke them. Declan stirred first, amazed that they hadn't moved position since they fell asleep at around five a.m. His watched displayed half past ten. He slid his arm from beneath Tara's neck and went to open the shutters and the windows. An indigo sky stretched above him. Tara stirred, contentedly.

It's going to be a fantastic day.

I just know it.

Two hours later, Tara looked on in admiration as Declan expertly purchased two Métro tickets for them.

"Deux cartes pour le jour seuelement, s'il vous plaît."

They exhausted the Latin Quarter of Paris on foot, visiting many contemporary design shops, places all well known to French interior designers and stylists. Tara had insisted to Declan, "Interior design-wise, the backstreets of Saint-Germain-des-Prés and the Latin Quarter are where we need to be! They're *full* of small boutiques."

Tara had delighted in Créateurs, a small shop whose mission it is to bring young artists to the attention of public without charging exorbitant prices. Maison des Designers gave Tara great insight into bringing a chic style to a kitchen. Declan had shook his head as she succumbed to buying a famous Alessi biscuit container. As they'd circuited Rue Saint Sulpice, Rue Lobineau, Boulevard Saint Germain and Rue Jacob, Tara had sketched and noted an abundance of ideas for the French themed *Home Is* feature. She'd noted Joseph Hoffmann glasses, Enzo Mari paper knives and a crystal bowl by Borek Sipek. She'd tried to avoid the cliché of the colourful furniture straight from a country house in Southern France, opting more for contemporary French designs with a determination to move on from Baroque and Art Deco styles. She realised a passion for Garouste and Bonetti, Van der Straeten, Dubreuil and Brazier-Jones that she hadn't realised existed.

By late afternoon they were heading for the Marais district which was sandwiched between Bastille and Les Halles. They needed to take the Métro from Mabillon to Rambuteau. As she walked arm in arm with Declan, feeling surprisingly comfortable, Tara realised that this was the Paris she'd intended for her honeymoon. The narrow streets of Marais were the epitome of French chic: little boutiques, shirt shops and amazing modern jewellery. Along Rue des Rosiers in the old Jewish quarter she found L'Eclaireur and Lolita Lempicka. In Rue des Francs-Bourgeois, she located Nina Jacob and close to the junction with Rue de Turenne she found a bag shop with the most amazing bags in all shapes and sizes, leather and synthetic.

Paris may have its Bon Marche, Galeries Lafayette, and Au Printemps, but when it comes to real shopping in Paris, forget the department stores and bury yourself in the backstreets of Marais . . .

Chapter 14

Ciara O'Rourke was barely able to lift her head from the suede beanbag that she lay on. Or rather, was sprawled across. One of the downsides to her quest for taking things one step further meant that she was now hooked on drug-cocktailing. Her swift dissatisfaction with things "new" made her forge ahead as one of the most inspirational contemporary designers. It also meant that the predictable highs that individual drugs brought to her now bored her. She still wanted something more. She'd heard from her London set about a "CK Sling", a combination of cocaine and the powerful tranquiliser ketamine. She'd wanted to try it. She detested being the last to know. That's what had upset her with the George and Den affair. She'd been the last to know. Declan O'Mahoney had known they hated metallics. She'd been the last to know. Again.

She was also one of the last to know that after recreational poly-drug use it would take days to come down. On her sofa lay the list she'd written after the phone call to London. It read:

Honey Oil Headbanger (Ecstasy & ketamine)

Disco Daiquiri (LSD & ketamine)

Blue Horse Haiwaiian (heroin & a tranquilliser such as Valium)

She was a professional.

She was a fool.

Ciara had spent her life trying to better everybody that she came into contact with. Even to the detriment of her friends and family. Her ambition had always been strong and huge, but her ruthlessness was ugly and it had alienated her from friends and family for years. If she had spoken to any of her London set for a reasonable length of time, she'd have learned that she was in for a mental and physical rollercoaster. The combination of a stimulant and a depressant would send her brain into overdrive. But she liked being out of control. Temporarily. Away from the public eye. She was tired of being in control. Sick of it. A light breeze blew in through the open window, gently lifting her fringe and moving it slightly. It blew her list onto the floor. The page flicked over.

CK One (ready-mixed combination of crack cocaine and ketamine)

Brown & White (heroin & cocaine)

Vicodin or Vike (US prescription painkiller, replacing cocaine in Hollywood celebrity circles)

As she drifted into an almost unconscious sleep she

was unaware that her phone was ringing. It rattled and vibrated in her pocket.

Her brain did the same thing inside her skull.

Declan pressed the button on his Nokia to disconnect the call.

"Well?" Tara asked. He'd never seen her so relaxed.

"No answer. She's probably busy with some young lad or something." They laughed at his jokey tone, but both suspected he could be right. It was now late afternoon and they were almost finished their research in the Marais district. Tara had three notepads full of sketches, comments and ideas on contemporary French designers whom she felt a passion for, new and established. As she completed her notes in Via, she viewed the current thematic exhibition. Via was not merely a shop, but also a gallery where you can see the latest trends in the French furnishings industry. The exhibition changed every six weeks, focusing on different subjects. Tara and Declan had both fallen in love with the building itself, located under the arches of an old viaduct.

There was only one fly in the ointment as far as Declan was concerned: he'd wanted Ciara's advice on the kitchen for the French-style makeover. Despite Tara's flair for interior design, he'd really have liked Ciara's expertise. Or, to put it another way, he was nervous about what would happen when Ciara found out she'd been side-lined . . . Now Tara was on the verge of making a decision for the makeover – it seemed he would have to give her a free rein.

Ciara would be the last to know.

"I am totally knackered!" Tara laughed as they sat in The Quiet Man, one of a large selection of Irish pubs in Paris. "The trouble is my head is still buzzing! I'm mad to get out there and look for more ideas. Shame my feet don't feel the same way."

"Don't stress, we've done marvellously today. You've nearly four books full of ideas. Feel any preferences yet? Got the form sorted in your head for this makeover?"

"Completely sorted!" She oozed confidence in a way that Declan hadn't noticed before. "But is that OK? Or would you like me to discuss this with Ciara first?"

"Well, of course, you will need to do that when the time comes."

As they sipped at their drinks Declan took in the surroundings of The Quiet Man. He found it hard to believe they were actually in Paris and not in Kerry or somewhere in the west of Ireland. They'd already been into Coolín, an Irish pub with a totally different atmosphere, when they'd exhausted the Latin Quarter. Where The Quiet Man was supposedly authentic Irish, Coolín seemed to successfully combine chic Parisian café culture with the energy and spontaneity of new generation Irish. They'd sat on the large terrace on this tranquil left-bank street and discussed how they wished there was enough time to come back one evening to see its transformation into a rocking pub with live DJ's. They both knew that a couple of days in Paris was far from enough.

They also knew that any more time spent together could easily push the boundaries of their professional relationship.

"I'd love to head back to our hotel for a quick freshen up before we go out tonight. Do you mind?" Tara asked Declan.

He smiled at her. "Of course! Fancy Crème tonight?" he asked, with a smirk on his face.

"What? Crème? What's that?"

"Just another restaurant I know. Reckon you'll like it."

Since when did it matter what I liked?

"Jesus, Niamh, look!"

Anna turned the pages toward Niamh, her face drained with dread at what she'd just discovered. They were back in the General Register Office trying to find more information on Slimey Simey. Niamh scanned the directory to locate the source of Anna's horror. There it was in small black print.

"4th September 2000, Simon Anthony Cullen, Howth, aged 34."

"You're not bloody serious!" Niamh shouted, much to Anna's embarassment.

"Sssh, will ya! 'Course I'm serious. It's there in black and bloody white! But what does *this* mean?"

"It means," Niamh hissed, "that bastard has been married *twice* before!"

"The question is," whispered Anna, "has he been divorced twice before?"

They took the book for the third quarter of 2000 back to the desk where the clerk behind the counter was now on first-name terms with Niamh and Anna.

"Finished?" she asked with a happy face.

"Yeah," Niamh replied, somewhat preoccupied, "thanks. Could you put in this code please."

The clerk typed it in and wrote down the full details, handing them to Niamh.

Anna was surprised to see that Niamh's hand was shaking as she took the paper.

"Mary Ryan. The bastard!" She turned to face the clerk again, "So if you *were* divorced and wanted to get married again, how do you do that?"

"Well, you have to give at least three months written notification to the Registrar for the district in which the marriage is to take place. If either party has been previously married they have to produce either a Divorce Decree – Absolute – or a death cert."

"That's if they *admit* they've been married before," Niamh confirmed.

"Of course. They have to fill in a form consenting to disclose any impediment as to why the marriage can't go ahead," replied the clerk, who they now knew to be Jenny.

"Bastard!" spat Niamh as she pushed the phone number into her jeans pocket.

"Niamh, it's no good losing your temper." Anna tried to calm the situation, ever fearful of Niamh and her hot head.

Jenny whisked the register from the desk and turned

to slot it back into its rightful place. As she turned back to face them she saw Anna link arms with Niamh, as if to calm her down.

"You know," joked Anna in Jenny's direction, "men are bastards. They're like holidays," she quipped in a girly-let's-be-pals kind of way, "they never seem to be long enough."

Jenny blushed and went back to her work, but not before hearing Niamh's bitter comment as they exited.

"Yeah, the bastards are more like bank accounts – withdrawn and rapidly losing bloody interest."

She looked stunning. Declan actually caught his breath as she opened her door to his light knock at seven thirty. Every time he looked at her she seemed more beautiful. And then, slightly embarassed at his admiration, she stuck out her tongue cheekily at him, revealing the dazzling piercing once again.

"Are you coming in? Or do you want to stand out there all evening? I don't bite, you know."

Feeling slightly awkward at his gawping, he lightly cleared his throat, entered the room and closed the door behind him.

"Em, you look fantastic."

She smiled, "Thank you."

He watched as she smeared on a light glossy lipstick and admired her silently. The beaded silk chiffon dress with spaghetti straps really skimmed over her hips in a most flattering way. And he noticed that when she walked the "kick" of the gathers at the calf-length hem really gave her a sexy sassiness. She pulled on a pair of tan, knee-length high-heeled boots. He knew that if it was Paula standing there in front of him, she'd put on a strappy pair of high sandals to go with the dress. But that was what he loved about Tara. She was even sexier because of her refusal to do what was expected.

They were booked in for eight thirty and arrived ten minutes early. Tara would never have noticed the restaurant – its small, inconspicuous door was virtually invisible amongst the neon lights of Paris at night. But once inside she realised that the jazz soundtrack, the handsome grey interior and the friendly welcome were a winning combination.

As they sat down, enjoying the friendly welcome and the saxophone-swamped soundtrack, Declan said, "Saw him at Vicar Street."

"Who," she teased, "the waiter?"

"Ha ha ha," he pulled a face thick with sarcasm. "No, Jim Byron. He's been voted 'Best Saxophonist'."

"Ah, you can't beat great sax!" she joked. "I love the saxophone. I'd love to have a go at playing it."

"It's supposed to be quite difficult. It relies on a mouthpiece and a single reed, just like a clarinet, to produce the vibration. It's mad really, a brass instrument, being a woodwind."

Tara was lost and turned the conversation back to Jim Byron. "Yeah, that Jim Byron is good. You know, I could get into this jazz thing. There's only one problem though. I still don't get it."

"It's not there to be 'got'. It's kind of musical

improvisation. There are so many instruments and styles, you're bound to find one that clicks with you." He paused and then asked, "Have you ever heard of the festival at Marciac?"

"No. What's that?"

"It's a French jazz festival. It's fantastic."

"Have you ever been to it?"

"Twice. Look, forget New Orleans, Marciac is one of the world's best music festivals. And it's hidden away in a beautiful corner of south-west France – in Gascony."

"But isn't New Orleans the jazz-capital of the world?"

"That's what I'd always thought – until I found Marciac."

Tara smiled, and leaned across the table slightly. "So," she glowed in the half-light, awash with hormones, "how long is it on for?"

"A fortnight. It's magic. I think there are more ducks in Gascony than people – every field and farm you pass by has a 'foie gras sold here' sign outside. And the duck-related produce! Fritons de canard, confit de canard!"

"Mmmm . . . sounds amazing."

"It's usually on in August. The town's poshest hotel is the Hôtel de Bastard. Maybe we'll stay there?"

She raised an eyebrow. "Really. And who is 'we'?"

"You and me. If you decide to come with me, that is."

Excited, all she could do was smile.

Despite the bustling restaurant they never once, in the three and a half hours spent there, felt rushed or awkward. They dined on an hors d'oeuvre of lobster bisque followed by starters of grilled scallops and salad and roasted langoustines. Overcome by the romantic mood, stimulating company and fine food Declan suggested champagne.

"The vintage?" he asked Tara, as the courteous waiter hovered.

"Why not?" she grinned, "After all, it's been a long time."

Tara felt a heady, almost romantic feeling as she looked into Declan's sparkling eyes over the popping of the champagne bubbles and candlelight.

They moved on to a quiet bar where they began to learn more about each other. It seemed their mutual politically-incorrect interests began with cigarettes, Tara enjoying the French Camel brand whilst Declan preferred Gitânes. Their conversation was interrupted by an almost chocolate-brown market trader carrying around wooden carvings and figurines with a distinct ethnic, even tribal appearance to them. Tara was intrigued by the carvings of a small male figure and bartered the price down to nine euro, which she handed over willingly.

"You know," she giggled into her wine as she eyed the wooden figurine, "he kinda looks a bit like Simon."

Declan was surprised at the mentioning of his name. He'd deliberately avoided the subject for fear of upsetting her, yet she seemed keen to discuss it now.

She continued, "He was always kind of stiffened up. Uptight, I suppose you'd call it. I don't really know why I wanted to marry him. He was so bloody precise about everything. Right from the start I felt like he was almost booking in time with me. He'd be forever consulting his poxy leather diary and marking off days here and there."

"Didn't you see much of him at all then?"

"Not really. He was a sales director and that meant he was constantly travelling around Ireland. Sometimes he'd go to London or Manchester for a few days too. But he always made me feel like I was second fiddle to his work. Still," her tone dropped to a mere whisper, "no reason for treating him like shit though, is it?"

"How do you mean?" Declan desperately wanted to find out more, but didn't want to push it too far.

"Declan," she placed her hands on the table and looked him square in the eye, "I had a bloody affair. There. You've got it in one. Not even married a year and I had an affair."

"But why? There must have been a reason!"

"Yeah," Tara shook her head and picked up her drink, downing it in one, "there must have been. But I don't know what it was."

He leant across and took her hand in his, smoothing its pale skin affectionately, "Tara, you're no cruel woman. Don't berate yourself so easily. You're a kind, considerate and fun lady."

"Lady!" she smiled in mock amazement, feeling tears spring to her eyes.

"Well, OK then – girl?" he teased. "You know, they say that voodoo is a great way to rid your mind of torments. You could start on that doll there. Especially if he's so much like him."

Tara laughed and ceremoniously named the doll "Simon" and then proceeded to poke at his bum and head with her cocktail stick.

Relieved that the conversation had lightened up a little, Declan then went on to make another suggestion. "How are you feeling then, after the day we've had?"

"I've had so much wine I can't feel beyond my knees. So I must be fine!"

"OK then, fancy a bit of a jig?"

"A jig?"

"A little ould dance? Thought we might head for Batofar."

"What's that? God, you know everything about this city, don't you?"

"Not quite," he replied softly. "But I want to do everything – it's so much more fun with someone as lovely as you."

OK, I'll admit it, I said to myself. I like him. I'll fall in love with him, and he'll be nice to me and then it'll settle into a routine and then what?

It's just not worth the heartache . . .

"So Batofar it is then. But where is it?"

"It's a bright red tugboat moored near the Bibliothèque Nationale de France."

"OK, in English. Please?"

"It's a rollicking dance-spot on the River Seine. Top quality DJ's and there's even a Batofar bus to take you home. It's a bit hardcore, but hey – it can't all be jazz."

Sure, I was probably ten years too old, but fuckit!

Chapter 15

Niamh's head throbbed in percussion to the click of her boots as she strode along Grafton Street. The Long Johns had been as fantastic as usual and she'd left the The Yacht with Adam. She cursed herself for drinking the vodka last night and despised herself for playing passion roulette.

Once again.

Sex without a condom just *wasn't* what she should be at. Not when she was looking for a good-looking guy with an arse-pocket full of euros. Or pounds, or yen or dollars. C'mon, she wasn't *that* fussy! It had all been fine until Adam had actually rung rather than text her. She hadn't really intended to go. She was tired and jaded after the revelations about her best friend's bigamous husband and was yearning for a quiet night in with a bottle of red. Or two. But when he'd rung, making her laugh and, more scarily, making her feel old for wanting to stay in she decided she needed the company. Especially with Tara away. It had been going great guns until they'd decided to go back to her place and then he'd nipped out and returned with a large bottle of vodka and a rather small bottle of lemonade. And so, as she confided in him about the revelations of Slimey Simey, one thing led to another.

As he'd pulled on his jeans that very morning, preparing to go to work, he'd turned at the doorway of Niamh's bedroom and joked, "But, Niamh, I won't have it. If my boss tells me one more time! She's accusing me of being truculent. Truculent! Stupid bitch, I mean I can't even *drive!*"

She laughed at him and threw a cushion at the closing door.

Rubbing at her temples, she mentally prepared herself to meet the record company's new protégé whom she was to "shoot" and prayed that he wouldn't be yet another boy-bandy geek. As a supposed runner-up at last year's Pop Sensation she supposed that he'd have a shelf-life of about nine months. Walking down Grafton Street she listened to the street musicians of Dublin – some fetching, some retching – as she pondered over Carolyn's advice on attracting monied-men. She'd suggested that Niamh swap her jeans for a pencil skirt, a cashmere jumper and court shoes. She'd insisted it was the perfect way to get the wave from the passing Bentleys. Niamh wasn't so sure she'd fit with the image and had began to even doubt her lust-for-the-upper-crust when she'd told her not to play too hard to get. "Millionaires are far too busy to be messed around."

To the melody of "Eternal Flame" she stopped at a newsagent's and pulled a twenty euro from her jacket pocket and asked for twenty scratchcards. It had been some time now since her last scratchcard-addiction phase. Looked like another was starting up. As she scratched, she reiterated her belief that every woman has a check-list when looking for a man and that money was at the top of hers. In the meantime she'd take photos and scratch at lotto tickets – ever hopeful. She scratched at sixteen of them, discarding the pile of grey shavings and the useless tickets, and shoved the last few into her pocket, reprimanding herself now for wasting the twenty euro, and continued her walk. "Of course," she daydreamed as she rejoined the walking masses, "I want a 'D4' really." As Dublin's most desirable postcode she'd set her sights on a man who lived there, or in Dalkey. She often drove around the village of charm, which had been dubbed by the media Bel-*Eire* or Dalkeywood due to the influx of international celebrities choosing to buy homes there. She'd usually park her car and walk past Dalkey Island along Coliemore Road until she reached the most exclusive address in Dublin – Sorrento Terrace. She admired the great houses carved out of the hill which faced the view that had often been compared to the Bay of Naples.

Turning off Grafton Street and down a side street she was overcome by the smell of a wet skip, a huge stinking carpet overflowing from it. Her thoughts had now turned to her concern about Tara. The smell of the wet carpet must have brought on thoughts of Simon –

that already-been-married-twice husband of hers. She knew that she and Anna would have to talk to Tara soon. She pulled out her phone and set a couple of reminders. The first was to contact Anna and agree when they'd tell Tara and the second was to buy a couple of bottles of wine so that she could welcome Tara back from Paris tonight. She knew she had to get home early tonight to clean up. She had every intention of intercepting Tara on her way back from the airport and *insisting* that she call around to Niamh before she went home. She had a load of clearing up to do at home, but she couldn't wait to sit down with Tara and pull the bones of the Paris trip apart. It was so obvious Declan fancied her. She turned into an old stone building, the converted warehouse where the photo-shoot was to take place. She'd already sent her equipment there with the photographic assistant who had brought two of her friends along to watch. "Do you mind?" she had squeaked.

"Only if they're quiet and stay out of the way." Niamh retorted, immediately switching into professional mode. She asked her assistant to set up the equipment while she scratched at the last four grey lotto cards with her thumbnail, prior to going over to meet the record company rep. Niamh's assistant watched as she concentrated on the few cards and, showing off to her onlooking pals, teased, "Niamh, really! How many scratchcards do you have there? Must be costing you a fortune!"

Niamh was irritated at her sudden outspokenness,

suspecting she was showing off in front of her friends. The nervous adolescent onlookers were huddled like pool-cues stacked against a pub wall as Niamh retorted, with a glare, "Yeah, don't worry, I'm not pulling it from your pocket!"

Approaching the small office at the back of the shoot venue Niamh confidently stepped in over the doorstep to see an exquisite young lady, nothing like the styled yet vaguely spotty teenager that she'd been expecting.

As Niamh began the shoot, she delighted as Dublin's newest black soul singer needed only slight instruction to be near perfect – she was a natural. Niamh really enjoyed this type of shoot, where everything seemed to flow to perfection. She had given the singer a few hints prior to the shoot and was extremely pleased to find that she'd only needed to be told once.

"Posture improves with time – see early Spice Girls or Madonna. Being relaxed is vital and hands are an unnecessary distraction – they should be clasped or behind your back."

Fulfilled and excited about developing her six rolls of film, Niamh left her assistant packing up the bags whilst she nipped out for just another twenty euros worth of scratchcards. As she stepped from the cool, stone building into the warm sunshine she watched as a magpie pecked at something caught between two cobbles. She made a conscious effort to look at him twice. "One for sorrow, two for joy," she whispered to herself. She was a great believer in doctoring proverbs and kidded herself that if you see the one magpie, you can look at it twice and pretend you've seen two.

Declan checked his watch – still a few hours before they needed to leave for the airport. Perfect. He'd had every intention of getting some personal business attended to during his short stay and had planned to do it that morning, but after a great night at Batofar they had slept rather late and had both been slightly the worse for wear all day. He glanced sideways at Tara as she scribbled furiously in her fifth notepad while they walked along. His mouth smiled involuntarily – it always did when he looked at her. She made him feel that way.

"There's something that I need to look into now," he said.

"Oh yeah, and that is?" She continued to write.

He wondered how she'd ever be able to read it once back home.

"I've been thinking of buying a property here."

"Oooh, more money than you care to mention, eh? Well, look, if it's burning a hole in that pocket of yours . . ?"

He took her hand, steadying its frantic movement. The pen remained suspended between her fingers.

"The thing about money, Tara, is that the Beatles were dead right."

"Eh?"

"It can't buy you love."

"Did the Beatles say that?"

He ignored her question. The truth was he wasn't too

sure – they'd sung something about buying love, but he wasn't confident enough to be quizzed on it. He carried on, "Money *can't* buy love. But a lack of money, especially in our materialistic society, burns away at people's values and self-respect. And it's the values and self-respect that make fulfilling relationships possible."

She pulled on his arm to stop him.

"What?" he asked, looking slightly awkward at his own profoundness. She leant forward and kissed him lightly on the cheek.

"You're a lovely man, Declan. And what you've said is very, very true." She raised her pen-clad hand as if holding a glass of something, "Here's to values and self-respect!"

"You're taking the piss."

"Declan." She caught his hand and held it firmly. "I surely am not. If only there were more people in the world like you! She turned her head away as she felt a gush of heavy tears speeding their way to her eyes. She whispered, still clutching his hand, "If only more people respected others' values then so many people wouldn't get hurt."

He changed the subject. "I've been speaking with an estate agent about properties in Paris and I've found out a few interesting things." He scanned his pocket map as they strolled, trying to seek out the Métro station Brochant. "It seems that while British and Irish buyers are usually delighted with period features on Parisian properties, they are often disappointed by the quality of specifications."

Tara was interested. "Such as?"

"Well, often the electrics are out of date and the kitchens aren't usually very good quality. And then, of course French bathrooms are another hurdle. Compared to what we're used to they tend to be cramped, and often flats are only equipped with the one. Mind you, having said that, I could get a cheap loft in the seventh *arrondissement* which I could afford to do some work on."

"It sounds fabulous!"

"Or a quiet turn-of-the-century apartment in an old freestone building in the seventeenth *arrondissement* for roughly €110,000. I've seen the brochure on it and there's a living-room, one bedroom, a bathroom, kitchen, cellar *and* a view."

Tara's eyes were wide open with excitement.

I wanted to go and look at these places!

"So where's the seventeenth *arrondissmement*?"

He checked his map again. "Slightly north-west of Montmartre. Fancy a look around? "Or," he'd now taken out some folded papers from his pocket and was reading from them, "a large, one-bedroomed apartment on the second floor of an eighteenth century block in the Marais. Close to the Pompidou centre – could cost me up to €360,000 though."

"Buy it!"

He folded the paper up, laughing, "Yeah, sure. God, I'm thirsty, fancy stopping for a drink first?"

"Great."

They stopped at a pavement café and sat in the window to enjoy a quick drink, their continuous conversation punctuated by the squeaks of the gendarmes on the street. There were two of them, with whistles permanently stuck in their mouths and guns resting in holsters on their hips. As always, it slightly unnerved Tara.

Relaxed with each other and entertained by the passing parade of people, they lingered over their drinks and then ordered another, eventually deciding there wasn't quite enough time left to go flat-viewing.

"Perhaps we'll make that another trip?" said Declan. She smiled at his cheek.

He took her for a walk past the Louvre and then on through the Jardins des Tuileries and beyond. She enjoyed this elegant and imposing part of Paris with its wide open spaces and views through to the Place de la Concorde.

Nearly two hours later, he eventually dragged her back to the hotel. The taxi would be soon arriving to return them to the airport.

"You know, a wonderful place to visit around Christmas is the Patinoire de l'Hôtel de Ville."

"What's there then?"

"An outdoor ice rink in front of the city hall. It's there till the end of February usually."

"That sounds fantastic! It's a bit Rockefeller Center, isn't it? Pity it's not Christmas! I'd feel like I was in New York or somewhere." She smiled, Doris-Day'ing at him.

See? My Christmas bulimia could be cured! It was possible that Declan's presence could rid me of my nausea around the festive season.

"Don't worry, perhaps we'll come at Christmas and do it then. Mind you, there's usually one at Smithfield in Dublin. It's fantastic at night – it's all lit up by the thirty-metre-high gas braziers."

"We *have* to go. How long's it there for?"

"Usually until mid-January. We'll make it a date, eh?"

Can you see me saying no?

"Ready for the airport then?"

"Never. But what choice do I have?"

It was tearing at me now to distance myself from Declan.

It would be hard – especially now he'd tempted me with the excitement of helping him find his Parisian pad. I mean how many times in your life are you asked to help someone spend a quarter of a million euro? I was determined to regain the professional working relationship that we left for Paris with. Instead, as I sat on that boring plane sipping orange juice, I knew that he'd enjoyed my company too.

She could now see the rooftops of Dublin and the Liffey snaking through the city and she was no further toward reverting to their professional manner than she was in Paris. The hotel room break-in had brought them closer together than they had anticipated and she was still reeling.

On arrival at Dublin Airport Declan hauled her luggage from the baggage-reclaim carousel, and she blushed slightly as he grimaced on lifting it.

I told Niamh I was taking too much. How embarrassing! I could tell by his pained expression that he couldn't believe I packed so much for just a few days.

As Declan watched the selection of bags for his own, Tara waited with her gigantic suitcase. She watched as Declan pulled his light sportsbag from the carousel and rested it down beside Tara's case. She was alarmed at how it was dwarfed by hers and grabbed the handle to push her one forward. Without conversation they made their way through customs amongst a variety of tourists. Tara always loved the airport catwalk of arrivals.

You see, Irish skin simply wasn't created for sun-worship. I looked to my right and saw a bustle of sombrero'd holidaymakers. And then to my left? A sleek figure, its freckled tones clad in couture-cut silk pants and jewelled sandals.

Tara was watching a hen-party arrival, their blotchy skin and sunburn indicative of the sun and sangria'd time they'd had. Dressed in Penney's shorts and their sea-ravaged jellies it was obvious that they'd left in a hurry. They looked like they needed a week to recover from it and Tara wondered when the wedding was. The sight of them bought back memories of her own hen-night which had been fantastic. They'd spent the weekend in O'Callaghan's bar and Tara couldn't remember much about it other than a huge collection of chocolate willies and monstrous bridal wear that Niamh, Anna and their other friends had conjured up.

I'd been told it was a great craic anyway.

I couldn't remember much about it all.

Her voyeurism was interrupted by Declan.

"It's still only early. Fancy Mange Tout? Seared beef

with blue cheese and salad leaves? That's my favourite anyway."

God, I'd have loved to! Any excuse to spend more time with him.

"Oh, I'm sorry, Declan, but I really want to get home now. I was hoping to prepare all my research for tomorrow."

"But Tara, the French job in Dingle isn't for another six weeks!"

"I know, but I've done prep for the next job and, in any case, I need to write down this lot from today whilst I can still decipher my scribble. I kinda wanted to hit the ground running with Ciara, you know."

He stopped and tenderly touched her shoulder, causing her to let go of the trolley and turn to face him.

"I really enjoyed it, you know."

"Me too."

"Maybe we can spend some time together alone again?"

Tara shifted. She so much wanted this. "Look, Declan. I really enjoy being with you. But you know what happened in my marriage – you know what kind of a person I am. This opportunity for me with *Home Is* – I just don't want to ruin it. Let me go at my pace, eh?"

He smiled, warmly, unfazed by her hesitation.

"No problem, Tara. And don't worry about our working relationship. I am, in fact, the king of tact. No-one will ever know what a fantastic time we had in Paris – for the benefit of the *Home Is* team, it was all completely professional."

"Even Batofar?" she teased.

"Like I said, king of tact. I have the enviable ability to make guests feel at home – when that's exactly where you wish they were!"

She smiled and, oblivious to the crowds around them, leant forward and hugged him. "Thanks, Declan."

"No worries. C'mon, I'll walk you to your car. There's no way you'll be able to lift that monstrosity of a suitcase into your boot."

She allowed him to take the trolley and they made light conversation as they walked through the breezy multi-storey. She pressed the remote key which caused her headlights to flash a few times as they approached her car, and she watched as Declan opened the boot and painlessly lifted the huge case and placed it inside.

"There. I'd offer to meet up at your place to help you in with it, but I wouldn't push my luck."

"Right. You're dead right," she laughed.

"OK then, see you tomorrow at work?"

"Fine. And Declan?" He turned to face her. "Thanks for a great time."

He smiled and leant forward to kiss her cheek.

"Tara. Just remember this old saying: it doesn't much signify whom one marries, for one is sure to find the next morning that it was someone else."

She blushed. "Meaning?"

"Meaning," he whispered, his whiskers grazing against her soft cheek, "you're not as much to blame as you think you are. Meaning – things happen for a reason."

I pondered on that for hours after. The "things happen for a reason" thing. If that was really the case then all Declan had done was to worsen my dread that Simon would rear his ugly head and ruin my five minutes of fame. It's an exciting gut-churning time, starting to be famous. I'd body-slammed from chronic diarrhoea to days of a dry spell since I'd started on Home Is. I suppose the culmination of nerves and excitement does it. And then there was the way that people had started to recognise me on the street. It's funny really, their reaction. There are neighbours of mine who have completely ignored my presence for years, who now take delight in a wave as they drive past, or a "hello" in the corner shop. The four-page spread in the RTÉ Guide went a long way toward it. It's strange how affected by the media we all are. You know, I hadn't really realised until now. So given that "things happen for a reason", I was now in a state of anxiety worrying whether Simon had heard the news of my RTÉ links and I was expecting a kiss-and-tell any day now. So I still couldn't fully enjoy my new-found kind of fame, because I was fretting. And then there were the exes. Loads of them! I was already cringing at the prospect of opening up the News of the World to see my acne'd teenage gob plastered across the pages, with the likes of Tommy or Paddy's stories about how we got pissed at seventeen and then went at it like rabbits in my parent's bed! Or even how we used to go for expensive meals and then clamber out of the toilet windows to do a runner. It was really only a matter of time before Simon revealed what a lousy cheating wife I really was. And how I couldn't even make it to our first anniversary.

It was only a matter of time before the bubble burst.

Chapter 16

At ten thirty, two days later, Niamh and Tara were entering the lift at the RTÉ studios, ready for a briefing of the next makeover.

At the same time the Jack Russell who belonged to Ciara's neighbours, and who usually barked at every slight sound, was quietly but resolutely dragging his backside along Ciara's small back lawn.

In the west of Ireland, at exactly the same time, a young woman was ringing the Irish Adoption Service looking for her natural mother.

Whilst this was all going on, on the northside of Dublin, a tabloid photographer was developing his own photographs under the red lights of the dark room in his studio. As a contorted image of the celebrity interior designer's face emerged on the Kodak paper, the young man smiled.

"Mizzz O'Rourke," he whispered to the developing

photograph as it swooshed in the tray beneath the solution, "I never realized you still had it in you."

Over the years Ciara's drug abuse had worsened her unsociable tendencies. Flashing her new bracelet under Niamh, Tara and Handyman-John's eyes she gloated, "Mikimoto – originator of cultured pearls – New Bond Street, London. The Gala Collection, prices *from* £5,100 – *sterling!*"

"Yeah, right. You think we *care*?" deadpanned Niamh.

They turned their backs on Ciara and continued their conversation. Ciara was intensely irritated at the way they ignored her, trying to belittle her, and with nearly eight grand in euros worth of pearls on too! She brazenly re-entered the conversation,

"So Tara, how did you get on in Paris? Of course, I hope you're not too naïve to realise that there's absolutely no such thing as a free lunch."

"Pardon?" Tara turned to Ciara, her stomach flipping at the insinuation that she'd one day have to pay for such a great time with Declan or perhaps even that she'd be called to task regarding her interior-design opportunity.

Ciara knew she had her attention and attempted to reel her in.

"Well, you hardly think that Declan doesn't expect some kind of 'return' on his investment, do you? And you a married woman? Oh, sorry, should I say, separated woman?"

"Bye, Ciara!" Niamh sang, turning her back on her

and dragging Tara's arm around so that she followed suit.

Ciara wasn't to be ignored so easily this time.

"I've heard he doesn't even know the basics, like, should I swallow before kissing?"

Tara reddened, too embarassed to confront her nastiness.

Niamh laughed, retorting, "Oh fuck off, you shabby imposter! I mean, look at yourself! If you jumped up and down you'd bloody rattle! You're like a bloody duty-free shopper with your logo'd bag and sunglasses and contrived jewellery. Remind me, Ciara, what kind of image *did* you intend to put across?"

Ciara exploded. "How *dare* you! How dare you! Do you realise how much these cost me? You have absolutely no idea what you're on about. You're nothing but a second-class –"

"C'mon," Niamh interrupted Ciara's outburst and tugged at Tara to walk away with her. "Here, try a couple of these for luck." She handed a few scratchcards to Tara. "Anything to take your mind off that lunatic."

Tara glanced, amazed at the bulk of scratchcards that Niamh had pulled from the left thigh pocket of her combats. There had to be at least forty in there.

"Libya? I didn't touch her, Libya!"

"OK," Declan interrupted the cackles of Niamh and John as he caught the end of the joke. "Thanks, John, I think we all get the idea of what *that* was all about. OK, so job number six takes us to Galway, Clarinbridge. Nine miles from the city centre in a beautiful location where Clarinbridge river enters the oyster beds of Galway Bay."

"Mmmm," Niamh interrupted, "Clarinbridge, oysters."

"You know," Ciara couldn't help but join in, "Clarinbridge oysters are justifiably among the most famous in the world. I simply love the festival! Never miss it."

"Well," Niamh smirked, "looks like you've missed it this year. Hasn't it just ended?"

Ciara scowled as Niamh continued, "Of course, Ciara, the aphrodisiac qualities wouldn't play any part in dragging you there, would they?"

Ciara simply pulled a face at Niamh.

"They look awful though," Tara stated. "I've seen people at the Saturday market at Meeting House Square eating them, slurping them. Prying open the shell and throwing the insides down their necks. *Urrgh!* I couldn't!"

Declan smiled and winked at Tara. She blushed at the double entendre.

Ciara took the reins, "'Course you could. Tip the entire contents, salty watery stuff and all, into your mouth and don't chew. Just let it sit there for a moment . . . and let it *sliiiiide* back down your throat."

Niamh had to say nothing, but just open her eyes wide toward Ciara for a split second. Ciara knew well enough what she was just dying to say and so promptly changed the subject.

"So, what's the brief?" Ciara showed off.

"New house – see the slides."

Declan nodded to his assistant to hit the lights as he led them through the slides.

"Large and airy entrance hall, glass panels between that and the dining-room. Colour and warmth added by wall hanging. Extremely minimalistic and clean. Yet warm. Ash flooring and chrome bannisters."

Ciara blurted, "Christ, doesn't anyone realise? Minimalism has had its day – decadence is back, flashy is forté. It's all about the 'in-yer-face' brassy and ostentatious look now."

"Nothing like you then, eh, Ciara?" Niamh couldn't resist.

Declan swiftly continued. "They'd like to Feng Shui the bedroom. Perhaps an oriental theme, recognising the difference between Chinese and Japanese styles."

He showed a detailed slide of the bedroom.

"It's a very lofty and spacious room, but needs to be bought to life."

"So we're looking at the high-street style *again* then?" Ciara sneered, leaning back and folding her arms, "Well, roll in the MDF – hell! At least the monkeys will be busy."

Everyone ignored her arrogance. The three handymen on the *Home Is* team were far from being monkeys. Tara stared at Ciara from across the table.

She really was a wreck lately, what with her chapped lips and bleeding lipstick. It was such a shame, she could be so nice. I couldn't understand why she's so angry at everyone.

The rumour was that even her agent was getting fed up with her bad attitude.

Tara suggested Farrow & Ball paints, their subtle, muted tones excellent for the minimalistic look. Ciara laughed.

"No love, Farrow & Ball aren't at all right for an oriental theme. Seriously, *do* you want this to reek 'high street'? I'd go for the Kelly Hoppen Perfect Neutrals range. The Shell, Limestone and Incense shades would be a perfect backdrop. And it would still fall into that over-rated 'minimalistic' category."

See, she really did know her stuff. I could learn so much from her. If only she was a little more approachable.

Tara made notes to check on the Bonsai Shop in Powerscourt and to look in Kinsella Interiors in Bray for some Ming-styled Irish furniture.

"I would suggest," Declan sat as he talked, "that subtlety is the key here. We're talking bamboo on the windowsills rather than red lettering stencilled on the walls. Still, I'll leave you to look into it, you have a few days. We're heading up on Friday, we'll spend the weekend getting to know the place and then we start filming on Monday."

He handed out the detailed paperwork and photographs to the team and they grappled with them enthusiastically. Declan sat back with his arms folded and watched as a long strand of hair, usually tucked neatly behind Tara's ear, fell forward onto her face as she read.

He hadn't felt his stomach do a somersault for years.

And here it was virtually auditioning for the I'm-in-love Olympics.

Tara was relieved to be home. After such a heady few days with Declan she felt as though her head was out of control. She had so many emotions coursing around her body that she wasn't sure where the truth began and ended these days. It was as if life was going faster than she wanted it to, but she had to hang on for the ride anyway.

Not literally, the "ride" you understand. As if! I was hardly in a position to be thinking that way. After what I did to Simon and all . . .

She decided she'd go to bed early and put on her velour track suit, and apply a warm face mask. As she lay back on her bed, soaking up the sounds of Nina Simone's angst at 'I Wish I Knew How It Would Feel To Be Free' she felt the mask begin to slowly tighten. She'd really enjoyed the last couple of hours. She had called into her mum's to collect Ruben and the three of them had gone for an easy walk.

I loved chatting to Mum, but I really missed the closeness that some of my other friends had with their parents. We were so close when I was a child. I never knew my father – but more recently, ever since she got together with this new boyfriend of hers, I could feel a new distance between us. I suppose my shock wedding announcement didn't help. My family had enjoyed the actual day, but I know they were amazed at the swift nuptials. Four of my cousins actually asked me when I was due!

Before Nina Simone had got to the end of her melody Tara's face began to feel irritated and itchy. Disgruntled at the intrusion on her relaxing, "me" time, she got up and went into the bathroom. Before she had a bowlful of warm water and her flannel at the ready, her skin felt as if it was wearing a mask of fibreglass. She quickly washed off the offending mask, annoyed that she hadn't been able to go the full twenty minutes recommended. As she splashed her face with cool water she looked up into the mirror to see her reflection.

My God, I gasped. I looked as if I've exfoliated with a wire brush! Blotchy and red and very, very tender. Great. Just in time for my next appearance on TV . . .

Ciara found it hard to orgasm lately. She was both disturbed and annoyed by the fact and wasn't sure whether it was due to her age or to her chemical dependency. She couldn't really explain why, as her sexual appetite was virtually insatiable these days. She knew she was becoming obsessed with the idea of climbing "Mount O" and reaching the top, and yet found that the more she sought it out, the more elusive it was becoming. The nineteen-year-old lad from last week had really caught her imagination. He'd been so teasing and suggestive. It was one of those chemical attractions. Ciara couldn't get him out of her mind. She'd had sexual encounters before that had made an impact on her, but there was something about the young man that she was drawn to, in her dependent state. She couldn't quite put her finger on it, but there was something there. She was grateful for the day off and made her way out to her garden taking an orange with her. She sat at the patio table, resting her legs up on the chair opposite her. The orange glowed in the sunlight and in her day-dream-like state she stared into its dimpled peel. She loved her home, with its busy view of Sandymount Strand and the wide expanses of sand exposed when the tide was out, and she revelled in the tranquillity of her back garden. She'd taken her design element to its extreme, and so enjoyed a streamlined lawn, topped with stepping stones, patio, pergola and an array of explosively coloured flowers. As she sat on her decked patio, tormented by her thoughts, she reached out to the orange and small vegetable knife that she'd carried out and placed on the patio table. Still daydreaming, her thoughts battling loudly in her perturbed mind, she lightly scored around the orange peel with the sharp, glinting knife. She always tried to get a good dose of vitamins into her; between oranges and cranberry juice she felt she was going someway toward eliminating the toxins that drugs pumped into her system. As she absentmindedly segmented the orange, her troubled thoughts turned to Tara. A wave of hatred welled inside her, threatening to burst through her skin. There was something about Tara that incensed Ciara. The truth was, she'd tried many times to turn a blind eye, to put her head in the sand, but in fact she knew what it was. Tara would be the same age as "her" now. And, Ciara suspected, probably looked a little similar. But what really angered her was Tara's talent and relaxed attitude. She reminded her so much of herself years ago. Almost without thinking Ciara drew the blade of the small knife across her forearm. She gasped slightly at the sting and then smiled as she looked down at the superficial wound. It always alarmed her, almost frightened her sometimes – the sight of the streak of blood as it fattened and then dribbled. She could never quite understand how, but the release of the blood, the opening of her skin was always a relief. It was as if her pain and anger were being released from her. It was a way out for it. As the blood threatened to drip onto her leg, reality kicked in and she quickly rushed to the kitchen, grabbing the tea-towel and putting pressure onto the cut. She was used to this and as she pressed the towel down onto her arm she viewed the other pale streaky scars which were swiped across her forearms. The downside was, she always had to wear long sleeves.

Once the bleeding had calmed she felt able to breathe again and was more relaxed, almost as if a painkiller had taken effect and lightened her load. She felt ready to face the world again and so, pulling up her bag from the kitchen floor, she grabbed her mobile, desperately seeking out the young lad's number. She just had to meet up with him again. Soon. As she flicked through her address book she came across the number for Ray, the sculptor in Kerry who specialised in oriental ceramic sculptures. She set a reminder to ring him in the afternoon. Finally locating the boy's number, under the entry for 'ne-ne-ne-ne-nineteen' she felt her heart race as she pressed OK to call.

Tara and Niamh decided to drive across to Galway together, on the Thursday night, a decision which was made immediately on finding out that The Hothouse Flowers were playing in Niamh's favourite Galway pub on Dominick Street.

"But I've never heard of it." Tara felt muddled, her skin still angry and red after the face mask.

Niamh grabbed her car keys and laughed. "'Course you haven't. How would you?"

"So what's the attraction then?" Tara questioned.

Niamh turned to face her, "Tara! This is one of the most hip and happening places in Galway. It's the top of all music acts there!"

"Wow . . ." Tara shrugged her shoulders, unable to understand how that could be something so great.

They put their cases into the boot of Niamh's car and she negotiated their way out of Baggot Street, heading for the motorway and their three-hour drive across the country to Galway.

As they hit the M4 Niamh began to relax a little, glad to be away from the early-evening traffic which bumped its way around Dublin.

"So, you still haven't told me about Paris."

"I have. I told you the other night."

"No, Tara. You have avoided the subject since your return. You don't know how excited I was about you coming back. I even bought you wine and made a carbonara!"

Tara smiled, "Oh, so that's what it was all about then. Fishing for info."

"Noo," Niamh laughed, "just interested in my old friend's love life, that's all. Just a healthy interest."

Tara had expertly dodged every question regarding Declan on the night of her return.

And I'm doing the same now.

Before they knew it they'd reached Ballinasloe and decided to stop there for a quick drink and a wee before completing the journey through Loughrea to Clarinbridge.

I knew Niamh was annoyed that I wasn't telling her the ins-and-outs of my time with Declan. You see, the truth is, I was so afraid of my feelings for him, that I couldn't admit to them . . .

Maybe not even to myself.

Yet.

In the pub toilets at Ballinasloe Niamh reapplied her lipstick. They'd made good time so far. At this rate they'd be checked into their room and into the Roisin Dubh before it got too packed.

Staring in the mirror, she once again wondered if she should talk to Tara about Simon that night. It constantly nagged at her that she wasn't being completely honest with Tara. She was desperate to tell her about Simon's two previous marriages, but knew she had to hold out to find out more. On the trip, she'd asked a few light, innocent questions about Simon's life before Tara and his thoughts on marriage.

Locking herself back in the cubicle she put the lid

down on the toilet-seat, sat back down, and rang Anna.

She replied almost immediately and Niamh whispered, "It's just dawned on me. Now I know how and why Simon was so good at the wedding plans and so charming at the reception."

"Why are you whispering?" Anna asked, a little slow on the uptake.

"I'm in the loos in Ballinasloe. I don't want Tara to hear me. Listen, Anna, I haven't got long. It makes sense, doesn't it? Why he'd known where to arrange for the wedding list to be held and all that. How he seemed to suggest so easily that any English guests could use the list held at Debenhams. How he was *so* composed during his speech. Do you remember, we couldn't believe how he took to it like a duck to water? I mean, of course he did! Hadn't he already done it twice before?"

"But, Niamh, he was so in love with Tara. He was so nice to her. Remember how he sent her a bouquet that very morning of the wedding? We were so jealous. And it had all started with us laughing at her for proposing. You must remember how charming he was."

"Anna, of course he was. Listen to what I'm saying – he had done it before!"

"So what now?"

"Well, we know he's been married twice before. But we must find out whether he's been divorced twice before too."

"How do we do that?"

"Anna, I don't think we can!"

"Niamh? Niamh? You still in here?" The echoey, vacuous sounds of Tara's voice bounced off the tiled walls of the toilets.

"Have to go. I'll ring you back in five," Niamh whispered, clicking off her phone. "Yeah, just coming."

She flushed the chain for good measure.

Declan O'Mahoney was half-watching *Sky News* in his house in Dalkey. Half-watching and half-packing his bag – but he couldn't stop thinking about Tara. It was obvious that she was cautious of men and quite evident that she still felt terribly guilty about what she had done to Simon.

"Still," he said to the large blue remote control, "I've decided. I'm going to ask her for a date in Galway. With any luck I'll take her back to Paris."

He knew she would refuse.

But decided to anyway.

Niamh had managed to get back into the toilets just before they'd started off again for Galway. Anna was reading aloud from a book. Wedging her phone under her chin as she turned the page she could hear Niamh's gasping at the other end.

"Niamh, stop breathing like that, I can't concentrate."

"For fuck's sake, Anna – I'm crouching in the loos. Get on with it! Quick, carry on, you were saying: characteristics of bigamists are . . ."

"Right, listen now then. They don't actually lie – rather they just don't give the full facts. It often doesn't even occur to women that they are married. Usually in a relationship he is seen to make suggestions but will always have the final decision on their lives."

"God, Anna, it sounds just like him. You must get onto the Family Law office as soon as you can."

"Are you going to tell Tara?"

"Dunno. I'd kinda like you with me really."

"Oh Niamh, does she *have* to know?"

"'Course she does! She's been feeling so guilty about the affair. It'd only be right that she knows. The question is when."

"And how."

"Yeah. You realise that this isn't actually bigamy?"

"How come?" Anna queried Niamh's sudden change of direction.

"Anna," Niamh hissed, "this is fecking polygamy!"

"What's that?"

"Being married and not divorced *more* than one time!"

"Look, Niamh, this is all serious stuff. I mean he could go to prison for something like this. Don't you think I should go back to the records office and just check one more time?"

"Anna, we've both seen the entries in the register. Do you think we're *both* cracking up?"

"No, but you know how sensitive this is. I'll just go in and check one more time. Just to be certain, you know."

Niamh was irritated at Anna's caution, but could understand where she was coming from. "OK then, if it'll make you feel any better. But let me know anything as soon as you do."

"OK, talk later then.

"Bye."

Chapter 17

In Ciara's book there was only one thing worse than waking up with a hangover.

And that was waking up with a hangover in a room that you didn't recognise. A room that you didn't recognise, an alarming disarray of tablets on the bedside cabinet and five empty bottles of champagne on the floor. Must have been a good night. Shame she didn't feel like it had been though. She repeatedly shook her head in a panicked attempt to rid it of the cotton wool that seemed to be filling it. She sat up in the bed and felt the cool air pinch at her bare shoulders and chest. Nervously she squinted around the room and smoothed her ruffled hair down. She decided to get up and dressed before someone, she couldn't remember *who* it might be, came into the room. She hated herself when she did this! Dressing quickly, fastening her completely-inappropriate-for-daywear Agent Provocateur lingerie, she slid on her skirt and blouse, finding her high shoes beneath the bed. She was aggravated that there were no photographs or clues to give away the identity of whoever she'd spent the night with. Tentatively opening the bedroom door she padded out into the lounge area. She could see from the French doors that she was in a flat.

"Hello?" she called lightly.

Silence.

She coughed to clear her throat. "Em, hello? Anyone in?"

The quietness would have been deafening but for the sound of her own blood coursing through her veins and her head, and the sound of her pulse banging in her neck. Pulling open drawers and rifling through magazines and paperwork she frantically tried to put a name on the owner of this flat. This flat which, by the view from the window, was somewhere around the Drumcondra area.

"Shit!" she cursed at herself, frowning. "How the *hell* do I get myself into these situations?" Her long red nails rattled against her car keys as she rummaged in her bag.

Truly disgusted with herself, she opened the front door, closing it behind her, and rushed down the stairs to the carpark.

Her car was nowhere to be seen and she was sickened. She was lucky enough to stop a speeding taxi on its way back from the airport and hopped into it. Anxiously she checked the call register on her mobile. The last number dialled was that nineteen-year-old's and that was two nights ago. It started to slowly come back to her. She remembered arranging to meet up with him. She *wished* she could recall his name. They'd met in Yamamori Noodles in South Georges Street. Ciara remembered driving and leaving her car nearby. So that solved *that* mystery. She called to the taxi-driver to take her there, relieved that she'd remembered so much. If only she could remember his name. And if only the damned driver would stop talking! As they drove slowly, passing one of Dublin's larger bookstores, she saw the window display, dedicated to her fifth interiors book along with posters and merchandise. This only served to disgruntle her more. OK, so it was selling, but not with the verve of her previous ones. The taxi-driver recognised her from the posters in the window and decided that he was her new best friend.

"You know, I've had Bonio in my cab."

"Who?" she spat.

"Bonio, you know, the singer from U2. They used The Dockers' Pub when they were recording in Windmill Lane studios."

Ciara ignored his ramblings. Scrolling through her numbers for ne-ne-ne-ne-nineteen's the droning of the cab driver interfered with her concentration. She pressed OK to dial the young man's number; he answered after a few rings.

"Yeah?"

Ciara felt a lump in her throat and closed her eyes. "Em, hi. Erm, a bit embarrasing really, but tell me this. Did I spend the night with you last night?"

"You *are* a naughty girl, aren't you?"

Ciara desperately wanted to tell him to cut the crap. The fun had gone out of it all now anyway.

"Please. Look, I'm not the kind to go begging and grovelling. I have to be in Galway today for RTÉ and I must know what happened last night."

"Last night?" She could hear the smile in his voice. "Miss O'Rourke, last night I was out with my friends in Kildare. Miss O'Rourke, I am *still* in Kildare. Do you, perhaps, mean what happened *Thursday* night?"

"Thursday night!" She poked the taxi-driver on the shoulder causing him to jump, his podgy neck craning round to look at her. She covered the phone with her hand. "What day is it?" she barked at the taxi-driver.

"Saturday, missus. Can't you tell by the traffic?"

"What? So where was I this morning?" she asked the young man. "I've woken up today in a strange and empty flat in Drumcondra. I can't remember *who* I was with on Thursday night and I *cannot* believe I have been there for the last thirty-six hours!"

"Look, you wrinkly old bag," his tone changed, chillingly, "you met me on Thursday night, over-indulged in your pathetic tablets and left with another fella. I haven't a clue *who* he was. And hey, you dried-up old tart, don't ring me again, eh?"

As he hung up two huge tears appeared in Ciara's eyes. For the first time in years. Her habits and cravings really were beginning to get her into very serious trouble. Her stomach churned at the thought of who she might have been with and what she might have been doing.

And to top it, she should have been in Clarinbridge *yesterday!* As the taxi stopped at yet another set of lights, she hurriedly opened her door and, leaning out toward the road, was violently sick all over the double yellow lines.

Declan was furious at Ciara's failure to arrive. Friday had been set aside for the designers to check out the house, discuss the owners' expectations of the makeover and to attempt to source some local produce in keeping with the angle for Irish themed art. Tara was slightly concerned at Ciara's failure to answer the many calls that Declan had put her way, but not enough to stop her from enjoying herself. Now, as the designated "head" designer of this makeover, she took great delight in meeting with a local rug-maker whose latest work would fit perfectly with the brief for this house in Clarinbridge. She'd taken great pride in finding a craftsman who worked with oak and had sculpted a fantastic incense holder and candle holders which would embrace both the oriental and Irish themes. He'd explained to her at great length how the sacred oak was associated with St Bridget and how oak symbolises, in the Celtic calendar, the seventh month – the month of the all-important summer solstice. He'd enlightened her how, because it can live for a thousand years, oak was a symbol of strength to the Celts and how its fruit and bark were used for healing.

When Ciara finally showed her face on Saturday

afternoon she looked and felt absolutely dreadful. She'd realised only a couple of years ago that she'd gone up a generation when it came to socialising and was horrified to realise that she was now in the menopausal age-bracket. It had been a severe shock to her to find that her age-group were amongst the ones who had grey roots and had begun some rather strange, erratic behaviour. She'd refused to succumb to HRT, strangely claiming that it wasn't a natural product. Strange when she'd taken so freely to poly-drug usage. Once she'd located her car on the Dublin street she had driven home, nervously looking over her shoulder the whole time. She had called in briefly, packed a small suitcase for her stay in Galway and left quickly. How relieved she was to get out of Dublin for a few days – she really needed to get her head together. She felt violently sick for the duration of the drive to Galway and, on checking into the hotel, took a few minutes to compose herself with a further few tablets. Unpacking her clothes and hanging them, she slid on her Levi's and a ruffled white shirt. Slipping on her Aztec beaded sandals, she grabbed her bag and made for her car in the hotel carpark. As she got in, checking the directions to the house in Clarinbridge, she slipped in her Nirvana CD and recalled her last heavy-sex session last week with the young nineteen-year-old. His question of "I suppose a ride's out of the question?" had been so blunt, yet Ciara couldn't help but fancy the young man's sexual confidence. His thick accent had helped too. She felt sad as she recalled what fun they'd had exploring their bodies to the sounds of the heavy rock music. Berating herself now, she knew she had to stop picking up strangers from bars, but her sexual appetite was only growing with age, not diminishing. She was insatiable at the moment. Ambition always bought this out in her. Determined not to ruin her reputation as an interior designer, she forced herself to cast it from her mind for a few days, in the hope that it would all die down in time. Although it still tormented her that she didn't know *whose* flat she'd been in and *who* she had left the pub with.

As she rang the bell of the house in Clarinbridge she was greeted by a pleasant, but housewifely-looking thirty-something.

Same old, same old, she said to herself, as she shook hands and exchanged niceties. She could hear Tara's voice coming from the open patio doors at the back of the kitchen. As she breezed through, desperately trying to exude an air of professionalism and confidence, she saw that Tara was out talking to the "monkeys".

"Well, how have you been getting on without me?" Her crisp, cut tone immediately made the hairs on the back of Tara's neck rise.

Did the woman have no conscience? She had strolled in two days late and, and, and . . . did she really think we couldn't manage without her? Force yourself to smile, girl, I said grimly, it just isn't worth the aggro.

Tara swung to face Ciara with a smile, and even managed to place a warm, friendly hand on her arm.

It killed me really – to do that.

Especially as she shrugged it off as if I had leprosy or something!

"Ciara. We were just discussing the designs for the MDF."

Ciara sneered.

I would rise above it. I would rise above it. I would.

"I know you don't like it, Ciara, but you must realise what a limited budget we're on. Especially in the light of the oak pieces too."

"Oak? For an oriental theme? Bloody oak!"

"They're matching incense and candle holders. The clients really like them and they embrace both the Irish and oriental theme."

John the handyman could see the tense situation between the women and so decided to break the ice again.

"Well, gals, there's going to be a lot of work here, so be prepared to start talking dirty."

Tara tried to extend the jokey atmosphere. "Oh, come on then, John, talk dirty to us," she teased.

"Bricks and ballast, paint and glue. Will that do you?"

Ciara simply scowled and walked away. She'd had enough sexual innuendo to last her a few weeks.

Maybe a few days.

As she light-footed up the ash stairs to the bedroom she felt overwhelmed with hatred for Tara. She couldn't bear her down-to-earthiness and easy manner. Her mind worked overtime as she spoke to herself: *Doesn't she realise how lucky she is being brought into this game just because Declan the Dick fancies her? I've* worked for years, networking and researching interiors and sourcing new craftsmen!

The thoughts of her flagging fifth book hit her between the eyes. She refused to believe she was only as successful as her last book. Refused to accept that perhaps she should give in to the new ideas of a younger generation.

If only she could see that she was her worst enemy, she'd be taking a first step in the right direction.

Tara continued to laugh and joke with John and the lads as they finalised their ideas for the bedroom. Despite her smiling exterior she couldn't help but be disturbed by Ciara's attitude. It was clear she did have a point about the MDF and Tara admired her refusal to accept what she didn't believe in. She had some great ideas but coupled with a bad attitude.

It was bugging me why she was so defensive and rude. Just what was that woman so angry about?

By Monday the team were set for filming. They'd cleared out any excess clutter that the cameras didn't need to pick up. Niamh was ready with her cameras and the production team were raring to go. They had enjoyed the company of these clients who had been willing to give the team a freer hand than most. It seemed it was going to pay off. Tara sat with the couple at the kitchen table, ready for filming, whilst Ciara was to be filmed up in the bedroom, to explain to the cameras what the intention for the room was. Tara had her "design kit" laid out on the table and was ready to offer advice such as, "I have glass colour spray for smoking the glass in the MDF screens that John will make" and "Always use a mask".

The next two days of filming were great fun. They even got some great footage of Tara trying to measure a window frame only to find that the cheap measure insisted on bending and drooping. She'd got annoyed at the measure and just when they thought they'd have to cut filming, to try again, she'd said, "Damn things never stay up when you want them to." To which John had added, quick-witted, "You must be using the wrong things then." Declan knew they'd have to cut out a section where Tara had genuinely taken great pride in their work and had stood back, hands on hips and said, "It looks really great. I'm really pleased with this one." To which Ciara had pushed past her, nudging her shoulder as she did so and muttered, "You're obviously getting more and more affected by the paint fumes."

But hey, I was getting more and more thick-skinned by the minute.

As the strong evening sun filtered in through the cream muslin curtains, creating exciting muted shadows on the freshly painted walls, Niamh clicked her shutter repeatedly. The oriental-themed bedroom just exuded an air of tranquillity. The wooden floors shone handsomely and the six ceramic pots of bamboo lined up on the windowsill gave the room the breath of fresh air that it had needed. Tara really had excelled herself this time.

Chapter 18

"She's an embarrassment to us."

"All I can say is thank God for the cutting-room. At least they'll cut it out. Looks like it'll be your smiling face at the end of *that* one, Tar."

"And you know something? I'm getting to like this 'celebrity' lifestyle. I mean, to think only weeks ago I'd have *died* if I thought I was going to be on the box. I'd even dive into the kids' clothes shop on Grafton Street if I could see an RTÉ or TV3 camera looming in the distance."

"You're doing really well, Tar, fair play."

"Thanks, Niamh. I'm really putting my heart and soul into it though. I still have to pinch myself to remember how much my life has changed in the last year. I still feel terrible about what I did to Simon and that'll always be with me, but I suppose, in a way, I'm much happier now than I was as a stay-at-home wife. I've got my independence back."

Niamh felt nauseated and was desperate to part with the information that was screaming to get out. She decided to change the subject back to Ciara, a topic of mutual interest.

"It's a shame about Ciara really. She used to be so popular. Especially when the interiors thing really began to take off."

"But she's not nice, is she, Niamh?"

"'Course she's not! And she looks so desperate too. Spaced out half the time, I reckon!"

Tara shifted in the passenger seat of Niamh's car as she reached to turn down the music. "It's the colour of her though. It's unnatural. I mean she has to be tanorexic."

"You mean anorexic?"

"I don't. I mean she'd probably feel ill without a tan."

They laughed, Niamh squinting as she gripped the steering wheel with her left hand and lit up a cigarette with her right. As she blew the smoke out she tested Tara with, "So what do you reckon about Stephanie?"

Tara felt an inward jolt, but prided herself on the fact that she didn't show it. Instead she pretended not to know her.

"Who? Stephanie who?"

Niamh didn't make eye contact. "The blondey researcher who's permanently flirting with Declan."

As if I didn't know!

"Oh, she's lovely. She'd make a great girl-next-door. Any man would be delighted!"

"You think so? I took her as more of the sexy kind."

"Ha," Tara laughed, hopeful that she sounded as casual as she'd tried to be, "she's hardly a sex symbol now, is she?"

"I dunno, she's always around Declan. Apparently she was seen in the late-night chemist at Salthill last night buying a packet of twenty-four condoms. Twenty-four!"

I wished she'd change the subject. The disturbing fact was, I had noticed the way Stephanie flirted with Declan and it was starting to annoy me.

And that was starting to annoy me too!

"Well, I'd say she's either in for a good week or a shit month," said Tara.

Niamh giggled, turning to face Tara.

Not a good idea when driving . . .

"You really are trying to be a cool cookie, aren't ya?"

"What do you mean by that?"

"Oh, come on, Tara. It's obvious Declan fancies you like mad. And I've seen you, cheekily sticking out your tongue at him when you think no-one's looking. Flashing that raunchy old piercing of yours."

"It's just a bit of harmless fun. You know how men misconstrue a woman's signals. I mean, really, they're from a different planet."

"Yeah," Niamh threw out the half of her fag that was left burning, "but it's always a planet that suits 'em!"

They were driving to the restaurant in Galway City for the meal that Declan had promised them all.

Ciara had embarrassed the whole team at the end of the makeover.

It was just on that sensitive end part.

The "Close your eyes . . . open them!" bit – the "reveal" as we in the trade call it.

Hark at me!

Ciara had tutted and rolled her eyes just as the couple gasped with delight at their peace haven of a bedroom. I'm not bragging, but it really was beautiful. And Ciara had groaned, "Isn't it amazing how people react so positively to a room full of MDF!" *just a little too loudly. I mean, that was bad, but we could have cut it. But then she laughed and said,* "Jesus, you'd think they were whiter than white! Yeah, love, we saw your armory of sex aids left beside your bed when we arrived. What was that all about? Fancied your chances with oul' monkey-man John?"

We just didn't know what to say. And neither did the couple. Luckily I managed to ad-lib over her moanings and talk the cameras through what we'd achieved. And there they'd been, hugging and kissing with tears of joy welling in their eyes too. And then Ciara had her say and they were ferocious! It was true, of course. I was gobsmacked at the way people left their houses when we arrived. It wasn't as if they disn't know we're coming! Honestly, I'd come across dirty laundry (I'm being polite here), strange magazines and even foodstuffs beneath the bed. So Ciara was right, but she should have been in the business long enough to know when to keep her mouth shut. I still couldn't figure why she was involved in the series if she was so sceptical about it all.

It's a wonder she wasn't given the boot!

As they gathered at the bar of the restaurant Declan was pleased to see Niamh and Tara arrive before either

Stephanie or Ciara. He could at least spend a little quality time with some *good* company before the others turned up. It was a shame about the bad atmosphere that Ciara O'Rourke was whipping up and he was beginning to worry about the success of the programme. He'd already had complaints from his boss about the way things were going and what a notorious liability O'Rourke was. Slipping his leather jacket back on as Tara approached him, he cleared his throat, bracing himself to keep his promise. He was going to ask her for a date before the night was out.

Little did he know how short it was going to be.

I was absolutely gutted.

I mean I knew that Niamh was in a strange mood. She's known for liking her red wine, but five glasses before we'd even sat down was pushing it. Even by her standards. And it wasn't even the fact that Declan cornered me only fifteen minutes after I'd got there and asked me if I'd like to go to Vicar Street with him next weekend. I knew he was tempting me with the latest jazz musician on tour from New Orleans. Ordinarily I'd jump at the chance – both for a night out with him and to go to Vicar Street – it's a fantastic venue. But he knew how I feel about the man-woman thing.

But it was all just much, much worse than I'd originally thought . . .

Declan was a lovely guy and yeah, I did like him, but his timing stank. It was bad enough being backed into a verbal corner, forced to think on my feet for a non-offensive reply to his request without what happened just as we sat down at our table.

All fifteen of us. There was Declan and me – him embarrassed at asking me only to be knocked back, and me awkward at having to say no when I really wanted to say yes. So we were feeling suddenly uncomfortable and slightly embarrassed in each other's company and trying desperately not to let it show when Niamh got out those bloody scratch-cards again.

On reflection I was glad that Ciara was at the other end of the table.

Declan tried to break the glassy atmosphere with a jibe about Niamh's escalating gambling and no-one was more surprised than me when she bit his head off. And downed another full glass of red. In one go! Shortly after, she asked me to go to the toilets with her. I'd suspected it was because she was feeling sick or pissed or something. If she wasn't – she should have been. So I did. I went with her. It was all a bit "dancing-round-your-handbags", but under the circumstances I was glad to be out of Declan's company for a few minutes. It was when we got into the toilets that she slumped down onto the bench by the cloakrooms and gushed:

"Tara, babe!"

Rather, she slurred.

"There's something I *have* to tell you. It's not nice and I know this isn't the right time but, although that Declan's a bit of a bollocks, it's obvious you like each other."

I just looked at her. I wasn't giving anything away at this stage.

Niamh had held her head in her hands and sighed.

"It's like this. Remember how George from Carlow said he didn't recognise you from that wedding that Simon had gone to?"

I still neither nodded nor agreed, nor smiled. I was waiting for the punchline.

"Well, I know we should have told you before, but we didn't want to upset you without knowing for sure." Niamh stood up to face Tara, eyeball to eyeball.

Although hers were more bloodshot and glassy than mine. And who's 'we'?

"You see, it's like this. Oh feckit, I wish Anna was here."

"Just say it, Niamh. Please. Just tell me. Whatever it is."

I still can't believe how calm I was when I said that.

"Tara. Babe. Simon is a polygamist."

A wha'?

I'd tried to crack a joke. I often do that when I don't know what to say.

"What's that? Someone who plays many *games*?"

Niamh didn't get the humour of it.

"No, love."

She reached forward and cupped my quivering chin.

"It's a person who has been married many times."

"And? So?"

Although I knew what was coming next. I was just plastering on as much brave-face as I could muster.

"And has never divorced."

"How *many* times?"

"Including you?"

Tara nodded, the colour completely drained from her face, her expression child-like.

Niamh whispered, "Three."

And so my body did things it wasn't supposed to.

My stomach wrenched – without a toolbox.

My head swam – and it had no armbands.

My mouth watered – without a tap in sight.

My knees went to jelly – without having time to set.

And then I puked, severely, all over Niamh's suede trousers and snakeskin boots.

"Taraaa!"

All the guilt and hate and sorrow, like poison inside my body, projected itself out through my lipsticked mouth.

It had been a long time coming.

It was pure coincidence that Declan had to take his starter back up to the waiter. Possibly it was a strange luck that put that curly hair in amongst his egg mayonnaise. Whatever it was that had propelled him to be standing within hearing distance of the ladies' toilets, he'd been in earshot when Niamh had shouted, *"Taraaa!"*

Without hesitation he'd made a dart for the ladies' toilet door, and had opened it. Only to see a retching, vomiting Tara spilling a rainbow'd concoction of colours down Niamh's beige trousers and tan boots. He'd initially felt humiliated that by asking Tara for a date he'd caused her to be physically sick. It was only when Niamh implored him with her eyes for help that he snapped back to reality. Considering the half-inebriated state that Niamh was in, he, gallantly, insisted on driving the pair of them back to their hotel.

For the duration of the journey, the full ten minutes of the silent and stenchy journey, he was desperate to know what had gone on there tonight. It was only when Tara had quietly asked to get out at the hotel reception doors, prior to Declan parking his car, that he had the opportunity to ask Niamh what had happened. She had refused to tell him, on the basis that she felt bad enough already, that she should never have told Tara the bad news tonight.

"No, Declan, I'm sorry. I've caused enough upset and it's Tara's business. No offence."

"No. None taken. I understand."

He felt slightly guilty, as if him asking her out had caused Niamh to tell her this terrible "news" tonight. Instinct told him that the timing was something to do with him. And so, instead of making life better for Tara, he felt he had now made it worse.

As he pulled into a parking space in the spotlit carpark Niamh turned to him and asked, "You wouldn't come up to the room with me, would ya?"

"I'm probably one of the last people she wants to see right now."

"No. I'd say that was probably Simon. Please, Declan, you're her friend. Plus I'm terrified she's doing something stupid up there."

"OK, come on then."

Niamh opened her door and bent forward, unzipping her boots. She tugged off her sodden yellow socks, scrunched them into a ball and fired them high into the decorative bushes of the hotel carpark.

"Niamh!" Declan couldn't help but smile. She was a bit wild, but you just couldn't help liking her.

"I'm bad enough going in like *this*. Without worrying about my damn socks too."

They walked together toward the hotel, Niamh barefoot, her glistening and yet tainted boots swinging from her clasped fist.

On entering the reception, a hub of businessmen were gathered at the bar and Niamh noticed the overnight dry-cleaning service offered. She looped her arm through Declan's, his leather jacket cold against her wrist.

"Would you drop my trousers into reception on your way out for me? With any luck they'll be recovered by the morning."

He just couldn't say no to her. She was too charming.

As they entered the unlocked room they saw Tara lying under the covers in her bed, with her back to them. Declan noticed her jeans and shirt lying in a heap beside her bed. He could see from her shoulders that she'd left her t-shirt on. He felt terrible that she was in such a desperate state. Niamh had tried to make light of it by quipping, "And after all that wine I thought *I* was the one going to be sick tonight."

Heaving with remorse he waited in the quiet bedroom, the only sound being the hum of the extractor fan from the bathroom. Niamh was in there removing her suede trousers and he could hear her rustling with a carrier bag as she'd folded them up inside it. As he looked at the back of Tara's head, her soft spiky hair flat against the pillow, his heart ached for her. Fighting an overwhelming urge to go over and hug her, he shook his head in despair. He was desperate to know what had been such bad "news" that she'd been so violently sick. Niamh reappeared, wrapped in the hotel-issue bathrobe and handed him the carrier bag, thanking him for his trouble. She'd seemed to sober up pretty damn quick. As Declan left them and walked toward the staircase, he realised how awkward he'd felt at Tara's silence. He hoped that Niamh could comfort her in some way. Maybe even make her see sense about it all. Making his way, with the stinking bag, to the receptionist, he felt overwhelming sympathy for her.

Of course, by all accounts it should have been raining now. Not just a sprinkly kind of shower, but that rattling pounding rain that hits off the window with a vengeance. But it wasn't. True to form for the typically untypical Irish weather it was actually a nice evening – weather-wise. It would probably be a heat wave by Christmas.

And that was something else I couldn't bear to think about right now – my first Christmas as a wife was to be followed by my first as a third wife!

Anna decided to ring Niamh relatively early the next morning.

She had more bad news. Niamh answered her mobile, leaving Tara to sleep. She was sure that she wasn't sleeping, but was still in exactly the same position as last night.

She hadn't moved all night, although Niamh had heard her sniffing and snuffling into her pillow a few times. Niamh slipped on her Nike trainers quietly, deciding to go for a short walk whilst talking to Anna.

"Jesus, Anna, you won't believe what happened last night!"

"Go on." She was expecting one of Niamh's bawdy tales about a new sexual encounter, but wasn't quite up for it.

"I only went and told her, didn't I?"

Anna rubbed at her fuzzing forehead as the remains of alcohol consumed the night before trickled through her body. "You did what? Oh Niamh, and how is she today? Why didn't you wait for me to be with you? I thought we were going to do it together."

"We were! I know, I know, I'm sorry. I'd had too much to drink and one thing led to another. I just couldn't bear for her not to know. I mean, she's tackling her life differently because of her guilt! It's not fair on her."

"So where is she now?"

"In bed. Where she's been since about nine o'clock last night. She hasn't moved."

"Well, you're going to hate what I've found out then."

Niamh groaned, as she rummaged in her pocket for her cigarettes and pulled out an empty pack.

"I've just left the registry office. Thought I'd call in there early this morning. I needed to do something to clear my head – heavy night last night. But, by mistake I picked up the wrong year."

"What do you mean – the wrong year?"

"I mistakenly read the register for 1999."

"Oh Anna! What a bloody waste of time then! Can't you go back?"

"Not now, I have to go home and get into bed. Me head's splitting. But Niamh, listen. Simon was in there."

"In there? What was he doing there?"

"Not *in* the Registry Office! In the register!"

"But, Anna, he can't be. His marriages were September 2000 and June 1998."

"Yeah – *and* December 1999."

Niamh wished she had a cigarette to light at this moment and so screwed up the empty packet and rebelliously threw it onto the pavement. She stopped and leant against the redbrick wall of a corner house.

"What? Are you telling me there was *another* marriage? Please, be clear. I'm a little hungover and stressed today."

"Yes. Simon has been married *three* times. He married again on New Years' Eve 1999. 31st December."

Now it was Niamh's turn to go dizzy. This was information-overload in a short period of time.

"OK, so tell me from the start. When, where, who and why?"

"Right, concentrate now: 31st December 1999 in Abbeyleix. He married a young girl, Christina Appleby. But why, Niamh? I simply can't tell you why."

"So, oh God, Anna I feel sick. So, Tara is Simon's *fourth* wife."

"Seems that way. Look, I have to go, Hugh's trying to get through."

Niamh came to life. "Oh, is he a millionaire yet?"

"I'm still finding out!"

"You dark horse, you!"

"Had a good teacher, babe – you! Talk later eh, but listen, don't tell Tara yet. She has enough to cope with right now."

"Bye then."

It had all been very hard after that night. Declan had called in to see her the next afternoon, only to find her still in bed. Although she'd changed position by the afternoon, she was lying on her front, crying into the pillow. He was relieved that she didn't seem to blame him for kickstarting this whole thing, but she still didn't seem able to talk about it. Niamh, tactfully, left them alone.

"Tara," he'd softly asked, "why don't you take some time out?"

Due to the very nature of the programme they had already assigned each of the four designers to projects. All it would mean was a little rejigging to give Tara some time. "Perhaps it might help you to come to terms with whatever has upset you so badly."

It seemed to Declan that a lot needed to be found out about this bastard Simon.

"Tara?" he'd said softly, stroking her ruffled hair. "Let Ciara and the other two guys sort out these next two makeovers."

"What are they?" she'd whimpered, muffled by the pillow.

Despite my condition I still didn't want to miss out.

It's a woman thing – isn't it?

"Kilmainham, a two-bed semi, and Drumcondra, a one-bed flat."

He sighed deeply, genuinely feeling sorrow to see her in such a state.

"You know," he said softly as he stroked the back of her neck, "I'd love to hold you. To hug you like we did in Paris after that hotel incident. I'd love to just hug you and hold you – to keep you safe in my arms."

To which Tara had sobbed uncontrollably into her pillow.

Again.

Counsellors comfort the bereaved with a forecast of emotions to be expected.

These emotions range from loss to anger to hurt. On the journey back from Galway Niamh watched as Tara experienced all these and a few more. She went from being quiet and withdrawn for the first hour of the journey to a sobbing wreck by the time they'd deviated off route and stopped at Abbeyleix. Tara had no idea why Niamh wished to stop off at Abbeyleix and paid no attention to the fact that she'd gone into the post office, spending a good fifteen minutes in there. By the time she'd gotten back into the car Tara had discovered Anger. Of the raging kind. She hated Simon for putting her in this position. She was disgusted at herself for being so shallow and proposing to him in the first place. She even went as far as blaming herself for being so desperate.

"Remind me, Niamh," she'd spat, "who was the one in Luigi's that night who had sang 'thirty-three and des-peride'?"

Niamh flushed a little, certain it was her.

"Well, it was bloody well true. As if it isn't bad enough with life taking the piss outta you, your bloody friends have to do it too!"

Niamh thought it best just to let her get it off her chest and by the time they'd reached Tara's house it was nearly dark and she'd reverted back to quiet mode. Niamh helped her in with her bags and watched as Tara simply padded up the stairs to bed, but not without first grabbing a handful of Penguin bars from the kitchen. It brought back alarming memories of a few months ago when she'd been confined to her bed for days on end. Niamh knew when to take a hint and genuinely felt bad for breaking the news to Tara in such an insensitive way. It was nearly enough to make her stop drinking.

Nearly.

She had wanted to tell her about Anna's phone call that morning with the horror of the fourth marriage to Christina Appleby. It would have to wait – she'd caused enough devastation. She closed Tara's glossy front door behind her carefully and drove to the newsagent's by the junction. After buying twenty euro worth of scratchcards she rang Adam. There was nothing like great sex to destress the mind and clear the head.

Chapter 19

Tara had decided to take Declan's advice. On the basis that she needed to get her head straight, she opted out of the Kilmainham and Drumcondra makeovers.

She knew she was feeling low – even The Shed couldn't drag her from her depression. Instead, she lay dozing on the settee mid-afternoon and was jolted from her sleep by the sound of Ruben's bowl rattling on the kitchen tiles. Any sounds that suddenly woke her from her sleep brought back disturbing memories of the break-in in Paris. With her heart thumping in her chest she sat up in alarm and then, on realising there wasn't a burglar in sight, she rested back down on the soft cushion, staring at the wrought-iron fireplace.

And to think that I'd been glad that he moved in with me, and not the other way around.

The bastard probably didn't even have a house of his own. And why would he need one, with three wives to look after him?

friendly, close way and respected the way that he didn't approach her man-to-woman-like. She was too fragile. And he knew it. It was an hour and a half later that they turned the corner of the block, and approached her house at the end of the street.

"Did I tell you what I heard in Phoenix Park last week?" he asked.

"No." She smiled, turning to face him.

He continued, looking ahead as he spoke. "I was sitting on a park bench reading a newspaper and an old fella came and sat next to me. I paid no attention to him, but shortly after, a small boy with his bigger brother ran over and they both sat on the end of the bench too. I could see their mother walking an Alsatian. She had her eye on them, you know."

"Yeah?" Tara was expecting some tragic, terrible story.

"Well, I had to laugh at the younger lad. He ate one chocolate bar after the other. He was onto his fifth or sixth when the old fella next to me began to shake his head. 'Son,' he tutted, 'eating all that sugar isn't good for you. It will give you acne, rot your teeth and make you fat.' The small boy stared at him, completely unimpressed. And do you know what he said?"

"Go on," egged Tara,

"He said, 'I don't care. My grandad lived to be 103 years old!'."

"Go 'way!" gasped Tara.

"No, listen," Declan continued. "He said, 'My grandad lived to be 103 years old!'" The old man smirked and said, 'But did your grandad eat *six* chocolate bars at a time?' To which the little fella sneered, just before he got up and ran back to his mum, 'No, he just minded his own fucking business!' I tell you, Tara, I nearly died laughing. You should have seen the old guy's face. It was priceless!"

Tara laughed out loud for the first time in days and just as Declan opened the gate to her house, she turned and stopped him.

"Thank you."

"Eh? Go on! Don't be daft."

"No, thank you. You've been a great friend. Coming in for a coffee?"

"I'd love to. Go on, Ruben," he patted the dog on the rump, "lead the way."

Declan led Ruben through to the back garden while Tara put on the kettle and rang Four Star Pizza. It had only taken a week for her to become the regular customer that she used to be.

"So when do you start on the two-bed semi in Kilmainham then?" she asked as she spooned sugar into mugs.

"Day after tomorrow."

"Who's doing it?"

"The two lads. I've told Ciara to give herself a week to sort herself out too. You know I got some bollocking over that outburst of hers. The executives want me to axe her."

"Literally?" teased Tara.

He smiled at her.

"It's a shame," she continued, "I kinda like her. She's obnoxious, rude, brassy and arrogant. But there must be a reason she's so angry. I can't figure why."

"Tara," he spoke softly, resting down carefully onto the settee, "she's a druggie. You must have noticed the distant look in her eyes half the time. And the mood swings."

"I have. But I can't help feeling sorry for her at the same time."

"You're just too nice."

"Too stupid, you mean."

He ignored her, leaning forward to rest his mug on the antique table, noticing the collection of mug-ring stains already there.

"You see the thing about Ciara is that she always has to go one better than everyone else. If you told her you'd been on holiday to *Ten*-erife she'd have to tell you she'd been to *Eleven*-erife!"

"Ha – ha."

It was a crap attempt at a joke, but he was just trying to cheer me up.

The next day seemed to start much better for me right from the beginning. Now, I don't know whether Declan's company had rubbed off on me in a good way, or what, but I woke up in a great mood. He'd stayed for pizza the evening before and had left about nine. It was then that I'd started to get my head around the travesty of my marriage to Simon.

The next morning Anna turned up unexpectedly. I think she was surprised to see me up and dressed.

"Oh, hi. Thought you would have taken to your bed to watch George Clooney videos."

"No. Been there, done that." Tara tried to talk through the foam of the toothpaste. "Come in. Stick the kettle on there, I'll be a couple of minutes."

"And here was me expecting that time would have changed nothing. I was half expectin' you to be confined to the bed."

"No chance. Not again."

Over herbal tea, they discussed Simon's marriages at great length, and, as they sat in the sunshine once again, Anna inside and Tara outside The Shed, she gently broke the news of the fourth wife, the marriage to Christina Appleby in Abbeyleix. Initially, Tara had been angry at Niamh for not mentioning this, until Anna made her see sense and calmed her down. Anna explained how she'd accidently found the entry and had rung Niamh the very morning that Tara was crying in her bed at the hotel. Tara asked Anna if this had anything to do with Niamh stopping at the post office in Abbeyleix on the way home from Galway. Anna knew nothing about their stopover and so couldn't honestly answer her. An hour later she had managed to persuade Tara to go to Joyce House, the Registry Office, with her, to show her the three entries. As expected, Tara had broken down and cried for a few minutes, but Anna sat quietly, patiently rubbing her back in comfort.

"*Four* wives, Anna," she sniffed, "and here was I only wanting to ever get married once and in doing so I'm now somebody's fourth wife! Is this what they call *four*-play?" She attempted to joke as she wiped her wet cheeks dry.

Told you I did that when I didn't know what else to say . . .

"Nooo, love," Anna cooed, "this is what they call illegal."

"So what do we do now? I just can't go to the police yet. It's all too new and too raw."

"I know. You might be interested to hear though that I've been doing a bit of research into the characteristics of typical bigamists."

"Jesus, you mean there's a *type*? It's all a bit too much Hannibal Lecter for me. You're telling me they have a psychological profile?"

"To an extent. I've read of reports that, generally, bigamist men are communicative, funny and keen, often preferring the 'chase' to anything else. But there are also stories of men *and* women who are just addicted to the idea of a wedding."

"No *wonder* he knew so much about wedding planning. Oh Anna," she began to cry again, "I've been made a complete fool of, haven't I?"

"How the hell were you supposed to know?"

"But when I look back on it. All those calls to his mobile that he'd said were work. All the nights out and disappearances that he'd blamed on work. I'd had no reason for suspicion. I was so gullible."

"Now, now. Don't go tormenting yourself. We can sort this out between us. That's if you don't think we're interfering. We just want to help you, Tar."

Tara held her hand softly, "How could I think you

were interfering? You are two of the best friends any girl could ever have. Thank you so much, Anna. I'm just not strong enough for all this right now."

"No worries. Have you told your mum yet?"

"No," she groaned, "I haven't told anyone. I'm just too ashamed."

Niamh was waiting at the entrance to the indoor market at Moore Street. The curtains at the window of Adam's flat were open, and he'd said they'd meet at eleven. It was now five past. She looked left and right, up toward Parnell Street and down Moore Street for a sign of him. She stood by a stall watching the bustling African community as they went about their business. It was hard to believe she was actually *in* Dublin. The stall, laden with pounded yam, cassava, plantain and a selection of types of rice, was thronged with women, their brightly coloured ethnic clothes providing light relief from the dull greys and blacks of Dublin's commuter belt. The sound of heavy hip-hop thumped out from the barber's as an easy buzz breathed energy into this ugly corridor of architecture. A group of very westernised coloured women bustled by, their thin, stretched carrier bags loaded with produce. A stark contrast to the traditionally dressed women, these all had their Afro hair straightened into very stylish arrangements and were dressed in glamorous, tight-fitting dresses and killer heels. Niamh set a reminder on her phone to bring her camera with her next time she visited Adam. A sharp slap on the bum made her jump. She turned to face a grinning Marco.

"Christ, you frightened the shite outta me."

"Haven't seen you for a long time. What you doing around here? Come to look at the grotesque architecture?" he deadpanned.

She laughed, throwing her head back in a flirtatious manner, making a mental note to contact him again soon – it had to be at least two months since their last time.

"Of course! And what else would I be doing here?"

Their conversation was interrupted swiftly by a female voice calling Marco's name. They both looked around to see a blonde stunner, something straight out of a men's mag, striding toward Marco. Niamh could literally see the swell in his trousers, but also noticed the shifty expression that shot across his face.

"Niamh? This is Courtney. Courtney, Niamh."

Niamh extended her hand to shake the limp wrist of Courtney.

"And how do you two know each other?" Courtney's husky voice drawled.

Marco sprang to respond, "Oh, I've known Niamh for years." He put his arm around her shoulder and slapped her chummily on the top of her arm. "I've known Niamh since I was . . . em, we were . . . Niamh? What would you say? Ten years or more?"

She was aware of the desperation in his eyes urging her to comply. She didn't let him down – the humour value alone was priceless.

"Oh yeah, definitely. At *least* ten years. And Courtney, how long have *you* known Marco?"

Courtney melted into a lip-glossed smile and sidled up to Marco, causing him to drop his grip on Niamh's shoulders.

"Marco and I have been engaged for the last two years. I'm still waiting for him to make an honest woman of me."

Niamh's eyes flicked from the vacuous wiggling Courtney to the fidgety and pensive Marco. So he'd been engaged all the time that he'd been sleeping with Niamh. She wasn't particularly bothered from her point of view – he was just another guy – but poor Courtney! Her thoughts went immediately to Tara and Simon and his extra-curricular shenanigans.

"Well, Courtney," Niamh shook her soft hand again, "very nice to meet you at last. I have to go, sorry, Marco. And you should have introduced me to Courtney long ago."

Enjoying Marco's discomfort, she gave a sarcastic smile and stuck her tongue out as they parted company, and so decided that she'd go up and knock on Adam's door – she'd been waiting far too long already. As she nipped in through the side door from the market up to Adam's flat a small mongrel followed her, close on her heels. As she knocked for Adam the dog waited obediently by her side and, as Adam answered, the mutt walked in with her. She took little notice of the dog, pinching Adam's bum as she jibed at him for not being ready.

"Sorry, sorry," he panicked, "I got stuck on the phone to me sister. She'd talk forever if you'd let her. She's got IBS today."

"Today? Can that come and go then?"

"Irritable Bitch Syndrome? Oh yeah, I understand it's very common."

She sat down on the sofa and threw a cushion at him as he ducked, tucking his shirt into his jeans. The small dog circled his coffee table and stopped, cocking his raggedy leg up and piddling on Adam's floor. They both watched in amazement.

"Do you mind him doing that?" Niamh was shocked at his lack of reprimand.

"'Course I do!"

"So why don't you say anything to him?"

"I thought he was *yours*!"

"And I thought he was yours!"

They both laughed as Adam shooed the pup out the front door, calling after him as Niamh fetched the mop from the kitchen.

"So come on then. Where's your car parked?" he beamed.

"That way." She pointed toward the right and they were soon making their way down along Moore Street, Adam irritatingly pinching at her bum the whole way.

As he sat into the passenger seat of her car, she teased, "Anyway, if I had an arse like yours, I'd keep away from other people's backsides."

He smiled, "Meaning?"

"Well," she turned the key in the ignition, "it's hardly small, is it?"

Adam laughed, stretching his legs out, "Well, babe, you know what they say about big arses on men?"

"No."

"You need a big hammer for a big nail . . ."

They reached Abbeyleix in record time. Niamh had enjoyed Adam's company in the car. She even began wishing she wasn't so intent on finding a man with money. Adam was her perfect match in every way. Except for the wallet department.

"So, how you gonna play this then?" he asked her, unsure as to what she really hoped to achieve from the trip.

"I've got her name. I managed to get the address from the lady in the post office here – Christina Appleby, Mount Prospect. I suppose I'll just wing it. Perhaps we'll sit outside for a while and see who goes in or out of the house. Then I suppose I'll just go and knock on the door."

She was aware of him frowning at her as she drove. She continued to watch the road.

"I have to do this. For Tara."

"And what if he's living there with her? What if she's a psycho? What if *he's* a psycho?"

"Adam babe," she smiled, rubbing his muscly thigh, "that's why you're with me."

"Great," he moaned.

Tara had steamed in with her preparation for her next job, Job number 10, for the Francophile couple in Dingle.

I needed something to take my mind off the impending Yuletide shenanigans. Whatever your religion or perspective, like it or not, Christmas is rammed down your throat. I was resisting all twinkly warm ideas this year. The trouble is that takes dedication and concentration because wherever you look – it's there!

So I welcomed the job. Just reading through my file brought back lovely memories of me and Declan. I felt so comfortable with him and a little guilty at not telling him why I'd been so down.

To Tara, the antique shops of Dublin were the first places that came to mind to source Irish art for the makeover, but she was finding this more of a challenge than she'd expected. She had spent her few days off very well, leaving early one morning for the Powerscourt Interiors Gallery in Powerscourt House, Enniskerry. A fond devotee of that shopper's paradise she had sat in the restaurant, sipping her coffee on the terrace which overlooked the splendid lawns. She had taken immense pleasure in attending the RHA paintings auction at DeVeres, which had brought flooding back many memories of the days she'd spent working in the gallery for Mulligan.

And now, as she sat at her kitchen table, fighting with the array of swatches and colours in front of her, she was puzzled.

I knew the brief was for the kitchen and bedroom – I'd seen the photos – but the question was, just how "French" was the rest of the house? I mean, to what extent are they Francophiles? If the house was completely awash with eighteen century furniture and indulgent frou-frou then I'd need to be rather bold in my approach. On the other hand, if this was a relatively new thing for them I'd be better to introduce a few subtle touches like gilded mirrors and painted armoires, pretty textiles and fresh flowers – a bit dated, I know, but it'd get them started. I decided to check with Declan next time he rang.

She took the liberty of provisionally deciding on paint for the kitchen walls from the Fired Earth range, opting for *Salle de Musique* in an oil eggshell with *Maison Jaune*.

When Declan called in later that evening, diverting his journey back from the Kilmainham job, she asked him, "Have you met this couple?"

"No, we've spoken over the phone. I think Stephanie met them though."

"I'm fascinated by them. Do you reckon they'll be there offering us ripe brie sarnies and vintage champagne? I just can't wait to meet them!"

"Well," he relaxed into the armchair, "anything'd be better than where we are the moment."

"Is it that bad?" Tara looked up momentarily from her swatches.

"It's worse. The place absolutely stinks! The only good thing about it is that John keeps making me laugh. He's such a mad bastard. And he's taught me a few tricks with that drill of his too. I'll be Mister DIY soon."

"Yeah, I am kind of missing some of the crew now. I haven't heard from Niamh for a few days either. Is she OK?"

"Seems to be," Declan closed his eyes and rubbed his temples. "Bit stressed. I think all of us can't wait to get out of Kilmainham."

"But isn't the next one the Drumcondra one?"

"Yeah, the *Ciara* one."

Tara laughed, "Glad I won't be around for that then."

"Make the most of it. You're on the one after that with her."

A few minutes' silence passed as Tara pondered over the idea.

"Declan? Could you let me see the full brief for Job 10?"

He opened one eye and looked at her. "Oh Tara, you know I can't really do that. Not the full brief. What about Ciara? You are both in it together, don't forget. I know she's a nuisance, but it'll only rub her up the wrong way if you've seen the full brief and she hasn't. It's not worth it, Tara. Sorry."

She smiled at him. "But I need to know what the rest of their house is like. It'd be pointless me going in there with bold ideas if it'll just alienate the makeover rooms from the rest of the place."

I really, really tried hard to pull my sorrowful face. I didn't even make eye contact. Just pouted and pretended to busy myself with the swatches. I heard him shifting uncomfortably on the sofa and then he said it:

"Alright then. I'll bring it all around tomorrow."

It worked. Yippee!!

"Thanks, Dec, you're a pal."

Little did she know how he wanted to be so much more . . .

Niamh and Adam sat outside the house in Abbeyleix

for the best part of the afternoon. Just as she was beginning to succumb to Adam's suggestions of spending the night together *again* and was enjoying listening to what he was intending to do to her, a young woman stopped, rummaged in the rain-cover of the buggy that she was pushing and pulled out a key. Alerted by her close proximity to the house they were watching, Niamh slid down in her seat a little.

"Look at you, ya nutcase! What're you doing?" He began to laugh. "Do you think you're on *The Bill* or something? Look at ya hiding!" Adam was bursting with laughter at Niamh's attempt at discretion.

Reddening slightly she sat up again, smoothed her hair and watched the young woman enter the house. This must be either Christina Appleby or her daughter. *Their* daughter maybe!

Feeling slightly nervous, but mustering confidence again, Niamh got out of the car and went and knocked on the front door. The young woman, still taking off her coat, opened it wearing a confused expression on her face. Niamh suspected she was the young woman that Tara had seen Simon with in McDonald's earlier in the year.

"Hello?" she asked, lightly.

"Em, hello," Niamh faltered. "Ah, is your mother in?"

"My *mother*?"

"Well, you see I'm looking for Christina Appleby."

"That's me. Well, I used to be Christina Appleby, I'm now Christina Cullen."

Niamh felt sick.

This was his wife.

A toddler ran into hallway, stopping in his tracks when he saw a stranger at the door. He rushed to his mum, grabbing onto her leg.

"Well," Niamh continued, "Mrs Cullen. Yes. Is your husband in?"

"No, I'm afraid he's away on business for a fortnight, can I help you?

Niamh relaxed at the news that Slimey Simey wasn't here.

"Em, look, I need to talk to you. My name is Niamh Connolly and I'm a photographer. You see, well, it's kind of delicate. How long have you known Slimey, em, I mean Simon?"

"What *is* this?" demanded the young woman, as she folded her coat in her arms. She placed it down in a strange neat square and faced Niamh, annoyed at her line of questioning.

"Look," Niamh whispered, struggling with her words, "I know Simon."

"He's a friend of yours?"

"Yes. Well, no, not exactly. A friend of a friend, let's say. I know you married him on the 31st of December 1999, here in Abbeyleix and I need to talk to you about him. Urgently."

Christina looked both panicked and freaked at the same time. "Is he hurt?"

"No."

"You'd better come in."

Adam watched from the car, relieved at the easy transaction. Obviously Simon wasn't there and so Adam's services weren't required. They had agreed, before she'd gone in, that she'd send a blank text in an emergency situation.

Niamh sat on the veloured sofa, perched on the edge anxiously. It alarmed her how similar her taste was to Tara's. They had the same rug in front of the fireplace, the same photo of Simon in the same frame. Only where Tara's used to sit on the side-dresser, Christina's took pride of place on the fireplace. She sat opposite Niamh, her young son perched on her lap. Niamh's stomach churned. She hated to be the bearer of bad news. Again.

Thanks to the emotional aftermath she had experienced with Tara, Niamh *half* knew what to expect from Christina. As expected she had first denied that it was possible. That her husband Simon couldn't possibly be married again. It took Niamh a lot of calm persuasion to make her understand how he had married her friend Tara only the previous year. The young woman was angry and indignant, hurt and then tearful. Niamh found herself hugging her and comforting her, even offering to make her a strong cup of coffee while the news sunk in.

As she delivered the coffee she also parted with the double-whammy that he hadn't only married one more time, but three. Christina sobbed into her young son's neck, causing him to cry too. By the confused look on the tot's face he didn't really know what he was crying for, just the unsettled vision of his mummy in distress was enough to upset his apple-cart. Niamh wished she was good with kids, but she just wasn't – she'd never needed to be.

She finally managed to compose Christina with the promise that she'd be in contact again soon to help her sort this situation. If she wanted her to. The young woman nodded, her hair beginning to stick to her tear-ravaged face. Stopping at the front door, Niamh turned and pressed a piece of paper with her phone number on it into Christina's hand.

"I'm so sorry to break this news to you. And you with a young child too. Is he Simon's?"

Christina was unable to speak and merely nodded, her lips clenched tightly together as she welled up again.

"How about I come back at the weekend and bring Tara with me. Perhaps the best way to sort this out is between all of you?"

Christina shrugged, too intent on preventing another outburst and so upsetting her little boy.

Niamh left her with a hug and a kiss on the cheek and felt like shit as she got back into the car. Lowering herself into the seat and closing the door, she slapped Adam on the leg as he snored. He wriggled but settled again so she started the car, causing him to waken.

"Well," he yawned, "how did it go?"

Niamh choked back an uncharacteristic tear. "Fucking terrible. I feel just terrible about this. She's so young, Adam, and that little boy is Simon's too."

"Jesus. He's some bad bastard, ain't he?"

As she headed away from Abbeyleix she stared at the road, determined.

"Now I have to find the other two. Una Slattery and Mary Ryan."

Chapter 20

Niamh sat, legs akimbo on her huge beanbag, busy sorting the reels of film and stills for the Kilmainham makeover. Out of every batch she'd usually have to discard about a third. Sometimes more. She wriggled slightly, uncomfortable as her thong cut into her. She cast her thoughts back to the night before when she'd spent the night with Adam – again. She laughed at the expression "spend the night". It sounded so innocent, almost like it was something boring!

"Ha," she laughed into her empty room, " he's taken over from Karl as Cunnilingus King!" She'd gotten him to gargle with crème de menthe first as she'd heard the tingling sensation was mind-blowing. The rumours were true. And then he'd taken her by surprise and had started to softly "humm" as he went to work on her down there. The deep vibrations of his voice-box made his whole mouth buzz. It had started as very exciting, although she had begun to feel a little like a woodwind instrument towards the end. Her relaxed attitude as a self-confessed "tri-sexual", in that she'd try anything, meant that she had more men on the go than she could keep tabs on and was coming to the conclusion that she was now at least two men over the legal limit. She was singing lightly along to her Nelly Furtado CD and her mind raced. Before she knew it she was talking to herself as she sorted the photographic images before her.

"Perhaps it's time for a male lodger. Maybe it'd make me a little less likely to keep bringing home these guys." Pondering the idea for a few minutes, she then answered herself, "No, men lodgers are bad news. They pee on the toilet seat for a start. They're sick in the sink and *never* clean it up properly." She laughed at her ramblings, then she came up with another, "*And* they laugh at your erect nipples on a cold morning."

Dismissing the whole idea she sorted the pile of photos into three, ranging from "excellent", "so-so" and "crap". Hauling herself up from the floor she checked her watch. It was great to have a couple of days off before the next job started. She was enjoying the constant work of *Home Is*, but had already turned down three commissions due to lack of time. It was all starting to feel rather contrived and, dare she say it, a little samey. If it wasn't for the fact that she and Tara had such a great time laughing at Ciara then she might feel even more desperate about it. Her thoughts of Tara bought on a wish to see her. They hadn't really spoken properly since before the Kilmainham job had started.

Niamh had been deliberately keeping out of Tara's way for a little while – especially in the light of the fact that she had since been to see "wife-number-three" and hadn't yet told Tara. Grabbing her denim jacket from the banister she scrunched it under her arm, pinched her car keys from the key rack and swung her bag up onto her shoulder. She was going to see Tara.

Tara was surprised to see her at the door.

To be honest, I'd thought she was avoiding me. It had been bugging me a bit really, but I wasn't sure whether she was embarassed about the night at the meal or felt awkward. What with me being married to a polygamist and all . . .

"Hey, stranger." Tara smiled warmly as Niamh stepped in over the doorstep.

They embraced and kissed each other on the cheek.

"Are ya busy? What ya up to?" Niamh dumped her bag in the hallway, completely relaxed in her surroundings. It was a home-from-home really.

"Oh, just trying to sort the French job."

"The *French* job? You sound like a mafia hood." Niamh frowned.

"No, I don't mean the French job, as such. I mean the makeover in Dingle. Don't tell Ciara, but Declan's given me the full brief."

"Good on ya!" Niamh teased.

Tara blushed, disguising it swiftly with a turnabout to the kitchen with the excuse of switching on the kettle. "So, what have you been doing?"

"You mean apart from shagging my way around

Dublin and photographing numerous 'before' and 'after' shots of suburban living-rooms?"

"So nothing's changed then?"

"Well, a few things. But we need to sit down for them. What about you?"

"Like I said. I've been immersed in the idea of moving away from the painted armoires, silk bedspreads, antique French bedlinens and delicately decorated glassware. I'm now trying to look at more of a Terence Conran interpretation of Parisian chic. To be honest, I can't wait to go back to Paris again for another look around – he has a couple of shops in Paris, I think."

Niamh watched Tara prepare the mugs and an instant distaste for domestic hot drinks came over her.

"Get your jacket, we're going out," she instructed.

"What? Where?"

"Oh, just get it. I'm taking you out for lunch. Café Alpha do you?"

"Great. Just wait while I go to the loo."

Niamh waited while Tara bombed it up the stairs, two at a time. Casually looking through her prep work for the Frenchy job in Dingle she was amazed at the effort that Tara was putting into it. Feeling a pride at Tara's latest talents and yet a sympathy for her dreadful situation, Niamh decided she'd have to explain to Tara about Christina.

They were disappointed to see that the Café Alpha was jammed to the rafters with corporate lunch-timers and tourists and so instead settled for Luigi's.

Sitting in the cool restaurant, Niamh leant across the

table and asked, "So, how are you feeling about Slimey Simey now?"

Tara looked up from the menu, squarely into Niamh's face, and spoke softly, "You see the thing is, Niamh, *that* piece of paper and two rings are only the by-products of a marriage. But it is so much more than that. It's the emotional commitment and the frame of mind that you're in at the time that means so much. Like a mental illness, your intentions and dreams can't always be seen. My attitude towards marriage was that it was for *life*. And I *know* I had the affair. But somehow that's faded into insignificance now – now that I know that Simon, *my* Simon, is already married. But, you know, I still miss him. I still love him too, in a way, and that torments me as well."

Niamh listened with a sympathetic ear, silently applauding her own sexual liberation and yet sorry for her friend.

"Well, I've got some more to tell you actually."

Tara sipped at her chilled white wine. "Go on."

"Simon's been married another time."

"I know. Anna told me."

"Oh. Anna found out by mistake. It seems he married Una Slattery first. She's the one that George saw him with at the wedding. He then went on to marry a Mary Ryan. So far I don't know any more about her other than that. And then Anna found out by mistake that, well – you know the young girl you saw him with in McDonald's?"

"No! That was *her*!" A sob escaped from Tara's

mouth, so loud that the waiters looked over. One even grabbed the first aid box.

Niamh put her hand over Tara's.

The colour had drained from Tara's face. Niamh took a deep breath and dived in, "And I've been to see her."

Three bottles of wine later, Niamh had persuaded Tara that they should go to Abbeyleix the following weekend – the Saturday after the Drumcondra makeover – so that Tara and Christina could meet. They were, albeit rather slurringly, in agreement that the only way to get back at Simon was to do it together.

As promised I was staying away from the Drumcondra job, although if Niamh's tales were anything to go by I was almost sorry about that. For some reason Ciara was like a woman possessed. Niamh was finding it hilarious, like they all were, at how she was so permanently edgy.

I'd done well on my French research, but since talking to Niamh about Simon's many other wives I found I was in a strange mental state. I was desperate to get back to work to take my mind off things and yet at the same time I was lolling around, analysing every word, every action. And I knew it wasn't good for me. It was all made worse by the fact that I remembered, once I'd sobered up, that Niamh told me how Christina and Simon have a son! I mean it's one thing hurting us women – aren't we big enough and ugly enough to look out for our pathetic selves? But children? Bringing children into that mess was completely unforgivable.

What was even more disturbing – did that make me a stepmum?

I was, after all, married to his father.
Along with three other poor bitches.

Ciara was on the brink of a breakdown. For some reason she was no longer able to hide her feelings. Somehow she was being haunted by something that had happened over thirty years ago and, as hard as she tried to continue turning her back on it, she simply couldn't.

Her head now buried into her cushion as she sobbed, full of self-inflicted humiliation, Ciara cursed herself for hating Tara as much as she did. She knew it was unfair – she couldn't help looking like she did. Ciara was becoming completely obsessed with her irritation at Tara – her natural flair and ambition. Nausea swept through her once again, like a thick barium meal. She'd wanted so many times to opt out of the celebrity production line that she felt she was on. She often wondered whether age was catching up with her – there had to be some reason for her recent reminiscences. If only she didn't hate herself so much. As she sobbed into the saturated cushion she craved more drugs, but knew it would mean that she'd sleep for another twenty-four hours afterwards. A rush of thoughts hurtled through her mind. A rush of get-out clauses so that she didn't have to appear in front of a camera ever again. She wanted out of *Home Is*. She wanted away from Tara and her painfully familiar air, and features that so reminded her of somebody else. She'd decided to feign illness at first, just to get out of it all, and then, while she'd sat on the loo in a disturbed state, had even planned how she'd slip on the wet tiles and hurt herself. Bravely, she had finally decided that she wouldn't be defeated. And so, in typical Ciara style, she swallowed a handful of tablets and steamed through. And so, the walls had been painted a vivid and very trendy red which contrasted boldly with the white marble fire-surround. A few zebra-printed cushions were added and, coupled with the wrought-iron light fittings and candle-holders, the finished product was one that lent a great theatrical feel to the room. Ciara actually preferred the finished product more than her own house. It had more class and style. But it made her feel as though she were losing her touch.

And so the final day had come for the "Close your eyes . . . open them!" that Ciara hated so much.

With the Drumcondra job out of the way, Niamh and Tara were on their way to Abbeyleix. Christina was expecting them at lunch-time and, whilst they were all nervous, Tara was actually quite intrigued about what she'd be like.

There's something exciting about meeting your husband's other wife. Apart from the fact that it's extremely weird. It's a bit like meeting your ex's new girlfriends – only worse. It's that time when you invisibly measure yourself against her. And you know damned well she's doing it to you too.

"And so," Niamh continued, her chatter non-stop since they'd left Dublin, "Ciara's face completely drained of colour. There she was, all snotty and miserable, jeering and pre-empting the owners' reaction, when this young couple walked in. I could see Ciara throwing tabs down her neck like she'd never be able to swallow again. She must have taken too many, she literally turned the puce of the marble fireplace! And *then* the colour of the walls."

"What colour where they?"

"Tomato red! It was obvious that she was struggling to compose herself and Declan tried to come to the rescue."

"And?" Tara was munching on toffees and was grateful that Niamh was rattling ahead at such great speed.

"And Ciara almost passed out, she was so drugged up. I reckon Declan was relieved that the owners were so pleased with the results that he didn't need Ciara's ad-libbing. Ah, she's just a dried-up old bag anyway. Who cares? She's a lost cause if you ask me."

If you ask me there's no such thing as a lost cause. Maybe that's just the humanitarian in me. Or possibly Anna's charitable influence. It had been obvious to me for a while that Ciara had her problems and maybe something was terribly wrong there. As horrible as she was, I wanted to help her. Yeah, I know I'm a mug – I've proved that already, haven't I?

It's just a crying shame I'm not as vigilant in my own relationships.

As Niamh pulled up outside Christina's house, Tara began to feel extremely nervous.

It was just so awful that they had a young child. And

from what I could remember from McDonald's, she was just a child too!

So though it started as an awkward and stilted meeting, Tara, Niamh and Christina found, nearly three hours later, that they had a lot in common.

Apart from Slimey.

They had soon begun to laugh at his idiosyncrasies, such as his predilection for takeaways. They'd soon began to gasp and cry at his perverse flower knowledge and felt cheated and sad at the revelation that they both received fresh red and white chrysanthemums every Saturday morning.

He certainly kept Interflora in business.

It was then that Christina had got upset and angry at the huge deception and his long spells away from home.

"Didn't you say that he's away on business at the moment?" Niamh asked. "Where is he supposed to be?"

"Belfast, I think? I can't always keep track of it."

"Convenient. For *him!*" Niamh commented.

"I found that too," Tara whispered. "His arrangements always seemed to change at the last minute. He was never where he was supposed to be."

"Literally," deadpanned Christina, without a trace of emotion in her voice.

The most chilling part though was when Christina told me that his parents were killed in a car crash when he was a child! And he'd told me there'd been a massive family bust-up and they now lived in Chicago. How would you know what to believe from somebody like that?

Niamh suggested that they try and keep tabs on him, eventually tracking him down and confronting them. All four of them.

It all sounded too Ruth Rendell for me really. I knew where Niamh was coming from, but this was a sensitive issue and I didn't think we should play with emotions. Christina, Una and Mary might have truly loved Simon and, where I felt humiliated, they might feel truly bereaved. I thought it was best to make them aware, but then to withdraw and let them make their own decisions.

After all, there could be even more children involved yet . . .

Chapter 21

Ciara was completely gutted. She'd spent yet another night off her face, but this time she was at home. She had decided she wouldn't go out for a while; it was safer to get rat-faced at home. And she didn't even seem capable of knowing who she was going home with lately. There were so many disturbing, unanswered questions. She churned them over in her dependent, confused mind. Her head felt as if it was being squeezed, both from the inside and the out. She knew she'd overdone the tablets yet again, and the three bottles of Krug on her sideboard were a sickening reminder of her addictions. Yet she knew she had to punish herself. Pulling on her rubber gloves with a "snap" she filled a bucket with piping hot water and an overabundance of bleach. If she couldn't have a "clean" body, she'd sure as hell have a clean house.

Three hours later her hangover was threatening to put her to bed. Despite the painkillers and water, cranberry juice and two oranges, all she'd managed was to successfully go to the loo. Four times. Her kitchen was a gleaming, shining Mecca yet she still felt terrible. She knew she was avoiding the issue and eventually flopped down onto her plush settee – tugging at the yellow rubber gloves as they stuck to her sweaty hands. She hated cleaning, but this was punishment. Only to Ciara it wasn't enough. Once again her mind drifted back thirty-three years. It seemed it was time to face up to her past.

It had been her last year at University and she had been so close to completing her studies – to her delight, interior design had been more elite-ist then. Now she often scorned the latest fad for home makeovers, yet knew that they paid her bills, but had so much preferred it in the seventies, when it had all been new and fresh. Only the crème de la crème could afford an interior designer and she had bought into the whole idea that she was something special – something different. Her eyes now filled with tears as she dug her long fingernails deeply into her wrist, oblivious to the red swollen mounds of skin that surrounded her nails. She thought back again to those last few months of training. She'd been top of her class and was operating a consultancy way before she'd even graduated. She'd been offered a fantastic contract by a Moroccan millionaire, who had insisted that she complete her training first. She really had felt that the road to success was already paved before her. As she sat bolt upright on her settee, she continued to track back the thirty-three years in her head and didn't notice the mushrooms of blood escaping from her wrist as she dug her nails in even further. Her tears fell involuntarily from her eyes, dropping onto her wrist and diluting the small red domes that were now dribbling down into the palm of her hand. That tutor had been such a bastard. And she'd been so young. She knew that was why she was filled with such self-loathing and hatred. She suspected that was the crux of her drug problem. And she was well aware of the fact that he was behind her insatiable anger. But there was no way she could have kept that child. And so now, thirty-three years later, she was being haunted by a living person, who didn't even know her and who she didn't know.

As she rubbed her eyes, the stale wet mascara falling in small clumps on her cheeks, she reflected back on her life a little more. For the last thirty-years she had mistaken her desire to be loved for lust. She knew, at her age, her behaviour was completely unacceptable, but for some reason the older she became the more desperate she was. She felt as though her life was spiralling out of control. She simply couldn't understand it. But she knew one thing: something was going terribly wrong. Somewhere, somehow. She looked down to her smeared bloody wrists and hands, as if she'd only just realised what she had been doing. Sighing deeply, she stood and slowly made her way to the bathroom. Turning on the tap slowly, she rested her wrists beneath the lukewarm water and watched the pinky swirling water gurgle down the plug-hole. She looked up at her reflection in the bathroom mirror, her panda'd eyes red and swollen from her tears.

"Perhaps," she told herself, "it's time to track her down."

Declan caught Tara's arm as she passed in the nylon-carpeted RTÉ corridor.

"Hey, I was thinking – now don't take this the wrong way – how would you fancy a night of fireworks and opera? My treat."

What did he mean by the 'wrong way'? Anyway, at least it would take my mind off Chrimbo – Christmas, that is.

"OK –"

I know, I know – I was never good at playing hard to get . . .

"– on the condition we go Dutch."

"Oh, I was actually thinking of Wexford." Declan grinned cheekily. Tara pulled a face at him.

"The Opera Festival starts on Thursday," he went on.

"Wow! Sounds cool."

"Well, it's mainly opera, but there's a fantastic firework display on the opening night on the quay – and there are lots of art exhibitions and a few great late-nighters."

"So, when then?" she pushed it.

"How are you fixed for Thursday? It'd be nice to stay longer, but I've got that big meeting on Friday, and the fireworks are only on Thursday night."

"You know me. As long as I can get Mum to look

after Ruben, I'm a free-agent up until the Dingle job."

"Right then, I'll go sort out the hotel now. Hope you're alright with this, but I've already got the tickets for the late-night event."

I love a man who's impulsive.

Well, I don't actually love them. You know, not in the true sense of the word.

"But what about the briefing this afternoon?" She was a little anxious about this.

"No problem, I'll be back before then. See you at the office at three?"

She smiled warmly at him.

Could be that he was my perfect man.

If there was such a thing.

What was it Niamh had said about my proposal to Simon? A Mr Right for Little Miss Not-so-Bright?

Declan bustled into his office at quarter-past three, only to see a room full of faces stare up at him in unison. He was flushed and puffed, but grappled his coat off with a wide smile. They all noticed the wink towards Tara.

"Sorry, lads, got caught up in town there."

He hung his casual jacket over the back of his chair as Miss Day handed him the file of papers.

As he talked us through the form for the makeover in Dingle I couldn't help but notice my stomach fluttering. Constantly! The slides and descriptions he gave regarding the kitchen were so familiar to me. Little did they all know, Ciara especially, that I'd already decided what colours to

*paint the walls! I must never let them know that I'd already
seen the full brief!*

Tara watched Declan as he handed over to Stephanie
the researcher to fill in the gaps regarding the Dingle
clients.

*The truth is, I'd probably given far too much time to this
job, but it was the French thing. I reckon I'd really risen to
the challenge.*

Declan caught Tara looking at him and smiled,
winking again and nodding slowly.

*I took the wink and the nod to mean that we were "on" for
Wexford.*

That was probably what the fluttering belly was all about.

*I mean, although we were staying over, it wasn't an
'official' date.*

Was it?

As they gathered for coffee and biscuits after the
meeting, their light-hearted chatter filled the large
office. Declan had managed to get away at one point,
following Tara to the toilets and pulling her into the
stationery room for a minute – just to confirm that
they'd head off on Thursday afternoon. She was
suddenly concerned that Ciara would find out about
their night away and that she'd lose the professional
edge that she'd taken such effort in building up. Declan
rubbed her arms briskly, as if she was cold, telling her
that Ciara wouldn't even put two and two together –
she was so caught up with her own life.

But it was a simple matter to put two and two
together, in fact. They'd all noticed that Declan had left

the room only seconds after Tara. They also noticed that he returned only a minute or two before her. Niamh nudged Tara and whispered, giving her a sideways glance, "Following you to the loo now, is he?"

"Shutup, Niamh. I'll tell you later."

"What are you two up to?" Niamh now wanted to know, still standing beside Tara and pretending to sip at her coffee.

"Keep it a secret, eh?"

Niamh nodded, with a mouthful of cookie.

"We're going to the Wexford Opera Festival. Day after tomorrow!"

"*Woooooooohh!*" Niamh cat-called, rather too loud for Tara's liking.

The others slowed their conversations and turned to look at them.

Then, just as Ciara swanked past them, Tara badly judged her proximity and hissed at Niamh, "We're having separate bedrooms though!"

At which point Ciara stuck her head in between them and jeered, "Jesus, I've heard of 'Around Ireland with a Fridge', but what is this – 'Around Ireland with a Frigid'?"

"Feck off, Ciara," Tara sneered back at her.

"Yeah," added Niamh loudly, "and while you're fecking off you might want to check your septum. Your nostrils are looking kinda *huge*, love." The others heard her and the room was filled with a tittering sound, which rose above all conversation.

Ciara glared and left.

Slamming the door behind her.

Niamh and Tara said their goodbyes in the RTÉ carpark. Niamh kissed Tara on the cheek, with instructions to travel safely and, most importantly, to enjoy her time in Wexford. And Declan.

Tara had laughed it off, saying how could she *not* enjoy a culture-filled evening with Declan? To which Niamh had hugged her and whispered that she really did mean *enjoy*. In the light of Slimey Simey and her now misplaced guilt, she suggested that perhaps it was time for Tara to start to *really* relax in Declan's company.

Tara knew what she was saying, but didn't let on. Grabbing her hand and giving it a tight squeeze, she promised to ring her as soon as they were back on Friday.

Niamh stopped at the Esso garage a short way up the road, parted company with a fifty euro note and drove home with her denim-jacket pocket stuffed with a roll of scratchcards. The trouble was, the adrenalin rush didn't last long and she wasn't even really enjoying it as much as she used to. While she was pleased that Tara was having the opportunity to let her hair down, she felt slightly unfulfilled in her own life. Her photography wasn't going like she wanted it to and she was already bored with the "homes" thing. She much preferred the freedom of "shooting" celebrities for their publicity shots and CD covers. Her love life was full in the physical sense, but emotionally there was only one of her men who really gelled with her mentally. Impulsive as ever, she picked up her phone and sent another photo message to Adam. This time it was a photo of her house and she knew he'd understand. She'd need some help with the scratching tonight anyway. Fifty cards would take her at least fifteen minutes.

What had I agreed to?

A night in a hotel. With Declan.

And so soon after the Paris trip?

The question was, what would I wear? I had learned from the last visit to wear comfortable shoes during the day – at the risk of sounding like my mum! Perhaps Declan could show me the Wexford arts scene. He was so well-informed in the arts. He'd already told me about the Wexford Arts Centre, Padraig Grant's photography, Karen Nolan's paintings, Elizabeth O'Brien's sell-out exhibition and Myriad Dance's quayside dancers. See – I was learning! And then there was the firework display on the quay!

You know, I thought, maybe my pre-Christmas nausea is clearing up.

Who can resist the lure of Wexford in the late autumn?

The drive down to Wexford was fabulous. The coastal road led them past Bray and Wicklow, then Arklow and Gorey as they avoided the commuter traffic. He'd known it'd be a great idea to leave in the afternoon.

As his car zoomed along the clear roads, the cotton-wool clouds sat lightly in a clear blue sky. Tara smiled at Declan, "I love these open spaces, don't you?" she breathed, completely relaxed.

"Yeah, great, isn't it? The blue sky and sunshine just make all the difference, don't they?"

"Yes, but it's not only that. It's the freedom. The potential."

The potential.

They both held that thought . . .

They arrived at the delightful hotel just as dinner was being served and the smell of enticing cooking immediately warmed them as they stepped in from the chilly air, their noses a glowing pink.

"Fancy a quick drink?" Declan grinned after they'd checked each other's rooms out and Tara had hung up her more delicate clothes. She was standing at her window which overlooked the large quay. She was checking for external staircases or any other possible entry point for undesirables.

"A brandy'd be good." She spoke without thinking.

"A woman after my own heart."

"And I thought I was the only one who could down a brandy this early in the day!" Tara gushed, suddenly slightly embarassed.

"Seems we have more in common than we thought." Declan smiled at her and watched as she locked her bedroom door behind her in the plush carpeted corridor.

They sat in the bar, sipping at the thick, cool drink as it swirled and clung to the fat-bottomed glass.

Declan continued his line of conversation, "So what else do you like?"

"Let me think . . . you know, it's not easy when you're put on the spot like that. Right, OK, I like going to the cinema. I love films, but I also like turning round and looking at people's faces in the dark. Especially at a weepie or a horror. They look so gormless, some of them."

They both laughed. He was intrigued by her, more than ever. She was completely different when she was away from the *Home Is* set.

"So," she disturbed his rambling thoughts, "what do you like?"

"Oh I like reading autobiographies, brandy and . . . I don't know."

"You don't know what you like?"

He realised he sounded really pathetic and so threw in, "I like peeling off really huge strips of wallpaper in the one go."

She threw her head back and cackled at his reply.

Yeah, he'd caught my imagination all right.

Cheeky, eh?

They sat in the Italian restaurant on the crowded Main Street of Wexford. Opera Festival time was always busy and the influx of American tourists surprised them. It had been a struggle to get their windowside table, especially as they'd heard a crowd of American women asking for the table that Drew Barrymore had once sat at.

It was obviously our one.

"Romantic, isn't it?" Tara sighed as she watched the families pass by, wrapped up in their coats and scarves. She noted the couples, dressed in tuxedos and velvet evening wear as they linked arms and strolled easily.

Declan smiled at her, his eyes dancing in an almost teasing fashion.

She continued, ignoring to his expression. "I love the autumn. The chill in the air, the kids in their woolly hats and scarves, the leaves, the dark afternoons."

Declan smiled. "That depends on how romantic your perspective is."

"Yeah, there's a lot to be said for runny noses and flu." She raised her eyebrows in sarcasm.

"Romance is like beauty. It's in the eye of the beholder. If you love the one you're with, then romance can be a cup of tea and a digestive."

"I've never felt that way about anyone, have you?"

"I did with Paula, at first."

"So what happened?"

"Probably what usually happens. I got too comfortable, started taking her for granted, got used to seeing her slop around the house in her pyjamas and felt like my head was being squeezed with it all."

"So where is she now?"

"She's living in Malahide with a fella. I can't stand him."

"You still love her?"

"No. At least, to an extent. It's a question of letting go. I'm nearly there."

I wished I was. Although maybe I'd already let go before I met Graham. Maybe it just all seemed different now.

Now that I knew he was unfaithful to me before he'd even accepted my proposal.

Feeling more comfortable after a sit-down and some

food, they walked through the crowds on the narrow cobbled Wexford streets as they made their way to the quayside for the firework display. Tara delighted at the illuminated, ornate shop-window displays which were expertly dressed to complement the operatic and arts festivities. They opted to watch the fireworks from one of the pubs which lined the quay. They watched the children playing with their three euro glow-in-the-dark gadgets and then marvelled at the fantastic firework display, which was conducted to extremely loud opera music. The crackles, thuds and *"aaahhs!"* reverberated through the air as the black sky was splashed like an artist's canvas with colour and shape, only to be reflected back in the black water of the River Slaney. The vision struck an emotional chord with Tara as she realized, playing with the stem of her wineglass, that she hadn't been as happy for a long time. She held the glass daintily, raising it aloft. "Here's to self-respect and values!"

Declan obliged. They clinked glasses and drank.

"You know," she sighed, placing the half empty glass back onto the table, "I married a polygamist."

"You what?" He couldn't believe what she was saying and wasn't expecting such a revelation.

"I did. I still am, actually." She seemed very easy with the news. "I only found out a few weeks ago. Niamh told me."

"Was that what upset you so much that night in Galway?"

She nodded.

He asked quietly, "Is *that* what made you so sick?"

She nodded again, smiling gently.

"Is that like a bigamist?" He folded his arms and leaned on the table, the fireworks forgotten.

She smiled. "It's worse. A bigamist is married twice. A polygamist is married more than twice. My husband is actually married four times. I'm the fourth. You must have heard of the First Wives' Club? Well, I'm in the Fourth Wives' Club! Honestly," she tried to laugh it off, "it's ridiculous even by Hollywood standards."

"Christ!"

"I know. Sorry, I'm not embarrassing you, am I?"

"No. Not at all. I just feel for you, that's all."

"Thanks, but there's no need. It's just a hideous marital shambles really. And to make it worse, *I* proposed to *him*."

He grinned. He couldn't help himself.

"I did! 29th February. You know the old Leap Year thing?"

"So, you're a traditionalist?"

"Hardly. More like an idiot."

As she unravelled the lengthy tale to him he listened, sympathetic and then horrified as she'd unfolded the illegalities of her "husband". Towards the end of her story he noticed the tears brimming in her beautiful eyes and swiftly steered the conversation back into a light, convivial mood.

"Hey, at least you got to keep the wedding pressies!"

"Yeah," she sniffed and giggled, "I suppose. Mind you, he could have kept the bloody barbecue."

"Yeah," he comforted her, "it's a real man thing, isn't it? I remember when I was first cohabiting. I was hosting a tragically naïve version of a barbecue – as you do when you're in the early stages of marriage – and I'd burnt all of the meat on the outside, but it was raw in the middle. There were twenty people in Rathfarnham with diarrhoea for a week!"

She truly laughed this time, the tears dissipating once again.

"So," he added, slightly more serious this time, "what are you going to do?"

"Oh, I don't know," she dismissed it, sniffing and wiping her eyes. "Probably torture him. Maybe I'll tie him up and find a really big chain and then weave it between his toes. Maybe you'd like to give it an almighty tug then, or something?"

He grimaced. "God, you're evil!" he teased.

"You'd better believe it. But seriously, maybe I should just do nothing and hope that he gets his come-uppance elsewhere."

"No, don't let him get away with it!"

"I just can't face it at the moment, Declan. The fact is Christmas is right on top of me and I'm consumed with the dread of spending it with my mother again. I thought I'd got out of that when I got married and here I am – one year later, back at me ma's."

"Well, look," he reached over and caressed her forearm lightly, "if you ever need a friend, you know where I am, don't you?"

"Thanks," she smiled. And she meant it.

"You could have him up in court though."

She ignored that statement, choosing instead to delve into her packet of cheese and onion Tayto and cram a huge cluster into her mouth.

The late-night event was great.

At least I thought it was.

The truth was, I was pissed. I'd pigged out on red wine and everything was pleasingly blurry.

Declan was no better. He'd gone to town on the brandies.

Great, eh?

As the clock ticked rapidly towards the early hours Declan suggested that they make their way back to their hotel. She knew it'd be hilarious trying to walk in the crisp night air. She knew they'd be wobbling and waddling into each other.

They were both on the wrong side of being sober.

Chapter 22

As they crossed the street-lit paved square that fronted their hotel, Tara realised she was seeing double. There were twice as many of the long sash windows, twice as many conifers flanking the door – the two doors. Clinging onto each other's arms, they bumped and nudged into each other as they walked, still giggling. They chuckled and tittered as they got into the lift and joked at the *"ping"* as it reached the third floor.

"Ping! Ping!" trilled Tara as she bumped her way along the corridor, clutching onto her litre bottle of Ballygowan. She stopped at her door and turned to Declan, "Coming in?"

He looked slightly uncomfortable, despite his half-pissed state. "Oh, I dunno. Maybe not."

She feigned offence. "Rightso, a wink's as good as a nod." She fumbled with her key and then dropped it and began to laugh. They bent together to pick it up and crouched, their noses almost touching. She whispered,

"Don't worry. I'm not going to ravage you. What do you take me for? After all," she began to cackle, "I am fucking *married*!"

But it all went wrong. And now in the cold light of day I could only remember half of it. Well, most of it. I thought.

My head was sooo sore and there was a vice-like grip around my temples. I felt sick and bad and disgusted. There was no way I'd be able to journey back to Dublin with him that afternoon. Just no way. Even worse, there was no way I could even face him again. You see, one thing just led to another and then it was just sex sex sex all the way. It was the damned hairy chest that got me. That and the tender and loving way he touched me. He held my face like it belonged to a porcelain doll and kissed me so beautifully. It made me want to cry. At first. Not all the time. Declan was raunchy and good. After all, it had been a long time. It had all seemed fine at the time. It was only after that it hit me. We'd lain there together, snuggled up, and I'd started to get spinny-rooms. I could have sworn the bed was levitating! He was snoring — don't they all — and then it hit me.

Suddenly, it hit me.

I realised that he was just taking the piss out of me.

Course he was!

Preying on my vulnerability.

There I'd been, stupid and loose-tongued in the restaurant telling him all about how Simon shat on me. What was he supposed to think? I was virtually letting him in on the secret that I was gullible and easily manipulated and stupid!

After all that bullshit about self-respect and values! He had used me.

He had even said he loved me.

My God. He said he loved me!

Or did he?

Maybe he said he thought he loved me.

As if I'd believe such a thing. After all, he'd got what he wanted from me. He'd looked so upset as I pushed him out of my room. But we know what good actors men can be when it suits them. Just look at Slimey Simey for evidence of that one.

What Tara didn't realise was that she was taking her anger at Simon out on the wrong person.

The person who really *did* love her.

Chapter 23

Tara woke again at midday. The two Nurofen and litre of water had helped. That and the extra four hours' sleep. She slouched, propped up against the restored antique headboard of the wrought-iron bed and listened. Through her closed shutters but slightly open windows she could hear the sounds of Wexford on a bright and busy day. She felt as though she were dreaming. Checking her watch she wondered what time he'd planned on leaving for Dublin.

She wondered whether he was up.

She wondered whether she'd be able to face him.

She cried softly at the thought of him. She really wanted him to hold her again and wished they could have spent the whole night together, but she was very, very confused and knew she'd have great pains in trusting anyone again. Ever.

I was feeling and confused and guilty. And that *was making me feel even more confused and guilty!*

Shaking her head in an attempt to clear it a little, she pulled back the covers and took a deep breath as she prepared to go vertical. Clenching her eyes closed, she swung her legs up and out of the bed and stood quickly. She balanced perfectly and her head wasn't being squeezed. Opening her eyes she was relieved that the hangover seemed to have passed. Feeling emotionally bruised and still slightly fragile, she went into the bathroom and refreshed herself with a shower. Her invigorating shower gel really stood true to its claims of being "reviving and refreshing". An hour later, after drying her hair and relaxing on the bed with a magazine for a short while, she began to quietly pack her case, disappointed that such a fantastic time had ended with such bad feeling.

I really enjoyed his company. I'd felt more relaxed and happy in the last twenty-four hours than I had for over a year.

She reflected over the time they'd spent and paused with her white cotton shirt in her hands, mid-fold. The Italian meal, the brandies, the art exhibitions, the fireworks.

Our fireworks.

She sat down on the end of the bed in a slump. Staring at the floor she continued to think. The arts exhbitions, the music. Her body tensed as she held the tears back. It took great effort to blink them away. There was no way she was getting in that car this afternoon with tears in her eyes.

No way.

They met in the hotel reception at midday. She'd taken

a couple of hours in Wexford alone and had shopped at Sasha, had panini'd and cappucino'd at Into The Blue.

I'd been wishing I could stay longer and then I realised that I could.

I would.

I simply couldn't sit beside him for two hours while we drove back to Dublin in silence. I'd go back to the hotel and meet him and I could tell him then. I'd make my own way back on the bus or the train or something. I needed more time alone.

Not least before I faced Niamh!

As they faced each other she felt uncomfortable at the pained expression on Declan's face. She felt guilty and yet angry, more confused than anything else! Before she could get a grip on trusting her mouth not to reveal her true feelings, Declan apologised.

"I am so sorry, Tara. I really didn't mean to upset you."

She shrugged.

"Really. I didn't. You took it all the wrong way. You have muddled it all in your head and made *me* out to be the bad guy. Tara," he lifted her hand gently, "you might not believe me, but I told you last night. I love you. I'd never do anything to hurt you."

She looked deep into his eyes for a split second and then pulled her hand away lightly.

"Please, Declan. I'm confused enough as it is. Why don't you just get back to Dublin, eh?"

He couldn't leave it like this.

"How could you think that 'that' was all I wanted

from you? Tara, we've had a fantastic time, no-one can deny that. No-one can take that away from us. If sex was all I wanted I could have stayed in Dublin."

She turned her back on him. The receptionist pretended not to be listening. She was expert at it now and took great delight in pretending to be on the phone or e-mailing someone whilst intently taking in every word, every flicker of emotion.

She even pretended not to notice how Tara cried when Declan finally turned his back and left her standing there.

Sitting in her hotel room, full of self-pity, she mentally tormented herself with her recurring feelings of guilt about the affair with Graham, and hated herself for being in a production-line of wives. She had managed to apologise to Declan for her outburst, but still felt it safer to keep him at arm's length from now on.

I seemed to cause trouble wherever I went. Perhaps it was better for me to concentrate on life without a man.

The journey was miserable. Declan reprimanded himself for the whole two hours and felt terrible at his weakness last night. He should have known not to go into her room. Especially given the way he felt about her. Glancing down at his mobile, he pondered whether to text her. He hadn't been happy leaving her in Wexford, but she'd insisted. Thinking better of it, he turned off his phone as if to dispel the temptation.

He'd trodden all over the eggshells now.

It was too late.

He supposed he'd ruined everything.

I can still see the pain in his eyes.

I can even remember counting – he had seven *frown lines running across his forehead. They weren't there all the time, mind. Only that day.*

The extra couple of hours in Wexford had done Tara the world of good. She didn't feel any better about herself – it was more a case of taking her mind off her situation. She'd enjoyed the many fringe events that accompanied the Opera Festival time and had lost herself in the various galleries and the numerous visual art exhibitions and cafés that lined the Wexford streets. She had wished she could stay longer to see the Paul O'Brien play that was being performed over the next few nights, but she'd already bought her Bus Éireann ticket for her journey back to Dublin. She was catching the early evening bus. She dragged herself from the Greenacres emporium, but not before buying some fresh fruit and exotic spices and a bottle of expensive vintage champagne, and made a mental note to return for a holiday the next year to really enjoy all that Wexford had to offer. She started to feel tired again as she made her way back to her hotel.

It was the effects of alcohol-induced insomnia again. I'd spent the first two hours in bed with Declan, the next two feeling angry with him, and the next few virtually unconscious.

And now I was paying for it.
All of it.

Tara no sooner had her bags in over her doorstep when the phone rang loudly, rattling on the hall table. Ignoring it, she watched as the red light on the answerphone flashed annoyingly. It whirred and then cut in, as Niamh's exasperated tones echoed through her empty house. Tara couldn't bear to regale her with the few days. Not tonight. She'd managed to sleep for a couple of hours on the bus, but she still hadn't come to terms with her emotions. As Niamh finished her message and the machine whirred again, Tara pressed the red-light button. All six messages were from Niamh. She could wait until tomorrow for the news. Half an hour later she'd made a steaming mug of hot chocolate and was hugging it as she curled up on the settee. The phone rang again and, not wanting it to disturb her whole evening, she picked it up.

"Hi, Niamh."

"How'd you know it was me?" Niamh screeched, amazed.

"How many messages have you left this afternoon? Six or seven, maybe?"

"So, how'd it go?"

"Fantastic and fatal."

"What? I wasn't expecting that. Shall I come over?"

She could imagine Niamh, chomping on the bit to get all the juicy info.

"Not tonight, I'm shattered. Late night, too much to drink, you know."

"You didn't, did you?"

Tara was irritated at her assumption. "Didn't what?"

"You know! Did you? You and Declan?"

Tara sighed at the memory. "Yeah. Like I said, fantastic and fatal."

"How come?"

"I got pissed and told him about my arsehole of a polygamous husband. Then we went back to the hotel and I was easy meat. He obviously realised how pathetic and gullible I was after confessing *that* to him!"

"Pathetic and gullible! Don't be ridiculous! Tara, I don't mean to rub it in, but you seem to forget, *you* proposed to Simon. And *you* had the affair. You're hardly a victim, are you?"

"I disagree. I really meant what I said in those marriage vows and, although I went off the rails with Graham, I really wanted our marriage to mean something! "

"I think, babe, you're suffering from a classic case of wanting something you can't have! Grass-is-greener syndrome?"

Tara was tired and Niamh's accusations were outrageous. "How the hell is that then?"

"You didn't really want Simon after the first few months anyway. You knew you'd made a mistake marrying him – that's why you got together with Graham. And you only felt guilty 'cos you were found out! If Simon hadn't have caught you then you'd still be seeing Graham! It's only now that you've found out what a louser Simon is that all of a sudden you want him and only him!"

"You're out of order, Niamh!" said Tara, shocked at this. "I didn't realise you felt this way! My God, I don't know what to say to you. I thought you were my friend!"

"I am your friend, Tara – that's why I'm being honest with you."

"Well, how's this for honest? I *did* want to marry Simon and, contrary to your beliefs, I *am* sorry for my affair with Graham. I knew it couldn't continue, however much I felt for him. But Niamh, my heart was in the right place when I married Simon and he has completely shattered my illusions about marriage!"

"So Declan pays for Simon's indiscretions?"

"Indiscretions? That's a fucking strange term for it anyway!"

"Look, Tara, you're obviously tired. We'll talk tomorrow, eh?"

"Fine. Goodnight."

Disgruntled and ruffled at Niamh's attitude, Tara stamped up to the bathroom, turning the taps on full blast. Pouring slightly too much bubble-bath in, she spun around and lighted her scented candles, dimming the lights. Pulling off her clothes as she stormed into her bedroom she pushed the ON switch of her CD player and then pressed PLAY. As she wrestled with her bra-strap the mellow sounds of Ella Fitzgerald filled the room. She turned the volume up high and got into her relaxing bath, pondering over her situation.

I didn't know who I was anymore! I wasn't a wife and I so wanted to be. So then I was a wife. Then I was an adulterer and a wife. And then I wasn't. Either.

So what was I now? Apart from a sad act. Was I legally a wife? I was confused. Perhaps it was time to get some legal advice.

As she got out of the bath and dried herself with the warm fluffy towel, tiredness washed over her again at the end of an emotionally exhausting day. Opting for an early night, she slid naked under her cosy plump duvet. Enjoying the freedom and lack of restriction of clothing she snuggled down, still toasty warm after the bath. But as sleep began to take her, suddenly she was woken by a screaming change of perspective.

Look at it this way, at least I retained some power by having the affair. Strange as it might seem. But with hindsight it spurred the bruised-ego'd Simon to leave me. If I hadn't had the affair then maybe he'd still be running rings around me – feigning trips away while he spent time with his other three wives!

Maybe I wasn't such a sad act after all.

She slept sounder with the knowledge that, in his eyes, she hadn't been a victim. Although in her eyes she still felt it.

She still wasn't quite the "top-dog".

Tara woke the next morning to a sun-filled bedroom. Feeling slightly guilty again at her outburst to Declan, she acted it out again in her mind. She knew how she felt about him really. He was so lovely, but she couldn't help but feel that her confession about the polygamous marriage hadn't helped.

With a renewed vigour and confidence she decided

to focus on her career, determined to make the best of this next makeover. So much had gone into it so far. Climbing out of bed she dressed in her joggers and baggy sweatshirt, first ringing her mum to bring Ruben home. She loved spending time with Ruben. Moreso than with her mother really, but she knew she'd stop for a chat and a few cups of tea anyway. As she tidied and listened to her CD's she decided to take her lead from the artists of the Place du Tertre, and so dug out her easel. As she assembled it she began to feel excited at the prospect of starting to paint again. She hadn't tried since she'd left UCD. She pulled out her boxes of watercolours and dusted off her paintbrushes and began to copy a postcard she'd brought home, swiftly throwing together a pleasing sketch of the Moulin Rouge which she'd begun to colourwash when her mum turned up.

It wasn't too bad. She actually stayed for a few hours. We even had a nice chat together about Wexford and painting and Simon. Yes, I told her about him. It wasn't easy, but after the initial shock she was quite supportive, even offering to come to the police with me. I wasn't ready for that yet though. But it was nice to know I had her support.

By early evening she had walked Ruben and then, on remembering she was off again for Dingle in the morning, had to ask her mum to have him again for a few days. Feeling like a child as her mother moaned down the telephone line, Tara managed to get around her and with the promise of dropping Ruben off early in the morning she settled down that night, ready for the challenge of the next job.

Chapter 24

The walk along the coast of Sandymount was a beautiful one. The tide was out and Ciara breathed the fresh morning air deep into her lungs. She'd hoped it'd clear her head too, but the intake of breath went downwards instead of upwards. She used to walk here all the time, but had been dragged into the mess of her life more recently. She dug her hands deep into her pockets as her mind raced.

She had needed a walk after the morning that she'd had. She had finally decided that she would try and trace her daughter. Not that she wanted any huge reunion or anything, but she felt it might calm her mind if she got the ball rolling. She nervously rubbed her arms lightly; the most recent evidence of her self-harming was throbbing and sore. She knew she had a problem and knew that she'd be unable to pull herself out of it alone. She needed help – desperately.

An hour later she had walked along the hard sand

from one end to the other and on her way back she'd sat on the bench, taking in the fantastic views. In the midday sunshine she rested back on the bench, putting up her feet, and wishing she could roll up the sleeves of her pink cotton shirt. Realising that she'd only be exposing her self-hatred, she placed her hands in her lap and thought about her own childhood.

Melvin and Josie O'Rourke had been the most loving parents and had completely immersed themselves in Ciara's life. She'd had a solid and stable upbringing, and had been encouraged to form a wide circle of friends, many of whom she had now lost all contact with. In fact, it had all been fantastic until that last term. She'd often enjoyed spending time with her tutor – he'd even helped her set up her consultancy and, if the truth be known, she'd always enjoyed their lovemaking – even though he was rather cocky about it all. She often reprimanded herself for not realising at the time. After all, her clothes were getting tighter and she had started to feel slightly different, but she'd just put it all down to the fact that she'd been sitting and slumped as she revised night after long night for her final exams. And then, just as she'd completed her final papers and had begun to make her way out of the examination hall, she'd felt strange. The sounds of her friends' laughter as they celebrated their final exam seemed to be distorted, the doorway which she was heading for shook and bent as if in a hall of mirrors. She hadn't even felt the desk when it knocked against her thigh as she fell.

She'd woken later in a hospital bed, its clinical

starchy sheets cold and rough against her legs. Ectopic pregnancy they'd suspected. Hell, she hadn't even known what one was! The next ten hours were a flurry as the doctors diagnosed ectopic, made her sign up to consent to a laparoscopy to determine their diagnosis – the proviso being that if they found a dangerous situation then she was also consenting to them removing her fallopian tube and ovary. Her mind spun as she'd lain in the hospital bed, watching the peeling green paint suspended from the walls. She was too young to think of pregnancy and yet was aggrieved that she'd leave the hospital with only one ovary. She didn't want either option – to be pregnant *or* to have a major part of her anatomy removed. And yet, when they'd finally decided that there was no ectopic and no need for surgery, she had felt dizzy and sick as they'd informed her that she was five months pregnant. And she really hadn't had a clue.

Now, relaxed on the bench, she felt the strong sun prickling on her cheeks as it began to burn her face. Holding her hands up to her warm cheeks she began to talk to herself.

"And so I gave her away. What a complete bitch!" Once again the tears began to fall. Ciara didn't notice. "I was so weak. And that's what I hated about myself – my weakness. And yet, maybe I've been too strong. Or pretended to be. I've sacrificed love in my life for success." She wiped at her tears, aware that the couple that were walking past with their dog were watching her. "It seems I've got my priorities all wrong."

She sobbed into her hands, suddenly dismissive of any spectators as she reprimanded herself for giving away the daughter that she'd had. She felt as if she'd literally spat the child from her body and from that day onwards hadn't given her a second thought.

And now it was all catching up with her . . .

Tara and Niamh were restless as they endured the journey to Dingle.

"We seem to be forever in the bloody car!" moaned Niamh.

"Yeah, but I have to say, I'm really looking forward to this job."

"I should think so," chided Niamh. "You've put enough planning into it!"

Tara fell silent. Niamh lit up a cigarette, and smiled as she puffed out the smoke through the half-opened window.

"You going to tell me what happened in Wexford then?"

"Do I have to?"

Niamh held her cigarette and wiggled it between her two fingers, grinning at Tara, "The sooner the better, babe, the sooner the better."

It took Tara over an hour to get it all out. By the time she'd finished, Niamh had got through half a packet of fags and Tara was bright red and blotchy with nerves. She'd worked herself up to fever pitch as she'd deliberated over their fantastic time in Wexford, giving Niamh every detail in a step-by-step narrative. As she'd reached the climax of her tale of woe Niamh was dragging on the cigarette for all she was worth. And then Tara finished.

Niamh sucked on the fag for another two or three pulls, and then threw the stub out of the window and looked at Tara.

"Tar, love. There's *no way* Declan was taking advantage of you. How *could* you have thought that?"

Tara shrugged. Again.

Niamh continued. "Why do you think *you're* the victim here? I don't get it. You had the affair. You clearly weren't happy with Simon or you wouldn't have gone for some extra-curricular with Graham. I don't get it, Tar."

Tara whispered quietly, "Neither do I. Perhaps you were right. Perhaps I am suffering from a case of grass-is-greener syndrome."

OK, so maybe I was a bit OTT. Still, I did feel vulnerable and exploited. There must be hundreds of women who feel uncomfortable or uneasy after a sexual situation. But hey, I enjoyed it. And I suppose he was right. It was my own lack of self-esteem that brought on those feelings.

Niamh was still rambling . . .

"Hell, girl, try believing in life *before* death, eh?"

I had to change the subject . . .

"Like you?"

She laughed, "Yeah, if you like. Like me."

"Go on then, so what's the latest on Adam?"

"Adam! Why do you ask?"

"Because you've seen more of him lately than any

341

other of your guys. And he doesn't even have a trust fund – what's going on, Niamh?"

"Really, I don't know. I'm getting a bit fond of him, you know. A little bit too much. Really."

"That's not such a bad thing though, is it? He's a great guy and you seem very compatible."

"It's getting bad. He stayed over for two nights on the trot last time. I nearly had to kick him out."

"Niamh," Tara rested her hand on her jeans-clad leg as she drove, "you're a match made in heaven. Hang onto him. You're both as cracked as each other."

"Don't rush me now. I'm not sure I'm ready for that emotional roller-coaster."

"'Course you are. Go on! It's good for the soul!"

"So, why don't you believe your own advice then?" she challenged. "Give it a go with Declan. What harm can it do? God forbid, you might even find happiness."

Tara stuck her tongue out at Niamh. "I'm looking for perfection in a man now."

Niamh sneered, "You'll never get it. You're simply looking for Maxwell House in a Lidl jar!"

What?

Her phone bleeped to indicate a text message. She smiled as she read it was from Adam.

He'd texted "FAN C A KWIK 1 L8R?" To which she'd quick-wittedly replied, "ONLY IF IT'S A LARGE 1"

"You really *are* seeing a lot of him lately, aren't you?"

"Maybe."

"But seriously, what about your man with moolah?"

"Tara, I'm still looking, still looking. But there's no need for a famine while you're waiting for your feast, is there?"

They finally arrived at the Dingle house and Tara was extremely disappointed on meeting the clients. She'd expected elegance and quality, haute couture, bouillabaisse, and twelve types of fromage. Eight types of jambon.

Instead she got more fake designer labels than you could shake a bread-stick at and English shoes.

As she politely made her way around the house, ducking and steering around the research team, camera crew and John and the handymen, she realised that her initial concern for blending the makeover with the rest of the house was less of a problem than the slides had even indicated.

Whatever we did with that house would only enhance it.

As Declan gathered them for a quick introductory speech Tara stood amongst the throng, looking around the room at the few, small French pieces. It was virtually a blank canvas. As Declan got the niceties out of the way, Tara and Ciara caught each other's eye. Tara noticed the sadness there much more than before.

The early-forties aged husband-and-wife team who had requested that the *Home Is* crew invade their house made up for their lack of Frenchness with their hospitality. It was the only makeover that they'd started where the owners had provided a continual flow of tea and coffee and dusted mince-pies. As they took a break in the back garden, seated at the resin table and chairs, they explained to Tara and Ciara how their neighbours had recently bought a French property.

"So we'd heard all about their fantastic place and thought it'd be a great thing to invest in. They've shown us the photos and everything."

His wife continued. "Their house is beautiful. It has those shutters and twirly wrought iron around the windows and inside it's all parquet floors and peeling paintwork. Very charming. They were lucky in that they had sourced a lot of their furniture from the Parisian flea markets and they've really gone for the shabby chic look."

The husband carried on where she left off, "Apparently there are very few homes magazines in France. One of our neighbours' biggest problems is filling the large rooms."

Tara took a gulp from her tea. "People don't often think of that. I have a friend who owns a beautiful converted bungalow near Waterford, but her rooms are twenty-five foot square. You know, that takes a fair bit of planning and money to make it work. I think they take a lorry over to IKEA for help now."

Ciara put her mug down and walked away.

Ciara had felt the shift in atmosphere the minute they'd walked into the house. It was obvious by the blotchiness of Tara's neck and cheeks that she was under pressure. Everyone on the set had noticed her unusually subdued personality, although she remained very professional in front of the cameras and the clients.

Ciara was intrigued as she noticed Tara spending as little time as possible with Niamh and Declan. It took the weight off Ciara's shoulders and she warmed to Tara. She didn't feel as though they were ganging up on her. Although she had to wonder whether the few days off the tablets had gone any way towards her different opinion. It had to be admitted though, the second Declan walked into the room – Tara walked out.

Ciara brought in a scorched-oak vase and some tafetta-and-organza-mix cushions. Tara fell in love with them and she noticed how the crew were speechless at their unexpected camaraderie.

They finished on the first day before five o'clock. The day had been fraught with tension.

More so than usual.

Handyman John had been using his power saw to cut some MDF for a mirror frame and the dust had blown straight onto my freshly-painted walls. Of course, it had stuck to it like flies to . . . ! I tried so hard not to, first, lose my temper and then second, cry. Ciara had pulled me aside and helped me with the situation. I couldn't believe it.

"OK, guys, we'll wrap it up there for today. Be back here tomorrow at nine," Declan boomed.

As Tara silently tidied her design kit and gathered her belongings, Ciara approached her, "Busy now?"

"Sorry?" Tara looked up at her, not used to the approach.

"Are you busy now? I wondered if you'd like a bit of a walk along the beach."

"Yeah," Tara relaxed and smiled, "I'd love to."

"Anything to get away from this lot, eh?"

Anna knew she wasn't doing very well with her job-hunting. The trouble was she was just too engrossed now in the Tara saga. And then there was the trouble of thinking about getting in a suitable lodger to help pay the bills. And then there was her love life. It just all got in the way. Her parents were still urging her to move back to Scotland and now that they knew she'd 'left' her job – she couldn't tell them the hideous truth – they seemed more intent on pestering her about a homecoming.

While Anna would have done anything to help Tara, she wasn't sure that Niamh's steam-in approach was the best way. She'd managed to track down Una Cullen, nee Slattery, easily. She'd not only got married in Foxrock, she also lived there, went to school there and was christened there. She hesitated in contacting Niamh with the news, knowing full well that she'd do a George Bush, and go in with all guns blazing. As far as Anna could see, the reality of parading around the country, confronting Simon's wives and bearing bad news would achieve nothing. With a surreptitious look over her shoulders, she clicked on the Internet Explorer icon on her screen. She reckoned she'd have about ten minutes before they were back from lunch. She keyed in the words "bigamy" and then "polygamy" only to find numerous websites *promoting* polygamy and even adverts from American sects touting for women to join! As the gaggle of women returned to their desks Anna quickly disconnected and, heaving the large telephone directory from the floor beside her desk, she flicked through until she found the pages for solicitors. Running her finger down the list, she finally found one that she'd pass on the way home. She rang for an appointment and was lucky to get one for five o' clock.

The solicitor's office was refreshingly trendy, with its bright blue interior walls and orange and yellow abstract squares hanging loftily above the reception area. She flicked through *Hello!* magazine while she waited, but had only reached page seven when a hunk of a solicitor breezed into the reception area and stood in front of her.

"Sorry to keep you waiting. Would you like to follow me?"

Anna nodded, inanely. "Of course," she replied. And she meant it!

Her half hour with the solicitor was worth every cent. It seemed the legal viewpoint on bigamy and polygamy was a complicated one. He had told her that the law of bigamy is one of the least used pieces of legislation on the statute books. Because of this, the government seemed unlikely to restructure it. It seemed that prosecutions under this law are extremely rare and, even if allegations are reported, prosecutions may not proceed. In his experience these allegations usually arise after a remarriage following a Catholic Church annulment or a foreign divorce.

"You have to have laws which define who is married

and who isn't. The complicated thing is that marriage is tied up with succession rights, family rights, taxation and the rights to occupation of property amongst other things."

Anna scribed frantically in an attempt to write it all down. He continued.

"Divorce is now legal in Ireland, so there really is no excuse. But in order to help your friend properly I would really need to see her. Is there any chance she can make an appointment to see me?"

"She's away at the moment," Anna replied, putting the top back on her pen and folding her notepad, "but I will talk to her when she gets back. Thank you for your time."

She stood and he followed suit, leaning across to shake her hand.

Ciara and Tara were strolling along the warm, but breezy beach. It seemed almost surreal that the two women were being civil for once.

"So tell me, Ciara, how long have you been working in interiors?"

"Over thirty years now."

Tara noticed her face darken as she spoke. Wary of upsetting her and tempting the wicked side of Ciara that she was so used to, she decided to let it go.

"So," Ciara clipped, "what's with the atmosphere?"

"What atmosphere?"

"I'm not stupid, Tara. It's obvious as the pimple on Niamh Connolly's arse."

"What pimple?"

Ciara scowled, "God, everyone can see it. All the cameramen and monkeys are laughing about it. I suppose she'd help herself if she didn't insist on wearing those skin-tight jeans."

Tara made a mental note to tell Niamh.

Not before I'd checked it myself though.

"So? The atmosphere? What's happened between you and Declan and Niamh?"

"Oh that." Tara sighed. "Nothing really. I've just got a few problems, that's all."

"Haven't we all? I've got more than a few myself. I've begun wondering whether I'm getting too old for all of this, you know."

"You're not serious! How old are you, Ciara?"

"Never you mind. It's not how old I am, it's how old I feel."

Tara knew exactly what she meant. She'd been there herself many times in the last year and a half.

"Put it this way," Ciara divulged, "everybody knows I've got a problem. It's common knowledge now. But I'm not really such an ambitious, hard-faced bitch. I do have feelings too."

I was dying to know more, but didn't want to push her. Anyway, who was I to make judgements on people's lives? Look at the mess I was making of my own.

Chapter 25

Given the amount of effort I'd put into research for this makeover, it was very disappointing. The clients' hospitality was overwhelming, yet did little to mask the fact that their knowledge of things French was limited.

Extremely.

Put it this way: if only they'd done half as much research as I had. They hadn't liked the idea of the antique chair that I'd uncovered from Mother Redcap's market. To her credit, Ciara had eventually managed to persuade them that it was from the same period as the furnishing in their neighbours' house in France. It had taken us the whole morning to convince them that it was very "gay Pareee". And then they had only consented to include it in the makeover if I re-upholstered it in the chequered fabric that they'd stored in the loft. That took another two hours!

(And it was gruesome).

The Louise O'Murchu oil painting had been another bone of contention – the husband loving it, the wife detesting it.

We left them to battle that one out between them.

He must have won though – it was on the wall above the fireplace when I looked again.

Ciara and Tara bumped into each other on the stairs, both exasperated by their difficult clients.

"If only the fecking cameras would stop, I'd tell them what I *really* think of them," Ciara growled under her breath to Tara.

Tara smirked. "Yeah. It makes me wish I'd bought them back a souvenir from the Erotic Art Museum now."

"Christ! That'd make his hair curl anyway!" They both giggled together, for the first time on-set. Ever.

Their friendliness hadn't escaped the rest of the crew. Niamh was even distracted enough by it to take a few snaps of them, tittering and chuckling together.

"What's with your new best buddy?" she asked Tara, passing her in the hallway.

But Tara was cool with Niamh and pretended not to know what she meant, only irritating her all the more.

At the end of an exhausting two days, just prior to the "close your eyes . . . open them!", Ciara's mobile vibrated in her pocket, causing everyone to look.

"Surprised she hasn't got it stuck down the front of her knickers!" Niamh heard Handyman John murmur.

Handyman John was bulkier than the rest of the team and the camera loved him. Tara had seen him many times rubbing his muscly arms with oil off-camera and he knew how to play up to the image of handyman. She suspected he was the housewives' darling and was sure that his exposure on *Home Is* had guaranteed him a career on the telly. His appeal was magnified by his ability to ridicule stupid expressions that everybody used, but nobody really knew why. Niamh and Tara had screamed with laughter only earlier when Declan had insisted that Tara play up to the camera and turn to Ciara and "whisper out of the corner of her mouth". Handyman John had jumped at the chance.

"The *corner* of her mouth! Since when did mouths have corners? Christ, Tara, I knew you had a big mouth," he'd teased, "but I never knew it was square!" He'd also bought to light the ridiculousness of sayings like, "she's getting better to die" and the response that Ciara often gave of "Well, yes – and no". Tara and Niamh had playfully dubbed him the King of Crap Expressions.

At the end of a long day and tired of John's playfulness, Declan was relieved that Ciara had responded to her shaking mobile by taking it into the privacy of the back garden, leaving Tara to wind up the programme.

Ciara snapped down the phone in a hissed whisper, "Who *is* this?"

"You don't know me."

"So! Who are you?" She was very impatient and irritated.

"This *is* Ciara O'Rourke, isn't it?"

"Yes, yes, yes. Now what is it. I'm busy here."

"Miss O'Rourke. I am your daughter."

The lump in her throat threatened to choke her. She blushed furiously.

"Don't be fucking ridiculous!"

"Miss O'Rourke," she laughed anxiously, "I swear. I'm serious."

Ciara felt sick. Violently. She stammered, whispering, "In the name of God. This can't be true."

The other woman spoke through gritted teeth. "It is very true, Miss O'Rourke. My name is Melanie Bishop and I live with my husband in Kerry."

"What?" Ciara gasped, she hadn't suspected that *she'd* ever track *her* down.

She continued, not giving Ciara any time to think clearly. "I was adopted by a couple – Dennis and Mary Collins who moved to Kerry when I was six. I'm now married to John Bishop, an architect, and we live near to my adoptive parents."

Ciara's eyes filled with heavy tears. She was unable to keep that first sob from her voice. "Please. Hold on. I can't take this in. I need to meet you." She sobbed openly.

The line fell silent.

She thought she'd gone.

Until she heard her say lightly, "Ciara, you're a grandmother."

Her head swam, causing her to clutch onto the back of the garden chair and then flop down into it.

When she listened again, Melanie Bishop had hung up or been disconnected. Holding her mobile in her hand she stared at the grass, aware of the *"ooohs"* and *"aaahhhs"* coming from inside the house as the new interiors were revealed, but not really hearing them. She felt the bright flashes of Niamh's cameras as she took the photographs of the finished product, capturing their ecstatic faces for the series book. Her world was turning upside down. A huge wave of self-loathing was building momentum inside her. Her *daughter*! At last.

"Holy Jesus," she sobbed into her hands as she covered her face, "I've never even seen her." She managed to muffle the sounds of her crying, smothering her face with her two hands as she broke her heart in that back garden in Dingle. She'd travelled all over the world since handing over that baby over thirty years ago, all in a bid to follow her precious career.

All over the damned world.

Sydney, San Fransisco, Johannesburg, London.

India, China, Canada.

All for it to come to a head in Dingle.

Its ridiculousness nearly made her laugh. Nearly. If she hadn't been so overcome with a mass of emotions: humiliation, regret, sorrow, anger, shame. Taking a deep breath, she tried to compose herself. She wiped at her saturated cheeks and tried to dry her eyes without smudging her make-up. She looked down at the phone in her lap. As she churned her mind back to that day – the 4th of June – when she'd given birth to a baby.

She hadn't wanted to know what sex it was even. She just wanted rid of it. Yet, as she had expelled the small body from hers an overwhelming love came over her. Though she had insisted that she didn't even want to *see* the child, she couldn't help but grab a glimpse of its black wet hair as she looked down between her wide-open knees. All her hatred and fears were washed away as she cried and asked if she could hold the child – just for a minute. She had always remembered how the nurses looked awkward between themselves until an older midwife had wrapped the baby in a blanket and handed it to Ciara. Ciara had lain there sobbing as she cuddled the bloody, smeary black-haired baby.

"What is it?" she had whimpered.

Just as the senior obstetrician had whisked the bundle from her she heard him bark, "A girl."

Steadying herself in the garden chair she could see a faint reflection of her face as she looked down at her mobile. Staring at her greeny-tinged image she saw a crease under her chin where a second one was forming. Her swollen eyes protruded in an ugly fashion and the "puppet strings" from the corners of her mouth to her nose were exaggerated by her pose. Taking four or five deep breaths to compose herself she went back into the house to catch the tail-end of another of a selection of Handyman John's jokes.

"Tommy Cooper joke now: two aerials meet on a roof – fall in love – get married. The ceremony was rubbish, but the reception was brilliant."

Everyone roared, Declan especially – all this made for excellent television and the cameras picked it all up. Only when they stopped rolling and Declan toasted another successful makeover, did everyone notice Ciara's red face and eyes.

It was only Tara who approached her.

"Hey, you OK?"

In the light of our newly formed "friendship", I thought I was within my rights as new buddy to ask.

Ciara stared into Tara's eyes, suddenly feeling guilty and sad at how she'd taken out her feelings on her. No doubt Melanie looked nothing like Tara and she now regretted her treatment of her. Ciara quickly averted her eye contact and sniffed as she walked away.

"Maybe I'm just a mess, eh?"

OK – so I was confused . . .

As Tara was packing up her design kit, wondering what had happened to change Ciara's swinging mood, Niamh knelt beside her, helping her to drop the small dyes, sprays and swatches into the silver knarled hold-all.

"I've just had Christina on the phone. She's in a right state."

"Why?"

Niamh continued to put bottles and tubes into the wrong compartments.

"She's shitting one. Simon's due home next week and she doesn't know what to do with herself. I think we should go and help her, Tar."

"No. We can't get involved."

"Pardon me? Honey, you *are* involved – like it or not."

"I'm not really. Not in Christina's life. She has her

own family and friends. It's not right for us to interfere."

"Tara!" Niamh was clearly annoyed at her lack of support for the young mum.

"We're not vigilantes, Niamh. It's not a witch-hunt for Simon! Anyway, I've decided what I'm going to do."

This was news to Niamh and she was desperate to know. "Go on," she coaxed her.

Tara stopped what she was doing. "I'm going to the police."

"We need to talk about this."

"No, we don't." She stopped and turned toward Niamh, oblivious to the clattering of the camera crew as they disassembled their equipment all around them. "It's not a game. It's not a joint decision. It's my life and I've decided."

"OK, point taken. I just thought you'd go for a little more action, that's all."

"I just *don't get you!* Do you think everything's like it should be in the films? Oh let's see, so I'm Meg Ryan and Simon is, who could he be, Nicholas Cage or Antonio Banderas or someone? Yeah, OK, and then we all club together, all us wronged wives – we could be Goldie Hawn and – and – Sharon Stone maybe. And with the help and solidarity of women we would all march in together and defeat him with our strength and girlpower? Niamh, get real!"

"Yeah," she shrugged, half smiling, "I thought that sounded kind of cool. But you never said who I was. Who could I be then? How about the karate-kicking Lucy Liu or Angelina Jolie?"

Tara relaxed, shrugging her shoulders, and laughed. "You really believe it all, don't ya?"

Niamh kissed her lightly on the cheek. "A bit of fantasy goes a long way in getting me through the day, babe."

"Get out of it," she laughed, shoving Niamh gently on the shoulder causing her to topple from her crouched position, straight onto her bum.

Wonder if it burst the pimple?

Ciara knew they were all talking about her behind her back. It was obvious, what with her red swollen eyes and blotchy complexion. But she didn't care. She was a grandmother! She was waiting for the idea to repulse her, yet a warm rush of something, she couldn't quite figure what, was giving her a glow. As she tidied up at the end of the Dingle job she was overcome with emotion. She felt as if the last thirty-three years were ready to burst out of her and she knew she was completely unable to stop it. Like a tidal wave or something as forceful – this unrelenting Mother Nature force had started and she knew nothing would stop it. The ball was well and truly rolling. Packing her tricks of the trade into her design-kit hold-all she felt the surge from the pit of her stomach somewhere and knew it was only a matter of time before the emotions hit her eyes. She stood, deciding that if she was going to burst into tears again, it was better that she do it outside. As she walked across to the front door she cursed that her feelings weren't considerate of her surroundings. Here she was, in "professional" mode, amongst a crowd of virtual strangers and she knew she was about to collapse in a flood of tears. Tara caught sight of her pinched expression and knew she had to help her.

It was obvious she was heading for a breakdown. I just couldn't sit back and pretend not to notice.

Ciara grabbed the latch of the front door and swung it open desperately. Tara just caught the door as it swung back and followed Ciara along the path.

"Hey, Ciara!"

Ciara dug her hands deep into her pockets, pulling out a handful of coloured tablets – some pink, some white. Before she could raise her hand to her mouth, Tara grabbed her arm, causing the candy-coloured chemicals to shower down onto the grass.

"Hey!" Ciara blurted.

"Ciara," Tara spun her to face her, "what's going on, eh? Look, I know you don't like me. I don't know why. I don't care. You're in a mess and I want to help you."

Ciara stooped to collect up the dangerous dolly-mixtures that she'd scattered, in an attempt to conceal her brimming eyes. Tara bent with her and tried to grasp hold of her hands.

I didn't mean to be so rough, but she was pulling away from me. She was desperate. I accidently tugged at her shirt-sleeve as she went to turn and I was chilled at what I saw.

"Leave me alone! Don't look at my arms!" Ciara spat.

Tara knew she was trying to sound rough and tough, but instead her pleadings came out as almost childlike as she frantically pulled her sleeve back down. Tara's heart broke for her. She was in a worse state than she'd ever imagined.

"Did you see that?" Niamh gasped at Declan as they stood at the bay window at the front of the house, peeking out through the net curtains. "Did you see the state of her arms?"

"Christ, yeah." Declan was virtually lost for words.

"Jesus, I never thought she was *that* bad." Niamh couldn't get over the sight of Ciara's scarred and mauled arms.

Declan didn't reply, instead watching Tara as she put her arm around Ciara's wracked shoulders and led her to the car.

"I was just on the brink of leaving uni. I'd just sat my last exam." Ciara sniffed as she sat in the car, unable to make eye contact with Tara, preferring instead to stare at the screwed-up, knarled tissue in her hand. "My life was just beginning. Everything I'd worked so hard for was falling into place. I'd even set up my consultancy!"

She was forced to stop by the sob that escaped suddenly. Burying her face in her hands she cried thirty years' worth of tears. Tara was an excellent listener.

Sure – I'm great at solving other people's problems! Aren't we all?

She tried to ignore the twitching curtains from the bay window as Niamh and Declan, she suspected, wrestled for pride of place.

"It was a terrible way to find out I was pregnant. I collapsed in the exam hall and was rushed to hospital. And do you know what?" she stared Tara squarely in the eye, the tears subsiding, "that bastard never came anywhere near me again. He knew I'd been rushed to hospital. He'd heard the rumours. That cocky little bastard didn't give a damn about me." She began to cry again, whimpering, "And I've hated him ever since."

"Who was he?" Tara felt slightly nervous at prying, especially given Ciara's temper and highly emotional state.

"My tutor. He's probably spent a lifetime bedding his students." Ciara blew her nose, making a loud rasping sound. Tara felt an urge to giggle.

"So when I found out I was pregnant I simply couldn't face the idea. I didn't want to acknowledge it was true. The only person I wanted to be with was him. I felt so alone. So I decided to have an abortion. I made all the plans to get the boat to England, telling my parents all kinds of lies about wealthy clients in London who were interested in my interior-design work. And so I set off one evening, alone. I actually got to the clinic the next morning and was like a robot. I completed all the forms, saw the counsellor and went through the motions. It was only when I realised how far gone I really was and what a risk I was taking that I knew I couldn't go through with it. I'm neither for nor against it, generally. I truly believe that every woman has to do what is right for her. All of our lives are so different, who are we to stand judge over somebody else's decisions? I mean, Jesus, isn't it all hard enough without judging each other?"

Tara was transfixed by this stage. "So what happened then?"

"I walked out. I cancelled the appointment and went home. For the first few days, I felt quite relieved, which was strange. Then I began to feel anxious again. I was beginning to show and my phone was constantly ringing with interior-design bookings. And so, while looking though a magazine one day, I saw a story about adoption. It felt like fate that I'd come across this, and so I rang for details."

"So what did your parents say?"

Ciara's eyes clouded over once again. "They didn't know. They never knew. I went off to a friend in Youghal for a few months on the pretence of a large, lucrative interiors job. It was there I got fatter and fatter until I finally had the . . . had . . . had the . . ." She burst into tears once again, sniffing and sobbing uncontrollably. "I can't even bring myself to say it. After all these years!"

Tara put her arm around Ciara's wracked shoulders and rubbed them gently, whispering comforting words as she did so.

Ciara finally managed to regain control. "And so now you know it all." Ciara sniffed, relieved that she'd recounted the full story for the first time ever, still fiddling with the few small pink tablets that she'd been able to pick from the grass.

"But you were so very young. Nobody can blame

you for what you did. You went through with the pregnancy. You did the right thing for you and had the baby properly adopted. Why so much guilt? Why so much hatred?"

Ciara began to cry again. "I don't know. I thought I was coping with it all. I'd accepted the fact that I'd never see her and, of course, I thought about her every year on the 4th of June. The sorrow never really went away. But Tara, you reminded me so much of myself. Your talent and ambition. And my, em, my," she laughed ironically, "my daughter – Melanie – she'd be about the same age as you. For some reason, I had the notion she would look just like you too." Ciara took hold of Tara's hand, offering sincere advice. "Enjoy your time on *Home Is*. Enjoy your career as a designer."

Tara giggled. "If I have one."

Ciara wouldn't be side-tracked and nodded seriously, "Believe me, Tara, you *have* one. But don't ever – *never* – put your career before your family, before your life. I've let my career rule my life and while I've enjoyed it, it's also meant that I've ended up a sad, lonely woman."

Her words reverberated through Tara's mind as she reflected on her own situation with Simon and how now she was holding Declan at deliberate arm's length for fear of her feelings.

Ciara continued, pulling up her shirt sleeves brutally, "Look. Look at my arms. And it doesn't end there. My breasts, the tops of my legs. I'm a fucking mess. It was the only way to release all the pain. That and the drugs. I just can't see an end to it all."

Tara was shaken at the state of Ciara's arms and shuddered at the thought of the extent of her self-abuse. She was glad that the windows of the car had begun to fog up slightly with their heavy conversation and tears.

Ciara gently rolled down the shirt-sleeves and rubbed at her sleeved arms lightly.

"So, Ciara, what now?"

"So now I don't know what to do. I just don't know if I can cope with actually *seeing* them. Although really, that's all I want to do."

"So go ahead."

"But," she emplored, "what if I want more? What if I want to actually make up for the lost years? Can I ever do that? What if it isn't enough? I need to question my need to go into their lives at this stage. And in my condition! I'm a bloody drug addict, you know. I'm hardly stable, am I?" Ciara began to sob uncontrollably again. In between gasps of breath she whimpered, "And they mightn't really want me."

Although Tara had made her decision she was worried about Christina and had to ring her.

By the time she and Niamh had reached Dublin they were exhausted. The journey to Limerick alone had been bad enough, with Tara listening to Niamh singing and rambling. She had been relieved when Adam had rung. It had kept Niamh on the phone for nearly an hour of the journey, giving Tara time to work out what she was going to do. When they'd finally reached Dublin, Tara asked Niamh for Christina's number – she was sure she had it somewhere, but couldn't think where.

"Why?" Niamh asked, the orange streetlights of Dublin city making her eyes glow in the dark as they stopped at the red light.

"I have to explain to her what I'm doing. It's only fair. And there's a few things I need to tell her too. It's bad enough being involved in this disgusting mess, but right on top of Christmas too. Christina has a child to think of."

Niamh handed over the number and, once she'd pulled in outside Tara's house, Tara took the opportunity to ring Christina. She felt her heart beating heavily as the car windows fogged up. Niamh sat next to her in the dark carpark, starting to feel chilly as the heat went out of the day. The phone rang for quite a long time before it was answered.

"Hello?" Christina's voice sounded wary and anxious. Tara's heart went out to her – stuck there on her own with a small child and her so young herself. It wasn't fair.

"Christina. It's Tara. Niamh told me that you rang her."

"I did. I'm so worried, Tara. You see, I can't tell anyone up here about Simon – they'd kill him if they knew. I've got so many friends up here and my brothers would go to town on him. I just can't do it."

"No. You're right. Christina, I'm going to the police about Simon. I can't be bothered chasing him around the country, trying to catch him out. I know some people may think that's the right thing to do, but it's just not me."

Niamh nudged her and poked out her tongue.

Tara continued, pinching Niamh on the side of her leg. "Christina, you do realise that our marriages are null and void?"

She simply sobbed into the phone.

Tara waited for Christina to speak. The line was silent.

"I'm sorry," Tara whispered.

Still she said nothing. But Tara could hear her heavy breathing down the line.

"Perhaps you should try and act normally with him. Don't let him know that we've caught him out. Don't try and have it out with him. I was lucky in a way that he left me! But I really feel for you – I don't know the other two wives, but you have a young son to protect and that must come as top of your priorities."

"So what should I do?" Christina's fear and anxiety rattled down the telephone wire like electricity.

"I think you should carry on as normal. Bide your time. I'm going to the gardaí tomorrow and I'll give them everything I know – all the dates of his marriages and the names of his wives – including yours. Just tread water and let the police take the reins. The first thing they'll do is go into Joyce House and check out the registers. That won't take them long – I have it all written down. Just let them sort it and follow my lead."

Christina began to cry, frightened. "How long will it take, do you think?"

"I don't know. But I will tell the police that you have a young child – and suggest that they give you a look over first of all. But Christina, if you need me you must call me."

"I will. Thank you."

"And Christina?"

"Mmm?"

"Sorry."

"S'OK."

I don't know why I said sorry – but I was. I was so lucky that I was led astray by Graham – it turned Simon away from me.

How lucky for me.

I'd never thought I'd be saying that!

I was worried about Christina though. She was so young. And I would be there for her if she needed me.

Strange alliance.

Two wives – married to the same pig.

Chapter 26

Niamh was barely home when Adam rang her again. She was a little annoyed at herself – such enthusiasm would usually have her running, but with Adam she didn't mind so much. In fact she rather enjoyed it. She hauled her bags and equipment hold-alls up onto her kitchen table as she spoke to him, cursing herself for losing her edge and reminding herself of her lust-for-the upper-crust, the search for the monied man.

Hearing her pant as she struggled with the heavy bags, Adam teased. "Hold on! You sound like a perv, all that heavy breathing."

"No chance," she puffed, finally resting the heaviest bag down and unzipping it, "just unpacking all my stuff."

"Damn. And here was me getting all excited."

She laughed at him, rooting into her jacket pocket for her cigarettes. He recognised the sound as she clicked her lighter, paused, and inhaled as she lit the cigarette.

"That's why you're puffed out. Those cigarettes."

"Yeah, yeah. One my many vices, but hey don't knock 'em. My vices keep me going."

"And there's a particular vice of yours that keeps *me* going too!"

She pulled out a chair and sat on it, crossing her legs. "Oh I see, and which one would that be?" She grinned as she rested her elbows onto the table.

"You know damn well."

"Mmmn, not sure now, would it be the drinking? Or the smoking?"

"Bitch!" he laughed.

"Bitch? *Moi?*"

"If you're not careful I'll have to come over and remind you then."

"Oh Adam, and here's me so tired too."

"I'll do all the work?"

"Really? You mean I can just lie back and relax?"

"No problem."

"What you waiting for then?"

The phone went dead and Niamh laughed as she could imagine Adam tugging on his boots and making a bee-line for her place.

While she waited for him she unpacked her equipment and sorted her cameras and rolls of film, handling them lovingly and carefully. She settled them back into their foam casings within her hold-alls and went into the kitchen to pour herself a huge glass of red. As she watched the dark liquid swirl and splash as it caressed the bowl of the glass she was once again tormented by her feelings for Adam. In a way she detested herself for being so shallow and yet it would be whimsical to forgo her lifelong ambition to marry into money. Before she'd finished her wine Adam was at the door, dressed in a denim jacket, casual red t-shirt and a pair of stone-coloured combats. His lean feet were clad in cool tan mules. She felt her tummy squeal with delight at his gorgeous blue eyes, his broad shoulders and his tanned face. And yet once again the insecurities of her financial dream cut in. She composed herself and let him in, speaking as he followed her through to the kitchen.

"You know. I usually go for older men."

"Ah," he merely smiled, "the allure of the bus pass."

"Nooo," she swung around to face him, "the allure of sexperience. I mean," she ran her finger lightly across his collarbone and over his muscly shoulders, "there was a time I'd seldom consider a man without crow's-feet."

He nuzzled into her neck. "Well, I'm so glad those times have changed." She threw her head back, delighting in his kisses.

"You wouldn't last six months with a wrinkly – all that denture fixative and incontinence."

He stopped suddenly and held her at arm's length. "You know, your eyes are like spanners."

"What?" she screamed as she pulled back from him, an expression of mock horror on her face.

"They are! Everytime I look into them they turn my nuts!"

Niamh cackled, "Oh right, and what are you? Old Tool-Box Man?"

"What?" he grinned.

"Well, you keep on about your big hammer for your big nail, and now you're croaking on about spanners. I'm starting to think you want a job on *Home Is*!"

"Hardly," he retorted, "don't fancy that one bit. Mind you, I wouldn't mind seeing more of you though."

She teased as she tugged at her buttons. "No problem for you, Adam my man. Now, just which part would you like to see more of first?"

The next morning Tara woke at six. It was hard to stay in bed with the sun streaming through your muslin curtains at four-hundred watt. Her bedroom was awash with a luxurious aura as the curtains slightly altered the sunshine, and the heat was glorious. She lay back on her bed, on top of the covers, and star-fished, letting her mind wander, pretending she was on a beach somewhere exotic. She could almost hear the sea whooshing and lapping at her feet when an ambulance blared past at ninety miles an hour, breaking her fantasy. It was days like this she was tearing to get out to The Shed. By seven she'd let Ruben out, had tidied the house *and* vacuumed –

OK - don't make fun!

And was dressed in her charcoal-grey combats and pink t-shirt. She'd ruffled her hair quickly and went out to sit in The Shed, but the frosty chilly air was too much for her. Instead she took her book inside and flicked through the pages of *Patio Planting*. The sounds of commuter traffic building up outside merged strangely with the icy blasts of wind that buffeted down the chimney. She had arranged a selection of sized terracotta pots on her kitchen table and had already split the bag of compost, her small spade stuck down in it ready. Now it was just a matter of choosing what colours she wanted, and which bulbs for the spring she needed.

By nine-thirty she'd made a long shopping list to take to the garden centre with her, and there was little else she could do until she'd spent some money.

And my hands weren't even dirty yet! I just couldn't wait to get into it.

She tugged on her baseball cap and decided that she'd set out now for the garden centre. She knew deep down in her mind that there was another task that she intended to tackle this morning, but kept pushing it to the back of her mind. She knew she'd promised Niamh and Anna that they could go with her, but she felt *this* was something that she had to do alone. Well, with Ruben. That poor dog had lived through the whole painful process with her. The sun shone brightly as she straightened her t-shirt and ran her fingers through the tips of her hair which were jutting cheekily from the cap and onto her neck. She jangled Ruben's lead in a teasing manner. Ruben went berserk, barking and leaping up all over her. Tara had to laugh. "Calm down, now! Come on, boy! Walkies!"

She strode confidently, delighting at her calm and the beautiful day. It really did seem as if everyone was more relaxed, had a calmer demeanour on a warm, sunny day.

Perhaps I suffered from that SAD thing. Maybe I'd got the SADs. Wouldn't be bad though, eh? Your doctor would insist you spent the winter in the Maldives.

Either that or in front of a UV light every evening – not much of a comparison really!

She patted her pocket to make sure that the folded shopping list was still in there, but then walked straight past the garden centre, slowing down only to twist her neck and crane her head in as she passed by. She approached the garda station and paused at the bottom step, taking a deep breath in preparation. "Well," she whispered to the obedient Ruben who waited by her side, "here goes."

As she walked through the double swing doors, in from the cold sunshine to the artificial fluorescent lighting, she was confronted by two dirty-looking men who looked up accusingly at her. And they weren't even the gardaí! She delicately sat herself on the last vacant chair beside them, instructing Ruben to sit at her feet. She could smell the drink off one of the men, but had to satisfy her curiosity with sideward glances for fear of upsetting anyone. Instead she lost herself in reading the posters warning against having no car tax, drinking and driving and failing to security-mark your possessions.

She jumped as a young garda opened a hatch in front of her and smiled.

"Can I help you?" he asked, pleasantly.

Tara looked furtively at the two men beside her, neither of whom reciprocated the eye contact.

"S'OK."

The garda indicated that she step forward.

Feeling suddenly nervous she stood, Ruben leaping to his feet ready for the off, only to be disappointed three strides later when he was told to sit again.

Tara explained her marital conundrum and was soon taken through to a backroom, an interview room, to give a full statement. It was half an hour later when she'd finished that she realised that her t-shirt was gaping slightly at the front as she sat, and she cursed herself for giving the young garda a free flash.

"You know, there's little we can do unless you wish to make a public prosecution."

"I don't really know what I want to do."

He smiled at her again.

He probably thinks I'm insane, I said to myself.

"Take your time. We'll hold your statement here on file until you make your decision."

"Fine. Thanks."

"Thank you, Mrs, em, Miss McKenna."

She had never been so relieved as when he'd unbolted the security door that stood between the reception area and the office. As she scurried out toward the swing-doors and the sunshine, she realised that the two men whom she'd been seated with were both fast asleep – and snoring.

Well, that was that. I'd done it. At least it was all down on paper now. But did I feel any better for it?

Not really.
It was ironic really – all I wanted was Declan.

While Tara felt relief, and was certain she was walking lighter than before as she made her way back to the garden centre to buy her bulbs and plants, Ciara sat in turmoil at her home in Sandymount, pondering over her life.

She sat at her front window watching the families enjoying the winter sunshine on the beach, through the slats in her antique-pine Venetian blind. In particular she watched a young woman who was playing with two toddlers and a puppy – all three of whom were laughing and running, and then often slipping and falling. As the youngest toddler slipped and fell face-first into the solid sand she watched the young mother crouch down, cuddling and comforting her daughter. The tears welled in Ciara's eyes once again and she bought back the focus of her gaze to rest on the dust which had settled on one of the slats of the blind. As the tear fell, landing with a splat on her bare leg, she drew back and looked around her lounge: the high-design of the soft furnishings, the crème-de-la-crème of furniture, the most sought after and revered antique pieces which sat gathering dust. As her head bowed in sorrow she looked at the floor and noticed the few smatterings of tablets that she'd obviously dropped at some intoxicated time, which had rolled and rested just by the fireplace. She watched how the stripes of sunlight cut through the slats of the blind and shone through her many decanters of vodka, Jack Daniels, Martini and Bacardi, refracting as miniature rainbows of distorted colour across her wall. She sobbed once again, feeling vile and berating herself that she gave everything up for this.

"For this!" she spat angrily, throwing a cushion across the room. "You are a fucking fool, Ciara O'Rourke. Feargal was right – you are rude and boring. You gave up the chance of a family for this. For what? Possessions and recognition! You are a fool!" She rubbed lightly at her scarred forearms. Her passage of realisation was a painful one. She stood up and tugged at her pants, half of which were stuck between her bum cheeks, and went to lie on the couch. She hugged the cushion close to her chest and began to come to terms with herself. With her mistakes. Her mind raced through her life: her self-abuse, the drugs, the emotionless sex. She detested herself for letting too many inept novices use her body to clock up road miles. Her success in front of the cameras was a farce. It was real life that mattered and it had taken her too many years to realise that she had her priorities all wrong.

"The question is," she whispered into the cushion, "is it too late to change it all?"

As she calmed herself, feeling her heartbeat slow down a little, she thought of her young daughter and felt more than a little guilty that she'd been so horrible to Tara simply because she *imagined* that Melanie would look like her. And Tara had been so, so nice to her too. With the calm came some answers to her many questions and as she lay, full of self-pity, she made a few decisions.

The first one involved rehab.

The second one involved an apology to Tara.

The third was to make sure that she never put her career before other priorities in her life.

Never, ever again.

Chapter 27

It was a shame that both Ciara and Tara had one more makeover to complete for *Home Is Where The Art Is*. They were both beginning to focus on life after *Home Is* and felt slightly begrudging that they had to stick with it for a bit longer. Niamh was feeling rather the same. She had enjoyed the travelling around the country with the team and had used her opportunities to take photos for other projects at the same time as those for the *Home Is* publication. She now wanted to spend more time with Adam, as much as she hated to admit it really, but he was gorgeous, and they got on so well together. She found the reality strange that she was the only one amongst them that had a partner to share Christmas with. Tara had to face her mother, Anna usually spent her time in the soup-kitchens doling out coloured water and stale bread, and Declan was on his own for the first year too.

They were gathered back at RTÉ for the briefing for Job 14. It was Ciara and Tara's last, although the series ran to 15 – the two male designers were preparing for that one. As they gathered in the large meeting-room, cupping their mugs of latte, Tara made her way across to Ciara.

"Hi."

Ciara looked up at her, the evidence of her tears still in existence. Her slightly pink eyes smiled, nonetheless.

"Tara. Thank you."

Her voice was subdued, yet warm. Tara had never seen her like this.

Not in public anyway.

"No problem, Ciara. Whenever you need a friend. I'll always be there for you. Have you decided what you're going to do?"

"I have," she nodded.

Tara giggled, a little awkward. "Well, is it a secret?"

"No. Well, it is a secret to a certain extent, but I'll tell you. I'm booked into a rehab centre in the west."

"Fantastic! No, I mean –"

"It's OK," Ciara smiled, "it's long, long overdue."

"So what about your dau – em . . ."

"My daughter?"

Tara nodded, feeling stupid.

"I've got her address and I've asked to see the photos. I have to go and meet the private detective to see them. I've decided not to make any contact until I'm sorted out – properly. And then, when I am, I think I'll ask him to contact Melanie and see if she wants to see me. I'm not going to steam in there and mess up everyone's lives even more."

Declan and Stephanie came into the room and everyone shuffled to their seats, ready for the briefing.

"Ciara, I'm sure she will want to know you. Families are very important."

She rested her hand on Tara's arm. "You are very kind. Thank you so much."

Tara gave a quick grin. "Hey," she whispered, "I told you. I'm there for you."

They sat down amongst the team and listened as Declan led them through the briefing for Job 14.

"OK, so Job 14 is a thirties seaside house in Cork. Owned by a London couple who have had the house in their family since it was built in 1936. They've used the house as a holiday home for the last few years and have now moved into it as their permanent residence. You can see by the slides that the house sits on a huge blasted rock and faces the sea. There is already a mismatched nautical feel to the house, but Mr and Mrs Barker would like this theme continued throughout."

"We're doing the whole house?" Ciara interjected.

"Only in terms of continuing the theme, Ciara. There's very little to do in the kitchen and bedrooms, and we'll be concentrating on the lounge and bathroom."

Tara made notes frantically as she noted the large pieces of driftwood, old ropes and debris which the family had obviously collected from the beach. The decked balcony which surrounded the house stood on high struts, and was almost suspended above the beach. Tara felt envious, wishing she could exchange her Ballsbridge house for something as beautiful as this.

"From the front balcony Mr Barker has told us that the family have watched years' worth of sailing, climbing, crabbing and swimming. It'd be nice if we could echo the crashing waves, swooping gulls and colour schemes inside the house. Perhaps mini-lighthouses, even?"

"Declan!" Tara shouted out. "Tacky or what?"

He reddened slightly which made her want to laugh.

"OK, so I'll leave the design to you lot. And nothing tacky then, eh?"

She smiled at him, pleased that she'd caused him to squirm in front of the others – he was way too composed lately anyway. She returned to her notemaking, scribing a prompt to contact the sculptor that she'd come across in Kilkenny who made bronze fish sculptures and the craft worker in Wexford who specialised in papier-mâché seagulls.

Niamh was delighted at the prospect of shooting in such as exceptional environment. She'd get loads of material for her other projects too.

"OK then, team. That's about your lot. You have a week for research and we're off next Tuesday. And try to resist anything too 'Captain Birds Eye'!"

Their chairs scraped as they all stood, packing away their pens and notepads as they did so.

Declan crossed the room toward Tara, slightly nervous as they hadn't spoken properly since the night in Wexford.

"You really enjoyed that, didn't you?"

She knew he was smiling by the tone of his voice, but refused to look up at him, intent on rummaging in her bag.

"You did, didn't you?" he asked a second time.

Tara looked up at him and grinned, "Maybe."

"Are you OK?" he asked.

"I'm fine, Declan, thanks. Look, not being rude, but I have to dash."

"No problem. See you soon then?"

"Yeah, see you soon. Captain Birds Eye!"

The week flew by. Tara's Mum had taken Ruben again and she was on her way to Niamh's – this time they were heading off in *her* car. She had spent the last week planting her containers full of glorious bulbs of blues and whites, reds and oranges and was half loathe to leave her personalised Shed.

But hey, this is my last makeover for Home Is, *I reminded myself.*

And my last job with Declan.

And my first Christmas as a fourth wife!

They travelled down to Cork with the car heater on but their front windows half open. Tara loved the feel of the wind buffeting her hair lightly. They had the CD player up to number eighteen as it blasted out her 'Christmas is Crazy' favourites. Niamh stretched back in the passenger seat and closed her eyes.

"I love this weather, don't you?"

"Yeah? The icy roads and freezing fog?"

"No, the sparkling frosty fields and anticipation of Christmas."

"Maybe."

Niamh leant forward and turned down the music. "The sea is beautiful, don't you think?"

"I think everyone loves it, don't they? It's the freedom and power of it."

"You know," Niamh lit up – again, "during those few years I spent in London I frequented Chelsea Harbour quite a lot, in my search for a rich man."

"Did you? Is that where all the houseboats are?"

"Yes."

"So? Did you find a rich man?"

"I did, but there was a problem."

"What?" Tara was trying to turn to look at Niamh as she drove, but her hair kept flapping onto her face and across her eyes.

"I couldn't stand the smell of seaweed."

"Eerrgh!"

They both laughed as Tara turned the volume back up just as Shane McGowan growled the beginnings of 'Fairytale of New York.'

They arrived shortly after lunch only to find that Ciara and Declan were already there and the camera crew were beginning to set up their equipment.

"You know," Niamh said as they gathered their things from the boot of the car, "I reckon this is going to be the perfect job. Especially as it's your last of the series."

"Wonder if they'll have me back again next year?" she asked Niamh.

"'Course they will. You've been a great success so far."

"But they're not broadcasting till September. That'll be when they know for sure."

"Believe me, they already know."

As their unsuitable shoes clonked up the decking stairway Niamh nudged Tara as she noticed a woman she presumed to be Mrs Barker, untangling a string of Christmas lights as she stood on the non-windy side of the decked balcony.

Mr Barker met them at the front door, his London accent charming as he greeted them and welcomed them into his home. Tara noticed he had a slight limp. She glanced to her left to see Declan and Stephanie going through some paperwork in the lounge and she immediately noticed Declan glance up at her, a sad look in his eyes and new shoes on his feet.

As Declan sat, he curled up his toes awkwardly. His new shoes felt strange on his feet and he was starting to wonder whether he should have stuck to wearing the boots that he always wore. His dilemma was interrupted with the arrival of Tara and Niamh and he felt a warmth as he noticed her ruffled hair. He couldn't help but see, though, how Tara glanced scornfully at his new slip-on shoes. He knew that he'd blown his chances with her back in Wexford and now chided himself for even thinking that he could ever win her back again.

Tara instantly fell in love with the house. Its clean lines and yet warmth and colour, combined with the natural woods and the to-die-for blue Aga in the kitchen were simply fantastic. She knew that Niamh had been right – this would be the perfect job and it wouldn't be difficult to make this place look fantastic on camera.

It looked fantastic anyway!

She asked the charming Dave Barker where she could leave her design kit until they'd decided on the tasks in hand, and he'd led her towards the utility room. She opened the cream-painted wooden door to see a utility room, the likes of which you wouldn't see in Ballsbridge. The tongue and groove walls were also painted cream, and brass coat pegs, similar to those she remembered from her schooldays, lined the walls. Two small and three larger orange lifejackets hung from the pegs and a small wetsuit lay on a wooden bench by the back door. As she took it all in, the back door opened, making her jump, and Mrs Barker walked in, her slim body clad tastefully in jeans and a knitted jumper.

"Oh sorry, didn't mean to startle you."

Tara blushed. "No, not at all. I just wasn't expecting that door to open."

Mrs Barker introduced herself as Valerie and shook Tara's hand firmly.

"This really is a fantastic utility room."

"Yeah," Valerie smiled, picking up the small abandoned wetsuit and giving it a light shake. "A great room where the sand and salt can be hosed off and the swimwear and flippers just left to dry."

"So where is your washing-machine and tumble-drier then? You know, the *normal* things you'd have in a utility room?"

Valerie turned and opened another small door to the right. "In here."

"Brilliant. You don't really need us here at all, do you? It seems you've got this place pretty much sorted yourselves."

"We have, but I'd like to bring the nautical theme into the bathroom and lounge too. The trouble is that John is getting carried away with it all. He's even started to suggest that we have a huge stuffed bass on the wall."

"Yuk!" Tara grimaced.

"Exactly," Valerie giggled with her, "my sentiments exactly. I did wonder at a tropical fish tank in the lounge, but we need to completely rearrange the room. And I draw the line at port-hole type mirrors and light fittings."

"I know what you want. An echo of your environment whilst still retaining that fresh, crisp aura."

Valerie Barker took hold of Tara's hands. "That is *exactly* what I'm looking for."

"Come on then," Tara indicated toward the door, "let's go in and get some ideas down on paper."

Ciara was busy making plans for the bathroom. She'd seen so many sea-themed bathrooms that just screamed of amateur: the shell stencils on the wall, the different shades of blues to suggest the colours of the sea and the sky. She intended to tackle this from a completely different angle and she was currently sitting on the edge of the bath and sketching a mosaic design for the wall and had already decided that she'd like to resurface the old bath. She knew the new enamel surface took three days to cure and was contemplating speaking to Declan. Perhaps they could start that before filming.

Tara called in to check on Ciara and they sat together for half an hour discussing the re-enamelling of the bath. Tara was sure Declan would let her go ahead prior to filming and she encouraged her to go and ask him. Ciara went to butter him up and so Tara went down to her car, collecting from it the two large papier-mâché seagulls that she'd brought with her. As she struggled to close the boot, lightly hugging the large gulls, she was distracted by some whooping and squealing from the beach. She turned towards the sea, and spent some time watching a crowd of children playing on the glistening sand. She rested back against her car and lost herself in them – their gloved hands grabbing for each other and their scarves jumping as they ran. She stood up straight as she heard the front door open and then close, only to see Declan pussyfooting his way down the decked stairway, unsure of his new footwear. In an attempt not to chuckle, she turned her back on him, feigning a struggle with her car keys and the two gulls.

"Tara."

She heard him shuffle up beside her.

"Declan."

"Suppose you persuaded Ciara to soften me up about the bath resurfacing?"

"Hell, what harm would it do? We're not starting filming until Thursday anyway, are we?"

He relaxed against her car, as she did. "No, I suppose not."

"So what did you tell her?"

"What do you think?"

"Yes."

He nodded, and pulled a face of resignation.

"See," she said in a light voice, "you're not as bad as everyone thinks you are."

"Thanks," he deadpanned.

I knew I was being mean to him, but I just couldn't help it. It was all in the name of putting on a brave face. You surely understand that!

"You know," she said, tongue-in-cheek, "I like your new shoes."

"What? Oh fuck. They look ridiculous, don't they?"

It was that maternal thing again, I'm sure. He looked so forlorn and ridiculous then. I just couldn't help being nice to him.

"No, I'm only teasing. They look dead cool. Mind you, you're making them look daft, the way you're trotting about in them as if you're afraid they'll fall off any minute. Relax a little."

"Yeah, maybe you're right."

She laughed with him, and pushed him up jokily, back toward the house. "Come on, back to work. Here," she thrust a papier-mâché gull at him, "take one of these while you're at it."

By the end of that first day they were all exhausted and Tara took great delight in crashing out in her hotel room at ten thirty. She was asleep by ten thirty-two.

Declan fidgeted on the high bar-stool, keen to make amends with Tara, but unsure how to go about it.

Ciara lay in her bed and cried. Not the desperate choking tears of the last week, but a calmer more pitiful cry. The tears of regret and change. Niamh sat cross-legged on her bed flicking through the TV channels, looking for the three minutes of complimentary porn before you have to pay, and texting Adam at the same time.

By Thursday they were ready to start filming. They had decided on the look for the house and were ready to go. Ciara had some excellent ideas to update the mirror frame and for the mosaic design on the bathroom wall. Tara had excelled herself once again with suggestions for the soft furnishings and doors that had caused Valerie Barker to squeal with delight. They were ready for the off.

Thursday morning was even icier than the last few days and Niamh was finding it a problem with the lighting. Just as she was repositioning herself, crouching and bending to get the right angle, Handyman John appeared with his drill.

"OK, Tara, where do you want this light fitting then?"

Tara hopped down from her stepladder, wiping the paint from her hands with a cloth. She dragged the stepladder across to the windows which ran from one end of the sea-facing lounge to the other. "I want the spotlights here, here and here, John. Will that be a problem?"

We were putting on our best polite and pally voices because the cameras were rolling. I'd usually say something like, "Hey, you fat git, any chance of getting those lights up there now?" to which he'd reply, "Jesus, you're some bossy yoke!" and we'd both fall about in fits of laughter.

"No problem, Tara."

Now let me tell you the rest. I stood back with a smile as John, drill in hand, climbed the few steps up. As he plunged the drill bit in through the ceiling disaster struck. Handyman John hit a waterpipe! We all screamed – well, John kind of hollered – and the camera crew pulled their equipment back out of the spray of water. Declan came rushing in and slipped – his new shoes sliding across the wet floor – and landed on his bum at my feet.

"Turn it off at the mains!" yelled John from the top step, trying to hold his hands over the spray which was soaking them all.

All except Ciara.

She came into the room and saved the day. She turned the water off at the mains and as she walked back into the lounge she took one look at them all and began to laugh.

"You want to see the state of yourselves," she roared. "Honestly! Can't I leave you for a few minutes?"

It was Tara who laughed next as Declan groaned at

her feet and then tried to stand, his slidey new shoes still ungripping.

"You look like fucking Bambi!" Tara burst. With that, everybody began to laugh, even Declan.

A few minutes later, they were all standing out on the decked balcony, wearing an odd assortment of borrowed clothes while their wet clothes were being dried.

"Look, don't worry," Valerie Barker soothed, "it could have been very nasty. You were all lucky."

"Yeah, no panic," Dave shook his head, "we're used to water in the house, what with cousins and relatives over the years using the house as an extension of the beach."

"You're being very kind and relaxed about it all. Thank you." Declan rubbed the base of his spine as he spoke. "It'll be all sorted and cleaned up in a few minutes anyway."

"Look," Mrs Barker repeated, "don't worry about it. No damage done." Tara was amazed at Dave Barker as he carried out a large tray of home-made lemonade, pimms and smoothies, mulled wine, truffles and chocolate log.

Despite his slight limp he never spilt a drink.

"Here," he offered the drinks around, "let's take a break, eh?"

John snatched at a drink first. "Well, I'm going to need a while to fix that pipe and sort that ceiling out anyway."

"Back tomorrow then?" asked Declan.

"No," John scratched his head, "I'd say give me till three."

The *Home Is* team had never been in the company of clients who were so relaxed and hospitable and they spent the afternoon swapping disaster stories, whilst John made good the inside. Moreso than for a long time, the team's emotions were relaxed and spirits were high.

"You know," Declan informed them, "they reckon that DIY enthusiasts are being injured and sometimes even killed, by being led into over-ambitious projects."

"Don't be ridiculous," Tara challenged. "Killed! How?"

"Honestly! Some critics believe that these makeover-type programmes encourage people to take on jobs which are beyond their abilities."

"I read that too," agreed Niamh, "and they reckon that more victims add to the toll over public holidays like Easter and Christmas. I suppose that's the time when most people try out projects at home."

Declan continued. "It seems that when people watch these kind of programmes they assume it's easy and then think they can do things like the experts."

"So what kind of injuries are you talking about?" Tara asked.

Ciara answered for her, with the voice of experience. "Well, even a simple job such as putting a screw in. People are forever puncturing their fingers or hands. And then there's falling off ladders."

"Go 'way."

"Seriously. I suppose it's all about overreaching. Really, about seventy people a year are killed as a result of DIY disasters."

"Christ. Maybe that'd be a good idea to put in the *Home Is* book then, Declan. A kind of disclaimer or something suggesting that people always take safety precautions and read the instructions or something."

"It's already there, Tara. We can't take any chances."

The bleeping of Niamh's mobile broke the conversation.

"Excuse me," she said, and leapt up from the lounger.

As she walked off toward the back of the house Tara's mind turned to Simon. An awkward silence hung in the air, as if nobody knew what to talk about next, so Tara took her chance. "Excuse me too, I have a quick call to make."

She slipped on her jacket and took her phone down on the icy beach, searching for Christina's number in her address book. She walked slowly, relaxed as she held the phone to her ear, waiting for it to connect.

As she enjoyed the fresh breeze in her face she thought back to how she never dreamed, a year ago, that she'd be walking along this beach, so happy and relaxed. Ringing Simon's *other* wife to tell her that she'd reported his polygamy to the gardaí. The phone connected and she took a deep breath as she smiled, waiting to hear Christina's pensive voice.

"Hello?"

The male voice caused her to stop dead in her tracks. The relaxed smile fell from her face.

"Hello?" he repeated.

My God, I thought, it's Simon! I haven't heard his voice in over a year. He's bloody well there! It's completely crazy!

I was overwhelmed with an urge to let rip at him – let him know what I think of him. All that guilt I carried around for so long about the affair! That polygamous bastard, smug and contented at the end of the phone.

I was gonna let him have it.

"Hello?"

The voice sounded breezy and happy.

And charming.

I felt sick.

Struck dumb by the sound of his voice once again, after so long, she froze.

He spoke again. "Hello? Who's there?"

The voice now had the edge of irritability to it. Tara was immediately taken back to when he'd lived with her.

As man and wife.

How many times she'd heard him answer their phone that way.

I could see it now, in my mind's eye – me in the kitchen preparing dinner and him watching the telly or polishing his shoes. I could almost imagine his big bare feet trotting toward the phone before it would stop ringing. And then he'd say that.

"Hello! Ah!"

And he'd put the phone down with a few "fucks" and curses.

The anger surged in her like never before and just as

she opened her mouth to begin her tirade of expletives she remembered Christina. And the little child. To the sounds of Simon's "hello" a movie played at fast speed in her head: it was Ciara's dilemma about Melanie – the daughter she'd given away and now regretted. How Ciara's life had suffered because of that and how Melanie's life was soon to change, now that she had found out who her real mother was. The question Tara couldn't answer was – dare she interfere in Christina and her small son's future? Simon had done enough; she knew it would be all about damage limitation now at this stage. If she screamed and shouted at Simon down the phone, he would only turn on Christina and who knows what would happen then?

No. I had to let Christina deal with it her own way.

She hung up.

Chapter 28

Because of the unexpected shower that Handyman John had treated them to, the team had to work until the early hours of day two to make up for time lost and to complete the job.

"I'm shagged!" Tara sighed, slumping down on the wooden bench of the utility room.

"You wish you were," Niamh muttered under her breath from the lounge, where she was wearily packing up her equipment. It was all Tara seemed to see her doing lately – that and sending picture messages to Adam. Through the slightly open windows they could hear the majestic sounds of the sea although the black of the night prevented them from enjoying the view. Valerie had lit some scented candles just prior to the final "after" shots and their heady but relaxing aroma now filled the room. Tara pulled up her sleeve, looking for the time.

"Jesus," she hissed, "it's nearly half past one!"

"I'm knackered too," Niamh agreed as she knelt to shoe-horn the folded tripod into its slot.

"Here, everyone!" Valerie's voice was surprisingly bright and jolly considering the late hour and the heavy day they'd all put in.

Tara supposed it was helped by her delight at the makeover – she'd been truly overwhelmed. She placed a tray laden with various spirits and mixers onto the floor, dangerously in front of Niamh, as she then sat beside it adopting a cross-legged position. "Come on, guys – come and get a relaxer!" Before you could say "I've-no-intentions-of-getting-pissed-tonight" they were all relaxing into the huge cushions and holding out their glasses. When Dave Barker followed shortly after with two plates full of shiny hot sausages which rolled excitedly as he limped in with them, the mere smell of the cooking alone made everybody instantly ravenous. It seemed, after such a long and tiresome, yet satisfying makeover, nobody could resist those extra couple of hours indulging in great bangers, chilled alcohol and a bit of craic.

It was quarter to four before Niamh and Tara got back to their hotel, and already the beginnings of a headache was threatening. Ciara had bravely declined all offers of alcohol – *unlike me – who had to draw the line at two* – and had made the first exit back to the hotel. She was now so focused on sorting out the rest of her life she didn't want anything getting in her way. Tara knew how she felt – she'd compromised her priorities for too long.

And so as the white sky slowly cut through the darkness

I drifted into an exhausted but relaxed sleep, aware of the bleeping of Niamh's mobile from the next room. I was getting used to hotel bedrooms now – the paper-thin walls, the noisy plumbing, the roar of the bath taps from every room around you.

Niamh woke, straining to see the display on her phone, both for the time and for any new picture messages. She unwittingly stretched out her left arm, feeling the cool white sheets beside her, and then felt alarmed as she realised that she was actually feeling for Adam. Flopping her tangled head back onto the pillow, she clutched her phone and sent Adam the usual photo message of the two green monopoly houses which they both knew meant "Your place or mine?" She was resigned to the fact that her lust-for-the-upper-crust had gone bust!

Tara showered after a fitful night. She'd hardly slept and couldn't figure out her feelings about Simon. She had managed quite admirably – *or so I thought* – to act normally last night after speaking to him. She'd even managed to complete the makeover without a hiccup.

The hiccups came after the vodka!

It was very strange hearing his voice again. I'd forgotten what a deep mellow sound he made when he spoke. And here was me doing OK. Damn it, I was even beginning to really hate him, what with the polygamy thing. And now, after hearing him again I was all messed up. It had been a complete shock to hear him at Christina's house too. It seemed strange, ringing someone and hearing your husband answer! Of course, I was dying to know if anything had happened there. I didn't suppose it had though – in reality Christina probably wasn't strong enough to tackle the situation yet and I didn't really blame her. She'd got a young child to consider too. Made me feel even luckier really, that I was not in her situation. In comparison it was quite easy for me to let go of Simon.

As if I had any choice.

He left me – remember.

By early afternoon they were back on the road once again and heading for Dublin. Tara couldn't wait for the chance to get home and strip off yesterday's clothes. Niamh was equally tearing to get back to see Adam. Niamh's hangover quietened her down and the journey from Cork to Dub flew by as they were both lost in their own thoughts.

They didn't realise that only eighty miles ahead of them Declan was lost in his thoughts too as he drove home. He'd noticed that Tara's car was still in the hotel carpark when he'd left an hour before them. He gripped the steering wheel, enjoying yet another sunny afternoon. He had his Charlie Parker CD blaring and hardly noticed his phone ringing. Just as it rang off he grabbed it.

"Shit!" He threw the phone back down onto the vacant seat beside him and, just as he turned up the volume again, the phone jumped into life once more. This time he wasted no time and clutched at it vigorously.

"Hello!"

"Declan. David Cruickshank. I've got some good news for you, Declan. The property near Champs Elysses that you made the offer on? They've accepted!"

"Excellent. Thank you, David. I'm on the road at the moment, can I call you in a couple of hours?"

"Of course, no problem."

Declan threw back the phone once again and grinned as he wriggled into his seat, resting his head back on the headrest.

"Just what I wanted to hear. An extra little bit of sunshine on an already brilliant day."

As he drove on, his thoughts couldn't help but turn back to Tara. She'd shown so much interest in the places in Paris and he would really have loved to share his good news with her, but whilst they were now at least on talking terms, he felt as if he was bringing up that fateful night in Paris if he so much as mentioned the word to her. He was disappointed that she had completed her last job of the series and had already begun to figure how he could maintain some kind of contact with her. It was time for coincidences or excuses now. Now that he wouldn't see her every week through work. As he breathed deeply he thought of the three offers he'd made on the Parisian properties – the charming apartment in the Pigalle area, an elegant third-floor one-bed near the Champs Elysses and the extraordinary modern studio near Boulevard Pereire. He was ecstatic that the offer on the Champs Elysses one was the one to come back first – that was the one he'd really wanted most. His enthusiasm waned slightly as his thoughts drifted to the peeling paintwork and the completely white interior – all but for the wooden floors throughout. How he wished he was on better terms with Tara – she'd be great at helping him get sorted with it all. If only things were different. He wondered if she'd made any decisions about her farce of a marriage and decided he had the perfect excuse for contact. He'd ask her.

On arrival back in Dublin, later that afternoon, Niamh had pulled herself together a little. Tara had known she was heading straight for Adam's when, on hitting Newbridge, she'd pulled down the visor and had spent half an hour sorting out her make-up in the vanity mirror. Once she'd managed to recreate the I'm-not-wearing-much-make-up-but-really-I-am look she sprang to life.

"You wouldn't drop me off at Adam's, would ya?"

"You didn't even need to ask." Tara smiled.

"Why didn't I?" Niamh turned, her glossed lips glistening as she ignited her lighter for another cig.

"It's kind of *obvious*."

"Really," Niamh smiled, exhaling her first draw, "and how so?"

"You're done up like fecking J-Lo!"

"Yeah, and so will you be tonight."

"Me? I doubt it. Another evening in front of the telly, I think. My life's a strange mix of celebrity makeovers for RTÉ and then nights alone with Ruben watching Alan Titchm-arse and Jamie Oliver."

"Well, we're out tonight, so don't say you didn't have enough notice."

"Who's 'we'?"

"The three of us. I'll give Anna a buzz – she's always up for it anyway."

"Oh Niamh, I don't know."

"No! I'm not taking no for an answer. You've just completed your last job as a celebrity interior designer for RTÉ and to think a year ago you hadn't even set up the Tara McKenna Consultancy. We are celebrating, whether you like it or not. So you'd better get used to the idea."

I was flattered really.

"OK. Be at your place by eight, OK?"

"Great."

She dropped Niamh off near to Adam's flat and went home, tearing off her clothes the minute she walked through the door, desperate to get her scruffy home clothes on.

And then there was that watercolour painting I'd started last week. Maybe I'd have another go at that too.

Tara was ready by seven-thirty and made her way to Niamh's, although she knew she'd be early. When she arrived at Niamh's Anna was already there.

"Wow, don't we all look fantastic!" Anna gushed. Both Tara and Niamh had to admit it – they did. With plenty of skin on view!

Tara was delighted that she'd chosen to wear her lightweight cream trousers with the large floral print across the waistband which wasn't a waistband.

They were hipsters!

And her shoulders jutted out attractively from her fitted cream vest, a smattering of freckles like confetti across her back. Niamh had opted for a tight cerise sleeveless t-shirt and her hipster jeans which showed off her tattoo.

"So where d'ya fancy?" Tara asked, snatching the glass of chilled white wine from Niamh. "Apart from Adam's."

"Ha, ha, fecking ha. If you must know, I spent a fantastic afternoon in the sack with Adam. I'm just ready for a mad night out now."

"So, where then? 'Cos if I'm honest, I'm tearing for a great night too."

Anna dribbled her wine as she suggested, "How about JJ's?"

They all loved JJ Smyth's in Aungier Street, one of Dublin's longest-standing jazz and blues venues.

"It'll be empty early though." Niamh grimaced as she paused to reapply her lipstick.

"OK, so we'll head out that way anyway."

"No surprise there then." Tara laughed. "Do you think we're really getting boring – going to the same places all the time?"

"Not at all," Niamh retorted, smacking her red lips together as she blotted, "we're at the cutting edge of Dublin nightlife."

"We could always go to The Inn. Remember last time we were there we saw that Mexican group and their acoustic guitars."

"Oh yeah," Niamh giggled, grappling for her door keys, "they were gorgeous. It'd nearly make you emigrate."

"Niamh," Tara playfully jabbed her in the back as they congregated in the hallway, bustling for the front door, "you'd think you *had* emigrated after a night out in Dublin. It's positively swarming with tourists."

They grabbed their jackets and stepped out, a fit-looking trio.

My mum would have a fit, I thought – going out with no coat at this time of year!

Tara did feel cold in her skimpy jacket, but felt cosy at the sight of the Christmas lights and the mood of merriment that was around them.

OK, so I mean the mood of alcohol, but hey – this was Dublin.

Niamh then brought up a subject which dampened down Tara's good spirits.

"D'you know, I heard Declan telling Stephanie that he'd made three offers on places in Paris."

"Really?" Anna wanted to know more. "How exciting! Paris!"

You know, I really could have done without hearing that. That night of all nights. It was killing me that I didn't already know. If things had have been different between me and Declan then I'd already know that. And I'd know where the three places were and I'd probably know the ins and outs of all of them.

I might even have been to see them with him.

Perhaps I'd overreacted in Wexford.

Perhaps he wasn't taking advantage of me.

Perhaps I was just a confused fool.

They stopped off en route at a couple of trendy bars for pre-JJ's drinks and got caught up then trying to decide on Break for the Border or Hogan's.

"Oh no," Tara wailed as Anna stood at the doorway of a heaving and loud bar, "please let's not go in there. I get sick of the traditional music sessions. They're always choked with tourists."

"Yeah," Niamh dragged Anna by the arm, "let's try up here. Anyway, it cracks me up in those places, especially when they have their break and the bar staff put the modern music on." She started to "riverdance" on the busy street, exaggerating the moves as she lightly tapped her feet and high-kicked. "They don't know *what* to do with their arms!"

They finally stopped near to JJ's and went into a large bar there. As they huddled around the tall circular table, stirring their drinks excitedly as they chatted, they were approached by three Englishmen.

"Fancy a drink?" one of them asked, pleasantly.

"Yeah," Niamh challenged, "make mine a stiff one. Please."

The men exchanged glances and raised their eyebrows promisingly at each other. He didn't hurry to the bar.

"So, ladies, are you going dancing tonight?"

"Dancing!" they all shrieked.

"Now isn't *that* something we all do better when we're drunk!" Tara giggled.

"We're great dancers," boasted the dark-haired of the three.

"Well, that's definitely out then," Anna replied. "There's nothing more intimidating than being with a man who dances better than yourself. Sorry!"

"So you're not interested then?"

He was clearly the slow one of the three.

"No," Tara smiled. "Thanks, but – as they say – no thanks."

Niamh necked her Seabreeze, spitting out the small grapefruity bits at the bottom, but still asking Anna if she was going up for any more.

"Going *up*?" Anna questioned her geography. "How do you figure I'm going up?"

"Up to the bar!"

"So how's that up then? It's over. I'm going *over* to the bar."

"Oh fuckit, whatever. Just order 'em up again, eh? I've got a raging thirst on me tonight."

Anna obediently took her turn at the bar, bringing back three Seabreezes. The time alone had obviously got her mind working overtime, as she placed the three drinks down on the wet table.

"Talking of going up, guess what I did on Tuesday?"

"Dunno," Niamh was too interested in stirring her cranberry, grapefruit and vodka cocktail.

Anna leaned in closer to the table and whispered, "I went down on Hugh at the opera."

Tara burst into laughter, amazed at her confession. "You never did! Where?"

"What d'ya mean where?"

"What opera? Where?"

"Christ, Tara, does it matter where? Good on ya, Anna, you're keeping the side going. Well, you and me are – it seems Tara's spurning all male attention lately. She won't even talk to Declan anymore."

"Shuttup, Niamh. Don't bring that up now. Just 'cos you've got a few drinks in you." Tara tried to bring the subject back round to Anna.

"So how did this come about then? You hardly got down on your knees in front of everyone as they hit the high notes."

"Well," she blushed as she spoke, but it was clear she was loving every minute of her daring story, "it all began as a bit of a joke. We were sitting in the side stalls, and there weren't many people around us. Hugh's just bought this pair of really tight trousers –"

"Oh fuck, not those shiny ones again," Niamh teased.

"No! Shuttup and listen. And I was just joking and I said that they were so tight that I could see his willy. So he said, 'Yeah? Whaddya reckon?' So then, just kidding really, I said, 'It's grey and knackered-looking, a bit like yourself!' To which he said I'd better take a closer look. And so, I did! It was really exciting, but I was shitting meself in case the interval happened before I was ready for it."

"Jesus, Anna, you really are getting it on with Hugh, aren't ya?"

"Suppose I am. I really like him."

Tara spoke up quickly to prevent Niamh from jibing at her. "Well, good luck to you. I hope it works out."

"Thanks, Tara. Me too."

As the evening slipped by in an ever-increasing blur, Tara began to feel tipsy and turned her thoughts to the last makeover of *Home Is*, wondering how the last job would go for the two guys now that she and Ciara were "off the hook". She was glad she'd found the time to start her watercolour painting again and with four now complete and filed in her portfolio in The Shed, she was planning to do another eight or nine and had toyed with the idea of asking Mulligan if she could have her first exhibition there. Thanks to *Home Is*, the Tara McKenna Consultancy was doing very well and she was pretty much booked up with new clients for the next five months. Her reflections on the changes in her life were interrupted as Niamh and Anna returned from the toilets, Niamh complaining about a woman who she believed wore no knickers.

"And I said to her, 'Hey, there's an invention called panties – wear them, honey!' Jesus, she'd be better with a thong than nothing at all, surely!"

Tara wobbled as she stood, raising her half-full glass as she did so.

"I have a toast to make."

"Oh fuck, Tara sit down, will ya! You're making me dizzy." Niamh groaned as she tried to look up at Tara.

"Shuttup. And listen!" Tara held her glass high and continued. "Friendship, they say, is like pissing in your pants."

"*Eerggh*," Anna grimaced.

"Let me finish." Tara was trying not to get annoyed at the interruptions.

"Friendship is like pissing in your pants. Everyone

can see it, but only you can feel its true warmth. I'd like to say thank you to you both, for being the piss in my pants!"

By the end of the night they all needed three things: to lie down, a bowl and a taxi. It was agreed earlier in the evening that they'd all stay at Tara's for the night, on the grounds that the taxi would be cheaper and she had the most room. They joined the queue, which threatened to go right around the block at the taxi rank.

"Oh God," Tara whinged, now desperate for her bed, "if only we lived in a well-organised city like Paris or New York. You'd only have to stick out your hand and a cab would appear. This is ridiculous."

Luckily for them Niamh's gregarious chat-up lines saved the evening for them as she managed to chat up a suited business man who was heading southside also. He also happened to be very near to the front of the queue.

"Hey," she called as she looped her arm through his, "I've managed to blag us a cab-share!" Tara and Anna quickly left the swelling queue and stood with the sober-looking man.

"Ha," Tara giggled, feeling slightly embarassed at taking the piss so obviously, yet quite willing to carry on, "nothing like supply to demand, is there?"

Ciara carefully folded the last of her clothes and lay them gently on the top of the pile that sat in her suitcase. She was ready to leave soon. She had decided that she'd travel through the early hours for the West to arrive ready for her two months rehabilitation bright and early that morning and was actually looking forward to Christmas in rehab. She had been surprised at her composure when her agent had rung earlier that evening with the news. She thought she'd have lost it again when he told her that the tabloid newspaper had a videotape of her picking up men in a Dublin club earlier in the year. But she'd remained calm. Remarkably calm. And then as he'd stressed and worried down the line that they also had photographs of her taking drugs, she was able to merely shrug it off. She suspected that he was more concerned than her. He didn't realise her new priorities in life. He didn't understand. She was remarkably composed as she explained to him that she was going to rehab in the morning and wouldn't be in contact for at least two months.

"After all," she even managed to smile as she spoke, "it's not all about the media circus, you know. Some of us have better things to worry about. You do know, I'm a grandmother."

As she put the phone down on him he'd sat at his desk, scratching his head for a good hour, convincing himself that she'd finally gone bananas.

Chapter 29

They dropped off the "suit" first, at his insistence, and the three women had laughed and joked the whole way back to Ballsbridge, Anna gagging at the body odour of the taxi-driver. As the taxi pulled up outside Tara's house, flicking on his hazard lights as they rummaged for the fare, Niamh hopped up on to her knees on the back seat, staring through the back window.

"Jesus, Tara!" She sounded suddenly sober. "That's Simon!"

A chill ran down my spine quicker than a German looking for a Mediterranean sunbed. It couldn't be. Here? Now?

"What?" Tara dropped her change in the confusion.

Anna grappled on her hands and knees, hiccupping as she looked for the coins.

"I'm telling you, Tar, in that black Saab parked a bit down there. We just passed it. I'm telling ya!"

"Where? I can't even see it."

"There. Look, he's turned his lights on now." Tara

watched as the orange rear lights glowed into the frosty street-lit road.

"Found it!" Anna called, her hair scruffed on her head and in her eyes as she clambered out of the cab backwards, a fist full of coinage. Tara and Niamh could only watch as the black Saab sped down the road, its orange rear lights so glaring it was impossible to read the registration number.

That and our inability to focus.

As they stepped into Tara's house, the mood had changed slightly. Anna rushed straight upstairs to the toilet, but Niamh and Tara stood by the kettle waiting for it to boil.

"That can't have been him. *Him* in a black Saab?"

"How would you know what car he has now? If he's married three or four times, who knows what money he's getting from where? And it could be a company car."

"Yeah, suppose it could."

Despite her drunken state Niamh could see how Tara was bothered and decided it was safer to put her mind at rest. She stood beside her and threw an arm around her shoulders.

"Look, Tar. I'm pissed. It probably wasn't him at all. Don't mind me."

"No. OK."

I said that to make her feel better. But I have to admit, it was really niggling me now. What if it was him? Why was he there?

Tara made coffee for herself and Niamh, sending

Anna to the spare bed with a bowl. In typical form Niamh wanted food when she was pissed and Tara sat, half concentrating as Niamh stuffed two fish-finger sandwiches in a bid to soak up some of the alcohol.

As Tara lay in her bed she contemplated the inevitable dribble tidemarks on her leather cushions in the morning.

I'd left Niamh sleeping on the sofa.

And I had to give Anna a bowl. She'd already puked twice.

But she was reassured that Niamh and Anna were staying the night with her.

Then her phone rang, making her jump. Switching on her bedside lamp she grabbed her phone, wondering who the hell was ringing at this hour of the night. It was gone two a.m.

"Hello?" she whispered, her pulse banging in her neck.

"Tara?" It was a woman's voice.

Tara remained silent.

"Tara. It's Christina. Christina Appleby."

"Yeah, what's wrong? It's gone two!"

"I just had to tell you, Tara. Sorry it's so late, but I've been dancing around the phone all evening wondering whether I should tell you or not."

"What? What's up?"

"I've thrown Simon out."

"You've not!"

"I have." Her pride was swelling in her voice as she

spoke. "I had to. I was very calm and just told him that I knew about his other marriages."

"You didn't mention me?"

"No! No, I didn't."

"Did he say he was coming here?"

"No! Why would he? Why do you ask me that?"

"No reason." She dismissed it as putting two and two to make five hundred. "So? What did he say?"

"He said very little really. He cried and was very embarrassed and then he got a little annoyed and kept on asking how I knew. I didn't tell him, Tara, honestly."

"Wow! I didn't expect you to do that. You're very brave – well done, Christina."

"Thanks. And so he's gone. Probably to one of the other wives now for a while. I feel upset, but I feel kind of strong too. I never thought I'd have the guts to do it, Tara. But then I was thinking about our son and thinking how he deserved better than that. When you've got kids, all your priorities change, you know."

Tara smiled as her tipsy thoughts turned to Ciara. "Yes, Christina, I know."

"Well, sorry to ring so late, but I just had to tell you. Thanks for your help and support, Tara. Perhaps you'll ring me if you hear any more news."

"'Course I will," she said. "Keep in touch, eh?"

"Sure. Night."

"Night."

Tara wanted to rush down the stairs and wake up Niamh and chew the cud over this for the next few hours, but knew that she was wasting her time. Both

Niamh and Anna were virtually unconscious by now. It'd have to wait until the morning.

Tara's hours of sleep were punctuated by the telephone. She'd gone to sleep with the sounds of Christina's call ringing in her ears, and was woken too early by the sounds of the phone ringing again. This time it was Ciara. Tara lay in her bed, her monotoned replies more of a grunting as she "yeaahhh'd" and "nooo'd" and "ah-ha'd" answers to Ciara's chat. She really would have liked to have given Ciara more attention, but her head was spinning and she felt a little sick.

Ciara explained how she had just arrived at her rehab clinic and knew that she wouldn't be able to make contact with Tara for a few weeks. She asked Tara to apologise to Declan for not hanging around for the end-of-series publicity shots.

"You see," she rambled slightly, trying to be humorous, "there's more to life than faux cow-hide bags, Prada yo-yo's and Gucci cheese-graters. To be honest, Tara, I'm sick of the pretence. Who am I trying to kid? I'm a grandmother. I'm a mother. It's time for change."

And with the re-iterating of her new-found priorities Tara found herself agreeing with Ciara as she apologised. "And I'm sorry for being such a bitch to you, Tara. You'll do well with your consultancy. And if I can ever be of any help, professional or otherwise, please don't hesitate."

Tara actually managed, "No problem, Ciara. We all

make mistakes," as she then bade her good luck and goodbye for now.

Ciara's call didn't only wake Tara. It had jolted Niamh from her sweaty sleep on Tara's sofa and Anna from the bed. Anna couldn't believe that she hadn't needed the bowl and had slept through.

In all honesty, she looked the best out of the three of us!

They tentatively padded around, passing each other for the bathroom and toilet and then the kitchen, finally taking their places on the sofa. Over many mugs of coffee and water Tara regaled them with an account of her busy night.

"I feel like I've been doing a night-shift at a call centre!" she exaggerated, much to their amusement as she enlightened them both about Christina and Ciara's dilemmas. Niamh found it hard to concentrate, partly as her pounding head was aggravating her, but mainly due to the photo messages that Adam continually sent her all morning.

"Jesus, Niamh," Anna sighed, irritated by the continual bleeping, "does that thing never stop?"

Niamh grinned cockily and got back to tapping in her reply.

"Can't you turn it off? Tara's trying to tell us the gossip!" Anna insisted.

"Oh Anna," Tara quipped, "that's nothing, believe me. She's at it the whole time. My working week is dotted with news about Adam and Niamh, Adam and Niamh, Adam and Niamh!"

"Oh no!" Niamh gasped, staring up at them with a twinkle in her eye. "Say that again!"

Tara looked bewildered. "Say what?"

"That!" she wagged her hand frantically at her. "What you just said."

Tara looked at Niamh as if she'd completely lost her faculties, but offered, "Adam and Niamh, Adam and Niamh," and then she smiled as she continued, "Adam an' Eve, Adam an' Niamh, Adam an' Eve! Christ, Niamh – you're biblical! For the first time in your damn life."

They all screamed with laughter.

"My mother would be delighted!" Niamh joked.

"Well," Anna tittered, "I'd say he's taken more than a *bite* of your apple."

"Darling," Niamh replied, "what choice did he have? The cherry was long gone!"

By midday they'd talked it all out and Niamh and Anna had left – Niamh still picture-messaging Adam and Anna was off home via Hugh's.

I don't mean to feel jealous, but I couldn't really help it. They were both so happy with the men in their life. And here was me. Me and Ruben and The Shed. I'd have loved to ring Declan, but there was just something there getting in my way.

My bloody pride.

She slumped on her sofa, a box of Christmas cards beside her, but her mind racing with torment as she went over and over the black Saab of the night before.

Niamh must have got it wrong. I mean she was hardly coherent, was she? It was probably best I put it out of my mind.

By early afternoon Tara had abandoned the Christmas cards and had completed her latest watercolour piece and sketched out the beginnings of another. She had taken to spending most of her spare time painting and had begun to hope that the consultancy would keep her busy enough to keep her occupied. She knew that she was pretty much booked solid for the next five months and was extremely pleased, but still couldn't help worrying.

It was very expensive to advertise, but with the Home Is *exposure and word of mouth it seemed that was not a problem for me.*

Yet.

Having sketched out the new picture she decided it was time to take a break and collect Ruben from her mother. She knew it'd be a good opportunity to give her the Christmas present and card that she'd scrawled. Where she'd been dreading the full afternoon *and* dinner with her mother and new boyfriend, she was now relieved that Niamh had suggested all having dinner at Tara's place. Tugging on her Nikes she grabbed her car keys and hopped in the car. It took only minutes to get to her mother's.

Tara had reckoned that she'd want to chat, but she was in one of those I-want-to-be-alone moods and so Tara put Ruben into the back of the car and made for the Grand Canal for a walk. She loved walking along the canal by Portobello Road. In the summer months she'd loved watching the students as they lolled beside the water in the sunshine, the bohemian atmosphere permeating the air. Some Dubliners criticised the aura as contrived and forced, but Tara took it more on face value and simply enjoyed the walk along the icy waterside. Ruben enjoyed it too.

By six they were home, Ruben tired and very thirsty. Refreshed and relaxed, Tara felt a million miles away from Simon and Christina and Ciara and all the problems that went with them. Her red glowing cheeks shone healthily.

It was only now with hindsight I realised that my passion to be married was both immature and ridiculous. I should have listened to all my friends and family as they tried to advise me. And to think I thought they were jealous! But still, perhaps without the sadness of this last year I wouldn't be the person I am now. I certainly wouldn't be an interior designer for RTÉ with her own consultancy.

Perhaps Declan was right. Things do happen for a reason.

The weekends meant that Tara could rarely park her car outside of her house and so she had to take a parking space at least twenty doors down from her. With a spring in her step she clipped the lead onto Ruben's collar and they walked steadily along the road, both gasping for a drink of water. As she approached her house she noticed in the half-light that something was different. Something was wrong.

The fucking front door was ajar! I was sure I never left it that way when I went out! It was – the front door was slightly open. And there was a light on somewhere upstairs, on the landing probably – I was sure that wasn't on when I left!

Bringing back an adrenalin rush of all the fears and terror from the hotel break-in in Paris, the sight left Tara paralysed on the street. She felt as if the sounds around her were amplified as even the slightest rustling of Mrs O'Reilly-from-across-the-road's carrier bags, as she carried her shopping home, were right in her ears. She felt sick and then dizzy and then tearful. Extremely tearful.

I needed to ring someone, but I could hardly breathe. There was only one person I felt safe with and I couldn't even be sure he'd come running. After all, the way I treated him back in Wexford was hardly nice, was it? No point ringing Niamh or Anna – they'd be useless. Anyway they were probably both "busy" with their men. I couldn't ring Mum – she'd scream and have a cardiac on the phone. It had to be Declan. I couldn't think of anyone that I'd feel safer with.

And so pulling her mobile from her pocket she rested against the wrought-iron fence of the house five doors down and punched in his number, her breath short and quick.

It rang and rang.

Maybe he wouldn't answer! He might take one look at my name on his phone and decide not to. Please God, don't let that happen, I prayed desperately.

"Hello?"

Thank you, thank you, thank you.

"Declan," her voice was shaky and fitful.

"Tara. What's wrong?"

"Oh Jesus, Declan, there's someone in my house, I'm sure of it."

"What? Where are you?"

"Outside!"

"Outside my place?"

"No! Outside *my* bloody place. I was taking Ruben for a walk and I've come back to see the front door open. Please. It's just like Paris again, I'm so fucking scared. Please come and help me."

And do you know, he just couldn't resist it. Not that I can blame him really.

"OK, so the don't disturb sign is *off* the door now then?"

A sob caught in her throat. "Please, Declan, hurry. I'm terrified!"

To give him his dues, he was there within eight minutes. Although it seemed like eight hours. I just didn't know what to do! I could hardly stand there waiting on the street! I mean, what if the intruder came out? I'd have to go face to face! Ruben started to get fidgety and I knew he was dying for a wee so I walked back up the street, letting him piddle in the kerb, and then we got back into the car. From there I had a clear view of the house and I'd be able to see when Declan arrived. You know, as I thought about it, sitting there waiting in the car, I loved his valiant and yet vulnerable demeanour. He was such a knight in shining armour and yet he wasn't afraid to show his feelings too.

There was no doubt about it.

I was in love with him.

*For what good that would do me after the way I'd treated
him . . .*

Declan arrived and Tara and Ruben immediately got
out of the car and rushed over to him. The first thing he
did was put his arms around Tara to check that she was
OK, while Ruben leapt up on both of them. He could
see that she was shaken and so he insisted that she wait
outside with Ruben.

That was no problem! I didn't need to be told twice.

"But what if they're armed or something? They
might hurt you? Perhaps we should call the police?"

*Isn't it easy to be sensible when there's someone else there
to sound off against?*

"How long have you been waiting for me?"

She checked her watch. "Ten minutes or so."

"Well, they're not exactly in a hurry to get out, are
they? Whoever 'they' are. I'm going in, Tara. Please
wait here."

They took a deep breath together and, as Tara
watched Declan tread very lightly through her open
gate and then over her doorstep, gently pushing the
front door open, she began to feel extremely guilty.

*I thought, I can't let him go in there on his own. Jesus,
I've got Ruben here with me. It's not fair leaving it all to him.
I'm going in after him.*

The minute Tara and Ruben walked into the
hallway, Ruben began to bark. Tara knew she'd messed
things up and hoped that "they" hadn't come across
Declan yet. She hurriedly whizzed Ruben through the
dark kitchen and put him outside into the garden. As

she closed the patio door behind her she couldn't help but quickly glance at The Shed to check it was still locked. It was.

A mad priority, I know – but I loved that Shed!

Declan appeared at the foot of the stairs, making a "ssshh" sign with his puckered lips and finger. She tiptoed up the stairs behind him, careful to avoid step number eight – the creaky one. As they stood at the top of the stairs they could both see along into the spare room. The light was on and the attic hatch-door was hanging down. It was open.

Tara's pulse banged in her chest and her throat and her ears. She thought she was going to be sick, then she heard a rustling sound from the attic. She grabbed Declan's arm in panic.

"Any ideas?" Declan whispered.

Tara shrugged.

"Tara," he tried to talk some sense into her, "there's no sign of forced entry. This person hasn't broken in."

"What do you mean?"

I feel so thick at times, but my brain doesn't work properly in panic situations. I can't help it!

"I mean," he whispered, helping her walk backwards slowly toward the bathroom, "that this person probably had a *key*."

The penny dropped.

It all came back to me. I'd never taken the key from Simon when he went. The black Saab.

She tiptoed through to her bedroom and looked from the window down at the street.

There it was – just up the street. That fucking black Saab!

And strange as it may sound, all feelings for fear, all insecurities and all my femininity left me in one mad rush. I knew I was hollering like a market trader –

"Simon, you fucking creep! Get out of there now! What the hell do you think you're doing up there?"

She stamped over to the open hatch-door to see the soles of "office shoes" waving in mid-air to find the exit. Declan's eyes were wide with amazement.

"Get yourself down here *now!* What the hell!"

Simon landed on his feet with a thud right before her. As if he'd fallen from the sky, only not as angelic. It seemed strange to her, seeing him again after so long. Strange that he was back in their marital home.

Only it wasn't. It never had been. And it never bloody would be!

Simon looked over toward Declan who was still standing in the bathroom with his eyes wide open in shock. He'd been expecting perhaps a petty thief or maybe even Anna or Niamh or even Tara's mother. But not Simon. Not in the damned attic.

"Who's *that*?" Simon spat as he indicated towards Declan. "Oh no, let me guess – 'Graham'?"

The anger surged in Tara like a tidal wave and she punched and hit him on his chest as she contorted her face in anger.

"Don't you dare! Don't you fucking dare! That isn't Graham. I never saw Graham again – more's the bloody pity! That's Declan and he's a great friend of mine. Actually," she laughed, delirious now with her shoot-

424

from-the-hip talk, "actually I'm in *love* with him. OK? Suits you, does it? You adulterous, bigamous, no sorry, polygamous bastard! How dare you try and throw this back in my face. And, yes, it was me who told Christina that you were a polygamist. And I know all about Una Slattery and Mary Ryan. You're a sad man, Simon! And the police know all about you! It's only a matter of time!"

He reddened and shifted from one shiny-shoe'd foot to the other.

"Well, I never wanted to marry you anyway. You pushed yourself onto me. Proposing to me and all that – what was *that* all about? You were just a sad desperate thirty-something who wanted to be married. And I was the unlucky guy."

"So why did you say *yes*? I hardly had your arm up your back, did I?" She went eyeball to eyeball with him in anger. "I hardly dragged you up the damn aisle! You and your wedding plans and flowers and sugared fecking almonds!"

Declan didn't really want to be witness to this personal situation of Tara's and yet was still reeling from her statement that she was in love with him. In *love* with him! That was news to him. But it was good news. He decided to step forward and make some sense of it all.

"So what were you doing in the attic?" he demanded.

"Butt out, it's got nothing to do with you!" Simon sneered at Declan as he spoke.

Declan wasn't to be deterred; he'd handled worse than Simon Cullen.

"It's got everything to do with me. I'm in love with Tara and I've got her interests at heart. The bottom line is, Simon, that although you have a key you know that you're not welcome here. Tara hasn't seen you for over a year and you can't just swan back in here unexpected. Whatever you want from the attic, a phone call wouldn't have hurt. Tara could have got it out for you to collect."

Simon looked as if he didn't know what to say or how to react.

For a man who claimed to be so well educated, he was completely speechless.

And with that he pushed past the two of them, walked slowly down the stairs and left. Slamming the front door behind him.

The silence filled the house and released Tara's emotions. She broke down and sobbed.

The shock of the intrusion had overwhelmed her. Declan caught her just in time as her knees buckled under the weight of such intense emotion, and she sobbed into his warm neck. The realisation was simply too much. Amid the sobs, as she fought to catch her breath, she sank into the clean scent of Declan's t-shirt, warming to the prickly sound of his light whiskers on her hair as he enveloped her in his huge hug. She felt safe. Warm, protected, accepted. As safe as she'd felt as an eight-year-old tucked up in her warm bed, her heart full of excitement as she was unable to go to sleep for looking at her new bedroom furniture. As happy and safe as she could remember for a long long time. Safer than she'd ever felt with Simon. She could see now how she had tried to manufacture security, had attempted to plan a fulfulling relationship by asking him to marry her. How wrong she had been – it seemed so obvious now. As if suddenly woken from an extremely long sleep she could see it all so clearly. It all made sense. She didn't notice the shocked expression on Declan's face as she broke free from the security of his embrace. She didn't notice her diluted, Alice Cooper'd make-up as she ran past the hallway mirror. She didn't even notice the sharp cracking sound of one of the small glass-panes in her front door when it broke on impact as she flung the door open with such force. The sound of her heels echoed in the silent street as she ran along the path towards the two bright headlights. Fumes from Simon's exhaust buffeted into the icy night and she ran into the middle of the road in a bid to stop him from driving past her. He began to pull away from his parking space slowly and Tara ran faster, the chilly air stinging her throat as she gasped it in. She ran into Simon's stationery car, slamming her palms onto the bonnet. They made eye contact through the windscreen and she noted his swollen red eyes.

"Get out, Simon," her voice rasped.

He continued to stare at her. Her palms tingled and she realised she was still leaning on the car bonnet. She stood up straight and breathed deeply.

"Simon," her voice was now softer and yet more stern, "please. Get out."

Without breaking her gaze, he turned off the ignition of the car. The road was eerily silent as the smoke wafted away. Tara gasped in another deep breath as she prepared herself for this confrontation. Simon got out of the car, lightly pushing the door closed behind him. She ran her eyes from his polished shoes up along his pinstriped trouser legs, jacket, over the bulge of his Adam's apple and then across his whey-faced expression. She watched the pain and shame dance in his eyes as they stared at each other. She felt strangely sorry for him, which puzzled her. He looked so pathetic, so small, so desperate, that she nearly forgot what a bastard he'd been. How many lives he'd ruined.

"I'm sorry."

His voice was small and thin and yet his words hit her straight in the stomach. She didn't try and stop the tears which wobbled like mercury on her lower lashes.

"Thank you," she whispered. The tears leapt from her lashes, crash-landing onto her chest. "Me too." She heaved in another sigh, finding it hard to keep the emotion from her voice. "I'm sorry about Graham. I was losing my individuality and freedom and I suppose I resented it. We were both wrong."

"No, *you* were wrong. You completely shattered our marriage."

"What! There *was* no marriage! Can't you see? I've got the wedding photos and the memory of the 'day', but there was no marriage. There *is* no marriage."

"Love affairs are like wars," he quoted. "Everyone finds them exciting and yet we all know the risk of untold destruction."

428

"How dare you! You polygamous bastard! How dare you!"

She fought the urge to hit him.

He continued. "I never had an affair. I've *never* had an affair."

"*Oh woopie-doo!* Bring on the sainthood for Mr Cullen. He doesn't believe in affairs, but is a great fan of religious ceremonies."

She noticed his Adam's apple rise and fall quickly as he swallowed hard. He looked down at the icy road.

"Why? Simon, that's all I need to know."

"Perfection. I was looking for perfection."

"Perfection! So tell me, what makes a perfect wife? A good wife, even?"

"It's different for girls, Tara. Aren't women supposed to be the nurturing gender?"

"So you wanted a nurse-maid! Well, excuse me if I didn't fit the bill on your search for the ultimate high."

His voice rasped as he reached out and took her hand lightly.

"But don't you see, Tara. You *were* perfection. You were the most perfect ever."

"I don't see it. Why was I? How was I?"

"Tara. *You* asked *me*. How more perfect could it ever have been?"

She was stunned at the realisation of what he had said.

He continued. "You were fun and great and beautiful. And you wanted *me*. I didn't have to risk the shame, the humiliation of the proposal. *You* asked *me*."

"Jesus. But you were in no position to accept. Where is your emotional integrity?"

"I don't want to be another divorce statistic! That's like admitting failure. I'm not a failure. Isn't the skill in the choices? Isn't that what they say? It's been easier to walk away from you and pretend it never happened. Don't you see? That way I don't have to admit to the shame and disappointment of failure. I couldn't officially let go of the other marriages."

"Until now."

"Until now."

"*Simon,*" she virtually screamed, shaking her hand from his, "*you have a child!* Wasn't the impact of fatherhood enough to stop you? Wasn't *that* in itself perfection?"

He stared back at the glistening road once again.

She continued, her voice softer again. "I *know* I was wrong in having the affair, but do you know what? In a way I'm glad I did. I'm glad you found out! How long would it have been before you'd gone looking for 'perfection' again? I tried hard to keep the marriage going. I even tried to accept your patriarchal institution ideas as I tried to be your wifey ideal. Jesus, Simon, I made Marge Simpson look unreasonable!"

"You didn't need me."

"This is the twenty-first century! The sex-role stereotypes are long forgotten."

"All I wanted was a good wife. I wanted a reliable, loving partner. I wanted to come home from work to find dinner waiting for me. I wanted a companion.

Who said honesty was the best policy? You wouldn't have gone near me if I'd told you I was already married."

"Simon," she sneered through clenched teeth, "men always get one thing from marriage that women never do – *wives*! And as far as I can see you were looking for a mother-figure, a housewife, a nurse-maid. Like people collect matchboxes or stamps or coins or . . . or . . . or fucking *anything*! You were addicted to collecting wives."

"It wasn't like that. Most times it was too good to leave, but too bad to stay."

"What was too bad? The wives or their lack of domestic prowess?"

She looked at his grey face and suddenly realised how pointless this was. "You do know the police are onto you, don't you?"

He nodded.

"I had to, Simon. We were both wrong going into this marriage. I desperately wanted to be married and I realise now how shallow that was, but you were wrong to accept my proposal. You should have been more honest with me."

"I know. I *am* sorry."

She nodded her head in the direction of his passenger seat at the handful of papers that were strewn on the leather upholstery.

"Is that all you took from my loft?"

"Yeah, I've left most of it behind."

"What is it?"

"Evidence. Marriage certs, photos . . ."

"Sugared-fecking-almonds!"

"Yeah," he nodded, embarassed.

"So where's the rest of it?"

"Still in your loft."

"Do you really want it all?"

"No. Keep it, destroy it, give it to the detectives. Whatever you think."

The chill of the night made her shudder. At least she thought it was that, but perhaps it was the impact of their final conversation.

"You're cold. Go back inside."

"Simon," this time she took his hand, "I did love you. I was wrong – we both were, but I did love you."

"Me too," he whispered.

"Please try and get some counselling. It'll be better for you in the long run. And for your legal situation. At least try and put things right."

"I will. I'll have to. It's all come to an end."

She smiled warmly as she squeezed his hand. "Try and think of it as your new beginning."

Once again the tears rushed to her eyes and she was surprised to see that he had copied her. Blinking away the tears, he pulled his hand away and opened the car door.

"Bye, Tara. Take care."

"Bye, Simon. You too."

She stepped sideways onto the pavement as the engine purred into life and the headlights once again illuminated the half-lit street. He didn't make eye contact as he drove away, simply leaving her to walk through the exhaust-fume clouds as she was drawn back to the warm glow of orange lights that filtered through her lounge curtains.

She was now ready for that hug from Declan.

Declan held her in his arms and she snotted and wailed into his navy jacket.

"I feel like I've been punched by a nun," she whimpered as she began to calm down.

He held her at arm's length and looked at her, confused. "You what? How?"

She sniffed loudly, swiping at her runny nose with the back of her hand. "Well, it was so completely unexpected. Nothing could have shocked me more."

Declan tried to repress a snigger and so pulled her in for another hug, and comforted her. "C'mon. Let me get up there and see what he was after."

They went back upstairs and she watched as he clambered up into the loft. She heard him walking around up there and then his muffled voice gasped, echoing through the hatch,

"Oh my God! Tara! If only you'd known. If only you'd seen this months ago."

"What is it?" She was desperate to know what he was talking about. He reappeared at the hatch with a large wooden box in his hands.

"This."

It was nine o'clock and they were still going through the contents of the wooden box. They both sat crosslegged on her lounge floor listening to Ella

Fitzgerald as they went through the details of Simon Cullen's marriages. It was all there for anyone to see.

His marital box of tricks. If only I'd known it was there. It had probably been there since before we were married. He'd moved in with a load of stuff prior to the wedding. If only I'd looked up in the attic then, I could have saved myself from that disgusting travesty of a "marriage". But then I looked at Declan and realised that I had to go through this to get to him. I'd never have met him if it wasn't for Home Is Where The Art Is. *It was very hard looking at all that wedding memorabilia though. What was worse was that he wore a similar suit for all of the weddings, and the order of service was virtually identical, even down to the invitations! And here were his photographs and marriage certificates for all of his four weddings! Four weddings! All I was missing was a funeral – and that was not about to happen – please God! There was a day I felt like dying over Simon leaving me, but that was long, long behind me now. And get this, then I found a letter from his mother – his parents lived in Mullingar! Not quite Chicago, is it? I felt like I'd been on a production-line of wives for Simon Cullen. And then a thought hit me . . .*

"But, Declan, he still has the key! He could come back at any time."

"He daren't. Don't worry, we'll get the locks changed tomorrow."

"Tomorrow! What if he comes back tonight? He's so unstable and now I've told him about the police too. Oh Declan!"

He reassured her once again, "Look. He won't come back. I promise you."

"Declan?"

He looked up from the paperwork he was holding, "Yeah?"

"Will you stay here with me tonight?"

"Ohh, Tara. I don't know if that's a good idea."

"I know what you're thinking. It won't be like in Wexford. I'm sorry about that. I was very low and confused."

"Tara . . ." He moved nearer to her, cupping her face in his hands and grinning mischeviously as he spoke. "You said that you were in love with me earlier."

She blushed a little and stepped back.

Only a little bit!

"So?"

"So is that true?"

"Maybe."

God, there's nothing like being put on the spot, is there?

"Well, you do realise what this means now, don't you?"

"Go on."

"You're not a married woman. Not legally, not in any shape or form. You're free to do what you like. No divorce, no separation, no mess."

"I know. It's all rather hard to take in. My history has been rewritten."

"Tara, I love you. And I have done for months. I will stay here with you for the night, but I'll sleep in the spare room. I'm not rushing you into anything you're not comfortable with."

"It's OK, honestly. It won't be like Wexford. I really am sorry about that."

"I know. Forget it. Although I've felt kinda like a laughter surgeon ever since then."

"What do you mean – a laughter surgeon? What's that?"

"Someone who removes smiles," he grinned. "Or at least – someone who removes *your* smiles. I'm sorry too – I should have been more sensitive."

"Not at all." She sat upright and smiled widely. "It's actually quite liberating now that I can dig out my adulterous underwear without any hint of guilt."

Declan felt himself flush quite hot and he rolled up his sleeves in a bid to counteract it. He coughed lightly to clear his throat, although he could think of nothing fitting to actually say.

She put him out of his misery. "I suppose it's all about your frame of mind. I mean, is the glass half-full or half-empty?"

"Point taken," he had composed himself, "but the 75 per cent fat-free chocolate bar is still quarter laden with fat."

"Spoilsport!" she giggled.

He sidled close beside her and lightly touched her chin, turning her to face him at close proximity.

"Your glass may be only half full, but my feelings for you are whole. It is the whole of my heart that is in love with you and you will never know how terrible I've been feeling since the night we spent together."

"I wasn't that much of a disappointment, was I?" she attempted to tease.

It's more nerves than anything!

"You were fantastic, but you know what I mean. Do you think you might give some thought into jumping in with both feet one more time? Only this time there'll be a safety net."

"What safety net? What do you mean?"

"Have you ever thought of being a landlady?"

"A lady who works on the land?" she grinned, teasing.

"An owner of property who rents out and makes extortionate amounts of profit!"

"Never. Why?"

"Well, you know how men are only programmed to do one thing at a time? At least that's the theory."

"The fact."

"OK, the fact. Well, I've got something to tell you. To ask you."

"What?" Her blotchy face broke into a grin.

He raised his butt from the floor and dug into his track pants pocket, pulling out a folded sheet of paper with colour photographs.

"This."

Tara looked at the beautiful architecture of the Parisian apartment.

"Declan, it's beautiful. When are you going to look at it?"

"I've been."

"Oh," she couldn't keep the disappointment from her voice.

"Tara?"

"Yeah," she was still scrutinising the paperwork, trying to translate any of the easier words.

"I've bought it."

"You've wha'?"

He nodded, smiling. "Got the go-ahead on it. Offer accepted and everything. It's mine!"

"Declan!" She threw her arms around him and hugged him. "That's fantastic. Where is it?"

"Just off the Champs Elysses."

"Oh my God, it's beautiful! And look at the balcony with that lovely wrought-iron work around it. I suppose you'll be marking your territory with topiary trees next, like all the others."

"Maybe. But there's a lot of work to be done on it, Tar. And you know how men are programmed blah blah?"

She ignored his open question. "Well, there's not that much to do on it, surely." She squinted at the photo to try and get a more detailed look.

"There's not that many DIY places over there," he said. "The paint is poor quality and the plumbing is usually questionable. I'm going to need to spend a bit of time there."

And why did I feel so disappointed? My stomach had just lurched depressingly.

"It's handy though really. I've put it to the boss the idea of taking *Home Is* to Paris. What with the interest in French properties and the holiday home market that's growing so rapidly."

Tara's eyes lit up with excitement.

"So what did he say?"

"He said we'll have to research it, but he wouldn't be against the idea of running a mini-series on it.

Perhaps more of a European *Home Is* rather than a specifically French one."

"And would I be back on the team?"

I could hardly breathe with anticipation.

Declan smiled at her and punched her in the ribs playfully,

"Might be. Depends."

She hopped up onto her knees and rested in front of him.

"Depends on *what*?"

He toyed with her, pretending to look around the room as he thought,

"Depends on whether or not the Tara McKenna Consultancy will take on the commission on my Parisian place first."

She sat back on her bum in surprise. "You're not serious!"

"I surely am! You think I know what to do with that place? No bloody chance! The owner had switched on the electric fire to try and warm it up when I was viewing it. I cringed at the black plastic lumps that turned orange. We wanted heat and all we got was a bloody light show! It's serious, Tara. I'm serious. I love you. I need you."

"Ahhh Declan!" She squealed and threw her arms around him again, threatening to suffocate him. He tugged at her arms, pulling her away gently and they made eye contact. And then he kissed her. Tenderly and softly.

"Declan. I do love you."

"It just took you ages to realise it. You're stubborn."

"I know, sorry."

"So," he lightened the tone, "how are you fixed for next month?"

"Declan, I've got five months' worth of work set up. I can't let clients down."

"OK," he wasn't to be fazed that easily, "so you'll have to commute. Fit me in at the weekends and between jobs. Just think," he teased, "the flea markets . . ."

"Oh my God! What was it again? Saint-Ouen at Clignancourt! Oh Declan, how fantastic!"

"But you realise that it can't all be strictly business, don't you?"

She stuck out her tongue, playfully, the small stud glistening, and then wrapped her arms around his neck as she straddled him.

"Declan. I wouldn't really have it any other way . . ."

The End.